Dark Magick

ERICA RICHER

ISBN: 978-1-7770159-6-1

DEDICATION

This book is dedicated to my family, friends and especially my readers. It's amazing to do something you enjoy so much; and your continued support and interest is the reason I keep doing what I love.

CONTENTS

ACKNOWLEDGMENTS

I would like to acknowledge my husband and children. Only with their patience and support do I continue writing. Special thanks to my friends, Jenn and Danica, for helping me edit and talking "book" with me.

CHAPTER ONE

Rose

My vision comes back into focus and looking around, I recognize the simple cabin in the woods. The fire is out though, making the room chilly and dark. I let my hands fall from Gavin, instantly feeling the loss of warmth as he allows me to step back from him.

"Are you ok?" he asks, sympathetically.

"Y-Yeah," I say softly, starting to shiver.

I'm so not ok. Not even close. As much as I wanted to hurt Caleb, I can't believe I came here with Gavin, of all people. *What was I thinking?*

Gavin walks to the fireplace swiftly. There is a solitary log sitting in the fire and no other logs in view. I hear him mutter an incantation under his breath and watch as a fire erupts on the single log.

I inhale a quick breath in surprise.

"You really aren't familiar with magick, are you?" Gavin says with a small smile as he turns around.

"Not really," I say, seeing him out of the corner of my eye but finding myself unable to look away from the flames.

Morgan, Xander, and Jason kept their magick to themselves. As far as I know, they're the only ones that have any.

"That's a shame!" Gavin says, not so silently judging them.

"What do you mean?" I ask edgily, snapping out of my daze.

"They were so concerned with shielding you from the darkness in our world that they were hiding the light too," he says sadly. "I mean, I get it. There are a lot of dangerous and dark things and nothing is black and white, it's all gray, but there is beauty too."

"Like what?"

"Like being able to watch the same sunset or sunrise for centuries and watching the world change around you," he replies with a genuine smile.

"What else?"

"Having more time with the people you care about."

Gavin looks into my face with a sweet smile. His eyes betray him as much as his actions do. He acts so entitled and pompous, but he rushed to the fire when he realized I was cold, just like he rushed me here when I didn't want to be near Caleb. I can see the compassion in his eyes even if he doesn't want me to.

"Why didn't you take me to the Order?" I ask curiously. "I thought that was your whole agenda?"

Gavin's eyes drift away from mine for a moment. He looks torn. I'm too tired to find out what it means. *It doesn't matter.*

"It seemed like you needed some time," Gavin says gently.

He's right.

I should be relieved. I don't know if this is what I want. I'm so angry right now. I feel numb. I left with Gavin to hurt Caleb for hurting me, but I don't know if I want to go to the Order.

"I don't know what I want," I say, admitting to my own confusion.

"I know," Gavin says. "It doesn't matter right now but you do need to feed," he adds seriously, rolling his sleeve up.

I've been suppressing it, my hunger. I've been ignoring the itching and burning and stinging. Distracted by all the lies. Caring only about them. Now it feels like a hundred knives stabbing me all over.

The heat rushes over me, my fangs elongating. I don't cover them. I don't try to hide it. I'm too hungry. I don't have the energy to deny what I need.

I close the distance in three steps, pulling him to me. I go for his neck rather than his arm. The hum of his blood calls to me. I pause for a second before I puncture his skin, making sure he is alright with it first. He doesn't say anything or push me away. His hands are on my back, holding me to him. So, I bite him.

My teeth pierce his skin easily. The blood rushes down my throat and dulls the burn inside, but the ache remains. I become aware of his hands squeezing as I drink with less urgency. Although I know it's not Caleb or Morgan, I feel protected somehow.

I pull back, easing my fangs out and transitioning back to human. He's breathing a bit harder than before but seems otherwise unharmed. I've never fed from someone that I barely knew. I was so overcome with hunger that I didn't really think about it.

Now though, he still has his hands gently on my back and I'm going to have to look him in the eye.

The blush creeps in as I pull away and make eye contact.

His light brown eyes are focused on me. There's a slight pink to his cheeks. It might be from the sting of the bite, the loss of blood, or the moment. *Who knows?* It does make me feel better.

"Thank you," I say nervously.

"Any time."

"Do you…" I start awkwardly, pointing at my neck.

He smiles at me- a genuine smile, but he seems far more comfortable with this situation than I do.

"No. I'm ok," he says confidently. "You should get some rest. You can have the bed. I've got to step out. I'll be back."

He walks over to the bed and folds down the blanket. I follow him over. Days ago, Gavin had been an enemy, and this place had been a nightmare. Now, I'm here voluntarily. *My life is so messed up.*

I climb into the bed, not sure how I'm going to sleep right now. My mind is racing with what just happened. Sitting up in the bed, I look Gavin in the eyes as a stray tear escapes my eye.

My emotions are all over. I'm angrier than I have ever been, but I'm also inexplicably sad and hurt.

"How could no one tell me that Caleb is an incubus?" I ask bluntly. "How could he not? Why didn't you?"

Gavin sits on the edge of the bed with a big sigh.

"He thought he wouldn't have to deal with his past mistakes. Honestly, he's an idiot," he adds smugly. "I don't know why no one told you. As for me, it wasn't my place to say anything."

I chuckle a little. It's nice talking to someone who doesn't defend Caleb's choices, but can I trust Gavin?

"Why are you doing this?" I ask suspiciously.

"I don't know," he replies simply.

I can hear it in his voice, his confusion, it's real. He's helping me and he doesn't know why any more than I do. He rises from the bed and heads to the door.

"Get some sleep. I'll be back," he says, before shutting the door behind him.

I lay back on the pillow, wet tears running across my skin. I thought we had something so amazing, now my heart is breaking, shattering. *How could I have ever loved a monster?*

CHAPTER TWO

Jason

Caleb sits down on the grass, his back to a tree, a look of horror in his eyes, but he's silent. It's a behaviour that has me concerned; his eyes are shadowed, showing that there is too much darkness in him right now.

Xander is building a fire in front of him, quietly. He can feel it too, Caleb's mood- I can tell by the set of his shoulders.

Rose disappeared with Gavin a half-hour ago, Isaac took off to feed, Paige went to fill in Tyler and feed, and Xander and I stayed with Caleb. Right now he needs us more than he wants us to know.

I move a few feet from the fire, leaning back against a fallen tree. Xander sits next to me once the fire is burning strongly. We watch Caleb carefully, knowing he's so close to the edge.

"She didn't mean it. She's just upset," Xander says, trying to ease some of his tension.

"She absolutely meant it," Caleb says hopelessly.

"She'll come around after she cools down," Xander tries to reassure him.

"I don't think she will," he says, devastated.

"She doesn't understand. How could she? She doesn't know your past," I remind him.

"I need to see her. I need to explain." Caleb says- his voice a bit frantic.

"Are you sure that's a good idea?" Xander asks. "Maybe you should wa…"

"No," Caleb shouts, interrupting. "I can't leave her just knowing what she knows…and who knows what shit Gavin is telling her?"

He pulls a vial of blood out of his pocket, along with a knife. He's made up his mind. I know that there is no talking him out of this, but I have a bad feeling.

As the world comes back into focus, we find ourselves standing on a sidewalk outside a tavern. The sign says, 'The Late Night'. I recognize the name immediately- it's the bar that Caleb took Rose to when we were searching for Isaac to get information on Lord Dalibor.

True to the dream realm, we're completely alone in the dark in the dead of night. Caleb begins walking down the alley beside the bar, to the back, so we follow him. There is a fire going in the metal barrel at the back of the building, casting a glow on us and the lightly snow-covered ground. Xander and I gather around the fire, soaking in the warmth. Rose comes walking out of the dark behind us and Caleb is already facing in her direction.

Rose's eyes sweep over Xander and me before focusing back on Caleb. Her eyes are red; she has obviously been crying. She glares at him with a mixture of sadness, desire, anger, and fear on her face. Caleb is staring at her from a metre away, breathing heavier than he should be.

"You always bring me somewhere cold and dark. It makes a lot more sense now," Rose says coldly.

Caleb says nothing, but a spark of pain passes through his eyes. "I need to explain everything," he says.

"Now you want to talk?" she asks with exasperation. "I told you that I never wanted to see you again."

"You have to let me explain," Caleb pleads, ignoring her quips the best he can, but I can see him clenching his fists already as he steps towards her.

She takes a few steps back from Caleb as he advances, trying to keep her distance. He pauses, shoulders falling, fists unclenching- her reaction to him clearly hurts.

"I don't have to let you do anything," she snaps furiously. "I don't want to hear your excuses for justifying your lies."

"I didn't lie about what I was," Caleb defends himself.

"No, but you weren't exactly honest either. You intentionally let me think you were a vampire," she argues. "Did you ever even consider telling me the truth? You had plenty of opportunity."

"Of course I thought about telling you. I wanted to but..." Caleb says, trailing off.

My heart is breaking for them. I know they are both feeling so much pain. Rose feels betrayed- betrayal is always worse from someone you love. Caleb feels her slipping away and he needs her love more than he'll ever admit. Nothing I say will make this better.

Xander and I stay back and stay silent. They need to talk.

"But what?" she shouts.

In that instant, Caleb's restraint falters and he shoves her roughly up against the brick building, hard enough that I know she's going to have a bruise.

Xander and I take a few steps towards him cautiously. We were afraid of this happening. Caleb's running short on patience and compassion right now and Rose has a way of pushing his buttons.

Sensing our concern, he glances back at us, then releases her arms and takes a step away from her. He knows he's being too aggressive. She stays rooted in place, breathing hard and glaring up at him with so much anger.

"I know, but I didn't want you to know…"

She interrupts him. "Of course you didn't! You wanted me to fall for you and how would I fall for a monster?"

He cringes at being called a monster, but holds in his frustration. Rose watches Caleb for a few minutes, waiting for him to say something, to prove her wrong, but he doesn't. She turns to walk away. He covers the ground between them with a couple steps and reaches out to grab her, but stops himself- thinking twice about his actions.

Grabbing her attention, he gives her some honesty. "I didn't want you to know because I liked who you thought I was. I wanted to be who you thought I was," he says as Rose turns back to him. "I hate my past," he finally admits, as much to himself as Rose.

Rose's face softens as she looks into his eyes.

"How can I even believe who you are now?" she asks. "You of all people should know that you can't rewrite your past. You can only choose the direction of your future."

"I know. I'm sorry," he says.

"It's too late," she replies, fresh tears falling down her cheeks.

"Rose, please…" Caleb begs, "I need you."

She walks away before disappearing into the dark. She doesn't look back and all I can do is watch helplessly as my friend falls apart inside. His hands clench tightly and his back tenses while his breathing accelerates.

The dream realm fades away quickly and I prepare for the worst of Caleb's moods.

I can see it when he comes into focus- his face dark, gaunt, and sharp.

"Caleb…" Xander begins calmly, taking in his appearance.

He takes off with blinding speed to create chaos until he feels better.

"Well that's not good," I say.

CHAPTER THREE

Caleb

"Let her go, Caleb," Jason warns. "You don't want to do this."

I come back to the present. We're in an alley somewhere. It has been more than a week since Rose left. I disappeared right after. I don't know how I got here. Jason is several meters away, approaching slowly, cautiously. I have my hands around the neck of some young woman. My fangs are out- ready, eager. I want to bite her- to feed from her, to kill her.

"Actually, I do," I say cruelly.

"This isn't you," Jason says.

"It is now," I growl out. "Go away Jason."

"Yeh don' really wan' tha' mate," Isaac says from behind me.

"I do," I say adamantly.

The young woman whines and trembles in my grip. She feels my lack of concern and compassion. The pressure I'm putting on her throat keeps her from making any real noise. I can taste the fear in her blood already, and I haven't even bitten her yet.

I bring my mouth within an inch of her neck. I can feel the blood beneath the skin. *I want it.*

"You don't want this. You're hurt," Jason says, trying to reason with me.

I back off a little, deep in thought. I am hurt. They know it. I know it.

"It doesn't change what I am," I say with self-loathing.

"It doesn't matter what you are. It never has," Jason says firmly, "to anyone but you," he says. "She fell in love with you," he adds gently.

"She didn't know what I was," I remind him bitterly.

"It's not what you are that she fell in love with, it's who you are. It's the way you were when you were with her. It's how you made her feel," Jason says, resolutely. "It's not too late."

I know that he's right. I just hate myself so much. I feel so defeated and lost. I haven't taken an undeserving life in centuries and as much as I don't want to, I'm so tired of fighting it- the urge, my nature.

"I'm tired, Jason," I say honestly. "It feels pointless."

"Stop feeling sorry for yourself," Jason says bluntly. "This is just a bump in your story with Rose. It's not over. Hannah is dead. Our story is over."

"I'm sorry," I say, laden with guilt.

Jason lost his chance at love, yet here he is, trying to talk me off the ledge. It's not my proudest moment.

"Monsters don't apologize," Jason says with a grin.

"This is not who you are, Caleb. You're better than this," Xander says, walking around the corner.

I release the young woman and she stumbles away. I'm ashamed of myself. I would have killed if it weren't for the guys. *Again*!

"You had us worried," Jason says, approaching me with his hand up.

"No," I say, calmly shaking my head.

"I can help," Jason offers.

"I know. But I don't want it right now," I explain. "I need to feel my pain- at least for a while."

Jason looks at me carefully. There's worry in his eyes, but it's what I need to do. Rose is my first love since I turned into an incubus and reformed. These feelings I have are overwhelming, but having them makes me feel more human.

She had every right to ditch me. I lied to her over and over, and they weren't little lies, but seeing her in Gavin's arms broke me. Not to mention, she said she hated me. The pain is just too much.

"You're taking off, aren't you?" Xander says, walking up to us.

His voice is sad. He knows what I am going to do next. I need to.

"For a while. It won't be forever," I reassure them.

"I think I'll tag along, mate. It'll be jus' like old times," Isaac says with a mischievous grin.

"You wouldn't rather go after Rose?" I ask, raising an eyebrow.

I haven't forgotten that he bit her even though she was mine.

"Nah. As appealin' as the lass may be, I was only tryin' to get yeh to admit how yeh felt about the girl," Isaac says with an innocent shrug. "Yeh know how I get, lad."

I shake my head in disbelief.

Only Isaac.

I suppose his company wouldn't hurt. It might even help. I've spent so long repressing my instincts. Perhaps having a partner in crime will make it easier to let go a bit.

"Keep an eye on Rose for me," I say to both Xander and Jason, with complete trust.

"We will. We promise," Xander says, while Jason nods.

Before I can change my mind, I take off down the dark alley with Isaac.

Xander

We watched as Caleb left with Isaac. I wish he didn't feel the need to leave. It's been the three of us for centuries now. It won't be the same without him.

"Do you think Caleb will do something he's going to regret?" Jason asks, slightly concerned.

"Well I don't have a whole lot of faith in Isaac. His moral compass isn't exactly reliable!" I say with a smirk. "...but Caleb is better than he thinks."

Jason laughs to himself as we head out of the alley.

I try not to worry, but Caleb is basically my brother. He is impulsive and reckless at times. Isaac has no regard for rules. No doubt they're going to get into a little bit of trouble without Jason and I around. Caleb might act more like a vampire, but maybe it'll be just what he needs.

"So, where to?" Jason asks me with a sigh.

I cringe when I look at Jason. We're going to keep our promise to Caleb. We'll look out for Rose, but she may not be thrilled to see us.

"I think we're going to need some help," I say to Jason reluctantly.

"Well...we better find Paige then," Jason admits.

I grimace.

I know now that she never wanted to hurt Rose. She was just a pawn. And I was so cold and mean to her. I owe her an apology with or without her help.

CHAPTER FOUR

Rose

"What do you think?" Paige asks me, smiling happily.

I take another look around at the immaculate wooden floors, the kitchen area, and the living area.

"It's perfect," I say enthusiastically.

"Yay!" she says, excitedly. "I'll let the realtor know."

The apartment is located on the top floor of a seven-story walk-up in downtown Toronto. I smile at the idea of finally coming home, or at least being in my home country. I can't very well move home, being that my house burnt down, (another detail that Caleb kept to himself,) but this apartment that Paige found is the next best thing. *Because it's ours.*

I take a closer look around, examining the fireplace, the master bedroom, the smaller bedroom, and the den. Of course, my favourite; the large bathroom with a clawfoot bath.

"It's ours!" Paige says giddily, pulling me into a hug.

She came running into the master bedroom to find me after she hung up with the realtor. She's as ready as I am to have somewhere to call home.

"I can't believe it!" I say with relief.

It's almost June now. It's been over three months since I lost both of my best friends- my brother *again*, and the boy I fell in love with. For a while, at Gavin's cabin, I lost my will to live. My heart was broken. Now I'm finally starting to put myself back together. I haven't heard from or seen Caleb since. It's probably for the best.

"Let's go tell the guys," Paige says, interrupting my sad thoughts.

"Do you think Xander will mind not having a closet?" I ask innocently, trying to shake all the negative thoughts from my head.

"No," Paige answers with a laugh.

We leave the apartment and walk the few blocks to the pizza parlor at the corner. We walk right in, scanning the booths. Xander and Gavin are sitting in a booth at the back, talking about something and finishing their pizza. They smile at us when they see us coming.

About a week and a half into my stay with Gavin, Paige and Xander showed up. At first, I wanted nothing to do with Xander, but Paige and I had begun hanging out. She explained that he had apologized to her and eventually I forgave him too. Then, we decided to get a place together and they said it could be anywhere I chose.

So, I chose here.

Paige slides in next to Xander comfortably. Gavin gets out of the booth, allowing me to sit across from Xander before sitting back down beside me.

"So, what'd you think?" Xander asks us.

"We loved it. We said yes," I say, trying to hide some of my enthusiasm for Gavin's sake.

Gavin shifts his gaze from me to the floor. I've been staying in his cabin for the last three months and it's been surprisingly enjoyable. He's not quite the jerk that I thought he was. He's actually kind of sweet. He makes breakfast every day and he always lets me sleep in the bed. I think I'm going to miss him. If I'm being honest, I know I'm going to miss him. That's part of the problem.

"Great," Xander says happily. "When are we moving in?"

"Tomorrow!" Paige says hastily.

"Wow. That's soon!" Gavin says, trying to hide his disappointment but failing.

Paige gets up quickly, pulling a confused Xander out of the booth too.

"So, Gavin, why don't you take Rose back to your place, get her packed up, and bring her back tomorrow," Paige suggests, taking charge.

"That won't take all night," Xander begins, with annoyance. "Why don't…" Xander continues, until Paige elbows him in the stomach.

Xander looks at Paige with confusion. He has been a bit over-protective since he came back around almost three months ago. At first, I thought he was back because of Caleb, but after apologizing profusely, he stopped bringing him up altogether. Paige started coming around too. And before I knew it, it felt like I had my friends back. So, I embraced them.

"Sure," I say appreciatively, knowing Paige is trying to give me time to thank Gavin.

Paige says goodbye, shoving Xander awkwardly towards the door.

"Shall we?" Gavin says, rising from the booth.

I follow Gavin out of the store in silence. The sun is still bright in the sky (thank you summer.) We walk down the road and disappear down an alley.

"Ready?" Gavin asks, turning to me with an outstretched arm.

"Ready," I answer, sliding my hand along his and taking hold firmly.

Gavin

When the world comes back into focus, we're standing in my familiar cabin. Her hand fits in mine so perfectly. It makes me instantly warmer and I let go reluctantly. I only have one more night with her here and it feels like she just started to warm up to me.

I get it now- why Caleb was so hung up on her. Her innocence makes her so addictive. She's warm, radiates light, and makes you want to be a better person. I like having her with me. I'm going to miss her.

Caleb really is an idiot.

Rose comes out of the bathroom wearing shorts and a t-shirt. She's even cuter because she doesn't realize she is. She starts packing up her clothes without saying anything.

I make my way over to her, knowing I may not get another chance to tell her what she has become to me, but I know that she's not over Caleb yet. I don't want to scare her.

Rose

"You know that you don't have to leave!" Gavin says sweetly.

I stop packing and look him in the eyes. They're so sincere. I'm not leaving because he makes me feel unwanted, and I would never want him to think that, but I can't tell him the whole reason I'm leaving- because it's the opposite. I'm starting to want him. *And it hurts my heart.* I just put it back together. I'm not ready for these feelings.

"I know. But it's time," I say, trying to keep our conversation light.

"Of course," he says, but the hurt is obvious in his eyes.

This is not how I wanted this conversation to go. He has been so caring to me, and he doesn't lie. The last thing I want to do is hurt him.

"I need to be back home," I say solemnly.

I resume my packing as a way to avoid everything we're not saying, but I can feel it and I'm sure he can too- the tension. He sighs, but I can feel his eyes lingering on me. I finish packing my clothes and books, ignoring the thumping in my chest.

"Done?" he asks patiently.

I say nothing, out of embarrassment. I try not to look at him, knowing that he'll see all the unspoken words in my face.

"Rose?" he says firmly.

He puts a hand under my chin, forcing me to look up into his eyes.

"Please." I'm begging him to just leave it alone. I take a calming breath to steady my nerves, knowing that he won't.

"I don't want you to go," Gavin says softly, still cradling my chin.

My breath catches in my chest and my pulse quickens. I know he doesn't want me to go. I'm not that clueless; but as long as he didn't admit it, I didn't have to do anything about it.

I guess that plan went up in flames.

He stares into my eyes, which are brimming with tears. His eyes are searching for the feelings that I'm trying to ignore.

I try to shake my head free of his hand, but he won't let me look away.

"Gavin, please. I can't do this," I say, a tear running down my cheek.

He releases my chin and drops his gaze to the floor. I steady my breathing and we stand silently, unmoving, for several minutes. I'm both relieved and disappointed.

"I'm sorry, Rose," he says sincerely.

He turns to walk away from me, but I reach out reflexively and grab his arm. He looks at me with surprise. I let my fingers slide down to his hand and hold it.

I like him.

I didn't mean for it to happen. I'm not ready. It still aches when I think of Caleb, but my heart also holds a special place for Gavin- a piece that he helped to save when it shattered.

I find my way into his arms. They wrap snugly around me, giving me the comfort that I need.

"I'm not ready," I say nervously, hoping he will understand.

"I'll wait," he says affectionately.

I smile into his chest, squeezing him a little tighter, with a little more enthusiasm. I feel happy again, for the first time in a long time.

CHAPTER FIVE

Rose

I come out of the bathroom and walk into the living room/kitchen area. Paige is sitting on the couch reading a book, looking up every now and then to watch Xander at the stove.

I walk over and join Xander in the kitchen, leaning casually against the counter. He glances up from mixing the pasta and smiles at me.

It's the beginning of July. now. Paige, Xander, and I have been roommates for just over a month. We've become familiar and every day I feel more attached to my new life.

"Is Gavin joining us for dinner?" Xander asks, watching me out of the corner of his eye.

"Yes. He'll be here any minute," I reply, trying to hide some of my excitement.

I can't help but smile to myself. Gavin comes by three days a week without fail. He hasn't missed a day since I moved out of his cabin. He's reliable and I feel happier when he's around.

"He comes around a lot," Xander states, raising an eyebrow at me.

"We're friends," I say quickly.

"Are you sure that's all?" Xander asks, his full attention on me now. "It seems to me that there's something more between you," he continues.

"I don't think that's any of your business, Xander," Paige says suddenly, defending me and pulling his attention away.

I smirk to myself. I knew Paige would be listening to our conversation and I'm relieved she interrupted. I don't know how to explain my feelings for Gavin- especially not to Xander, who clearly would rather see me forgive Caleb.

"I'm just wondering," Xander says innocently, turning his focus back to the food.

Paige winks at me before turning back to her book. I smile gratefully at her. She really has become an amazing friend. A lot like Hannah.

Knock. Knock.

The sound ends my thoughts of my late bestie. I miss her, but I have to try and live. She'd want me to.

"Hey," I say, opening the door.

"Hey," Gavin says sweetly, his eyes locked onto mine, a grin on his face.

He's wearing dark jeans and a white t-shirt that looks like it was made for him. His brown hair is perfect and his caramel colored eyes sparkle. *Drool.*

I open the door wider to let Gavin in, while I try to ignore the feeling of Xander watching us a little too closely. I feel a slight blush creep into my cheeks at the whole situation.

"How's work going?" I ask, making small talk.

"Work is work," he answers casually.

"Hi Gavin," Paige says happily, acknowledging his arrival. "How are you?"

"I'm good," Gavin replies. "And you?"

"I'm good. I'd be better if I didn't have to work tonight," Paige says jokingly. "In fact, I better go," she adds, getting up from the couch.

She works part-time at Taboo, a bar not too far from the university. She really enjoys bartending. She likes socializing. She's changed- in a good way. Without Kiara around, she's become her own person.

"See you," I say.

"Bye, Rose," she says cheerfully. "Xander," she adds seriously.

The way she says goodbye to Xander makes me certain that something more had been said.

Paige closes the door behind her, leaving Xander, Gavin, and me in an uncomfortable silence.

"Dinner's almost ready," Xander says without looking up.

I give Gavin a sympathetic grin and lead him to the couch. Gavin likes me and I like him. We both know this. We're not keeping secrets, but I've been honest with him. I wasn't ready to make this a thing. But lately, it feels like maybe I am.

"How are you?" I ask Gavin as we sit down on the couch.

"Good now," he answers confidently.

His gaze is unwavering and warm. I feel the blush creeping into my cheeks. I don't look away. I stare into his eyes. I want him to see how he makes me feel.

"I'm happy to see you too," I confess, smiling like an idiot.

We share a moment, eyes locked, feelings apparent. In that moment, I feel things change.

"Dinner's ready," Xander says with a grumpy tone.

"I'll get it," Gavin offers, giving me a smile that melts my heart.

Xander walks over, plate of food in hand, and sits on my right. Gavin comes back with two plates. He hands me one with the cutest smile as he sits on my left. I turn the movie on and we all start eating in silence.

Xander

Gavin is sitting so close to Rose, she may as well be on his lap. I'm glad that Caleb doesn't have to witness this. Their affection is so obvious. It would destroy him all over again.

It doesn't matter. What Caleb and Rose have is unimaginable- they have so much passion for one another. They'll find their way back to each other eventually. He's my brother, so I'll do everything I can to help him win her back. Besides, I don't trust Gavin.

I promised Caleb that I would watch out for Rose. I have no intention of letting him down. Whatever I say, Rose can't know. We're going to have to do this in private.

I send him a message in his mind.

"What's your angle?" I ask Gavin with distrust.

"There's no angle," he replies back, eating his pasta seamlessly. "I like her. Plain and simple."

"She's taken," I say clearly.

"She WAS taken. If you can call it that," Gavin says smugly. "I don't see Caleb anywhere."

"You can't stop what they have. She loves him and he will come back for her," I reply.

"Maybe, but that's a risk I'm willing to take," Gavin says stubbornly. "Besides, she can make her own choices. She's a big girl," he continues arrogantly.

I watch Gavin look at Rose while she smiles at the movie. He's not lying. I can see it in his face. He's willing to risk it all for her. Things are going to get messy when Caleb comes back.

Rose

Xander gets up after inhaling his plate of food. He puts it away and stalks off to his room. I stare after him, concerned.

"I hope he's ok," I say, looking at the dark hall.

"He'll be fine," Gavin reassures me. "He's just not too happy that I've been around," he adds with a chuckle.

"He's just being protective," I say, annoyed.

I look at Gavin. He's already looking at me. He wants to gauge my reactions carefully. *I know what that means.* He's going to bring HIM up.

"It's more than that. He's loyal to Caleb- as he should be. They're friends and brothers. He sees you as Caleb's and he doesn't want anyone taking you from him," Gavin says calmly, with understanding.

"But you're not taking me from Caleb. He's a liar and I want nothing to do with him," I say defensively.

"I know…" Gavin says, trailing off.

He stares into my eyes hard. I find myself reaching up. My fingertips lightly trace his jawline. He makes no move to stop me, so I shift closer to him on the couch. I feel his hand close gently on my arm. I lean in, my lips lingering so close to his. I try not to overthink what I'm doing. I'm fully aware that I can't take it back when it's done, but he makes the choice for me. When his lips touch mine, the warmth and tenderness in them takes my breath away. He kisses me slowly, gently, knowing there is no rush, that we have all the time in the world. His fingers caress the skin on my arm, and I can feel his steady breathing as he inhales, pressing his chest to mine. His calm is intoxicating, his confidence unwavering, and I find myself melting into him.

He leans backwards, pulling me on top of him. I smile into his kiss, completely into the moment. I find myself falling for him more each day. As his hands run up and down my back, my excitement builds. I quickly find myself straddling him, and I don't feel uncomfortable about it. I'm not second guessing my behaviour. I'm just enjoying the way he's making me feel.

His hands slide over my butt and stop on my thighs. The strength he's using intensifies a little and it does something to me. I feel the fire in my belly build and I know that the heat is taking over. I haven't quite gotten a handle on it yet. I feel my teeth elongating automatically. He pulls away, brushing a few stray hairs out of my face and behind my ear. He looks into my eyes adoringly.

"We should take a breather," he says to me with a knowing smile.

I push back from him and give him an embarrassed smile. I feel the blush in my cheeks, but I ignore it. My fangs quickly retract.

"Ok," I say shyly, trying to hide my disappointment.

It's one of those times where his restraint was not needed. I liked the way he was making me feel. I don't think he knows what his touch was doing to me. Or maybe he does. I keep straddling his lap, because I do want to get back to kissing at some point.

"How is your job hunt going?" Gavin asks, with genuine interest.

"Good. I actually have an interview at a little bookstore near the university in a few days," I say excitedly.

"That's amazing Rose. I'm sure you'll get it," Gavin says. "Speaking of university, have you thought about it?" he adds casually.

"You're kidding, right?" I ask incredulously.

"No. I'm serious," Gavin replies, amused by my reaction.

I climb off his lap. This is obviously not going to be a quick conversation.

This has to be a joke. After the year I've been through, education hasn't even been a passing thought. Alex died, then was brought back. Hannah died. Morgan bailed. Dalibor tried to kidnap me and I'm sure I haven't seen the last of him…and let's not forget that Caleb utterly destroyed me. *Only I could fall in love with a monster.* But I can't exactly discuss all of this with Gavin.

"I haven't given it any thought. I didn't even finish high school," I say with a laugh. "Too much has happened in the past year," I add, not wanting to get into the details.

"You do remember what we are, right?" Gavin says, his eyes shining mischievously. "Graduating high school is a minor detail that can be altered."

I smile nervously. Caleb had always pointed out how important it was to finish school at least once in your life. Mind you, he'd probably just wanted me out of the way, at the time. But for some reason it stuck. Manipulating my way into university seems like cheating, though.

"I suppose," I say. I avoid mentioning the words of wisdom from Caleb.

"So…" Gavin pushes. "If you could go, would you?"

"I don't know," I answer truthfully. "University was always Hannah's thing and I'm pretty sure it's past the application deadlines."

Gavin sighs at me. He shakes his head and gently rubs my cheek.

"We don't live in a world where we have to follow the rules," Gavin says. "If you want to go, I'll make it happen. Just tell me where and for what."

"You make it sound so easy," I say, with disbelief.

"That's because it is," Gavin replies playfully.

"Can I think about it?"

"Of course. We have all the time in the world," Gavin says happily.

I can't help but smile at him. He's so sweet. The fact that he will get me into school if I want is so thoughtful.

I climb back onto his lap happily, grateful our conversation is over.

"Now- where were we?" I say, trying my best to be flirty.

He grins at me excitedly. I can see in his eyes that he also wants to pick up where we left off.

"Right about here," he says, wrapping his arms around me and pulling me closer until our lips meet and the fire starts in my belly.

Knock. Knock.

The sound puts a stop to our make-out session.

Come on, I think to myself as I reluctantly pull myself off Gavin to answer the door- flushed cheeks and all. I walk over and swing the door open.

"Jason," I say in surprise.

CHAPTER SIX

Rose

"Hi, Rose," Jason says with a small smile.

He takes a look at my disheveled appearance, my flustered cheeks, and I watch his eyes travel to Gavin.

He pushes past me and glares at Gavin.

"What are you doing here?" he seethes.

"Visiting," Gavin responds, unfazed by his tone.

He looks from Gavin on the couch and turns back to me. He figures it out quickly. I see realization dawn on his face. This only makes me blush more. Strangely, he looks hurt.

Xander walks back in the living room and sees the strange situation unfolding.

"Is there a problem?" Xander asks.

"No. I was just on my way out," Gavin says with a sigh.

He shuffles past Jason and gives me a delicate, lingering kiss.

"Tease," I whisper to him playfully.

"We'll talk soon," he replies with a smile.

I close the door behind him and turn back to the guys. Jason looks appalled and Xander looks unsurprised, but annoyed.

"Just friends, huh?" Xander says sarcastically. "That was awfully friendly."

"What the hell is happening?" Jason asks in shock.

I roll my eyes at the guys. This is more ridiculous than just Alex.

"What?" I ask, avoiding eye contact and playing dumb.

"You know what," Xander says with a smirk.

"Gavin?" Jason asks in disbelief.

"Why not Gavin?" I ask defensively, putting my hands on my hips.

"What about Caleb?" Jason asks with real confusion.

I pause for a moment as Caleb's piercing gray eyes pop into my mind. I shake the imagery away and give them my best glare.

"There is no Caleb," I say with finality.

"Why? Because he made a few mistakes," Jason says confrontationally.

"A few mistakes?" I say with exasperation. "Not telling me he's actually a monster was not a *mistake*."

"He's not a monster," Jason says with a warning tone, taking a heated step towards me.

Xander looks at Jason with mild concern. He also steps towards me.

"Your reaction is why he left it out," Xander chimes in calmly, backing up Jason. "He was afraid."

I can tell he's trying to de-escalate the situation because Jason is getting emotionally involved, but so am I.

"He intentionally misled me!" I accuse

"You expect him to be perfect. It's unfair," Jason says sadly.

"I have standards."

"And because you think he can't live up to them you'd rather be Gavin's plaything?" Jason argues furiously.

"Really, Jason?" I say, hurt. "I'm going to bed."

"Rose…" Xander starts as I stomp to my room. I slam the door and throw myself down on my bed and cry.

Xander

"That was kind of harsh, don't you think?" I ask Jason.

"I know," Jason says with remorse.

Jason walks over to the couch and sits down tiredly. I follow him over and sit with him.

"I get it," I say sympathetically. "You've felt his feelings."

"His love was…" he says, searching for the words, "everything. He still loves her…he has to."

"I'm sure he does," I agree. "Have you seen him lately?"

"No. I lost him two weeks ago and I can't find him," Jason says somberly. "When I last spoke to him, he wouldn't let me help him. I'm worried about him," he adds seriously.

"If he doesn't want to be found, he won't be."

"I didn't mean what I said," Jason says with a sigh. "She's just so frustrating."

"She's young," I remind him. "She still sees the world as black or white, no gray."

"She's unrealistic," Jason says. "But Gavin?" he adds with distaste. "If we told her about Gavin's past, it might solve the whole black and white problem," he grins at me.

"We all have a past. It's not our place to expose his," I remind Jason halfheartedly.

"Yeah. Yeah."

I'm not completely against the idea, though all I can do is shrug. Gavin was in the right place at the right time. That's how it started, but now, Rose glows when he's around- I can't take that from her. I still don't trust him.

"I'm going to keep an eye on Gavin," I say with distrust.

"Good," Jason says. "I'm going to try to find Caleb. See if I can reason with him."

"You going to crash on the couch tonight?" I ask kindly.

"Yeah," Jason says with a yawn.

Just then, the door handle jiggles. Paige comes in, but her eyes stop on Jason.

"What happened?" she asks tiredly, knowing instantly that something is up.

CHAPTER SEVEN

Rose

Knock. Knock.

Paige eases the door open and peeks her head in. I'm lying on the bed awake- my eyes red and wet.

"Oh, Rose…" Paige says, rushing to the edge of the bed. "Are you ok?" she asks.

"No," I answer honestly.

Paige leans over, wrapping her small arms around me in a comforting gesture. It's the kind of hug I'd expect from Hannah. Of course, this only makes me sob harder.

"Please don't cry," she says soothingly. "Xander told me everything."

I pull myself into a sitting position but squeeze the pillow that I've been crying into.

"Jason basically called me a whore," I say through fresh tears.

"He didn't mean it. He let his emotions get the best of him," she says reasonably. "He wants you to see things the way they do."

"That's impossible," I say in disbelief. "I'm not like them!"

"I know," Paige says sadly. "It's hard to see things the way they do; they're…unique," she finishes politely.

"What?!" I question, shaking my head.

"Alright. They're old," Paige admits sheepishly.

I laugh gently, but it's a genuine laugh. It's the same kind of laugh Morgan could always get out of me- one of real joy.

I release my pillow shield and drop back onto my bed with a loud sigh.

"Why would he say something so hurtful?" I ask.

Paige pulls her legs up on the bed and makes herself comfortable.

"It's hard to explain," she answers after a minute. "Jason and Caleb have a…special relationship," she adds, finding the words.

"What do you mean?" I ask curiously.

"Jason has an incredible ability. He can absorb pain; physical, emotional, whatever really," Paige says.

"I already know that!"

"He's been absorbing Caleb's pain. To help him," she explains patiently. "The pain from loving you and wanting you, but not having you- Jason has experienced it, like it was his own."

Paige watches as understanding flashes through my eyes.

The pain I felt from all the lingering gazes, the wanting, fighting the desire, the forbidden kisses and touches- Caleb felt it too. Because of that, so did Jason. It's no wonder he was mad about Gavin. It would feel like a betrayal to him too because he'll know how it would make Caleb feel.

Why would he put himself through that?

"Why would he do that?" I ask incredulously.

"Caleb isn't quite an incubus, but he isn't entirely a vampire either. He's a bit of both. As such, he struggles. He fights urges and desires that we can't imagine. An incubus is aggressive, self-serving- violent even. They want what they want- and they won't stop. He didn't want to be like that. So, he reformed," she explains.

"How?"

"By choosing to fight his instincts, urges and desires, everyday!" she says with admiration. "By taking away some of his pain, it helped him to keep control of his actions. Jason wants to help his friend, his brother."

"Is it hard for him?" I wonder out loud.

"I don't know," she answers honestly. "You'd have to ask Jason."

Finally, Caleb is becoming less of a mystery to me. No thanks to him. But it doesn't matter now. I don't want to talk about the one that broke my heart anymore.

"Anyway," I say, changing the subject.

Paige rolls onto her side to face me and smiles.

"Anyway…what exactly happened with Gavin on our couch?" she asks excitedly. "The guys couldn't give me a real answer."

"Well…" I say, smiling. "Nothing really, we were kissing," I add, blushing.

"Aww. He kissed you?" Paige says with delight.

"Yes, and it was amazing," I say, getting lost in my thoughts of his lips and his hands on my back. "If Jason hadn't knocked, we might have…you know."

"Slept together? Wait…are you…have you never been with anyone?" Paige asks in disbelief.

"…I'm still a virgin," I admit.

"But all those nights with Morgan?"

"We spent most of those nights arguing about Caleb," I reason.

"Fair enough! Did you ever come close with Caleb?" she asks.

"Not really. My feelings were always so messy. I was usually conflicted about whether I even liked him as a person. He was always so hard to read," I confess. "I didn't want to accept how I felt about him. By the time I did, things were too complicated."

"The best romances always are," she says knowingly.

She gets a faraway look in her eyes, like she's remembering something. It hits me then that she has a lot of history that I don't know about.

"Have you…had sex?" I ask shyly.

"I have," she answers confidently.

"Any advice?" I ask.

"Wait until you're sure," she says adamantly. "You'll want to remember it, so it should be special."

"Was your first time special?" I ask.

"It was," she says, remembering fondly.

I want that. I want to look back and say it meant something. I don't want any lingering feelings for Caleb. I know that that means I'm not ready. I need more time.

I stare up at the ceiling thinking about Gavin. He makes me feel so happy. I want to be his in every way, but talking about Caleb has made my heart hurt. I can't be with Gavin fully until my heart heals.

I fall asleep with Paige beside me.

Knock. Knock.

I wipe the sleep from my eyes as I realize that someone is knocking on my door. Sitting up, I notice that Paige is gone and someone covered me in my blankets.

"Come in," I say groggily.

The door opens just a crack and Jason pokes his head in.

"Hey. Can I come in?" he asks politely.

"Sure," I say, smoothing my blankets.

Jason walks in and sits down on the side of my bed. He's fidgeting nervously but looks into my face.

"I'm sorry!"

"I know," I say, releasing a deep breath.

"As your friend, I want you to be happy," he says. "But as his friend, I want it to be with him," he continues.

"I get it," I say reassuringly. "But it can't be with him."

"Why not?" he asks incredulously.

"Well for starters, he's not here. Secondly, I don't trust him," I say firmly.

"And thirdly?" Jason asks, humoring me.

"Thirdly, I deserve more," I say defensively.

"But he loves you so much," he says sadly.

"It's not enough," I say, a tear leaking from my eye.

"Why not?"

"Because it just isn't," I say angrily.

We both sit in silence. Him- thinking about what I said. Me- trying desperately to keep the tears at bay. It's been months and Caleb still wreaks havoc on my emotions.

"I'm sorry, Rose," Jason says affectionately.

"There can't be an *us* anymore," I confess.

Jason nods in understanding. He rises and walks to the door without another word, disappearing through it.

I grab my phone off the bed table and dial Gavin.

"Hey. Is everything ok?" Gavin asks with concern.

"Yes, everything is fine," I say.

"Are you sure?" he asks sweetly.

"I am. I'm sorry to bother you at work…"

"You know you can call me anytime!" he reminds me.

"That's sweet. Any chance you can leave work early?" I ask.

"Of course. I'll be there soon," he says.

"Ok."

I hang up, feeling better after hearing Gavin's voice. I get up, get dressed, and head to the living room. Paige and Xander are having a hushed conversation at the counter when I walk out.

"Hey guys. What's up?" I ask.

"Nothing," Paige says quickly.

"Where's Jason?" I ask, noticing his absence.

"He left already," Xander replies.

"Oh," I say, feeling guilty.

"It's not because of you, Rose. He had somewhere to be," he says, knowing I feel responsible.

"Ok…"

"What are you doing?" Paige asks, changing the topic.

"Gavin's on his way," I say.

"Already?" asks Xander.

"Yes," I reply.

It seems like there is more he wants to say but he decides not to. I'm relieved, because I'm too tired to argue more.

Knock. Knock.

I pull the door open and find Gavin standing there smiling at me.

"Hey," Gavin says smoothly.

"Hey," I respond, feeling my body relax.

I take him by the hand and pull him towards my room. I can hear Xander and Paige say "hello" before we disappear down the hallway and behind my door.

"What's going on?" Gavin asks.

His voice is laced with amusement and curiosity.

"I missed you!" I say shyly.

If he's surprised by my confession, he doesn't let it show. Instead, he smiles at me confidently and pulls me towards him. He doesn't hesitate to press his lips up against mine. The warmth relaxes me even more. I let my hands slide up his arms and over his shoulders. Our kiss deepens and he lifts me as he walks to my bed.

He stops in front of it and pushes me back gently.

"What's really going on?" Gavin asks. "Did something happen?"

I feel my shoulders tense slightly.

"No," I say too quickly.

He doesn't say anything, just looks at me.

I sit on the edge of the bed and fall onto my back with my hands over my eyes. I sigh.

"Maybe Jason said some stuff…" I admit.

"Stuff about Caleb?" Gavin says calmly.

"Maybe," I say uncomfortably.

I feel Gavin sit down beside me on the bed. He leans over me and moves my hands off my eyes. His caramel eyes sparkle at me.

"Are you alright?" he asks me sweetly.

"Yes," I answer with watery eyes.

"Are you still crazy about me?" he asks, brushing some hair off my cheek.

"Yes," I confess, unable to hide my smile.

"Good," he says smugly, "does my touch still give you butterflies?" he asks, his finger drawing circles on my belly.

"Yes," I say excitedly.

"Good," he says. "Does my kiss still take your breath away?" he asks, leaving a trail of light kisses along the side of my neck.

"Yes," I manage to mumble out.

"That's my girl," he says with a chuckle.

His lips find mine again and his kiss wipes all thoughts of Caleb from my mind. He leans in closer, pressing his body against mine. His one hand travels up and down my side until his fingers find the waist of my pants.

"I don't think I'm ready," I blurt out in panic.

Gavin smiles at me and takes his weight away.

"I swear that's not what I was trying to do," he assures me. "I was just having a little fun," he adds.

"Oh god…I'm so sorry," I apologize, feeling stupid.

"It's ok," he says with a laugh. "I'm sorry if you felt any pressure from me," he continues. "I like you and yes, I want you, but not until you're ready."

"You are unbelievably sweet," I say with relief.

He gives me a tender kiss and then rises from the bed. He's obviously trying to give me a little space after my awkwardness.

Knock

"Xander and I are going to get some Chinese food. Do you guys want some?" Paige says from the other side of the door.

"Sure. Thank you," I say.

"Ok," she says.

I listen to her foot-steps fade away. I hear the apartment door open and close.

I glance at Gavin quickly, feeling a mixture of shame and embarrassment. He's watching me silently.

"I feel so dumb."

"Don't," he reassures me. He sits beside me on the bed, giving me a serious look. "Are you a virgin?" he asks, raising an eyebrow.

"No-no, o-of course not," I say defensively.

I look away from him, but I can practically feel him smirking at me. I don't know why I'm so embarrassed.

He chuckles.

"What is so funny?!" I say angrily.

"You," he says bluntly. "Being a virgin isn't a bad thing, especially at your age."

"Yeah, right."

"It's not! It's beautiful," he argues.

"That's easy for you to say," I say with a pout.

"When it's the right time, it'll happen," he says confidently. "But if you really want to change that, I'll gladly help," he says with a smirk and a wink.

"Shut up," I say playfully.

I give him a gentle shove.

"But seriously, you don't need to rush it," Gavin says sweetly.

"Thank you."

I stare into his beautiful brown eyes. He's so sincere and I'm surprised at how easy it is to talk to him. *How did I get so lucky?*

He leans forward and gives me a light kiss on the lips before he gets up and swiftly moves towards my bedroom door.

"Come on, let's get a movie ready for the food," he says.

He reaches for the doorknob.

"I'm crazy about you," I say suddenly.

Apparently, I have verbal diarrhea tonight.

"I feel the same way," he says, gazing back at me.

It's then that I know that everything is going to be alright. I can feel his sincerity. What we have is real.

CHAPTER EIGHT

Rose

Knock.

I open my door, already knowing who it is.

"Hello beautiful," Gavin says, smiling his sweet smile at me.

He doesn't wait for me to reply before stepping into my room and pulling me into his arms. His lips are soft and welcome against mine. I wrap my arms around his neck, pulling myself up on my tip toes.

He holds me tightly to him, kissing me with very little concern for anything else going on around us.

"So…I'm going to go," Paige says, breaking our lip-lock.

She smiles at me as she smoothly passes by.

"Sorry," I say to her, still wrapped up in his embrace.

She slips out the door without another word. I know she doesn't take it personally. It is August now. Gavin has been my "boyfriend" more or less, for almost two months. Our public displays of affection aren't new. Everything changed after our first kiss. He always kisses me and touches me, no matter who is around. He's very open about his feelings. It's refreshing.

"Hey," I reply comfortably.

I pull his head back down until my lips connect with his again. I shuffle backwards, holding him to me. He lays me gently onto the bed and pushes himself on top of me.

He pulls back and brushes a few strands of hair off of my cheek.

"How's my girl doing?" he asks.

"Never better," I whisper.

It's true, though. I don't think I have ever been this happy. Here with this sweet, sexy, and amazing guy feels like heaven.

"I can think of a way to make it better," he starts mischievously, "but it involves less clothes," he finishes with a smirk.

"Of course, it does," I say with a giggle.

"That doesn't sound like a no," Gavin says, raising an eyebrow.

I roll my eyes at him playfully. *To be honest, I'm tempted.* I have been falling for Gavin more each day. Fortunately, I don't have to choose, because I was called into work at the bookstore a little while ago.

"I actually have to go to work," I say, avoiding his comment.

"Ugh," he groans.

Gavin rolls off me dramatically and lies on the bed like he's been gravely wounded. I roll on top of him, knowing I'm teasing him.

"You're awfully dramatic," I say, playfully.

He grips my legs, a smirk playing at his lips.

"Now who's the tease?"

I climb off him with a smile and make for my door. He'll wait for me; maybe we can pick this up after. *Maybe I'll run out of excuses.*

I whip back around, feeling brave.

"By the way, I thought about university," I admit. "I think I do want to go."

"Really?" he says with interest. "For what?"

"English, I think," I answer. "Am I too late?"

"No. I'll make it happen," he says confidently.

"Thank you."

I leave smiling.

The bookstore is dark and right now I'm the only one here. *Not that I mind.* I like the calm-the quiet. It's relaxing. I'm lost in thoughts of Gavin while putting some books back on their shelves in the back. The rows of books tower over me. There's dust gathering on the shelves. I make a mental note to come back with a cloth. Just as I place the last book up on the shelf, the lights flicker.

Jingle.

The bell above the door shakes to let me know that there is a customer in the store. I hurry back towards the front, but I have the strangest feeling that I am being watched. When I get there, I look around, but there is no one there.

Strange.

I grab a cloth and head back to dust. Thoughts of Gavin once again flood my mind. I can't deny that I want him. *Why wouldn't I?* He treats me like a princess. He really listens to me and cares about my feelings. I'd be crazy not to want a guy like that.

The lights flicker again but then shine steady. The building is old. *Stupid ancient wiring.* I finish dusting and let out a triumphant sigh.

Jingle.

The bell chimes again, so I head back to the front. Again, I see no one. I hear no one shuffling around. I look at the dark of the night through the window. The moonlight is hidden by clouds. The clock above the door says it is after nine- less than an hour left.

It has to be a prank by some bored teenagers.

I walk back into the store. When I was dusting, I noticed some books out of place. I still feel like I'm being watched as I walk through the shelves. The hairs on the back of my neck stand up. The air has gotten thick, making me breath harder. The shift has me on edge.

Jingle.

I hear the bell again, but I can't see the front from where I am. I stand and wait for either the bell on the front desk to be rung or for someone to call out to me. I hear nothing. My nerves start to get the better of me- a strange feeling urges me to run.

Strong arms slip around me from behind, soundlessly. I let out a scream and try to jump away, but they're strong and they don't let go. Instead, I turn enough to take them in.

"Surprise," the familiar voice says playfully.

"Gavin! Oh my god," I say, releasing my breath as I recognize the flirty voice. "You scared me!"

"Sorry!" he says apologetically. "Is everything ok?" he adds, watching me carefully.

He lets go, realizing that he genuinely scared me.

"Yes. It's just been a weird night," I say, thinking about the bell.

"What do you mean?" Gavin asks, concern in his voice.

"It's nothing, I'm sure," I say, feeling better about it. "The bell at the door keeps ringing, but no one is there. And I feel like I'm being watched."

Gavin looks distracted for a minute, but then the sparkle returns to his eyes.

"I don't think it's cause for concern," he begins. "If you're being watched, it's only because you're gorgeous!" he adds smoothly.

"Aw, Gavin!"

I reach my hands up to his neck and pull him into me. I kiss him lovingly, the fire starting in my belly. He pushes me back with his body so that I am pinned in between him and the solid bookshelf. My breathing gets quicker, rougher, my excitement mounting. His hands are grabbing firmly at my hips, the pressure increasing.

I'm aware that a customer could walk in at any moment, but that makes it better. *If that makes sense.*

He seems to read my thoughts, his body responding in the same way. His kiss gets more intense, his grip firmer.

He steps back, separating our embrace. He quickly drops his coat, no doubt too hot. I slide my hands down and quickly pull my shirt up over my head so that I am standing there in a simple gray bra. He takes a minute, his eyes raking over my body before stopping on my face. His eyes shine when they lock with mine.

We both know where we want this to go. Unspoken words pass between us and before I know it, he is removing his shirt and once again connecting with my lips. His chest is covered in muscles that ripple and flex with his every move. His hands explore my body with vigor, slowing and enjoying the feel of my bare skin. Our kiss deepens, lust taking over.

He reaches under my legs and lifts me up, wrapping my legs around his torso. His lips tear from mine and travel tenderly down my neck.

I grip at his shoulders, clenching the muscles with my fingers as I feel the sting of his fangs sinking into my neck. It hurts but in a good way.

I suck in air harshly, slightly out of breath, and start relaxing into him as the pain disappears. It feels better than I thought it would. This is the first time he's ever fed from me and the whole moment is more than amazing.

I feel his teeth exiting my skin carefully. I know that he's trying to be gentle. Resting his forehead on my cheek, I feel how his breathing has sped up. I know what he wants. I want it too!

"I want you," I manage to whisper out.

He stops kissing my neck, pulling back and looking into my face. His eyes are filled with desire, excitement, and affection.

"Are you sure?" he asks delicately.

"Definitely."

My answer is confident. I have no lingering doubts. I want this to be my first time. *It's perfect.*

Gavin's lips turn up into a smile and he confidently pushes back into me. His hands slide around to the button on my jeans, opening them easily. He places my feet back down on the floor and moves his hands to my zipper- never taking his eyes off mine. I feel his thumbs tuck into the fabric at the waist of my jeans and my heart rate quickens as I'm filled with nervous excitement. He slowly starts pushing my jeans down...

He knows exactly what he's doing.

"Well, well…" the shadowy figure snarls.

Our heads shoot in the direction of the voice and there the wraith is, waiting in the dark, red eyes locked on us.

Gavin tries to block me from view, no doubt because I'm standing in my bra with my jeans halfway down my hips.

"Wraith!" I say, fearfully.

"How sweet, you remember me," the creature taunts.

Scared and embarrassed, I tug my jeans back up over my underwear and pop my head out from behind Gavin's back.

I guess I know why I felt watched.

"What do you want?" Gavin demands.

The wraith peels his eyes off me to glare at Gavin.

"You're not Caleb," the wraith says with a snarl, and looks back at me. "Aren't you a naughty girl," it cackles.

"I said- what do you want?" Gavin seethes.

"Interesting choice, Rose," the wraith says sickly, eyes still on me.

"Why are you here?" I ask, fearfully.

"Simply to deliver a message," the creature laughs maliciously. "He'll see you soon!"

The wraith grins a twisted, sadistic smile. The lights flicker again and the wraith disappears.

What the hell just happened?

Gavin turns to me, placing a hand on each arm.

"Are you ok?" he asks, sweetly.

I look up into his eyes, so full of concern. I can feel the tears brimming in my own eyes. I nod unconvincingly.

"Mhmm," I mutter.

Gavin pulls me in for a hug, letting out a sigh. He knows I'm not ok. *How could I be?* The wraith ruined what was going to be a perfect first time. Now all I can think about is how Lord Dalibor is still out there, waiting.

"I'm never going to be safe, am I?" I say sadly.

Gavin pulls back to arms-length and looks into my face. A tear escapes down my cheek. He wipes it away with his thumb.

"I wish I could tell you what you want to hear," Gavin says empathetically, "just know, I will protect you with my last breath."

He holds me tight, calming me, reminding me that I'm not alone. His arms are strong and comforting, his heartbeat steady.

There will be another time for my "first time". He's not going anywhere.

He bends down to pick up our shirts while I do up my pants. When he hands me mine, his eyes linger on me. I'm sure he's as disappointed as I am.

Lord Dalibor

I sit in the armchair, only feet from the fireplace, soaking in the heat from the flames. I'm always cold- the fire never seems to penetrate far enough into me to fully warm me. Ana's touch, however, could warm me. Her magick helped me to feel alive, and less like a cold, dead *thing*.

I suppose that's one of the downsides to being an incubus.

I press my eyes closed, my fingers playing with the locket in my pocket. It won't be long until I have her back and I can stop reliving these feelings in memories.

"Well, don't just lurk. Get in here!" I say impatiently, sensing its presence.

The door opens and the smoky body of the wraith walks through, lingering in the shadows, red eyes blazing.

"Where is she?" I demand.

"Toronto. It appears she went home. When I found her, she was wrapped in the arms of another halfling," the wraith purrs.

"And Caleb?" I ask.

"Nowhere to be seen," it says.

This news surprises me. Informing Rose of Caleb's deceit worked out better than I expected, and it appears that she has a side I'm not aware of.

"Good."

Caleb was my only real obstacle- the others are inconsequential. This is going to be too easy.

"Do you really believe the boy will stay away?" it questions.

"It would be preferable…but, no. He's much too selfish to do what's best for her," I glower.

"There might be another complication, my Lord."

I sneer at the wraith, "what?"

"I've heard whispers that the vampires are making a move, that they have plans for her- none of which are pleasant," he smiles evilly.

"Yes. Yes. I've heard…It doesn't concern me. With the Dark Shadows under my control, there is no place she can go where I can't get to her," I remind the wraith.

"Perhaps you should let it play out. It could work in your favour if certain people were killed in that ordeal," it says cleverly.

"Hmm. You might be right," I muse.

I smile a twisted grin at the shadows, knowing the wraith looks forward to the chaos and destruction we're going to inflict.

CHAPTER NINE

Rose

It's the second week of September- four weeks since the wraith appeared and delivered the threat. Gavin was true to what he said, which is why I'm sitting on the campus of Toronto University, having dinner with Paige and looking for a little advice.

"I need some advice," I say bluntly.

"About what?"

"It's about Gavin and the night the wraith showed up."

Paige nods at me, wanting me to continue.

"Ok, so Gavin and I were alone, and things were getting…heated," I say uncomfortably.

"Heated? Like a great make-out session?" she asks excitedly.

"Well, it started out that way but then things got…serious," I say, with a blush.

"Did you have sex with him?"

"No, but it almost happened," I admit. "He finally fed from me, but the wraith showed up before anything else happened."

"And you haven't since?" she asks curiously.

"No," I say sadly.

"Do you still want to be with him?" Paige asks, confused.

"I do. Even more now, but…"

"But what?" she questions.

"Thing is, that whole night was flawless. How do we do it again?" I ask with frustration.

The truth is, I'm nervous. I was so in the moment that I didn't have time to overthink it. Since then, I've avoided even being alone with Gavin out of fear that we will try again but I'll just mess it up.

"That's absolutely awful," Paige says. "You know that you can't avoid it forever."

"I know," I admit.

"Just talk to him," she says with a sigh. "He seems pretty patient and understanding."

I nod at Paige while I fight back the blush from this conversation. This topic is new to me and while Paige is amazing, I still wish Hannah was here. I have so many questions.

We continue eating our dinner while all my thoughts, worries and questions consume me. I'm so concerned with the whole topic that I don't notice that Paige is watching me.

"Ok. What's on your mind?" Paige asks, pulling me out of my own head.

I look at her, embarrassed.

"Whatever it is, you can say it."

"What's it like?" I ask, blushing hard.

"What's what like?"

"Your first time," I say quietly, peering around to make sure no one is paying attention to us.

"It's hard to describe," she says thoughtfully.

"Try," I say eagerly.

"Well, it's overwhelming. It hurts a little, so it can be scary. But it also feels good," she says simply. "It depends on the situation and the person. It needs to be right for you!" she emphasizes. "If you have confused feelings at all it will definitely make it worse."

"Sounds simple enough," I say sarcastically.

"Just talk to him," she says with a smile.

She starts packing up her purse and gathering her garbage. Our dinner is over. It's time for me to head to the library anyway.

"I will," I say honestly.

"Good," she says, "are you coming home or are you off to the library?"

"Library. I have a paper to start," I reply.

"Ok, I'll see you at home," she says cheerfully.

Paige heads off with a wave. I send Gavin a quick text asking him to meet me later to talk, before I lose my nerve. I look up just in time to watch Paige disappear from sight before heading to the library.

The university library is huge and quiet. There's no one at the desk now and only a few remaining students. *It's perfect.* I find a secluded table in the back and start piling up the books that I need. To anyone else, it's a long night, but not to me. I love reading!

Before I know it, it's been a few hours. I notice that the remaining students have silently left, leaving me alone. I start putting books back, knowing that Gavin is probably waiting for me.

I'm putting the last book on the shelf when the lights flicker. I turn quickly, my back to the bookshelf, looking from left to right down the aisle. The last time the lights flickered, that wraith showed up.

"Rose," my name is whispered from nowhere and everywhere at the same time.

It sends chills up my spine and I feel the hairs stand up on the back of my neck. Instantly I race down the aisle, trying to get as far away from the voice as possible. The lights flicker again and I back myself into a corner, terrified. The oxygen in the room seems to disappear. I can't breathe. I don't think I'm alone anymore.

"Rose," the air whispers again.

I know that voice, I think to myself, frozen in fear and looking frantically from one aisle to the next.

"Hello, Roselyn," Lord Dalibor taunts, appearing half-way down one aisle.

His black hair is slicked back, not a strand out of place. He's staring at me with his deep black eyes, standing tall and proud. A sinister smile is on his lips. "You look lovely," he adds.

"Lord Dalibor...you're here," I whisper out.

"More or less," he answers distantly. "You didn't really think I'd give up that easy," he continues sickly.

I had hoped that he would, but I'm not naïve enough to believe that he actually would. I can't bring myself to speak to him though, out of both fear and anger. I don't know which emotion is more obvious. Instead, I stand there breathing heavily and trying to calm my nerves.

"What do you want?" I respond, my bravery wavering.

Lord Dalibor takes a few steps closer, his eyes watching intensely, appreciatively. He doesn't try to hide the longing in his face, and it makes the heat begin to rise in my own cheeks.

"I think you already know what I want. You!" he says with confidence.

"Why?" I plead.

Lord Dalibor stares at me quizzically, intrigue and interest written all over his face. He takes another menacing step towards me. I stand frozen with my back already against the bookshelf.

"You really don't know why, do you?" he teases.

"No," I say honestly.

"It is not only for your beauty or the spirit you possess," he says with amusement, "but because your power has been foretold by the sorceress."

"What power? I don't have one! What sorceress?" I ask, confused.

"You don't yet, but you will. It will come...and when it does, whatever side you're with will have all the power," he says excitedly, taking a few more steps towards me. "You could choose to come with me, and this could all be over. Everyone you love would be safe," he promises.

"No, I can't," I say, my voice shaking in fear.

Lord Dalibor eyes me with disappointment. As if he actually thought that I would choose to go with him. *Crazy!* Maybe he thought that he could confuse me by telling me about this so called "power" that I will have, and this sorceress that has seen my future. What even is a sorceress?

"You think that I am a monster. Perhaps I am!" he says thoughtfully, "but you will discover soon that there are all kinds of monsters worse than I," he adds with a look of disgust. "This world, *our* world, is made up of different kinds of monsters, each group with their own twisted idea of how this world should be."

"I doubt that anyone else could be as cruel and sadistic as you," I say scathingly.

Lord Dalibor stands up straight and sneers at me, his lip twitching.

"You will see. The wolves, the enchanters, even the halflings all have their own practices and traditions that are appalling and outdated. And then there are the vampires…well, their group is a special brand of cruel. I would know. I used to be one."

"You're lying," I say adamantly.

He laughs to himself and reaches a hand outwards to touch my face. I cringe as he is about to connect, but his fingers float through me like a cold breeze. I stare at him in surprise.

"More or less," I whisper mostly to myself.

That's what he had said about being here and I hadn't given it a second thought.

"Yes, I suppose even dark magick has its limits," he laments.

Lord Dalibor lunges at me and his body hits me like ice. His figure turns into smoke and dissipates. The lights flicker again and then everything seems back to normal.

I stand there in shock. *What just happened?*

I know better than to believe everything he says. He has a way of speaking cryptically and in a way of touching on the truth without really talking about it. Dark magick? Sorceress?

Why does it feel like there's so much more I should know?

As my breathing returns to normal and my pulse slows, I leave the library. I have to get home. I need to talk to Xander, Paige and Gavin about this.

CHAPTER TEN

Xander

Gavin and Jason are standing only feet apart while they argue. The tension could be cut with a knife. Paige is standing beside me, no doubt ready to help break up the fight.

"She won't do it," Gavin says quickly.

"Why not? Because you don't want her to?" Jason says angrily.

"No, because it's him!" Gavin says aggressively.

They are both standing in an aggressive stance, neither wanting to back down from the argument.

"We need her to do this," I explain to Gavin calmly. "She will want to help us if you're on the same side," I add.

"I won't stand in her way if it's what she wants to do, but even mentioning him hurts her," Gavin says matter-of-factly, "and that's on you."

"You're arguing over this and you haven't even asked her yet," Paige says observantly.

Just then, the apartment door flies open and Rose charges in.

"I need to talk to you guys…" she begins, "J-Jason?" she says surprised.

"Hi, Rose," Jason says sadly.

"Are you ok? What is it?" Gavin asks with concern, rushing to her side.

"I-it's not important," she says, brushing off his question and centering her eyes on Jason.

"What's going on," she asks nervously.

Rose

Gavin is standing at my side with his hand on my arm. I can sense his nervous energy, as well as the tension in the room. I don't know what they were talking about, but it can't be good.

"We need to ask you a favour," Xander says.

"Ok?" I say, a mix of concern and curiosity in my voice.

"We need you to talk to Caleb," Jason says hurriedly.

"What?" I ask in total disbelief.

"It seems Caleb has gotten himself in a bit of trouble. He's been killing people left and right," Gavin says bluntly.

"He's in a rough spot," Paige interrupts quickly, giving Gavin the first scowl that she's ever given him. "He took off from Isaac and he's heading down a bad path," she continues.

"I don't know what you think I can do," I say tiredly.

"He won't talk to me," Jason says sadly, "but I think he will talk to you."

"I don't know," I say uncomfortably.

"Please," Xander says hopefully.

I look to Gavin to see how this all makes him feel. I don't want to see Caleb, and I definitely don't want to talk to Caleb, but a part of me can't stand the idea of Caleb in trouble. For some reason that I can't understand, I want to help him, but not at the cost of my relationship with Gavin.

"What should I do?" I ask Gavin.

He is quiet for a moment, obviously thinking over his response. His facial features look sharp, as if he wants me taking no part in this. Then they soften, and he takes a deep breath.

"Jason and Xander are your friends and they need you. I think you should help them," he says assuredly, even though it's obvious he doesn't want me near Caleb.

"Ok," I say.

Gavin is right. Jason and Xander are my friends and I owe them this.

"Let's go to your room," Jason says.

We all pile into my room. Jason and I take our places on my bed for our dream walk. Gavin is to the right of the bed. I look to him, searching his eyes for the comfort I so badly need right now. He gives me a small smile and squeezes my hand. I want to be in his arms so badly.

Jason pulls a dagger out and drags the blade down across his hand. Blood starts collecting at the gash. He takes a glass of blood from Xander and downs half, clearly in a hurry to do this. He looks at me expectantly, holding the knife ready. My pulse speeds up and I start second guessing my choice.

"Let me," Gavin says, taking the dagger from Jason.

I look up at him, afraid of the whole process again. He gazes into my eyes with so much compassion. When he leans down and presses his lips against mine, I forget what I'm about to do. He pulls back reluctantly, holding my outstretched hand.

He doesn't take his eyes from mine as he presses the knife into my hand. He makes a small cut across my palm as I wince slightly. I take the glass with the remaining blood from Jason and chug it back. I lean back into the pillows and shut my eyes, trying to remember the taste of Gavin's lips on mine.

I feel Jason press his bloody hand against mine to make the connection. I hear him mutter the incantation that will take us into the dream realm. As the world around me spins, my breathing starts to feel more forced. Jason comes into focus while I struggle to breathe. We are surrounded by blackness.

"This is as far as I ever get. He won't let me in," he says in frustration.

"Jason…" I whisper as I collapse to the ground, heart beating out of my chest.

"Breathe, Rose. Just breathe," he says dropping in front of me. "Look at me," he adds calmly. "Just focus on me."

I do what he says, feeling my breathing returns to normal. I'm having a panic attack at the idea of seeing Caleb. I know it. Jason knows it. *This is humiliating.*

He helps me to my feet and as he does a fire and some trees materialize in front of us.

"He let us in," Jason says excitedly, still holding my hand.

I look around at the darkness, the nearest trees illuminated by the fire. *Where is he?*

"You found me," Caleb says, walking out from behind a tree in a gray t-shirt and skinny black jeans.

His piercing gray eyes are focused on me and only me. I'm overcome with relief at the immediate sight of him, followed by a storm of repressed emotions.

He looks as gorgeous as ever with his strong jaw and perfect black hair.

"We're so glad that you're alright," Jason says sincerely.

"Really," Caleb asks, still watching me.

"Yeah. We've been worried," he answers, despite the fact that Caleb has yet to look at him.

"Does that include you?" Caleb asks me boldly, ignoring Jason.

I open my mouth, but nothing comes out.

"She's here," Jason says, trying to affirm Caleb's thoughts.

"She is," Caleb acknowledges, stopping only feet in front of me and gazing at me with a familiar intensity.

"I didn't come for *you*," I say defiantly.

Caleb smirks at me, amusement sparkling in his eyes, challenging me. Something is different about him.

"Sure, you didn't," Caleb says, his voice heavy in disbelief.

"She came as a friend," Jason says, trying to compromise for us, but my anger is returning. My desire to cause him pain flares up again.

"I came as a favour," I say defensively to his attitude, "but I will gladly go back to Gavin now."

"He hasn't gotten what he wants and tossed you aside yet?" Caleb says hurtfully.

"What's wrong with you?" I ask, on the verge of tears.

He seems cold, distant, *cruel,* almost.

"His humanity is completely off," Jason says, the realization dawning on him. Worry settles in his eyes.

"Oh, very clever; took you long enough," Caleb says with a mocking clap, not taking his eyes off me.

"What does that mean?" I ask Jason.

"It means that he was overwhelmed by his emotions and turned them all off. It means he doesn't feel anything," Jason explains sadly.

"It means that I'm finally doing what I always should have," Caleb says coldly.

"You can't mean that," I say, not wanting to believe it.

"Oh, but I do," he says, stepping closer to me so quickly that I gasp.

"Backup!" Jason orders him while gripping my hand tighter.

Finally, Caleb looks at Jason and smirks in response.

"Or what?" Caleb taunts.

In that instant, I release Jason's hand and slap Caleb as hard as I can. I stand there in shock with what I've just done. Caleb looks from me to Jason, a grin playing at his lips.

"Don't..." Jason begins a warning to Caleb before he disappears into the blackness.

"Where's Jason?" I ask with concern.

"Awake. I only kicked him out of my head," Caleb says simply, refocusing on me. "That wasn't very nice," he adds, rubbing his cheek.

I back up in fear, with Caleb stepping every time I do, until I find myself up against a tree with nowhere to go. My chest is rising and falling raggedly with my accelerated pulse.

I'm alone with no idea how to wake up.

Caleb takes a final step, closing the distance between us. His hands press into the tree on either side of me, digging into the bark, and he brings his lips to my ear.

"Remember all those times we were alone? It was so hard for me not to kiss you, to touch you, and make you cry out my name," he confesses intimately with a whisper. His admission makes it that much harder to breathe.

"Without my humanity, I don't feel imprisoned by the same rules," he continues, pushing himself up against me intentionally.

He pulls away so that he can see my face, analyzing my reaction. His beautiful gray eyes flash silver in excitement. My heart feels like it's going to beat out of my chest. His words are aggressive and blunt, but they're tinged with a longing that he can't hide. I can't breathe. I don't know what to say.

"Caleb, please, this isn't you," I sob and plead. "I can't…"

He leans back in to whisper once more.

"Too bad," he says. "I guess I'll have to settle for a taste," he adds quickly.

I feel him change into his vampire form, his body radiating a restless energy. My hands fly up to shove him away as his words register in my brain. He is too strong. His fangs plunge into my neck, an immense pain radiating through my whole body. I scream out in helplessness, unable to shift into my halfling form out of pure panic. His body crushes me into the tree while I thrash against him pointlessly.

I start to feel dizzy and close my eyes, succumbing to the darkness.

Xander

Jason wakes up abruptly with a gasp, his nose suddenly bleeding. They've only been under for ten minutes.

"What happened?" I ask Jason as he comes to.

"He pushed me out when she let go of my hand," he replies with frustration. "It's what he wanted," he adds, annoyed that he fell for it.

"Well, where's Rose?" Gavin asks, voice full of concern.

"She must still be with him," Paige says, "but why would he push you out?" she asks.

"Because he's turned off his humanity," Jason says, devastated.

"But his incubus nature could take over," Paige says what we're all thinking.

"We have to get her out!" Gavin exclaims.

Jason reconnects his hand with Rose's and begins the chant. His eyes are squeezed tight in concentration, blood running from his nose.

"Bring her back," Gavin says angrily.

"I'm trying…he won't let her go, he's fighting me," Jason struggles.

Rose bolts upright, shuddering and crying, two punctures bleeding on her neck. She jumps into Gavin's arms and sobs. Jason collapses on the bed, exhausted.

"Never again!" Gavin says firmly.

We all exchange looks. Paige and I help Jason out to the couch, leaving Gavin and Rose alone. *This was bad!*

"Why would Caleb bite her?" Paige asks me as she pulls a blanket over a sleeping Jason.

"We're lucky that that's all he did," I say honestly. "You don't want to know what he could have done."

I don't want to think about the things he said and did to her while she was alone with him. If he was willing to push Jason out like that, then he might be too far gone. Not only was it a dangerous and painful event for Jason, but Caleb knows that he's a threat to Rose in that state.

His past is dirty and dark and littered with victims. We've kept this from Rose and everyone else. It's something you had to see to believe. He has killed hundreds of innocent people, all to satisfy his own sick whims. Although it wasn't entirely his fault, it was ultimately his choice. You have to really know him to understand that that's not all he is.

I hope Rose can see it.

CHAPTER ELEVEN

Rose

His arms are wrapped securely around me, reassuring me of my safety and comforting me in only the way he can.

As my breathing evens out, I can feel the warmth of his breath on the top of my head, hear the steady beating of his heart in his chest, feel the strength in his arms.

It's everything.

"I love you!" I say confidently.

He pushes me back at the shoulders until he can look into my eyes- the caramel in his eyes shimmering.

"I love you too!" he says with a smile.

He tips my chin up with two fingers- tears run down my cheeks. A single tear spills over the rim of my eye and follows the trail down.

Gavin presses his lips into mine sweetly, but he pulls away too quickly. I don't want to stop. I want to erase the memories of all the things that happened to me in the dream realm.

"Are you ok?" he questions, observing the punctures in my neck.

What kind of question is that? Obviously, I'm not ok. I wasn't prepared to see Caleb like that- I doubt I ever could be.

The things he said to me were cruel and detached, but he was honest. As horrified as I was, his confession was bringing up feelings that I really didn't want to have. I remembered those moments alone with him well. They will forever be seared into my brain. The desire was so intense that it was physically painful. Those are details that I will take to my grave.

"Not really," I say honestly.

He tries to wipe the blood off my neck, but it's already drying. He pulls me to the adjoining bathroom. He grabs my arm, spinning me towards him- so close that I can rest my head on his chest. He runs his hands down my hips and slips them just under my butt. He lifts me easily, bringing me up so that we're face to face. I look into his eyes filled with adoration and concern. He sets me down on the bathroom counter just behind me.

As he goes to back away, I wrap my legs around his hips and pull him against me tightly. I slide my hands up his chest and over his shoulders. His face shows his amusement and surprise as he leans into me. He caresses my cheek lovingly while I squeeze him with my legs.

"What are you doing?" he asks playfully.

"Nothing," I say innocently.

I push into him harder, making us as close as we can. His hands move around my back, gripping me firmly. He kisses me a little roughly, showing me his desire. I smile into his lips, enjoying the way I'm making him feel.

"We need to talk," he says breathlessly, between kisses.

"I don't think so," I whisper, "you're right where I want you," I add bewitchingly, squeezing him between my legs.

"Rose," he says, pulling his lips from mine, "you can't pretend it didn't happen."

His voice is serious now, missing its flirty playfulness. My legs drop, releasing him from their grip. I take a disappointing breath, missing the feeling of his body between my legs.

"Why not?" I ask in annoyance.

"That's not healthy," he says sympathetically.

He grabs a washcloth, wets it, and wipes gently at the dried blood on my neck. I grimace slightly as he cleans the tender area. I know he's right even if I wish he wasn't.

"You need to talk to someone," he says wisely, "even if you can't talk to me."

He keeps wiping gently at my neck while I think about what he said. There are certain details that I don't want to share with Gavin, but he looks so hurt that I am unable to talk to him. I make a choice.

"It was devastating seeing him like that," I say emotionally. "He was cold, detached. When he spoke, his voice was filled with hopelessness."

He finishes cleaning my neck and watches me intensely. I feel exposed and vulnerable, but it feels good opening up to Gavin.

"When he bit me…" I begin to say, but fall speechless. "When he bit me, it felt like I was dying," I say quickly. "The pain was unbelievable, but I felt his anger, hurt, fear- failure, too. I felt it all," I say grimly. "It was awful."

Gavin grabs my hand in a comforting way.

"What colour were his eyes?" he asks delicately.

I look at Gavin, slightly confused by the random question. Then it occurs to me that Xander is asking, not Gavin. They were letting me think it was a private conversation.

"They were gray, but darker and cloudy- silver when he turned," I say thoughtfully. "What does it mean?"

"It means he hasn't completely given up," Gavin answers slowly. "If he were an incubus again, they'd be black."

"Like Dalibor's?" I ask in a small voice.

"Something like that."

"Is that everything?" I ask, with more annoyance than I meant.

Gavin looks apologetic for what he's relaying. He knows that I have figured it out, and it doesn't take a genius to realize that I'm not thrilled.

"Will you tell us what he said to you?" Gavin asks hesitantly.

"No," I say firmly, leaping off the bathroom counter.

I brush past Gavin, feeling all kinds of hurt. Hurt from Gavin rejecting my fun in the bathroom, hurt from Caleb for disregarding my feelings, and hurt from being aggressively fed from. I drop down on my bed, the moon shining through the window, and close my eyes. *I'm beyond tired.*

Gavin walks over, rubbing my arm. He leans over, kissing me on the cheek.

"I'm sorry," he whispers. "I love you."

I grab his hand before he removes it.

"Stay with me," I say without looking at him.

He curls up behind me, draping his arm over my side and across my belly. I feel his breath on my neck while we snuggle.

I never told him what happened at the library with Dalibor. It seems like a minor detail compared to Caleb attacking me. *I can tell him later.*

"I love you too," I whisper to him.

I roll onto my back and stare up into his eyes, his fingers lightly running up and down my arm. I reach up and trace his jawline softly. *I'm crazy about this guy.* I bring my head up so that my lips can reach his and kiss him passionately. His hand cradles the back of my head, holding me to him. Our kiss is deep, full of love. I pull away from him, turning my head and exposing the uninjured side of my neck. I want him to feed from me- *need* him to feed from me, to erase what Caleb did.

I don't have to say it out loud. He knows what I need.

He brings his lips to my neck, pausing for a minute before kissing the spot delicately. I feel his teeth sink into my skin as gently as he can. The pain- a fraction of what Caleb caused. Naturally, my hand goes up and around his head, holding him to my neck.

His hand grips near my ribs with enthusiasm. It's obvious that he is fighting the inclination to be a little more handsy.

He removes his teeth carefully, his breathing slightly more rapid than before. He rests his nose in the crook of my neck, his eyes closed in appreciation. He moves his head after a few minutes and smiles at me.

I roll over quickly, pushing him to his back and straddling him in a teasing way. He grins up at me, impressed and amused. I use one finger to toy at the neckline of his shirt seductively. I lean in, kissing him sweetly before moving to his neck. Still holding his shirt, I let my fangs slide into his flesh like a hot knife through butter. The sting it induces only causes him to grab at my back tighter, which thrills me. A groan escapes his lips and it only makes it better.

After a few minutes, I pull my fangs out and lay my head down on his chest. The beating of his heart comforts me to sleep while he rubs my back lovingly.

CHAPTER TWELVE

Rose

It's been a few weeks since the whole dream walking disaster. Although I have healed physically, emotionally I am scarred. I haven't told anyone about Dalibor and the library. Things are just starting to get back to normal. I don't want to mess it all up again.

Gavin sleeps over most nights, but I haven't given myself to him fully yet. Not that I don't want to; it just never seems like the right time.

I wasn't completely honest with him about Caleb, about how a piece of me ached for him when he was so close.

Feeling dishonest has a way of spoiling the mood.

I know that I can't erase what I felt for Caleb, but I really wish it was that simple. *One can dream,* I think to myself as I walk home from the university.

It's later than usual- around seven. I lost track of time in the library, which was full of other people this time. As I walk down the streets, the wind giving me chills, I can't shake the feeling of being watched. There are a few cars driving nearby and the odd pedestrian, but everything seems eerily normal.

That's when I spot someone out of the corner of my eye standing near an alley. Dark jeans and a dark jacket with a dark hood covering their face. *It must be Caleb,* I think to myself. I cross the road and head towards them, against my better judgement. Before I can get close, they take off down the alley. They're running from me.

I follow them into the alley at a full run but come to a standstill because they are standing at the end of the alley facing me. Their lips are the only feature showing beneath the hood.

We stand there watching each other in a creepy silence. I can see that his fists are clenched.

"Caleb?" I ask, unsure.

"No."

Omg. I know that voice.

"Alex?" I ask again, my happiness building.

I take a step towards him, but he takes a step back quickly.

"No, don't go," I say fearfully, "please."

"It's not over," he warns me.

"What are you talking about?"

"He wants you…others want you…they all will come," he says. "He is dangerous, but he will protect you."

Who? His vague warning leaves more questions than answers.

"What…" I start, but stop when he disappears in an instant.

I consider chasing after him, but I know I'd never catch him. So, I continue on my way home, unsure what his warning was all about and wondering why he's coming to me now.

If he was talking about Dalibor, he has obviously been brainwashed. Then again, maybe he's talking about Caleb. He'd have no way of knowing he's turned into a psychopath.

"Is everything alright?" Gavin asks.

He's leaning back on my bed, watching me while I read. He raises an eyebrow with his question, a look of concern on his face.

"I'm fine," I lie.

I'm only mildly focused on the book while my mind is wandering to various thoughts about Alex.

After all this time and after everything, he is still nearby, watching out for me like he always has.

I feel Gavin watching me as my focus returns to my book. He knows that I'm not being entirely honest.

"I'm going to go with Paige and Xander to get the takeout," Gavin says, sensing my reluctance to talk.

"Ok. I think I'm going to go take a hot bath."

He gets to his feet smoothly and walks out the door, sparing a small, sad look at me. He wants to talk it out, but what the hell would I say? *Oh, by the way, Dalibor cornered me in the library, told me some cryptic nonsense about dark magick and a sorceress, and I saw my reanimated brother on the way home, who also revealed some vague shit about me still being hunted, and being in danger even when I'm safe. I don't think that would go over well.*

Maybe the warmth from the water will calm my mind and allow me to actually enjoy Gavin's company. It can't hurt.

The apartment door closes with a thud and I let go of the fluffy towel I'm holding around me tightly. It falls to my feet, where I leave it as I climb into the claw foot bathtub full of scalding hot water and bubbles, just the way I like it. When I settle myself into the water, the layer of bubbles come up to my chin. The heat instantly relaxes me as my hair floats around my shoulders. I sink deeper into the water, my back resting against the tub. I close my eyes and soak.

I needed this.

I try not to think about Alex, but his words haunt me. *"They all will come,"* that's what he had said. Why does it feel so foreboding? More so than just Dalibor coming after me. *Who? Why?* I just don't understand.

"What makes me so special?" I ask the back of my eyelids.

"I was wondering the same thing," someone replies.

My eyes don't fly open at the voice of the intruder. Instead, they squeeze tighter. My breath catches painfully in my chest. The water feels icy cold and panic consumes me as I recognize the voice.

Kiara.

I dare to open my eyes.

She is standing at the foot of the tub staring out the window, not seeming to pay me much attention. I know better. She knows exactly where I am, without looking. She is very strategic.

She looks gorgeous in a pair of skin-tight white jeans and a white formal jacket. Her blond hair shines in the light, her make-up is perfection, and her blue eyes are sparkling dangerously.

"W-what do you w-want?" I stutter out.

"Simple," she says quickly, turning to look at me. "I want you dead!" she snarls.

In an instant her features change- becoming sharper, deadlier and yet more beautiful. She has turned.

She jumps at me, forcing me beneath the water. I can't breathe. She's killing me and I can't turn. Her fingers grab at my hair, pulling me just above the water. I reach up in pain- it feels like she's pulling my scalp off. I cough out a little water that I swallowed.

"Why?" I ask, crying and screaming at the same time.

"It's all your fault," she screams furiously, shoving me back under the water angrily.

I flail against her from in the tub- fighting to get above water, to breathe, but it's useless; she's so strong. Just when all the air has left my lungs, she rips me up above the water by the hair again.

I gasp, coughing and choking.

"Caleb would have been mine if you had just stayed out of the picture," she yells hysterically.

She pushes me into the water again- my fingers wet and slippery, helpless on the rim of the tub. Again, I feel the water begin to seep into my lungs slowly as my body gives up. Darkness takes over my peripheral vision. My arms and legs weaken, losing all strength.

Just when I think it's over and I accept it, she drags me up again- right up and over the edge of the tub. I flop on to the floor, soaking wet- choking and coughing up water from my lungs. She let's go of my hair and I fall closer to floor.

"You're pathetic!" she spits at me. "What Caleb ever saw in you is beyond me. At least Lord Dalibor wanted to sacrifice you to bring back Ana. That makes sense," she adds jealously.

"I was never in the way," I say, still coughing.

"By breathing, you were in the way," she says bluntly.

I raise my eyes from the floor to rest on her face. I can see the blame and the hate in her eyes. She truly believes that I am at fault for everything. Nothing I say will matter.

Suddenly, she leaps on top of me and puts her hands around my neck, squeezing and suffocating me. The back of my head hits the tile. I'm too exhausted to put up much of a fight. I weakly attempt to pry her fingers from my throat and gasp for air.

"Lord Dalibor would have been the best way to go. It would have been quick and relatively painless," she says, straining. "I'm doing you a favour. This'll be better than the lifetime of torture waiting for you."

The bathroom door blasts open so hard that the wood splinters. Shapes rush by, pulling her off me and pinning her against the wall.

"Are you ok?" Paige asks, kneeling next to me and covering me with the towel.

I can't speak; out of shock, relief, and the fact that I am still gasping for air. I thought that I was going to die- *naked* none-the-less! I was sure of it.

Now I'm sprawled out on the floor, still wet and naked, but Paige is at my side. She helps wrap the towel around me and has a hand around my shoulders comfortingly, protectively. Xander and Gavin have Kiara pinned up against the wall. Stepping in front of her, Gavin places both hands on her head. He puts his foot on her stomach and propels off her. She screams out in anger and pain. A wet, ripping sound fills the bathroom as her head detaches and the screaming stops.

I watch in quiet horror as Kiara's lifeless corpse slumps to the floor and Gavin drops her head. The guys look at me in Paige's arms before glancing at each other. They're both breathing heavily. Xander nods at Gavin and he hurries to my side, replacing Paige. He pulls me against his chest. I look up into his eyes, intrigued in a horrified way by what just happened.

"Are you hurt?" Gavin asks me seriously.

"No."

"I'm so sorry! I couldn't feel your fear right away," he says apologetically.

Although I have some bumps and bruises and a sore throat, I think I'm physically ok. Mentally, well I was almost killed in my own bathroom totally naked…as a virgin. *Holy shit!*

I lean in and push my lips firmly against his. He doesn't fight me, just kisses me back. His arms wrap tighter around me.

I'm vaguely aware of Xander and Paige leaving the room. I can hear them dragging something by us and I can only assume that it is Kiara's lifeless body. I don't look- I don't want to. I just want to be with Gavin. It feels more important than ever.

I pull back slightly so that I can see his face, my breathing rate still elevated.

"I don't want to die a virgin."

It's honest. It lets me be vulnerable. It shows him that I'm serious about him. He knows what I'm getting at.

He scoops me up in his arms, without saying a word. The muscles in his arms harden as he gets to his feet. I can feel the steady beat of his heart through his chest. Paying no attention to the bloody massacre in the bathroom, he easily carries me to the bedroom. He closes the door with his foot and gently sets me down on the bed.

Gavin

She's absolutely captivating, sitting there, with her innocence shining through her green eyes- her skin still damp, her hair wet and cascading around her bare shoulders. I want her. I'd be an idiot not to have her in every way she'll have me. I'd be Caleb.

Then it makes sense why he never touched her, even though it probably killed him. I won't be him. I will sleep with her, but when the time is right. I want nothing more than to remove her towel and be her first, but it feels wrong given what just happened.

"I can't," I say hesitantly.

Rose

"You can't?" I ask with confusion and hurt.

I pull the towel tighter around me, wishing that I could magically be wearing clothes. This is not what I expected.

"Let me explain," he says, sitting on the bed.

"What is there to say? It's clear that you don't want me," I say defensively.

"You're wrong," he replies firmly. "I want to be your first, your last, and your in-between," he says confidently.

"Then what's stopping you?" I ask sadly.

"Your first time can't be after someone tried to kill you," he answers.

"Why not?"

My temper starts rising from being told what I can and can't do. I'm tired of it.

"You can't erase the bad simply by chasing it with something good. You'll regret it later. I don't want to be a regret," he says passionately.

My heart slows- the icy feelings I had melting away. How could he ever think he'd be a regret? He is more amazing than possible.

"You want to be my first?" I say, blushing.

"And your last and your in-between," he says smiling. "I love you!"

"I love you too," I say, tearing up. "I just wanted to take the next step."

"Then perform a blood bond with me," he suggests happily.

"A what?"

There's something I haven't thought of in a while.

"A blood bond," he chuckles. "It will bond us by blood. I will always know what you're feeling, no matter where I am. The same for you," he explains.

I want to say yes, but that means that I won't be able to hide my feelings for Caleb- the feelings no person in their right mind should have. Gavin will know. He'll know everything.

"I…" I begin.

"You're hesitating…I don't want to push you into anything."

"I want to," I reassure him. "It's just…"

"Just what?" he says patiently.

"There are things that you don't know about me," I say, on the verge of tears.

He moves to my side, his hand cupping my cheek affectionately.

"It's Caleb, isn't it?" he asks, already knowing. "I don't expect your feelings for him to disappear. As long as your feelings for me are stronger," he says with a small smile.

"They are," I say firmly, reassuring myself more than him.

He gives me a delicate, lingering kiss.

"Then bond with me," he says.

"I would love to."

He grabs me around the waist, pulling me to him. He kisses me sweetly- still cupping my cheek. I feel the heat rising as he pulls away.

"You've made me so happy," he says enthusiastically.

"How do we do this?" I ask impatiently.

"In a few days," he says with a sigh.

"What will we have to do?"

"Well, it's a ritual. So, there is an incantation, we share blood, then another incantation."

There's always blood. I don't know why I bother to ask anymore. It sounds simple enough.

Gavin smiles at me, his hands roaming the towel. I think he's already regretting his rational behaviour. Too bad for him, he's going to have to wait now.

CHAPTER THIRTEEN

Rose

"Oh my god. You're going to make a blood bond with him," Paige says with happy surprise, louder than I want.

"Shhh," I say, silencing her and glancing to see if Xander overheard. "Tomorrow, I think," I answer shyly.

We're sitting in the living-room chatting on the couch after dinner. The fireplace crackles. There's a movie playing, but we're not watching it. I can hear the shower going, so I assume Xander is busy.

"I'm excited for you. I've never felt the urge to have a bond with anyone," she admits.

"I want Gavin in every way possible. He wants this before we're physical," I confess to my friend.

"That's so sweet."

"But I'm nervous," I admit. "He'll know everything."

"Yes, but he will always know the second you're in trouble. After what happened with Kiara, it'll be a big relief for him," she says, shaking her head.

"What do you mean?" I ask, furrowing my eyebrows.

"Well, we were getting the food and all of sudden he said "she's dying" and he took off for the apartment. We followed him right away. He was so scared, you could see it," she says emotionally. "He really loves you."

"I love him too."

"That's amazing. I'm so happy for you!" she says sincerely.

I can tell she means it. She has no reason to have loyalty to Caleb. She may have no experience with bonds personally, but it feels like she's on my side. Regardless, there's something bugging me.

"Thank you, but…"

"But what?" she says, crinkling her eyebrows.

I pause, debating on whether I should say what's on my mind or not.

"What about what you said about Caleb? About our romance," I say, taking an uncomfortable swallow, "about how the most complicated romances are the best?"

"…It's hard to explain what I meant. You're so young…"

I sigh in frustration. *I get it. I don't like it, but I get it.* Maybe when I put a few centuries behind me, we can revisit this topic.

"You still have feelings for him, don't you?" she asks me steadily.

"I don't want to," I admit after several minutes, "and I know I shouldn't."

She looks at me with sympathy in her eyes.

"Maybe…" she says softly.

She doesn't elaborate, even though I know there is more that she wants to share. There are no valid reasons to excuse the way Caleb has treated me. *Right?*

"Should I be worried about letting Gavin in?" I say nervously.

"No," she responds. "Gavin doesn't seem to be the jealous type."

I was hoping she would say that. We fall into silence. She seems troubled by something. I'm about to ask her when Xander joins us.

"What're you guys chatting about?" Xander asks harmlessly.

"Girl stuff," Paige says without missing a beat.

He sits down in between Paige and me with a light chuckle. We all turn our attention to the movie, but my heads not in it.

When it's over we all head to bed. Xander stares after Paige with a strange look on his face. I give him a questioning look at my door.

"Night," he says quickly, awkwardly.

Yeah. We're going to talk about that, I tell myself- dropping onto my bed. I stretch out after ripping my pants off and pull on some pajama pants that were laying on my bed.

I drift off.

Coming to, I see a familiar campfire surrounded by trees, but not a soul in sight. I take a couple steps forward and freeze, the hairs on the back of my neck standing up. I turn around quickly- running being my first thought. I come face-to-face with Caleb, or rather, face-to-chest.

"No," I say, terrified.

Panic rushes through me, making me shiver with cold while pain pulses in my neck where he'd bitten me. My hand automatically flies up to the area. He's watching me, staring at me, analyzing my every move, but he hasn't moved, making this encounter even more eerie.

"Why am I here?" I ask weakly.

Caleb begins walking around me silently. My breathing gets rough.

"You're scared," he says, ignoring my question.

"You attacked me last time," I reply defensively; breathlessly.

He comes to a stop in front of me, looking both amused and proud.

"I wanted to see you."

His voice sounds more natural and even remorseful- almost like his old self. My hand is still on my neck, protecting it the best I can.

"Why?" I ask.

Caleb lets out a low chuckle.

"I'm not going to bite you," he says, stepping around me, "unless you want me to," he adds, overly confident.

I begin flushing when I should be disgusted by his comment. *What's wrong with me?*

He stops at the fire, staring into the flames and avoiding my question again. For a few minutes, I remain standing with my back to him, hand on my neck, trying to gather some strength.

I let my hand fall to my side and walk over to the fire, standing a few feet from him. I feel vulnerable standing here, trying to calm my breathing.

He glances at me, his eyes dark and cloudy, but I swear I see a sparkle in them when we make eye contact. It gives me hope.

"Why did you want to see me?" I ask more slowly.

He breaks eye contact, looking back to the flames- ignoring me and my questions.

"Perfect," I mutter impatiently.

I turn to walk away, I have no idea where, but his hand quickly goes around my arm. Despite the familiar tingle, I jump away from him. He lets go of me just as quickly, but he doesn't look amused or proud anymore. He looks sad, lonely, and pained.

"You're jumpy," he says, trying to lighten the mood.

"Being attacked over and over will do that."

"I won't touch you…just don't leave," he says, almost pleading. "What do you mean *over and over?*" he asks curiously.

I walk back to the warmth of the fire, giving him lots of space.

"You, Dalibor ghosted me in the university library, and Kiara paid me a visit at home," I say blankly. "I'm tired of people trying to kill me."

"I wasn't trying to kill you," he says, wounded. "You're going to University? And Dalibor did what?" he says, intrigued. "What happened with Kiara?

"She tried to drown me in my bath then strangle me beside it," I reply shortly, avoiding the school talk.

"What?" he says with genuine surprise. "I'll find her, she won't bother you again," he adds, his feelings betraying him.

It's not his job to save me anymore, though. I don't need him to.

"What are you going to do?" I ask angrily.

"I'm going to kill her," he says adamantly.

"You're too late. Gavin already did…when it happened," I say candidly, ignoring his affinity for violence.

"He was there?" he asks somberly, looking away from me.

"Yes, HE was there. He usually is," I say, almost wanting him to pick a fight with me.

"There's something you should know…about Gavin…about his work," he says hesitantly.

"NO!" I shout. "I'm happy. Why do you want to ruin that?"

His face softens as he watches me. I struggle to keep the tears from escaping. I'm so tired of the secrets. There are always going to be secrets. I don't like it, but I'm beginning to see that that's how it is.

I am curious to know exactly what he's talking about, but I refuse to give him the satisfaction.

"I'm not trying to make you miserable," Caleb sighs.

"That's a lie," I seethe. "You want me to feel as hopeless as you do."

"I don't," he says sadly. "I only want to protect you."

"I don't need you to protect me anymore," I exclaim, tears running down my cheek.

Using his vampire speed, he comes to a stop a foot in front of me. Very slowly, he reaches up. Using one hand, he wipes the tears from my cheek. His fingers tingle on my skin as I look up into his gray eyes, clearer now than they had been.

"You're so stubborn," he says, a hint of a smirk playing at his lips.

"And you're beyond frustrating," I reply with a small smile.

"What do you need me to do?"

I pause and say nothing. I don't want to say what seems obvious, but I know that I need to.

"I need you to leave me alone."

Caleb pulls his hand back reluctantly, looking devastated. His eyes grow cloudy again. This isn't what he wanted me to say, and it was hard for me to say it.

"If that's what you want," he says, his voice hardening.

"It's what I need. It doesn't matter what I want," I say resolutely.

"It sounds like you've already made up your mind."

"I have." My whisper turns into a sob.

We stare at each other, my heart-beat quickening and threatening to expose how much this decision hurts me. The lingering tingle from his touch taunts me, while the grays of his eyes continue to swirl with clouds. I feel lost in his eyes.

Suddenly, his hands are on both sides of my face and before I can think about what he's about to do, his lips are on mine. He kisses me passionately, his mouth acting for the words he can't speak. My hands reflexively rest on his forearms, feeling the muscles flexing beneath them. His kisses are hungry, his body wanting more, his tongue eagerly searching for mine. I find myself kissing him back despite my self-loathing.

After a few minutes, he pulls away slightly, letting me rest my forehead against his cheek. We're both breathing heavily.

He kisses me sweetly on my forehead, his hands still on my face.

"Goodbye, Rose," he whispers.

Before I can look him in the eyes, the world fades to black.

I bolt upright in my bed, alone and breathless. Silent tears stream down my cheeks- I know things have changed now. My heart's twisted and aching again.

That was his goodbye.

I fall back into my pillow, tracing my lips where his were.

"Goodbye," I whisper to my room.

CHAPTER FOURTEEN

Rose

"Are you ready?" Gavin asks.

"I am," I say.

Gavin is standing behind me and he moves closer, sliding his hands over my eyes. I lean back against his chest for balance; it's warm and I can feel his muscles.

He leads me forward as I push the door open with my arms outstretched. I can smell the flames while his hands are still covering my eyes, but I keep my eyes shut as I feel his hands slip away.

"Open your eyes," he whispers in my ear.

I do as I'm told. I let out a little gasp because there are candles sitting on every surface, but only one is lit. There are flower petals spread out across the neatly made bed. It's beautiful.

Tonight is the night. *Tonight we make our blood bond.*

He shuts the door behind us even though Paige and Xander are working, giving us absolute privacy. My heart skips a beat at the thought of what we're about to do.

"This is beautiful," I tell him.

"There's more," he says happily.

I feel Gavin's arms slide around my waist and pull me tightly against him. He kisses the back of my neck through my hair, making me smile and blush. He begins muttering an incantation under his breath. Within a minute all the unlit candles burst into flames. *They're beautiful!* It casts a warm glow through the room.

"I love when you do that," I say in awe.

"I know," he says.

I turn my body around in his arms so I can look him in the eyes. They emit a warmth I can feel. They're filled with adoration and love. It makes me so happy to see.

"You still want this?" Gavin asks, tensing slightly.

"Absolutely," I say.

He relaxes into me, wasting no time in pressing his lips against mine. He is kissing me gently but excitedly as we fall onto my bed completely wrapped up in each other.

His hands rub my shoulders, working their way down. They grasp at my hips enthusiastically and my heart starts to flutter. Using one hand, he pulls his shirt up and over his head, smiling at me as he tosses it to the ground. He smiles a sexy smile at me before sliding back into my arms and kissing me patiently.

My fingers brush over his smooth skin that feels hot to the touch. He allows more of his weight to press into me. He could have any girl in the world, but he chose me. Things feel so easy with him. I feel the fire starting in my belly before my fangs fall.

"That didn't take long," Gavin says, smiling into my lips.

He rolls onto his back, pulling me on top of him and causing me to straddle him. I give him a light peck on lips and smile. He pulls me down, putting all of my weight on top of him so that my lips are near his neck.

"Repeat after me," he says softly.

He starts whispering the incantation into my ear.

"Po moćima koje se," I say awkwardly. "By the powers that be, I take this man, Gavin Michaels, to be my blood bound partner," I finish.

He turns his head to the side, and I take the hint. I sink my teeth into his neck and drink only a little before pulling back and looking at him unsurely.

He pushes himself into a sitting position with me still straddling him. He stares into my eyes adoringly. His hands squeeze my hips. Without a second thought, I pull my shirt up and over my head, throwing it down with his. I'm sitting on top of him in a tiny black bra and the way he's looking at me makes me feel gorgeous.

His hand caresses my cheek lovingly and I flush. He lets the heat overtake him in seconds and runs his hand through my hair, brushing it off my neck. He brings his mouth to my neck, leaving several delicate kisses.

"Po moćima koje se, by the powers that be, I take this woman, Roselyn Parker, to be my blood bound partner," he says smoothly.

He tilts my chin, exposing all of my neck. Kissing it sweetly, I'm surprised when he sinks his fangs into my neck. My hands tense on his back before a moan escapes my lips- making me realize that the pain goes hand-in-hand with the pleasure. His hands rub my bare back as he holds me to him even when he removes his teeth, letting the heat leave him.

"Zahvaljujemo ti se," he says.

The candle flames flare for a moment before returning to normal. Gavin smiles sweetly at me.

"Is that it?" I ask, confused.

"It is. You should feed a little more, though…you didn't take enough. Besides, I like it," he says with a wink.

He pulls me back down on top of him.

"I think you just like me pressed up against you," I say seductively.

"Maybe," he says.

He doesn't have to tell me twice. I gladly sink my teeth back into the warmth of his neck and drink until I'm full.

"I love you," I say shyly.

"I love you too."

I rest my head on his shoulder. He holds me tightly and I'm happy about everything right now.

CHAPTER FIFTEEN

Jason

"It sucks being alone," I say to myself grimly.

It's late. I'm sitting on top of a bed in a run-down motel on the outskirts of a town in southern England. Clothed in a pair of black sweatpants and a white t-shirt, I'm about to eat and pass out. A pizza box sits open in front of me, but the smell of cheese and grease does little to bring me happiness right now.

I'm hurting. I still miss her- Hannah. I was falling in love with her. She was so full of life. Her happiness was contagious. And she would still be happy in this dingy old room with me.

Water and grime mark the walls. It's obvious no one bothers with much upkeep here. This place wouldn't be my first choice for a vacation. I'm here because Caleb isn't too far away and I have to keep an eye on him. *Someone has to.* Rose may have given up, but I haven't. I've felt his love for her. There's no way those feelings are gone. He has to be ignoring them, repressing them. I'm betting that *that* is the real reason he won't let me take some of his pain. It's easier to keep up his lie if no one knows.

Since Xander is busy keeping watch on Rose, I'm the logical choice- the only choice, really.

I lean back on the dirty bed, exhausted. My eyelids are suddenly too heavy to keep open. I let out a sigh, realizing what's happening.

My world fades into dark and a new place comes into focus- a place I recognize instantly.

Xander

I realize that I have been watching Paige a lot lately. Rose has caught me on more than one occasion, but she hasn't spoken to me about it- not yet. I'm sure she will. I can see it, she suspects it. Rose and Paige have become friends and when you have a friend, you take an interest in their romances. Not that Paige and I have one, but I think I'd like to.

I wiggle deeper into the soft blankets on my bed, a sudden chill coming over me. Both Rose and Paige are safe in bed, probably sleeping by now. Rose was sleeping when I got home, Gavin was here too. *Unfortunately.* I don't like him, but he's really been there for Rose. We may not have gotten to her in time that night that Kiara attacked her, if it weren't for him. He ripped off Kiara's head without a second thought, and Rose is happier than I've seen her in a long time. She deserves that.

My thoughts drift back to Paige. I haven't cared for someone in at least a century. I was accustomed to being the voice of reason without conflicting emotions, but when it comes to Paige- I am definitely conflicted. *More than I want to admit.*

I finally close my eyes, blocking out all of the thoughts in my mind and allow the sleep to come. I shiver slightly as my warm bed disappears and I find myself standing in a small camp.

Caleb

I watch as my camp materializes around the three of us. Jason, with his messy brown hair, sweatpants, and t-shirt, standing there with his arms crossed. Xander is in a pair of pajama pants and a t-shirt, wiping sleep from his eyes. A warm feeling rushes over me at the sight of them- my emotions are trying to regain control, but I ignore them and push them down.

I haven't been in the company of my friends in what feels like ages. Now there is less than a meter between us.

"Jason. Xander," I say, acknowledging them.

They both look at me- Xander with apprehension and Jason with anger.

"What the hell is wrong with you?" Jason asks angrily.

He lunges forward at me, stopped only by Xander. I stay where I am, unfazed. I expected no less. He's pissed about his dream-walk with Rose- when I forced him out and bit Rose. I know he doesn't care that it hurt him, but I hurt her.

Xander looks at me sadly, his hand still on Jason's shoulder even though he seems to have calmed down.

"He's right to ask," Xander says, "that was cruel, especially for you."

I laugh to myself. Have they grown so accustomed to me that they've forgotten what I am?

"Well, I am a…vampire…incubus," I say dryly. "Who really knows at this point?"

"You're a damn fool. That's what you are," Xander says, surprising both Jason and me.

I watch him, bewildered. He's usually not the one to call me out on my behaviour, it's usually Jason. Xander has always been the quiet, listening type.

"How's that?"

"You had her! She loved you!" he says, exasperated, "but you couldn't stop brooding about your past mistakes long enough to take her in your arms and show her that you loved her too."

"And now she's in HIS arms," Jason adds with displeasure.

I take a step back from the guys, feeling a pain in my chest at the thought. My breathing has accelerated at the discomforting words- my hands clench in fists at my sides.

"She learned what I am, and she ran," I fire back defensively.

"That's bull and you know it," Jason accuses me. "She ran because she doesn't understand our world. She needed your patience, understanding, and love. All you had to do was explain things when she calmed down so that she could process it. Instead, YOU ran."

"You left her to figure it all out- alone," Xander adds on the guilt.

I hate it, but they're right. I'm an idiot and I made a mistake- several. Now I have to live with the consequences.

I turn my back to the guys, breathing deeply to calm myself. Their words are hurting me more than I thought that they could.

"I brought you here for a reason," I admit, back still turned.

"Why?" Xander asks calmly while Jason fumes.

Why did I bring them? I knew this would happen. They have a way of seeing my life in a way that I can't, and they call me on it and force me to face it. It used to keep me in line; now it just upsets me that I can't take it back. Even worse, there's a part of me that doesn't want to.

"There have been whispers…" I begin, turning back around to face them, "that the vampires are going after her soon."

"When?" Jason asks, speaking to me once again.

"I don't know when. I just know that they know the halflings already have a plan in motion," I answer.

"Gavin," Jason says bitterly.

"Well, he *is* their collector," I say.

"We need to tell Rose. She deserves to know," Jason says.

"I tried. She didn't want to hear it," I say, thinking about when I brought her back here and kissed her for the last time.

"Maybe it's not Gavin," Xander says.

"Of course, it's Gavin. He's a bloody scavenger," Jason says with hate dripping off every word.

"But maybe it's not!" Xander argues.

"What are you talking about? You *like* the guy now?" Jason asks angrily.

"Don't be stupid! I know who he is, Jason," Xander quips, "but you seem to be forgetting that I live with her. I've seen them together, the way he protects her- the way he looks at her…" he adds, pausing and watching me. "The way he feels about her is obvious."

"He loves her?" I ask, not really wanting the truth.

"I think he does," Xander says gently.

"Does she love him?" I ask, regretting it immediately.

"It doesn't matter," Jason interrupts before Xander can answer, "she isn't going to appreciate it when he hands her over to the order."

"I don't know if he will," Xander says.

"He will," I say bluntly. "He's a soldier. He will follow orders, but he won't want to."

"So, what do we do about him?" Jason asks.

"Nothing," I shrug. "He's not hurting her right now. He protects her and he makes her happy. You can't do anything about him without hurting her. At least, not right now."

Jason and Xander look at me with curiosity. I know that they are wondering how I can talk about anything to do with Rose with such detachment. The truth- it's hard. I'm trying to swallow my feelings, to ignore how I really want to react. It helps that I'm planning to break twenty trees in half when I'm alone.

"We just let him have her, like she means nothing to you now?" Jason says furiously, stepping towards me.

I lunge forward and grab Jason's shirt at the collar with both hands, bringing us eye to eye. His hands go to my wrists in a weak attempt to pry them off. I want to scream at him, to shake him out of frustration, to tell him that despite everything I've done, everything I've become- that I still love her.

But I don't. I feel relief.

I shake him off and step back, understanding what he just did.

"Clever!" I say, feeling impressed and annoyed. "If she wants him, he can have her."

As he steps back, I can see that the fight has left him. Absorbing some of my pain tired him. No doubt he felt how conflicted I am or at least saw it in my eyes- the cloudiness swirling within. I know that I should be grateful for the relief, but I find myself feeling angry for feeling anything at all when I've been trying so hard not to.

"It's not as easy as you'd thought, to stop being human," Jason teases, reading my mind.

"It's harder when you're actually a good person," Xander adds.

"It doesn't matter. Gavin doesn't matter. Hell, right now Dalibor doesn't even matter," I say, gritting my teeth. "The vampires…the vampires should be your main concern. If you want to protect her, you need to move to another safe location."

"It'll take a couple of months to get a new place warded and properly hidden," Xander replies cautiously.

"That won't be fast enough, but do it," I advise him. "You know that the vampires are unimaginably cruel. They will pursue her relentlessly," I remind them with a cold indifference.

Xander nods in understanding.

He knows as well as I do that running will only delay the inevitable. If the vampires want something bad enough, they get it- even if it means manipulating the laws in their favour.

"We're done here," I say, anger threatening to overtake me.

"Ok," he says seeing the signs, "are you coming home with us?" he asks with hope, already knowing the answer.

I say nothing and look at the ground, unsure that I can cause my friends any more pain. He knows what my silence means and it hurts just as much as saying it out loud. His image fades away quickly as he leaves me and Jason in the dream realm.

"Is there something else?" I ask with a sigh.

"Why are you trying so hard to convince yourself that you don't love her anymore? I know you still want her."

"Of course, I still want her; she is delicious. Not to mention, hearing her moaning my name would be heaven," I say smartly, grinning.

"Caleb, stop it and talk to me. I know that you're still in there," he says. "I also know you're not done with her, even if you want us to believe that."

"I never claimed I was done with her. She's so fun to play with."

I move towards the fire and sit down. Jason follows me at a distance and sits near me, but not *too* close.

"That's not what I meant."

"I know what you meant," I say, all joking aside.

"You're struggling right now. I get that," Jason says. "It won't always be like this. You'll get a handle on it again."

"What if I don't? What if this is how I'm going to be now- fighting back the darkness inside?" I ask.

"Then we'll deal with it," he says, like it's no big deal.

"You don't understand. I'm always warring with myself," I say. "I feel like she's ripping me in two. I can't be what she needs- what she deserves, and I also can't be what I want to be or do what I want to do."

"Why not?" he asks.

"I want to touch her, to kiss her, to be with her without holding back," I say. "It's not in my nature to ignore my desires. I am what I am and what I am is dangerous."

"Maybe that's ok. Maybe that's all she's ever needed," Jason says.

"It's not," I say adamantly. "I can't be that guy for her. Morgan once said my affection was toxic. Turns out he was right."

"You may have become an incubus, but that's not all that you are," he stresses. "How many centuries are you going to torture yourself for the mistakes you made in the past?"

"As many as it takes," I say stubbornly.

Jason gets up from his seat and turns to leave.
"You're being ridiculous. I'm not going to argue with you anymore- I'm tired," he says, not looking at me. "When you're ready to get her back, let me know. Vampire, incubus, whatever you choose to be, I'll have your back. Until then we'll keep an eye on your girl."

"Thank you," I say, uncomfortably.

With that he disappears into the dark and I'm left with my thoughts.

CHAPTER SIXTEEN

Xander

"What is going on?" Paige asks me, shoving open the door to the men's room at the bar she works at.

She walks in confidently and for a minute I'm caught off guard as the only other person in the bathroom scurries out.

"Why are we here again?" I ask.

"Well, I had to work and you needed to give Rose some space," she says.

"Right," I say, annoyed.

"What is going on? You've been all over her every move for months."

"It's nothing," I say unconvincingly.

She watches me with her hands on her hips. Her hair is up in a ponytail, a few tresses hitting her cheek, and her blue eyes are shining bright. Gavin and Rose went to dinner to celebrate New Year's Eve and Jason went to check on the new house.

"Over two months ago you tell us we're moving to a new house, with no explanation. Jason has been crashing on the couch for the last two months, and you've been watching Rose like a hawk," she says expectantly. "So, what is going on?" she demands.

I sigh, knowing that I have to explain. I take a few steps towards her.

"Caleb warned Jason and I that there were rumours that the vampires would be coming after Rose," I explain. "We're just being cautious. Jason is at the new house adding some wards. We can move in tomorrow."

"Does Rose know?" she asks.

"No. I don't want to scare her. Things are just starting to get normal," I say.

"That's really sweet of you," she says, her stance relaxing.

My eyes run over her body almost unwillingly. She's wearing a flowy silk tank top and skinny blue jeans with little black heels. She looks good.

I notice her watching me and I tear my eyes away.

"I've also noticed you watching me," she says, taking a step closer.

I'm embarrassed. I guess I wasn't being as stealthy as I thought.

She takes the final two steps towards me and I look up, ready to apologize for being weird and explain that it isn't a disrespectful thing.

She presses her lips into mine, sweetly, for only a second before pulling away, even though I'd really rather she didn't.

"I like you too!" she confesses.

Her one hand is still on the back of my neck, her other hand on my arm. It makes me feel good. Suddenly, I want to give Rose some time with Gavin because I get it once again.

I don't feel alone.

CHAPTER SEVENTEEN

Rose

"Everyone must still be out!" Gavin says, pouring us some drinks.

"You mean we're actually alone," I joke from the couch.

It's New Year's Eve, so we went out for dinner- we just got back, but no one is here yet. Jason has been here for a couple of months and Xander has been more overbearing than usual. With there being five of us in this apartment, we don't get much privacy.

"It certainly looks that way," he says playfully.

He walks back over to me with two glasses, rye and coke for me and straight bourbon for him. He sits down on the couch with me and takes a large swallow of his drink.

"We should take advantage of this," I say seductively, setting my drink on the coffee table.

Gavin takes another big drink before putting his glass down. He smiles excitedly and leans into me. His hands squeeze at my thighs while my fingers lace through his hair.

"You don't have to tell me twice," he says happily, pressing his lips to mine.

He kisses me passionately, pushing his chest against mine, which thrills me. I can feel his muscles tensing against me. I pull away, my breathing getting faster. Gavin groans in disappointment.

"I want you to spend the night…" I say shyly. "With me," I continue quietly, biting my lower lip nervously and trying to read his eyes.

Gavin looks at me with surprise. His eyes sparkle with anticipation.

"Are you sure?" Gavin asks carefully.

"Positive," I reply without hesitation.

"There's nothing I want more," Gavin says.

"Good," I say.

I get to my feet, my drink in hand. I take a step backwards towards the bedrooms, hoping he'll follow me.

He rises to his feet, smiling at me confidently, and he swallows the last of his drink.

"I'm just going to get another drink. I'll be there in a minute," Gavin says, grinning and lifting his empty glass.

"Ok," I say, turning towards my room.

I hurry off, hoping to throw on something that is sort of cute. I don't have any sexy undies. I've never been that type. I settle on a black bikini cut panty with a black, cropped tank-top.

Shuffle. Thud. Shuffle.

I hear the noise as I check myself out in the dresser mirror. I grab my drink and head back down the hallway.

"Are you coming, Gav...?" I start asking when I walk into the living room, but I freeze at the sight before me.

Caleb.

I feel the colour drain from my face. As my fingers let go of my glass and it plummets to the floor, my breath catches in my chest.

He's looking right at me, his gray eyes staring with their well-known intensity, the cloudiness still swirling in them. He takes me in, but he's still got his hand around Gavin's neck, pinning him to the wall. I can't think. I can't speak. I can't even breathe.

It feels like forever when I finally snap out of my daze.

"Let him go, Caleb," I yell angrily.

Caleb looks from me to Gavin, obviously putting the pieces together. After a minute, he releases his grip on Gavin's throat and he takes a few steps back.

Gavin coughs as he inhales air. I want to rush to his side, but I'm still frozen to the spot.

"Are you ok?" I ask Gavin.

He nods at me as I look right past Caleb, not caring what he thinks. When I finally look at him, the hurt is clearly there.

"We don't have much time!" Caleb urges.

"Before what?" I ask, annoyed.

He uses his vampire speed to come up beside me. I gasp in surprise. His hand grasps around my arm and he starts pushing me towards the bedrooms while I try to avoid the broken glass.

"Put some clothes on. We have to leave," Caleb says harshly.

"What?" I ask, confused. "I'm not going anywhere with you," I exclaim with equal amounts of disgust and disbelief.

"Wait a minute, Caleb..." Gavin says, catching his breath and taking a few steps towards us.

"We don't have time for this," Caleb says with exasperation.

"Ouch," I gasp, stepping on a piece of broken glass.

His grip on my arm doesn't let up, but he stops shoving me down the hall when he realizes that I am hurt. The tiny piece of glass embedded in my foot is the last thing on my mind right now.

"Like hell! Get off of me," I shout, pulling my arm free. "What's wrong with you?"

I move away from Caleb awkwardly, rubbing the arm he had grabbed. He hurt me and he doesn't even seem sorry about it. He rolls his eyes as Gavin comes up beside me, comforting me and checking to make sure I'm ok even with the glass in my foot.

"You need to get dressed. They're coming," Caleb says to me, ignoring Gavin.

"Who's coming?" I ask skeptically.

"I'm assuming he means us," someone says from the doorway. "Although, I am curious why you're here."

My head turns in the direction of the voice. It's a cold, dangerous voice with a slight accent. The man speaking has dirty blond hair, dark eyes, and bears a striking resemblance to Caleb, being just as tall with a strong jaw. Of course, he's not alone. Four other men file in behind him, and they look just as mean.

"Who are you?" I ask. "What do you want?"

I glance at Gavin. He doesn't notice. He's watching the strangers with extreme focus. He looks…nervous. This only makes *me* more nervous. I can feel Caleb standing behind me, his tension palpable.

"Aren't you going to introduce me, brother?" the man says snidely.

Brother! What?

His gaze returns to me. He's watching me with such curiosity that it feels borderline inappropriate.

"What are you doing?" Caleb asks with a sigh. "Why are you here?"

"For her, of course," the man says with a twisted smile, "but, you already knew that."

Gavin steps in front of me, shielding me from the intruders. He starts slowly reaching out for my hand. I know what that means. He's going to get us out of here.

"I don't think Rose wants to go," Gavin says defensively.

"Too bad she's coming anyway," he says through a smirk.

"Over my dead bo…" he starts.

In the blink of eye, I see Caleb grab Gavin. In one quick motion, I hear the sickening crunch and I know what he's done. Gavin's body drops to the floor, lifeless.

I scream, dropping to Gavins' body. "What did you do?" I yell at Caleb.

I quickly rise to my feet and start beating my fists against Caleb's chest in anger. He doesn't even flinch. He just stands there emotionless, letting me hit him.

"Enough," the man says. "We're taking her."

"Not necessary. I'll bring her," Caleb says.

He grabs my wrist so hard it hurts and stares at me. "Why?" I whimper.

"Be happy," the man says, "he'll awake from a broken neck. If I'd had to listen to him any longer, I would've ripped his head off," he admits cruelly.

Caleb throws me over his shoulder and carries me to my room, shards of glass crunching under his feet on the way. His arm is wrapped around my bare legs, holding me securely.

"Caleb, put me down," I scream, but it seems pointless.

He shoves the bedroom door open roughly, throws me down on my bed, and stalks towards my dresser. He pulls out a pair of jeans and tosses them towards me, oblivious of the death stare I'm giving him.

"Put them on," he says, coming back to the bed.

"No."

"Either you put them on, or you leave in your underwear," he says.

"Are you threatening me?" I ask defiantly.

He leans towards me intimidatingly, grabbing my foot quickly. Without a moments' hesitation, he removes the piece of glass, ignoring my painful wince.

"Ow," I say, annoyed.

"Pants…shoes," he says, rolling his eyes at me and tossing a pair of shoes on the bed.

I pull on my pants and shoes- muttering hateful things at him the whole time. Then my anger gets the better of me and all my fear disappears.

"What if I refuse to go?" I ask.

His eyes sparkle with excitement, like he enjoys it when I try to be difficult. Meanwhile, I'm just trying to think of an escape plan by stalling, by being a pain in his ass.

"That's cute!" he says, amused. "It's not a choice."

He reaches out to grab me, but I climb off the opposite side of the bed. All he does is smirk at me from the opposite side.

"Knock it off. Let's go!" he says seriously.

"Come on, Caleb," his brother says from the living room, sounding bored.

He uses his vampire speed to get in front of me.

"Stop being difficult," he warns.

Seizing my wrist painfully, he pulls me back into the hall towards the strangers, who are waiting impatiently at the apartment door.

He stops in front of the intimidating group of men. I glance at Caleb's face as he is eye-to-eye with his so-called brother.

"What's the matter, dear brother? A lover's quarrel?" the man asks, clearly taunting him.

Caleb rolls his eyes at him as the man turns his devious grin on me.

"Who are you?" I ask boldly.

He reaches over to the coat rack and grabs my coat, holding it out to me with one finger. A twisted grin on his face shows off his bright white teeth, which makes him look downright evil.

"You'll see," he says. His goons chuckle behind him.

I yank my wrist from Caleb's grip and pull my coat on over my tiny tank-top. I look back at Gavin's body longingly for a minute. When I look back, the man is still watching me, seemingly interested in my behaviour.

"Well…" I say with attitude, gesturing to the open door they came in through.

He chuckles at the way I speak to him, which I find unsettling, before turning around and leading us out. Caleb reaches out and slips his hand around my wrist again. I try to pull away from his touch, but he only tightens his grip.

As we leave the building, it finally dawns on me.

I'm in trouble.

CHAPTER EIGHTEEN

Rose

The wind cuts through my coat and jeans, making me shiver. We've been walking for at least an hour, but I seem to be the only one affected by the cold. I can still feel Caleb's hand tight on my wrist, hotter than seems possible in this cold. I chance a look at him; I can see his breath in the air, but he doesn't seem to mind. He glances at me and for a minute, our eyes meet. His eyes are still dark and cloudy, his features sharper than I remember. He quickly looks forward again.

"There was a portal two blocks back," Caleb offers to his brother.

"I'm aware," he answers flatly. "We're staying at a motel for the night. The boys are hungry," he says, looking at me and flashing a dangerous smile.

My breath catches in my chest- fearful of his words.

"Sebastian," Caleb says, with a cautioning tone.

His brother, Sebastian, moves his attention from me to Caleb. He's apparently entertained by his reaction.

"Relax, Caleb. She's not on the menu…tonight," Sebastian mocks.

My body shudders at the casual mention of me as a menu item. I swear I feel Caleb's hand squeeze my wrist comfortingly, but it must have been in my head. *Why would he care?*

After walking a little further, Sebastian and his goons lead us into a motel. A chubby, middle-aged man is tending the desk.

"Two rooms," Sebastian says calmly.

The clerk busies himself getting the keycards and he peers up at me curiously, glancing at the guys surrounding me.

I'm still shivering from the cold and I wouldn't doubt that I look terrified right now.

"Are you ok, miss?" the clerk asks me nervously.

The thought crosses my mind to tell him I need help, but what is he going to be able to do against a bunch of vampires? Sebastian looks at me with a disturbing grin, letting me glimpse the reason he puts Caleb on edge.

"Yes. I'm fine," I force out.

"Ok," he says, unconvinced.

Sebastian turns back to the clerk, still smiling darkly, sparing an eager nod at his goons.

I only register what's about to happen when I feel Caleb press up against me and hold me with both arms.

"No. He said ok. He said ok," I start screaming hysterically, fighting against Caleb's arms, but he's too strong.

The clerk's fear probably matches my own terror as I helplessly watch Sebastian and his men descend on the unsuspecting man.

I see Sebastian rip the man's throat open. The blood pours out with a familiar gurgling noise. Caleb tries to turn me, but not before I see one of the goons tear the man's arms off.

With my back against Caleb and turned away from the struggle, I can still hear the poor man being torn apart, and the muffled blood-soaked cries. Then everything is quiet, aside from my ragged breathing, loud heart beats and silent sobs.

"Move the body," Sebastian orders, walking past us.

Caleb half drags, half carries me down the hallway to our rooms.

"In," he commands us.

Caleb shoves me into the room roughly, and I collapse on the carpet, devastated. That poor man didn't deserve that- no one does. I pull off my coat and throw it down, feeling like it's suffocating me.

I look up and watch him walk past me and go silently to the far bed. He sits on the edge, eyes glued to Sebastian behind me. I turn my head angrily as he shuts the door.

"Why would you do that?" I ask Sebastian in disgust.

"Why not?" he asks, showing the man's blood on him.

Without saying more, he moves into the bathroom, leaving me alone with Caleb.

I get off the floor, looking at the door to the hallway- the exit.

"Don't," Caleb says, reading my thoughts.

I roll my eyes at him without looking. I can't figure out if he's a prisoner as well, or a prison guard. I already know he's an ass, but that's beside the point.

The adjoining door opens suddenly and one of Sebastian's surly looking goons walks through. He's standing feet from me, smiling sadistically. I can smell the blood dried on his shirt. It makes me hungry and scared at the same time.

A warm hand closes on my forearm, making me jump a little. Caleb had crept up behind me and now he's staring down the goon and pushing me away.

The bathroom door opens, and Sebastian emerges. He nods at the goon, who begins stomping to the hallway with one last glare at Caleb.

"That's Rip," Sebastian says, gesturing at the guy in the hallway. "He'll be your babysitter this evening," he says to me. "Don't piss him off. He's already angry that he has to stay behind," he continues. "Or do."

"Where are you going?" I ask, confused.

"We're hungry," he says matter-of-factly.

I stare at him with disgust. If they weren't going to eat that clerk, why the hell did they have to kill him?

"You're psychotic," I say.

I can see Caleb tense in the corner of my eye. Sebastian grins at me sickly.

"Want to come? You must be hungry," Sebastian asks Caleb with a twisted grin.

Caleb's eyes flicker to the hallway door. He looks concerned about my babysitter. My heartbeat quickens at the thought of being left here with Rip.

"Rip won't touch her," he answers Caleb's unspoken concern. "Maybe," he adds, letting out an unsettling laugh.

"I'll stay," Caleb decides calmly.

I let out the breath I had been unknowingly holding. Caleb may be dangerous, but at least he isn't a psycho.

"Suit yourself," Sebastian says indifferently. "If you get hungry, she's here," he adds, gesturing to me. Caleb glances at me and I see the creature flash in his eyes. "She's yours after all, right?" he says more as a question, with a strange taunting tone.

"She is," Caleb says, smirking at his brother.

Sebastian's grin falters before he speaks. "For now," he says calmly.

He turns and leaves, the three other goons coming through the adjoining bedroom and following him out.

Caleb

Rose steps back and falls onto the bed, breathing roughly and letting out a few shuddering sobs. Her hands are on her face, covering her eyes, but I don't need to see her eyes to know that she's scared. *She should be.*

After a few minutes, she moves her hands, dries her tears and her fear is replaced with anger.

"I'm not yours," she says fiercely.

"Hmm," I chuckle.

"I'm serious, Caleb," she says harshly.

She sits up quickly on the bed trying to make her point. My chest stings from her cold words, although I was well aware of her status before. I feel a sliver of my own anger sneak in and a pang of hunger irritates me. I use my speed to rush in front of her, reminding her who she's talking to.

"I know you're not mine, but Sebastian doesn't, and it's in your best interest to keep it that way," I say.

She inhales sharply, clearly hurt by the way I'm speaking to her.

"I hate you," she says.

She lies down again, rolling over and facing away from me. She cries silently, but her arms go tightly around her own torso in an attempt to comfort herself.

Part of me wants to comfort her, but the other part of me can't stop thinking about how she tasted that night in the woods- my teeth in her skin, her body trembling against mine.

I've changed.

My own thoughts disturb even me as I watch her laying there in her tiny tank top and tight jeans. I lie down on the empty side of the bed, rest my arms under my head, and try to think of how I'm going to get her out of this.

Rose is asleep when Sebastian gets back, fortunately. He walks in covered in blood and heads for the washroom. He's in there cleaning himself up for a while. When he comes out, I have my eyes closed, but we both know that there is no way that I am sleeping.

"You missed out brother," Sebastian says darkly.

"Mhmm," I reply, hoping to avoid a conversation.

Luckily, he seems tired and falls asleep quickly. *I won't sleep.* I know better. Within minutes, a scream pierces the air from the room next door. Rose bolts upright, gasping in panic.

"I brought Rip back a toy," Sebastian says with a sleepy laugh.

I'm not surprised, but Rose looks petrified. I reach out a hand and gently squeeze hers- old habits. She looks relieved at first, and I begin to feel the familiar electricity, but she quickly pulls away and lays back down, looking away from me again.

The electricity fades, leaving me feeling empty, lonely, and mad again.

What is she doing to me?

CHAPTER NINETEEN

Rose

I wake up to light coming in through the curtains. I instantly recognize the motel room and my heart drops. I had been hoping that it was just an awful nightmare. My stomach squeezes at my realization.

I roll over slowly. Caleb is next to me with his eyes closed- maybe sleeping, maybe not. Seeing him there, peacefully, it's easy to forget that he may not be on my side now.

My wrist twinges, so I look at it. A purple bruise wraps around it from Caleb being so aggressive. I look back up and Caleb is looking right at me with his brilliant gray eyes- the darkness still clouding them. He glances at my wrist to see what I was looking at.

He holds my wrist gently, examining what he's done. I can't read his expression, but he is careful.

"My, my, brother…you should be more aware of your actions," Sebastian says, teasing Caleb as he gets up from the bed.

Caleb puts my wrist down slowly, but sits up and watches his brother. Sebastian pokes his head into the adjoining room. The smell that comes drifting out is overwhelming. It stinks of blood and death.

Caleb's hands clench at the blankets with startling strength. The veins under his eyes start pulsing, while a low growl escapes his lips. I climb off the bed and step back.

Sebastian watches us carefully, an eyebrow raised.

"Somebody is really getting hungry," Sebastian taunts Caleb. "Tsk. Tsk. Rose, don't you feed your man?"

"I'm fine," Caleb says quickly, trying to shake it off.

Sebastian smiles, obviously having the time of his life witnessing Caleb's discomfort.

"Caleb," I say, worried and forgetting how detached he has been. "When did you last feed?"

"I'd say it's been a week, at least," Sebastian says.

Caleb is still digging his fingers into the bed in pain. He usually feeds every day; sometimes more than once- even I know that. *He needs to feed.* I doubt Sebastian will do anything helpful, but I can't get past the last time he fed from me. I was unwilling and he took it anyway. It was so painful and yet there was also an unwanted pleasure of having him touch me. I just can't give him what he needs right now.

"Caleb...I," I begin, but hesitate.

Caleb jumps up from the bed using his vampire speed. He snatches the lamp and throws it across the room. It shatters against the wall on impact.

Sebastian is smiling excitedly at the scene before him when Rip pokes his head in, no doubt checking on his boss. I stay where I am, breathing hard, but Caleb won't look at me.

"Can we get moving?" Caleb asks with frustration.

"Sure," Sebastian drawls, still amused.

One of the goons takes the lead. Sebastian is walking with Rip, but he looks back, smirking at Caleb and I every few minutes.

Caleb still won't look at me, let alone touch me.

"Where are we going?" I ask Caleb, hoping to get him to look at me.

"A portal...to the otherworld," he replies somberly, without looking.

"Home, dear. We're going home," Sebastian contributes, proving he was listening.

The otherworld? I don't really know anything about it, but there seems to be one thing creatures agree on; it's awful.

CHAPTER TWENTY

Rose

We only walk for twenty minutes before we find ourselves in an alley behind some bars and small businesses. There's not a soul in sight, which is probably for the best. They'd probably end up like that poor hotel clerk.

Sebastian stops at a brick wall and turns to us.

"You two first," he says, pointing at two of the burly goons.

They step forward and pull out knives. Without wasting time, they drag the blades down across their palms, mutter an incantation, and disappear through the brick, which ripples like water.

Sebastian walks towards Caleb and me, my heart quickening as he draws near. He stops in front of us and gives a twisted smile.

"Hand," he orders me.

I give him my hand, knowing what's going to happen but not feeling any more prepared for it.

He pulls the blade heavily across my palm, holding my hand painfully still. My blood pools and begins to drip, much like the silent tears that escape from the pain.

I can see Caleb out of the corner of my eye. He tenses at the smell of my spilt blood, gritting his teeth and clenching his fists out of need. Sebastian seems to be enjoying our misery thoroughly.

He raises my injured hand to his face and inhales deeply. When he opens his eyes, they are big and bright. He looks thrilled.

"My, my…" he says thoughtfully. "I'll take our guest through," he adds, releasing my hand and licking his lips.

My heart pounds with fear. *I don't want to go through with him.* What if it's a trick just to get Caleb away from me? He moves to bring the blade down against his own hand but Caleb's hand shoots out and grabs the knife firmly around the blade.

"She goes with me," he growls.

Sebastian looks annoyed with Caleb and rips the knife down through his grip. He smiles as Caleb winces in pain, blood pouring thickly from his wounds. Caleb grabs my upper arm hard and pulls me towards the wall. He mutters the incantation and takes me through.

"Thank you," I say to Caleb.

He finally looks me in the eyes when I speak to him, and although I can see that I cause him pain, I can also see that he still cares. Even if wants to deny those feelings.

Sebastian and Rip come through the portal behind us, drawing my focus away from Caleb. Seeing me watching, he grins.

"Miss me?" he asks, pushing past Caleb. "They are expecting us."

I look over at Caleb, several thoughts going through my head. *Who's expecting us? Why? Where are we going? And are they going to hurt me?*

Rather than pulling me by the arm, Caleb places a hand on my lower back, gently guiding me to follow Sebastian. It's as if he knows that there are a billion things terrifying my mind right now and he's trying to offer me some sort of comfort.

We leave the portal area, which is a giant stone with symbols, surrounded by grass and a light dusting of snow. It's sitting on the outskirts of a forest. I make a mental note of where it is, just in case I need to find it in a hurry.

I notice it is dark here, the sun setting the sky ablaze like fire. This place looks as beautiful as it does foreboding.

"It's beautiful," I admit, unable to keep the thought to myself.

Caleb looks at me strangely, seemingly unsure if my reaction was a good thing or not, but his lips twitch in amusement.

Sebastian stares back at me, eyes shining in excitement. He knows something important that I don't.

It's quiet as we walk up the cobblestone streets despite the many homes and shops that we pass. Only a few people peer out of their windows, watching us curiously.

"Where is everyone?" I ask uncomfortably.

"Sleeping," Caleb says shortly.

The street leads up a steep hill winding through the village. At the top of the hill sits an extravagant property with a large stone castle in the middle of meticulously kept grounds.

"It's stunning," I say, unable to keep quiet when we enter the grounds.

"Of course, it is. It's home," Sebastian says smugly.

We walk in the giant wooden doors, attracting several stares from the staff. Honestly, it feels like I just walked into royalty's home. I'm clearly out of place.

Two of Sebastian's goons disappear down a dark hallway, but Rip stays at his boss's side. We're waiting, that much is obvious; I just don't know what we're waiting for.

After a minute, I feel Caleb's hand drop from my back, much to my disappointment and relief. Having him touch me in such an affectionate way was making it hard for me to hate him, and I want to hate him. I need to hate him.

"Sebastian. Welcome home," a man says with a heavy accent.

He comes out of a door in the dark hallway. He's beautiful in a dangerous way; commanding with strength in every step. With dark brown eyes, jet black hair peppered with gray, and a strong jaw.

The resemblance to Sebastian and Caleb is remarkable.

"Hello father," Sebastian smiles, not taking his eyes off me.

His eyes fall on Caleb and start twinkling with the same kind of perilous energy as Sebastian's.

"Caleb…what are you doing here?" the man says with surprise.

Caleb says nothing, but watches the man with anger. His hands are clenched in fists so tight that I can smell the blood that his fingernails are drawing as they pierce the flesh of his palms.

I remember what he said in the hotel about me being safer if they think I'm his. In what could be sheer stupidity, I lace my fingers through Caleb's and hold on. He doesn't show any discomfort, although I'm sure he feels it. He probably knows what I'm doing, though.

Sebastian looks at me curiously, cocking his head to the side. He has seen me be nothing but cold to Caleb, so he's probably not sure what I'm doing.

"You must be Roselyn," the man says, zoning in on me.

He steps closer to me, his white teeth sparkling brilliantly in the light of the oil lamps. I shudder.

"That's close enough," Caleb orders, stopping the man in his tracks.

The man looks from Caleb to me with interest, then back to Sebastian.

"I didn't know that Roselyn was taken," his father says, a look of annoyance on his face.

"I would have thought she wasn't," Sebastian says, smirking at me.

I stare back at him, refusing to give up this ruse.

"Hmm," the man looks thoughtful before backing away from me. "Aamily will show you to your rooms," he adds as a young girl comes down the corridor.

"We were going to stay together at my cabin," Caleb says abruptly.

"Nonsense. The cabin has been vacant for centuries. It will take a few days to prepare it," his father explains happily. "You will stay in the castle until then."

"Of course," Caleb says.

"Aamily, take them to their rooms," he commands. "Sebastian, a word…" he adds coldly.

He disappears down the hallway without waiting for Sebastian, who takes his eyes off me reluctantly and follows his father.

"Follow me," Aamily says politely.

William

Standing in front of the roaring fireplace in my office, I'm seething, waiting for my more impulsive son. Caleb being here causes a large obstacle in my plans. I hadn't expected to see him, although, I had heard rumours of his fondness for the girl.

I keep my face neutral when Sebastian comes in, closing the door behind him.

"So, the whispers are true. Not quite an incubus, not quite a vampire. But what is Caleb doing back here?" I ask, with obvious annoyance.

"He was at her apartment when we got there," he explains. "Would you rather I slit his throat and bleed him dry?"

"Please. You would have tried, and he would have killed you," I say, sparing no concern for his feelings.

Sebastian scowls at my comment- not appreciating the truth.

"Caleb is older and stronger…" I continue.

"He may be older, but he's not stronger," Sebastian interrupts indignantly. "His emotions make him weak."

"His emotions make him vulnerable, but they do not make him weak," I explain. "His appearance complicates things, though."

As my oldest, Caleb is a prince and the next to rule.

His existence was brought about during a period of weakness on my part. I was romantically involved with his mother for a short time, but it was long enough that she fell pregnant.

I didn't want a child; I wanted wealth and power. But she wanted to be a mother, so I let her keep it out of weakness. We wanted different things in life. So, I left, leaving her to raise the child that I never wanted.

When she died, I brought him to live with me because things had changed. I had Sebastian now, but he didn't take kindly to having an older brother taking his place as next in line to rule.

"He doesn't matter. He's been gone for so long, surely our rules don't extend to him anymore," Sebastian says pettily.

"Caleb's situation is…unique. It requires delicacy," I say sternly.

"Why can't we just banish him? Isn't that what happened to that Lord Dalibor?" Sebastian asks.

"Caleb is a vampire prince until he is deemed unfit by the council," I argue.

Caleb has always possessed a darkness, even before he turned incubus. When his mother died, it showed. He was cruel and twisted- more so than Sebastian. As the next to rule after me, he was often referred to as the dark prince because of his demeanor.

There has always been a sibling rivalry between the two of them, now they're fighting over a shiny new toy- Rose. In order to fulfill the prophecy, I need her to choose my side.

"He's half dead already," Sebastian says happily. "He hasn't fed in over a week- he's starving himself. If he doesn't feed from her soon, he won't be able to control his bloodlust."

"Not to mention that if he doesn't feed from her, he can't claim her," I offer excitedly. "And I don't think he will risk feeding from her. He's too hungry."

Sebastian's eyes grow big with sadistic excitement at what will follow.

"Then I'll be allowed to have her?" Sebastian asks, licking his lips.

"It would be best if she chose us. We must get her to fear Caleb," I say thoughtfully. "I see the way she watches him. It shouldn't be too hard."

"Then she's mine," Sebastian says, grinning.

"Yes son," I say with a sigh.

Rose

Aamily leads us up a staircase and down a few halls in silence while I still cling to Caleb's hand.

"Miss," Aamily says, opening a door and gesturing inside.

I release his hand, my fingers sliding out of his and I walk through the doorway. Caleb follows me in.

"No, Master Caleb, this is not your room," she says quickly.

I glance back to Caleb, feeling nervous once again that he is going to be sent away. However, his recent behaviour doesn't exactly instill confidence in my feeling of safety with him.

"It is now," Caleb says, closing the door between us and Aamily.

I want to fall to the floor, but I can't let him see that. Caleb stands behind me, not saying anything, but I can feel his eyes on me.

The room has a desk, armoire, dresser, and four-poster bed made out of solid wood. The fabrics are rich and vibrant, the patterns clearly very old-fashioned.

I muster all the strength I can and turn on shaky legs. I face him and stare into his murky, gray eyes, wishing that he could be the way he was before.

"I don't think you're supposed to be in this room with me," I say.

"I'm not," he says bluntly, "but IF you were mine, I'd never stay in a separate room," he says.

I feel the blush creeping into my cheeks at the thought he's implying. He walks past me, his arm brushing mine. He crosses the room to the window and peers out.

"You think they don't believe us?"

"It wouldn't matter if they did," he says nonchalantly.

"What does that mean? Why does it even matter then?" I ask with frustration.

In the blink of an eye, Caleb is forcing me up against the wall, pinning my arms above my head. I'm breathing heavily in fear. The last time he had me pinned, it was right before he took my blood. I look into his face nervously, noting the faint blue pulsing of veins under his eyes.

He's hungry. *Really hungry.*

I watch his chest rise and fall quickly, not from fear, but from the effort it's taking to not feed from me.

"Caleb…let me go," I say, as calmly as I can manage.

He ignores my request, his eyes glinting with a challenge. "As long as they think that you're mine, our laws dictate that they can't touch you without your consent," he says breathlessly, "but…"

"But what?"

He releases my arms carefully, the veins under his eyes still pulsing faintly, but he's fighting to regain control.

"I've…been away for a long time. The rules may not be extended to me anymore," he explains, taking a step away from me.

Great.

"What? I'm not a blood bag," I say, disgusted.

"Here, that's exactly what you are," he says, sighing. "Being in this part of the otherworld is like stepping back into the eighteen-hundreds. As a woman, you are seen as nothing more than a belonging, especially if you're not a vampire," he continues gently. "Feeding from you against your will is not the worst thing they will do to you."

"W-what?" I stutter out.

My heart skips a beat as I'm gripped with fear. The warmth rises in my cheeks as his piercing gray eyes sweep over me.

"There's more…"

"No more," I yell.

I stomp over to the bed and lie down, ignoring the nagging feeling of my curiosity. Silent tears slip out despite squeezing my eyes shut tight. The bed moves as Caleb lies down beside me. I can feel him studying me.

I open my tear-filled eyes and see him staring back- his face only a foot from mine.

His fingers slide up over my cheek, warmth radiating from them. My mouth parts slightly in surprise and a small gasp escapes my lips. He smirks at my response, his eyes growing brighter and clearer.

"I won't let them touch you," he promises me, touching my cheek affectionately.

CHAPTER TWENTY-ONE

Caleb

She doesn't deserve this. I think to myself as I watch Rose sleep. Her dark brown hair is spread out around her, with a few strands hanging off her shoulder. Her lips are parted slightly from sleep. She's exhausted from the constant terror she's been feeling and she may have passed out next to me, but I know that I scare her too.

She's smart.

She should be afraid.

Even I don't trust me.

That night I brought her into my head and attacked her was a night I will regret, but it's also the night I let myself be me. I messed up, letting the monster out for even a minute. She'll never forget that. The worst part is that it felt good- I liked it!

I don't want to be a savage. I've worked so hard to not be one and it's not easy. I fight my natural instincts everyday- wanting her but not having her hurts so much. I want her blood; more than that, I want all of her, I want her to be mine- and I want everyone to know.

Knock. Knock.

A knock at the door has her stirring, her eyes not yet open. She reaches out stretching, her arm landing on my chest. I can feel the warmth through my shirt, the familiar electricity tickling my skin.

Sometimes I don't feel anything anymore. I become numb when I shut down my feelings, but I don't have my guard up right now, not since I touched her cheek to comfort her. It scares even me at how easy it's becoming to turn it all off.

Her eyelids shoot open, revealing her gorgeous green eyes. She looks up at me, wide awake now, eyes shining, rosiness in her cheeks- she's beautiful. She pulls her hand back quickly and looks at me with a mix of fear and apology. The warmth is gone. I feel the anger creeping back in, the blood lust returning.

"Sorry," she says in a small voice.

I don't say anything. I can't. I'm fighting myself right now. I want to sink my teeth into her neck and have the warmth of her hands on me again. If I open my mouth, I won't be able to stop myself.

Knock. Knock.

Rose

Oops. He doesn't like when I touch him, I know that, but it was an accident. I removed my hand from his chest the moment I realized where it was. I can't believe how out of it I had been, with him right next to me no less. *Was he watching me the whole time?* His piercing gray eyes are glaring at me.

I don't know how I feel about it.

I rise from the bed, partly to answer the door, but mostly to avoid Caleb's overly intense gaze.

I open the door cautiously, peeking out. It's the same girl that brought us to the room, her arms full of things.

"Hello, miss. I'm here to help you get ready," Aamily says.

"Ready for what?" I ask suspiciously.

"Lord William is having a breakfast made in your honour, of course. I'm here to make you presentable," she explains.

Caleb chuckles sarcastically from the bed, but I open the door all the way and let her in. Although, I'm slightly offended that I don't look presentable, I was stolen after all. And why do I have to look presentable? Then I remember. Caleb said that being here is like being in the eighteen-hundreds.

Aamily stops when she sees Caleb.

"Master Caleb, would you prefer the bar while we prepare?" she asks politely.

"No," Caleb replies rudely.

He closes his eyes, resting his arms behind his head without any concern. Aamily swallows hard, obviously afraid of him.

"Of course, sir," she says with a slight bow.

She hangs up what is clearly a man's suit on the closet door, setting a pair of shiny dress shoes underneath. All black naturally. With her eyes down, she gestures to the bathroom.

I could fight them on getting dolled up- refuse to look nice for my captors. Until I know exactly who I'm dealing with, I guess I should try and make them happy, even if I am their hostage.

Caleb

Aamily and Rose go into the adjoining bathroom. They'll be in there for a while from my experience. My father will want Rose done up like she's going to a ball. I glance at the suit hanging up, so formal. He hasn't changed, not that I expected him to.

I hate this place.

After an hour, I walk over and grab the suit from the hanger, pulling on the black dress pants, dark gray button-up, dress shoes, and finally managing the black tie. I've always hated wearing ties.

I take a look at the mirror in the closet and manipulate my hair into looking good. I shut it with more force then necessary and slip the matching jacket on.

Just as I am walking back to the bed, the bathroom door opens. Aamily stops in her tracks and quickly looks down at the floor, terrified.

We've never met, so obviously she's afraid of what I am and what I am capable of. *Smart girl!* She hurries into the hallway.

When Rose walks out, I feel my mouth open. Her hair has been put up in intricate braids, revealing her neck, save for a few strands. Her make-up is dark but glamorous. She's wearing a black floor length dress made of silk, with a thigh-high slit. The top is a halter that covers her chest and comes together below her navel, leaving her entire back exposed. And through the slit, you can see a pair of designer heels, with ribbons that wrap up to the knee. It's not at all sensible for the cold weather, but she looks amazing.

"Your father doesn't believe in leaving much to the imagination," Rose says uncomfortably.

It takes me a minute, but I snap out of my trance. I won't lie, I was imagining ripping that dress off of her and throwing it aside.

"No," I say, trying to pull it together.

I lead her to the door hastily. I look at her face, so unsure.

"You look beautiful," I reassure her. "Just follow my lead."

She nods nervously and steps out in the hall.

Here we go.

Rose

As I walk out into the hall, I try to pull the slit in the dress together more. I feel so awkward and yet, attractive at the same time. It bounces right back to where it was sitting and balances on the edge of being an inappropriate outfit.

I sigh in defeat.

Caleb is walking beside me with his hand resting on the small of my back, which is completely exposed. So of course, my skin is tingling under the heat of his hand, making it hard to focus on anything else.

When he first saw me, he looked different. It almost looked like he was blushing. *I wonder what he was thinking about.* Curiosity sparks in me as we descend the staircase.

"Are you ready?" he asks, pausing at the bottom of the stairs.

"Nope. Not even a little," I reply, playing with my hair nervously.

He slides his fingers through mine so easily, you wouldn't know he doesn't like me touching him, and he leads me down the hall and through an open door.

Inside is a table that can seat more than twelve people, but only four spots have been set. Rip is standing off to the side, as-well-as two other guards. Sebastian is talking in low tones with his father but falls silent when we enter, openly gawking at me.

I shift uneasily in the dress as we walk towards them.

"You look stunning, my dear," William says.

"Good enough to eat!" Sebastian adds, his eyes raking over me.

I shudder and press into Caleb nervously. His arm goes around me protectively while he stares at his brother, warding him off.

"Enough, Sebastian," Caleb says through gritted teeth.

"Behave, Sebastian. Thoughts to yourself," William says, genuinely amused at something.

Oh god. He said something that he didn't want me to hear.

William heads towards the table with Sebastian close behind.

"What did he say?" I whisper to Caleb, wanting to know what kind of trouble I'm in.

He looks at me thoughtfully, deciding whether to tell me or not.

"Please tell me."

"My father complimented your dress and," he begins but hesitates, "Sebastian suggested that it would look better on his floor," Caleb says reluctantly.

I let out a small gasp, the heat rising in my cheeks, and I clutch at Caleb's arm as he heads for the table. He pulls me along with him, easily ignoring my resistance to go any closer to the men already at the table. I'm breathing faster than normal, feeling exposed, vulnerable, and more than a little terrified. *I don't think I can do this.*

Who wants to eat with their captors and pretend they aren't there against their will?

We're sitting in silence, but I can feel William's and Sebastian's eyes observing me closely. I try to ignore it and nibble at the food before me because I am hungry. Caleb doesn't touch his food, (not that he needs it,) while his father and Sebastian expertly move the food around on their plates to make it appear like they're eating more than they are. After a reasonable amount of time, William signals for the plates to be removed. The staff then brings out glasses of alcohol for each of us. Mine has a metallic smell to it, one I recognize right away. *Blood.*

Caleb drinks his greedily, although his doesn't have the smell of blood. He waves for the staff and they approach him cautiously. He whispers to a man who disappears behind the doors. When he returns, he pours Caleb a new glass of whiskey and sets the bottle down next to him.

William chuckles dangerously at this behaviour.

"Thirsty brother," Sebastian teases.

"I imagine he is…" William begins, "sharing this lovely girl must not be easy," he continues looking at me. "Does she choose her own lovers?" he adds with a twisted grin.

"She's mine," Caleb says with a snarl.

"That's not what it looked like at her apartment, when she was in her underwear with that halfling," Sebastian says, smirking.

"That was a misunderstanding," Caleb says, pushing back from the table and rising angrily to his feet.

I take a drink of my whiskey awkwardly, scrunching my face at the taste. They don't believe we're together, that's why Sebastian has been gawking.

"We were together…" I blurt out, "but we had a falling out. We're working things out," I lie.

"That doesn't make you his, dear," William says coldly.

"What does it make me?" I ask.

As soon as I ask it, I regret it. William and Sebastian both center their focus on me, grinning demonically.

"Well Rose, if he doesn't feed from you and doesn't fuck you, that makes you fair game," Sebastian says with a sick laugh.

"Must you be so vulgar?" William asks Sebastian rhetorically.

My cheeks redden immediately at the conversation. It's the kind of talk that you have with friends, not that someone says about you in your presence.

Caleb grabs my arm painfully hard, removing me from my seat. With the bottle of whiskey firmly in his other hand, he drags me towards the hallway. The guards flinch at Caleb's movement, but stay where they are.

He doesn't take me to the room. Instead, we keep walking until we're in a dark part of the house, covered in dust and surrounded by paintings.

Caleb sinks down against a wall, raising the bottle to his lips and taking a long, hard swallow.

"I'm sorry that he spoke to you that way," he says, his face showing more compassion than he's displayed in a while.

"But what he said is true, isn't it?" I ask.

I kneel down in front of him, the dress making me feel naked. He sets his whiskey down and slips his jacket off, sliding it around my shoulders and affording me a little modesty.

"It's..." he hesitates, "complicated."

"Isn't it always?" I ask smartly.

A little laugh escapes his lips before he has them wrapped around the whiskey bottle again.

"I suppose it is," he agrees. "I'm sorry you're trapped here with a bunch of monsters," he adds sincerely.

I look into his eyes, swirling with clouds.

"I'm sorry that I called you a monster," I say.

"Don't be. My behaviour was monstrous," he admits.

"You're not one, though," I say honestly, taking in how happy that makes him. "How long will we be here?"

"Until they decide that we can go."

"There you are," William interrupts as he comes around the corner. "I want to apologize. Sebastian has much to learn," he says to me.

I watch Caleb get to his feet, taking another long swig of whiskey on his way, finishing the bottle. He looks at his father and says nothing, out loud anyway. After several silent, uncomfortable minutes, William has finally lost his smile. Whatever Caleb said seemed to have gotten the better of him.

He lets the empty bottle fall to the ground and break, then he reaches out his hand for me and I take it, not because he is forgiven, but because between him and William, I choose him.

I can't believe I'm back here. I think to myself, taking a seat at the table which is set for eleven this time. Around the room, there are about six guards standing quietly. At the head of the table is William. Beside him, on either side, sit four gentlemen who are clearly older than they look- they eye me curiously. Sebastian sits at the other end of the table, staring with an inappropriate intensity.

"You're sitting beside me," Sebastian says smugly.

Oh god.

I glance at Caleb nervously. He puts his hand on my bare lower back and gives me a small, sympathetic nod. His fingers tingle on my skin again. I almost forgot what that's like.

Sebastian raises an eyebrow, noticing my reaction to his brother's touch. I flush with embarrassment at his realization. He looks like he has something to say about it as his eyes intentionally travel where they don't belong, making me breath faster.

"Caleb…" I start whispering, but stop when someone catches my eye.

A beautiful woman with ebony skin, long silver hair and light blue eyes glides into the room. Two men are at her sides- they take the seats opposite us. She is absolutely breathtaking wearing a sheer dress, revealing a perfectly fitted body suit underneath.

"Caleb…how are you?" she asks, unsurprised to see him, unlike everyone else.

"I'm sure you already know," he answers with a grin.

She smiles back at him playfully, as if they have an inside secret, but quickly turns her attention on me.

"And you must be Rose," she says knowingly.

"I-I am," I stutter out with confusion. "How did you know that?"

"This is Xomira," Caleb says to me. "She's a sorceress, and William's oldest…guest," he adds, rolling his eyes.

Guest? Is she a prisoner too?

"By now, I like to think of you as a friend," William says to Xomira, every word dripping with charm.

How long has she been here?

I open my mouth to ask more, but stop as William taps his wine glass with a knife, requesting quiet.

"Friends, family, council…" he says, glancing around at everyone, "thank you for joining us to celebrate Rose's arrival and Caleb's return," he adds, his eyes falling on us.

Everyone lifts their glasses to toast William's words, but Caleb simply stares at the table, leaving his glass untouched. Xomira lifts her glass with what looks like sadness in her eyes, taking a small sip. Sebastian simply raises his glass to his mouth and drinks the whole thing. I don't know what to do. How can I toast what has happened? I don't care how nice they're being.

Seeing my inner struggle, Caleb's hand lands on top of mine; his fingers grazing my bare leg. I blush immediately, but try to push it away. Caleb and I lock eyes for a minute, his gaze both calming and chaotic while at the same time comforting.

I start to relax, so I glance around at everyone pretending to enjoy their food or drinking their wine.

Suddenly, Caleb's hand clenches my hand and leg aggressively. My head swivels back to him, but he isn't looking at me. His eyes are targeted on Sebastian who is returning his hateful stare. They must be arguing again.

"Boys…that's enough," William warns, all joking aside.

He was clearly privy to the conversation.

Caleb removes his hand from mine, and I find myself surprisingly disappointed as his warmth disappears. He consumes his wine with silent moodiness as the dinner continues.

After plates are removed and new dishes are brought in, I start to think that it's really not so bad here if you can ignore Sebastian. There was even an impeccable desert which I happily ate.

"Shall we move this evening to the study," William says graciously.

Everyone rises from the table, each making their way to the study. Caleb leads me there with his hand on my lower back again. It's an enchanting room with a roaring fireplace decorated in luxurious fabrics, several oversized armchairs, and a couple loveseats.

"I'm going to take in air outside," Xomira says, excusing herself with her guards in tow.

Caleb stops under the arch into the room, looking around uneasily as the others sit down- the council and Sebastian.

"Let's go for a walk…" Caleb suggests nervously.

I'm about to agree with him when William comes up beside us.

"Take a seat," he commands us coldly.

Caleb takes me by the hand and leads me to the nearest armchair, which isn't big enough for two. He sits down roughly and gently brings me sideways onto his lap. As confused as I am, I know that there is usually a reason for his behaviour.

The councilmen are looking at me- some with disappointment, others with intrigue. Sebastian is gawking as usual, with amusement glinting in his dark brown eyes.

"I hope the company meets your approval," William says.

Six scantily dressed young women float into the room abruptly. Each is waved over to a man, including Sebastian. Some sit on their laps, some perch on the arms of the armchair. The sixth girl stands near William patiently.

"What's going…"

"Enjoy!" William says, cutting me off.

Without any hesitation, the heat transforms each of the men into their vampire forms. They sink their teeth into different parts of the girls right away. A collective moaning and groaning permeates the air.

I gasp out loud at what is happening around me. Sebastian is staring at me intently, while the girl straddles him, his teeth sunk into her neck as she grinds against him. I feel his mind having inappropriate thoughts of me while he smiles twistedly.

I look awkwardly at Caleb as heaving, petting and other intimate touches have begun all around us. The veins under his eyes are pulsing brightly as his chest rises and falls roughly.

He looks at me filled with need- so much so, it scares me, and my heartbeat quickens. My breaths come out in harsh bursts, betraying me and proving that although I'm horrified, I'm also intrigued.

Noting that Sebastian has left the room with his girl and that William is now busy with the sixth girl, Caleb pushes me off his lap and into the hallway, where he walks with purpose, dragging me behind him.

We find ourselves in the dark gallery room of the house again when he releases my wrist and steps away, keeping his back to me.

"What the hell was that?" I ask horrified.

I watch as Caleb says nothing, tensing his hands and then relaxing them, trying to suppress his bloodlust and regain control of his body. He's struggling, bad.

I walk towards him and place my hand on his shoulder in a show of support, but he shakes it off furiously. I gasp again, knowing firsthand what happens if he loses control.

I put my hand on his forearm and try to turn him toward me. He resists again, shaking off my grip more vehemently.

"I can't be around you right now," he says with desperation.

"But I…"

"Leave. Now," he pleads.

"C-Caleb…" I stutter fearfully.

"NOW," he yells, enraged.

I back away quickly, actually afraid. His voice is laced with darkness, making it seem threatening. I panic and take off in any direction that'll lead me away from here.

CHAPTER TWENTY-TWO

Rose

Leaning against the wall, I wipe tiredly at the tears that I am once again shedding because of Caleb. I heard it in his voice; he was losing it- his control was slipping. In that moment, I could see what it does to him, being near enough to protect me, but being unable to feed, even if it isn't entirely my fault.

In my rush to get far away from him, I end up in some remote, unused area of the home.

I'll admit that I may have panicked, but the memory of how cruel Caleb can be is still fresh in my mind; the sting of his threats won't be easily forgotten.

Now, I'm lost.

I wipe away the last tear, deciding that I'm going the wrong way. I spin around and Sebastian is right up in my personal space.

"Why the tears, darling?" he says.

I'm not an idiot. He doesn't actually want to know why I'm crying, not unless it will benefit him in some way. Reaching out, he twirls my hair between his fingers, taunting me as he circles me like a shark. My lungs seem to stop working properly as the air gets thicker and breathing becomes forced. I only hope he doesn't see how afraid of him I am.

"I…I…" I stutter, nervously.

So much for putting on a brave front.

"You're nervous," he says, stopping in front of me.

His eyes rake up and down my body, making me even more freaked out. I wrap my arms around myself in an effort to cover some of my bare skin.

"Y-yes."

He steps closer to me, making me step back until my back is up against the wall. A small gasp comes out from the cold wall touching my skin.

"Don't be. You might like the pain," he says with an evil grin.

"If you touch me, you'll be sorry," I say shakily.

"You think I care about Caleb's stupid little claim on you?" he asks.

"You should, he's your brother," I say.

His face changes, his smile disappearing completely. My comment seeming to have fanned his anger, which is the opposite effect I had wanted.

"He hasn't been in a long time," he says, sadness and anger showing in his eyes. "Things change."

He shoves me aggressively back against the wall, knocking the wind out of me and lunging forward while I am caught off guard. He slowly runs one hand up my side, wrapping his fingers around my neck so tight, that I can't scream- I can barely breathe.

"What a-are you d-doing?" I choke out, trying to distract him.

I keep talking to him, hoping that I can buy myself more time until I figure a way out of this mess.

He brings his mouth to my neck, letting his closeness torture me with what he could easily do. Panic makes my heart rate accelerate to uncomfortable levels when I feel his free hand on my leg where the slit in the dress ends.

"P-please, no. P-please don't," I beg, sheer terror gripping me.

Using both of my hands, I try to force his hand off my leg, trembling.

"Why not? It can't be the first time," he says jokingly.

Pulling his face back, he cocks his head to the side in thought. He had meant it as a cruel joke but as realization crosses his features, a deranged smile forms on his lips.

"It is the first time," he announces giddily with a laugh.

He uses his speed and strength to pull me off the wall and squeeze my back up against him, keeping one hand around my neck to force my cooperation. Not that I have a lot of other options. His free hand toys at the slit in my dress, threateningly. Fear rises in my throat like bile.

"This is going to be fun," he taunts me.

I squeeze my eyes as tight as I can and sob helplessly, trying to accept what's going to happen to me.

Caleb

"Are you alright, Caleb?" Xomira asks, walking up behind me.

She's wrapped in a warm coat, her silver hair blowing in the icy breeze. Her two guards are hanging back, but they don't look happy about it.

In a daze, I look around, recognizing the shrubs covered in snow. I seem to have found my way out to the gardens in my hunger haze.

"I'm fine," I reply. "You left just in time," I say, forcing a smile and changing the subject.

"I always do," she says knowingly. "I take it you didn't?"

"I tried, but William had other plans."

"How'd Rose take it?" she asks curiously.

"She was horrified."

"How did you take it?" she asks sensitively.

"Like a savage," I admit with a self-deprecating chuckle.

Xomira and I walk through the shallow snow in reflective silence.

"Did you hurt her?" she asks.

"No," I say firmly, "but I wanted to do more than that. The feeding, the touching- it triggered the bloodlust. I wanted her blood. I needed it. Not just any blood would satisfy me; it had to be Rose's. So, I scared her into getting away from be before it was too late."

I'm not proud of the way I behaved, but I didn't know what else to do. If she stayed around me, I was going to hurt her. I can't do that again. I owe her more than the way I have been behaving.

"So, you left her in there...alone?"

"The girls will keep the guys busy for a while," I say defensively. "I just need to collect myself. I'm protecting her, from me."

I feel guilty about leaving her in there, but I had to get away. The more time I spend around her, the harder it is to stay away, the harder it is to not touch her. Especially when I don't think she would stop me.

"Maybe you don't need to protect her from yourself," Xomira says.

"I have to," I admit with defeat. "If I take advantage of her, I'm no better than Sebastian and William."

"How do you know she wouldn't give you what you want willingly?"

"She wouldn't," I say adamantly. "She's in love with someone else."

"It's possible that she loves you too," Xomira hints, walking ahead.

My ears perk up at her insight. "What do you know? What have you seen?" I say, catching up.

"That's for me to know," she says playfully.

I smile at the familiarity of this conversation. She's the reason I left centuries ago. I used to be just like Sebastian, maybe worse, until Xomira told me about Jason and Xander becoming my family. She was vague then too, choosing to let me experience everything, the good and the bad.

I think she knows more than she lets on, but even I know that you don't mess with a sorceress.

"How is it...being back here?" she asks delicately.

I let out a dry laugh. "How do you think," I say with more frustration than she deserves. "Sorry."

She gives me a sympathetic nod.

"He's trying to bait you," she explains. "You know that, right?"

"I know, but it doesn't make it any easier," I admit. "She's my weakness and they know that."

"If you want her to survive this, stop seeing her as your weakness, she needs to become your strength," she says wisely.

"I know but how?"

"That means that you need to feed," she stresses, "from *her* if you can handle it. If you feed from someone else, it won't stay a secret long."

"What if I can't stop?"

"You're going to have to figure it out. You're no good to her like this."

We turn around, walking in silence again for several minutes before she brings up another problem.

"So…how much does she know about the prophecy?"

"Nothing," I sigh. "I tried to tell her when we got here, but she didn't want to hear it."

"You should tell her. Eventually she'll have to pick a side and the more she knows, the better," she says.

"I know, but there is no choice where her best interests matter most," I say sadly.

"But there is," she says adamantly. "You!"

I appreciate the thought, but I don't think she sees me as an option anymore. I made too many mistakes when it concerns her.

"I don't think I count," I say shortly.

"I wouldn't be so sure, Caleb," she says cryptically. "Aren't those the girls?" she asks nervously.

I turn around to see three of the girls walking down the driveway and if I remember correctly, the blond on the left had been with Sebastian.

Panic courses through me. Rose is somewhere in the house, alone, and so is Sebastian.

I run towards the house, unable to use my vampire speed because I haven't been feeding.

I have to find her.

Rose

"She said no, Sebastian," Caleb says sternly.

Caleb.

My eyes fly open with relief to see Caleb walking towards us. I want to run to him, but Sebastian still has his hand wrapped around my neck, keeping me firmly up against him. All I can do is look at Caleb with terror in my eyes.

He looks at me, our eyes connecting. Although he looks beyond furious-with his brother I'm assuming, he seems to have regained control from the bloodlust. He stops a few feet away and turns his attention on Sebastian.

"You look tired, brother," Sebastian says smugly.

"Not too tired to kick your ass, or have you forgotten," Caleb replies confidently, taking a step closer.

"We could have her at the same time," Sebastian suggests, making me cringe and tense up.

"This conversation is over. Let her go, Sebastian," Caleb says, a darkness noticeable in his voice.

A low snarl comes from Sebastian, but he takes the warning, releasing me as I suck in the air harshly.

"See you soon, sweetheart," Sebastian says to me, threateningly, before walking away.

Caleb leans against the wall unsteadily when Sebastian is out of sight. I hurry to his side, still a little winded.

"Caleb."

My voice is filled with relief for myself and concern for him, my hand resting on his chest. I take in his pale skin, dull eyes, and light layer of sweat making his shirt damp.

"I'm fine. I just need a minute," he says stubbornly.

"You're not fine. You're starving," I say, seeing the signs. "They can't do this," I add angrily.

"They can. This is their world," he says calmly. "Come on."

He pulls away from me, seeming to prefer that I don't touch him. I fall into step beside him, heading back to our room, but I watch him out of the corner of my eye with worry.

I watch Caleb lie down on the bed, eyes closed, clearly exhausted. I approach him slowly, not knowing what to do. I sit down on the edge of the bed and notice a sheer black teddy draped over the end. It is obviously meant for me. I hold it up, scrunching my nose in disgust. Caleb chuckles lowly. Clearly, he had been paying attention. He gets up from the bed, crossing the room gracefully, while I toss the barely-there pajamas across the room.

No way am I wearing that.

Caleb opens the dresser drawer and heads back towards me. He tosses the clothes at me, making his way to the bathroom.

"Why do they want me to wear this stuff?"

Caleb is standing at the bathroom door, hand on the knob, with his back to me as he speaks.

"That's what the women here wear," he replies simply. He turns his head to me, his eyes serious, "also, they're trying to tempt me."

After staring at me for a few minutes, he goes into the bathroom, leaving me to contemplate what he means.

I hold up the item he threw at me. It's a simple black t-shirt, but at least it isn't see-through. Taking off this too revealing dress, I gladly pull on the t-shirt. I lay down, already exhausted from all the stress.

Caleb comes back into the bedroom wearing some gray sweatpants. *That's. It.* Saying he's in shape is an understatement. The man is cut.

He glances at me before lying down beside me and closing his eyes.

He saved me.

He stopped Sebastian from biting me and being my first. He may not realize it, but it matters to me. I'm grateful.

I scoot closer and snuggle into his side, resting my head on his shoulder and my hand on his chest. I feel him tense up at my touch but after a few minutes, he lowers his hand, and I can feel him caressing my arm, my skin tingling under his fingers. We lay there in silence, just enjoying the comfort of each other's touch.

CHAPTER TWENTY-THREE

Caleb

Looking down at Rose curled up to me, in nothing more than my t-shirt, sparks a lot of feelings in me. Feelings that I thought I'd finally buried. Feelings that I can't bare for her to see again, because if she rejects me, I don't think I'll survive. Worse, they're feelings I'm not supposed to have. I thought I'd given up, deciding to follow my true nature, but then she needed me. Seeing her makes a part of me fight to be better, even if it's not what I thought I wanted. *I was wrong. I want her.*

She fell asleep so easily after cuddling up to me, listening to the beating of my heart and feeling the warmth of my fingertips brushing her arm. Now my hand is resting on her arm, holding her to me in what you would think is a sweet way, but I see things differently. I'm protective of her, possessive even. William and Sebastian have seen it in me, I know they have. I'm not stupid, I know what they're doing. They are starving me in the hopes that I will hurt her, forcing her into their arms, manipulating her. If she cooperates with them, I won't be able to save her. *All because of that damn prophecy.*

As I watch her, I feel a warmth spreading through me. She has no reason to trust me but here she is, fast asleep, her breathing relaxed and even, completely comfortable.

It's amazing. She's amazing.

She stirs slightly, nuzzling against my chest in her sleep. Her hand flexes on my chest so innocently. It's adorable. It pains me to admit that the thought of her blood is consuming me. Every nerve in my body feels like it's on fire, and not in a good way. I wiggle out from under her and roll over, not wanting to test my restraint anymore. Seeing her makes it worse.

She knows that I'm starving and it's more painful than I remember, slower too. I don't know how much longer I can keep the monsters away, me especially.

Rose

I wake up strangely alert and immediately notice that Caleb has rolled away from me. His back is to me, but he is finally asleep, something he does very little of. He's calm, his ribs rising and falling slowly with each breath.

He's still in there somewhere. I can see it when he looks at me. But if he doesn't start feeding, I won't be able to trust him.

My fingers ache to touch his chest and feel the tingle that his touch causes me, but I have an idea that may help him, and it has to happen now.

I gently slide off the bed, making as little vibration as I can, not wanting to wake him. I creep over to the door, sliding the deadbolt back carefully. Looking back over my shoulder, I can see that he is still sleeping soundly, and I slip out the door, grabbing a small blanket on the way.

Shutting the door quietly behind me, I head down the silent hallway on a mission; find blood.

It's quiet in the house right now. There aren't any staff going about their business in the hallways, not that I'm surprised. Everyone should still be sleeping.

Heading down the hallway in search of the kitchen, I tip-toe as quietly as I can. I doubt it really makes a difference as I am in a house with vampires after all.

If I were a kitchen, where would I be? I think to myself as I check all the open doors. There has to be blood baggies in the kitchen. I pass the study where William held that inappropriate after dinner party and scowl to myself but keep going.

After passing the dining room, I find the gallery again. Walking through the gallery, I find myself looking around in the dark at all the paintings. The room has no windows and is dimly lit by two gas lights, making the large pictures feel darker and more ominous than they had before.

I hurry through the room and down a hallway, finding a staircase behind a door. Going through, I descend the steps, a nagging feeling telling me to turn around- but I don't.

A door is cracked open on the right at the bottom. Ignoring my batter judgement, I push the door open. Inside, there are no windows, there is an oversized bed with black blankets lying haphazardly in a pile. There's a large dresser and lounge against the wall and a large bookshelf covered in books on the other side. I'd be more interested in the books, but I spot what looks like a mini fridge next to the bed.

I rush over and swing the door open. Inside are various bottles of tequila, vodka and scotch, but no blood, and it's not even a fridge, just a cupboard.

"Can I help you?"

Shit.

I slowly close the cupboard door, not turning around, while I straighten up. His voice sends shivers up and down my spine.

Sebastian.

I'm in his room. I start putting the images together, the black blankets, the lack of windows, all the alcohol, but the only thing that doesn't fit is all the books. I can feel his eyes drilling holes in the back of my head. I turn around and find Sebastian standing inside his doorway. His dark brown eyes are focused on mine, his dirty blond hair only slightly out of place, and he is still wearing black dress pants and a white dress shirt, his tie undone around his collar.

"This is your room?" I ask nervously.

"It is," he says smirking, an eyebrow raised. "And you're in it," he adds, as more of a statement than a question.

"You have an impressive collection of books," I say, taking a step towards the towering bookcase.

His smirk widens as I pointlessly try to distract him. I don't want him to know what I was really doing- he can't know what rough shape Caleb is really in right now.

He steps closer. "Thank you, but that's not what you were looking at," he says, still smirking.

He glances towards his alcohol stash and then back at me. His eyes sweep over me while I fidget nervously, tugging the hem of the t-shirt lower.

"If you wanted a drink, Caleb could have got you one," he says, pulling his tie off and throwing it across the room. "Unless…that's not what you came for?" he adds, his smirk becoming more twisted as he unbuttons the top two buttons on his shirt.

He takes another threatening step towards me, causing me to tremble a bit. I take a step back timidly, aware that he stands between me and the door. I was so concerned about keeping Caleb's condition a secret, it never occurred to me that he might think that I want something from him specifically. *Not good.*

"I was looking for blood," I say quickly, "for me. I'm hungry," I add.

Sebastian takes a couple more steps towards me, closing the distance, and putting me almost in arm's reach.

"Are you sure it's for you?" he asks knowingly.

"Yes."

"Caleb not enough for you?" he teases. "You won't find blood baggies here. We prefer it fresh," he continues.

"Oh," I answer, trying to hide my disappointment.

Now what is Caleb going to do?

"I don't usually share, but for you I'll make an exception," he says suggestively.

My eyes involuntarily go to his neck, making him grin again. He lets out a short laugh, drawing my attention back to his face, just in time to watch him lick his lips inappropriately. I find my own hunger lingering just below the surface and reacting to the thought of fresh blood.

"Sebastian? Rose?"

We both turn our heads to the sound of the voice from the door.

William.

I feel my breath rush from my lungs with relief at the sight of him. I walk around Sebastian, stopping halfway between him and his father. He's observing us with hidden curiosity.

"What on earth are you doing down here, Rose? Where is Caleb?" he asks with mock concern.

I open my mouth to speak, but nothing comes out.

"She was searching for blood. She's hungry," Sebastian says, butting in.

"Is Caleb not feeding you enough?" he asks, his lips twitching into a grin.

"Maybe he's not feeding her at all," Sebastian suggests to his father.

I freeze, unsure what to say.

"Of course, he is. She is his," William interjects.

"Y-yes, he is. I was just…r-restless. Caleb is sleeping, so I w-was hoping for a snack," I stutter out.

"Ah, I see. Sebastian will gladly help you out," William replies, his grin too wide for his face.

Sebastian steps up beside me, rolling up his sleeve. He holds his arm out to me, expectantly. I look from him to his father awkwardly.

"I'm feeling much better actually, but thank you," I say, taking a few tentative steps towards the doorway.

"Are you sure about that? I won't mind a bit sweetheart," Sebastian says, his voice as thick as honey.

He steps closer to me, and I become very aware that his father is blocking half the doorway.

"Mhmm. Yes."

"Rose?"

As if by divine intervention, Xomira appears beside William, looking at the strange situation suspiciously. I let out a loud laugh without thinking about it, almost crying with happiness.

"I'm just on my way out. Why don't I take you back to your room?" she asks, reaching a hand for me.

I gladly take it and let her pull me past an annoyed looking William. I don't dare to look back at Sebastian, knowing he won't be pleased either.

"Thank you," I say, as we head back up the stairs.

She doesn't speak until we get up the stairs and back to the gallery room.

"I don't know how you ended up down there, but you put yourself in a very dangerous situation," she warns me, stopping in place.

"I know. I was trying to find blood for Caleb," I explain.

"You're going to get yourself killed, or worse. Here," she says, handing me a bag of blood from the folds of her coat.

"I don't know how to thank you."

I take the bag of blood in my hands, holding it protectively to my chest. Happy tears start making their way down my face. I'm so relieved because Caleb needs this so much.

"Don't thank me, just listen to me," she says urgently. "I've been here for a long time, so let me help you."

There's a sadness in her eyes that I don't want to understand. When she says that she's been here for a long time, I'm inclined to believe her.

"Why are you helping me?"

"Because I've seen a different future for you, for Caleb- one that will benefit all creatures," she says vaguely.

"What did you see?" I ask curiously.

She smiles at me secretively. "I can't tell you everything. Just that you don't have to be a prisoner forever, but you have to be willing to fight for it, to be ruthless. You have to be smarter than them, and that means keeping Caleb close," she stresses.

"Why does that matter? It sounds like you're just pushing Caleb's agenda," I say with distrust.

She sighs and takes a step back, looking at me with understanding.

"Caleb is my friend and I'm rooting for him. He's been through a lot but he's still trying- he hasn't given up even if he wants you to believe that he has. I've seen the way he is with you, the way he looks at you- like you're his whole reason for existing. He loves you."

I open my mouth, but nothing comes out. What can I say to that? I don't know what to believe.

"I know it's hard to see and with more time you will," she assures me. "I'm not telling you this to argue Caleb as an option."

"Then why are you telling me this?"

"Because you need to understand how fiercely loyal Caleb is for those he loves. That list is not long; you should be honoured if you're on it. You'd also be an idiot not to accept his help. If you have any hope of getting out of here, it's with him by your side. You're going to need him, not just now, but in the future too," she says mysteriously. My advice to you is that whatever it is that tore you apart, get over it. Give Caleb what he needs so that he can help you."

"Excuse me?" I say shocked.

I stare at her with an incredulous look, and she returns it with an unreadable one. I don't care if she is a sorceress, *whatever that is*, I hate when people tell me what to do.

"Please," she starts patiently. "He's the only thing keeping them from taking what they want right now. You need him. And your pretense of a relationship isn't fooling anyone. Soon, they will tire of this charade and they will stop playing this game."

"I don't understand," I say. "What do they want from me?"

Xomira looks down guiltily.

"You."

"Why?"

"A prophecy was told about you, centuries ago. It spoke about your ability and your…children," she says hesitantly, resuming her walk in the direction of my room.

"My children? What about my children?" I ask, stumbling after her.

"I'm sorry, I can't say anymore, but what you need to know is that I'm suggesting you stop pretending. You're playing with fire and you're going to get burned."

"You're saying that the only way for me to get back to my friends is to give myself to Caleb and trust him?" I ask skeptically.

"Yes," she says seriously.

"I can't. I love someone else," I say adamantly.

"Did it ever occur to you that maybe you love them both, and that that's ok," she says with frustration. "Besides, I'm not telling you to abandon your love. I'm telling you to embrace what you have with Caleb."

"How?"

"Well, you could start by getting to know him, the good and the bad," she recommends, stopping at the door to my room.

I scramble up beside her, a million questions in my brain, begging to be answered but the door swings open suddenly. Caleb is standing there looking panicked and murderous until it clicks in his brain that I'm right here. His face relaxes a little as he comes towards me, pulling me into a protective hug, but not before I see the dark circles under his eyes, reminding me of why he needs this.

I'm surprised as he holds me to him, feeling the strength of his arms wrapped around me. *I thought he hated touching me.*

"Where were you? How long were you gone? What happened? Are you ok?" he demands answers, shooting off his questions rapidly.

"I'm fine," I say slightly smothered, but not bothered.

"She was wandering! I thought I'd bring her back." Xomira chimes in patiently.

I feel Caleb's grip loosen as he lifts his chin off my shoulder, focusing on Xomira.

"Thank you!"

"You're welcome. Goodnight!"

As Xomira's footsteps disappear down the stairs, Caleb pulls me into the room, slamming the door behind us.

"Do you have a death wish?" he roars at me furiously.

All relief is gone from his face, replaced with pure irritation. He stands a few feet from me, towering over me even from a distance. I'd be lying if I didn't admit that I was intimidated. He has a strange look in his eyes and he is starving, after all.

The blood.

I hold out the blood bag for him in one hand. His eyes start swirling immediately, the veins pulsing under his eyes. The heat takes him over.

"I just want to help you," I say tiredly.

I'm not looking for a fight, I'm tired of fighting. He takes the blood gently from my hand, but I can see how hard keeping his calm is. He bites into it, draining it in under a minute. I don't look away. It's not a shameful act. If they didn't add blood into my drinks, I'd probably be feral too.

"Thank you and I'm sorry," he says calmly, with sincerity.

"We're not done yet," I say, closing the distance between us.

I hold up my arm, offering it to Caleb, in much the same way Sebastian did to me.

"You want me to feed from you?" he asks.

His face and body give away his excitement and need, but he's watching my face, confused. Truth is, Xomira was right. He's my ally, so I need to help him.

"Yes. I need you. You said you'd protect me. In order to do that, you need me." I say confidently.

We stand silently for a minute, eyes meeting- understanding passing between us.

Caleb

I take her arm carefully, although I'd prefer her throat. This is going to hurt her enough. I don't need to pull her arm off in the process.

"I won't do this unless you're sure," I say, despite the fact that just the thought of her blood has me salivating.

She looks thoughtful for a minute, no doubt remembering the agony that my bite brought her last time.

A creature's bite also contains venom that causes differing amounts of pain, depending on the creature and the intention. An incubus already possesses the most painful venom, designed to torment the victim in the worst way. As much as I want to protect and care for Rose, subconsciously I also want to hurt her because of what I am and how vulnerable she makes me feel. Facts I haven't shared with her, but I know she'll figure out.

"I'm sure," she says, placing her free hand on my arm reassuringly.

Bringing her wrist to my lips, I hear her suck in a breath, preparing the best she can. My teeth sink into the delicate skin on her small wrist easily. A gasp escapes her lips as she clenches her eyes shut against the pain. I feed greedily, her blood flowing down my throat smoothly, knowing the torture I'm inflicting but powerless to stop it.

"Caleb," she mutters weakly, a few minutes into my feed.

I pry my lips from her wrist and apply pressure as she collapses into me, shuddering. I've taken more than I should have. I scoop her up in my arms, my strength returning because of what she has given me.

"You really do have a death wish," I whisper into her ear.

"Maybe," she whispers back to me, a small smile playing at the corners of her lips, her eyes still shut and her body sleepy.

I carry her with ease to the bed, indulging in the electric feel of her skin against mine.   I'm in no hurry to put space between us now that I am sated and pose very little risk to harm her in any way. With her blood coursing through me, I can easily ignore my violent and twisted urges. They're still there, but they can be controlled.

I lay her down on the bed, still in my arms as I brush a strand of hair out of her face. I stare at her for hours, wondering how she could be so selfless to give me the thing I need most.

Maybe she doesn't hate me as much as I thought.

CHAPTER TWENTY-FOUR

Rose

I wake up feeling hot- too hot. My eyes flutter open hesitantly. Caleb is staring at me already, wide awake. *Did he even sleep?* The heat is coming from his body, because I am still wrapped up in his arms, his one hand rubbing the back of mine.

"Watching me is not as charming as you think," I tease him groggily.

He smiles at me sweetly, not seeming to care. He's a totally different person when he isn't hungry.

I am still exhausted from sneaking around in search of blood and my encounter with William and Sebastian, not to mention feeding Caleb.

"How're you feeling?" he asks with concern.

I turn my wrist over to see that the punctures have almost disappeared, leaving a slight bruising.

"I'm fine," I say shyly, ignoring the twinge in my wrist.

I stare up into his intense gray eyes, noting that they are still cloudy, but they seem brighter, which is good to see.

"Are you sure?" he asks suspiciously.

"Yes. Why?"

"You slept through breakfast and lunch…it's almost dinner," he explains.

"What? Really?" I ask, floored.

"I'm sorry it's my fault. I took too much from you yesterday," he says apologetically.

"It's alright. I'm ok, just tired," I assure him. "What'd you tell your dad?"

"I told Aamily to tell him it was none of his business," he says.

"I bet that went over well," I laugh while he shrugs. "Wait. Did you sit here with me all day?"

"Yes. I'm not going to leave you unprotected," he replies.

"Thank you," I say enthusiastically. "Can we go for dinner?" I ask.

"Of course."

He climbs out of the bed, even though it's obvious that he would rather not. I miss the feel of his body right away and guilt starts to eat away at me. He hands me a pile of neatly folded, clean clothes- my jeans and cropped tank that I arrived in. Aamily must have brought them back.

"I thought these clothes were unacceptable."

"I think that they are perfect," he says honestly, staring me up and down and making no attempt to hide it.

I smile to myself as I head to the bathroom to freshen up and change. When I come back out, Caleb is sitting in a chair, waiting patiently. He's wearing some dark jeans and a black hoodie. *He looks hot.* He stands up, handing me a dark gray zip up sweater.

"To cover your wrist. They don't need to know," he says.

"Thank you."

I know that he doesn't care if they know. The discretion is for my benefit and I appreciate it, even if the whole point is to prove that I am his. I'm not ready for the prying eyes and knowing glances.

"She is still breathing," Sebastian says with amusement as we enter the dining room.

I blush a little at the attention, while Caleb scowls at his brother.

"There she…" William begins. "What are you wearing?" he adds, taking notice of our clothes.

"Does it matter?" Caleb says annoyed.

"I suppose not, but tomorrow be presentable," he says with displeasure.

I take my seat between Caleb and Sebastian, the latter eyeing me with interest.

"Nice sweater," Sebastian says in a hushed voice to me. "You're looking well today," he continues to Caleb.

Caleb smirks at him but says nothing in return. Sebastian doesn't seem to miss much, so it's likely he knows everything that happened. My absence, the sweater, Caleb- it's pretty obvious when I put it all together.

"I'm so glad you chose to grace us with your presence, Caleb," William says sarcastically. "There is business to discuss," he adds coldly.

"Like what?" Caleb says, only half-interested.

He's nursing his whiskey, no blood, and watching to make sure I drink my wine with blood to keep up my own strength.

"It seems that you're determined to claim Rose as yours…" he begins, both of us paying attention now, "and if that's what you want, the laws will only include you if you take back your title."

"As prince?" Caleb asks, almost spitting out his whiskey.

"What else?" he answers with a bored tone.

"What does that mean?" I ask, looking around the table.

"That means he will take the throne after our father..." Sebastian drawls, chugging his drink. "He will live here permanently, and he will be one of us again," he adds miserably.

"There will be stipulations of course..." William says coldly. "You will have to contribute to family business within the month and then there will be the induction ceremony."

Sebastian gets up furiously from his seat, draining his drink and storming off aggressively. Caleb doesn't even look up at him, but William looks in the direction he left.

"Think about it and let me know in the morning."

William gets up, takes one more disgusted look at our outfits, and leaves the room as well.

"Why is Sebastian so upset?" I ask.

"If I accept, Sebastian will only sit on the throne when I'm dead. It's a position he has always coveted, and he won't like me getting in the way. But he won't be allowed to hurt you without my permission."

"Why the hell would you ever give him permission?"

"It's rare, but some vampires are willing to share," he answers with a mischievous smile. "For the record, I don't share," he adds firmly.

Cocking my head to the side, "you don't say," I tease.

He gives me a smoldering grin, making me melt, as he grabs my drink and takes the last few sips, sitting it next to his empty glass.

"But..." he begins grimly.

"You'll have to do your fathers bidding," I say, realization dawning on me. "And he won't likely go easy on you."

"No."

"You can't do it!" I say fearfully.

"I have to. It's the only way to keep them away from you and to make sure I get to stay with you," he says desperately, clasping my hands. "I don't know what else to do, short of murdering them all."

"We'll find another way."

"This will affect me more than you, and I can handle it," he says, taking my fist and kissing it.

I don't like it, letting him be a martyr. But it's Caleb, when he makes up his mind, there's no changing it.

Knock. Knock.

"Come in," Caleb calls out from the bed.

We went back to our room right after dinner last night. I had trouble falling asleep though, even while Caleb was reading from a stack of books. I feel guilty about what Caleb is committing to do, just to keep everyone's hands off me. I guess it's just something I'm going to have to live with. Now, bring on the morning.

The door opens and Aamily comes in, hanging up Caleb's suit and taking my clothes to the bathroom.

It takes me about an hour to get ready with my hair, makeup, and clothes. Aamily helps me of course, putting my hair in an elegant bun, putting on my face and dressing me in skintight dress pants, knee high black boots, and a red silk dress shirt. I look very fancy.

Caleb is wearing black dress pants, black shoes, with a black button up shirt and a black tie. He never wears any colour, but he always looks sexy as hell.

"Are you sure about this?" I ask, tugging Caleb by the arm before we go in for breakfast.

"If it means keeping you safe, then yes."

"Something doesn't feel right," I confess.

"Rose…I know what I'm doing. This is the only option," he reassures me, sliding into the dining room before I can say more.

I follow him in, wondering how he could be so calm about this, when I'm a ball of worry for him.

Taking our usual seats, I dive right into my drink. This action has Sebastian smirking beside me. I actually wish there was more blood in my orange juice and vodka this morning.

"Caleb, have you considered my offer?" William asks pushily.

"I have. I accept."

"You're sure?" William asks, raising an eyebrow. "There is no going back from this."

"I know and I am," he replies confidently.

I swallow hard as William reaches out and pats Caleb on the back, smiling deviously.

"Excellent!" he says excitedly. "You should come to my office to sign some papers and I will catch you up on business."

Caleb glances at me nervously then at Sebastian with distrust. Sebastian grins smugly, taking pride in being the wild card.

"I'll be fine," I say, drawing his focus back to me.

"Of course, she will. Sebastian won't go against her will, right?" William asks his son.

"Of course not," Sebastian says.

Caleb looks at me nervously again, but I give him a calming smile.

"I won't be long," he says, following his father and sparing a glance back at me from the doorway.

"Guess it's just you and me, sweetheart. What to do?" he muses.

"Let's talk," I smile innocently.

"About what?" he asks.

"Caleb getting his title back," I say bluntly.

"What about it?" he asks, leaning back in his chair casually.

He waves his hand in the air signaling for the staff to remove the dishes. They bring more drinks as well and he tells them to keep them coming.

"What will he have to do?"

"That's hardly something I should discuss with you," Sebastian says snidely, "but I'm sure my father will put his...*talents* to use."

I really don't like the sound of that. Is he referring to Caleb's violent nature as an incubus? That's a highly addictive path for Caleb to be on. I take several large drinks.

"He could have chosen the easy route."

"Which is what? Giving me to you?" I ask smartly.

"It would have made things a whole lot simpler, but he had to choose the messier option," Sebastian sighs, chugging back two more drinks. "I suppose I can't blame him for wanting to be the dark prince one more time."

"What do you mean?" I ask.

"That's enough, Sebastian," William growls from the doorway, Caleb at his side.

"Yes, sir," Sebastian says mockingly. He grabs his fifth drink and heads towards the hallway. "You're only prolonging the inevitable, brother," he says lowly as he passes Caleb.

I drain my drink, feeling slightly tipsy and taking Caleb's outstretched hand, we leave a sour looking William.

I wonder what that was about.

Caleb

As I walk back to the room with Rose, hand in hand, I realize my suspicions were right. Sebastian's comment about prolonging the inevitable confirms what I've known all along. *I am temporary.*

When you make a deal with William, you have to know that he's doing it for his own benefit, and when it stops benefitting him, he will use a loophole that he's already thought of, to get out of it.

My father is as callous as they come. I knew this deal was too good to be true. He wants control over her because of the prophecy that concerns Rose's future children and is dependent on her having some. Incubus can't have children. That's why we turn incubus instead of being born one. He needs something from me and when he gets it, he'll find a way to get me out of her life.

What he doesn't know is that he's going to have to kill me to make that happen. *Maybe that's his plan?*

I just need to get her away from here. With this deal, I have the time, but she can never know their plans for me. She'll never go along with it, her heart is too big!

CHAPTER TWENTY-FIVE

Rose

It's been five weeks since I was taken from my home and forced to come here, and I still don't understand why, not really. I know it's because of some prophecy but everyone is very vague about it. Caleb seems to avoid the subject altogether, despite the fact that I let him feed from my wrist every three days. Knowing him, he's keeping something from me, but it can't possibly make things worse.

Our schedule has become routine, the faces familiar, but I miss Gavin, Xander, and Paige so much. I even miss Jason.

I follow Aamily out of the bathroom after getting ready. Caleb is waiting patiently as usual, in the chair by the door. He's dressed more casual today, wearing dark blue designer jeans, a black long sleeve shirt and a black sneaker. Aamily slips out the door after a quick bow to Caleb. She's still terrified of him and it makes me curious.

He stands up, taking me in, from my sleek ponytail and braid, low-key make-up, to my more casual outfit consisting of designer jeggings, black boots, and black cropped long-sleeve shirt.

"I think she knows something that we don't," he quips, making me smile as we head for breakfast.

Caleb

"Good morning," William says as we sit at the table for breakfast.

"Morning," I say without making eye contact.

I take my seat between my father and Rose, glancing at Rose as she sits. Both William and Sebastian are watching her closely. Sebastian looks up at me briefly, a hint of amusement written on his face. *That's never a good thing.* I return his grin with one of my own murderous and impulsive stares, making him grin wider. I don't bother trying to conceal my dislike for the way he rakes his eyes over her. I don't think he's a risk to her right now; he just likes getting under my skin, but he is unpredictable.

"Rose, it's your birthday in a few days, right?" William asks enthusiastically. "You'll be nineteen?" he adds with too much interest.

I look at him, eyebrows squished together, trying to figure out what he is up to, knowing it can't be good whatever it is.

"Yes," Rose answers, oblivious to my suspicions.

"That's wonderful. I hope you'll think of something we can give you," William says, feigning kindness.

"*I know what I can give her,*" Sebastian says clearly in my head, smirking twistedly at me.

"Screw off," I say back to him out loud, earning a confused look from Rose, and a dark laugh from him.

"Boys, don't start."

I stare at William annoyed that he's letting Sebastian voice his disgusting thoughts, even if they're in my head.

Rose places her hand on top of mine, calming me and pulling my attention back to her. She gives me a small smile that I feel in my chest. I stare into her bright green eyes while the electric charge from our contact continues.

"Today, you're going to put in some manual labour. I want you to collect some firewood," William says, disrupting my happy feelings.

"Don't you have people to do that?"

"Of course."

He stares at me expectantly. I know that this is a power play. He wants to prove that I have to listen to every menial order he gives me now, to punish me for abandoning our family way back. And to show others that he has an incubus under his thumb. I'll go along with it…for now!

"Rose is coming with me," I say adamantly.

"Shocker!" Sebastian says sarcastically.

Rose

"If William thinks that chopping wood is one of your talents, I don't think he knows you very well," I say playfully as we make our way across the grounds to the trees.

"He wants to make everyone think I'm at his beck and call," I explain. "He's using me to create fear."

We come to a stand-still beside a large pile of un-split wood, next to a wall of stacked split wood. I lean back against it as he dips down to grab the ax. Tossing his coat beside me, he begins swinging the ax over his head, bringing it down on a log and splitting it apart.

After an hour, Caleb has gone through a quarter of the logs and he's already coated in sweat from the effort. I don't know why he's not just using his creature self. He'd be closer to being finished and less sweaty.

He sets the ax down, pulling his shirt up and over his head, exposing all of his muscles glistening in the moonlight. After a minute, I realize that I am practically drooling and he's watching me. I shake off my attraction to him and pull my attention away from how cut he is.

"You're going to freeze," I say, pulling my coat tighter around me.

He uses his shirt to wipe the sweat off his face as he walks over to me, tossing the shirt next to his coat. He stares down at me, peering into my soul. When I feel his hands land firmly on my waist, I stifle a gasp. Squeezing gently, he lifts me up, setting me down on the other side of his coat, so that I'm sitting on the pile of wood rather than standing.

"I'll be fine. I run hot anyway," he says, smiling and returning to pick up the ax, unaware of how his touch still affects me every time.

He swings the ax over his head, splitting another log. I shamelessly ogle him as his muscles flex to control the action. *It's making me feel things I shouldn't be feeling.*

"Did you grow up with your father?" I ask, distracting myself.

He glances at me briefly, probably to gauge how interested I am before returning to his work.

"No. I did not spend my childhood with William," he says, continuing to split the wood with vigor. "I lived with my mother until I was sixteen," he adds after a minute.

"What happened?"

He stops what he's doing and stares at the solid log sitting before him, his shoulders tensing in thought. "She died in a fire."

He drives the ax through the log, letting out some pent-up rage and sending pieces of wood flying everywhere.

"I am so sorry, Caleb," I say sincerely, my heart breaking for him.

"It was a long time ago."

"What was she like?" I ask, feeling genuine curiosity.

He looks at me with a strange look- something resembling gratitude.

"She was warm, kind, and somedays her patience was limitless. She was also courageous- never backing down, and her laugh was contagious," he smiles with his memories. "She was meant to be a mother."

"She sounds perfect."

"She was," he agrees.

He splits a few more logs while I stare longingly at him. He rests the ax on the ground and gazes right at me with a knowing smirk.

"You're gawking."

I feel the heat rising in my cheeks as I blush with embarrassment- realizing that I'm being inappropriate, but I just couldn't help myself. He puts the ax down and strides over to me with conviction. *What have I gotten myself into?* My heartbeat picks up the pace while his eyes stay on mine, making me feel even more awkward. Thank god for the darkness hiding how truly flustered I am.

Caleb

"You don't have to stop," I say, my voice low and husky.

I walk up to her, sitting on the row of wood, spreading her legs further apart as I push my way in between them. My hands rest intimately on her thighs and a fire starts to burn in my stomach.

I stare into her face, her eyes wide with nervous excitement. She's fighting how badly she wants me. I saw it when she was watching me and I can see it now, even if she doesn't want to admit it to herself. I'm already hot from the physical effort of my punishment and hotter still from being so close to her. I'm sure she can feel the heat coming off me in waves. It does nothing to calm either of us as I force air in and out of my lungs and she tries to hide her uneven breaths.

I think it really overwhelms her when she sees how comfortable I am being up in her personal space. If anything, it makes it worse for me, making me feel reckless and fidgety. Especially when her blood starts calling to me.

I close my eyes and lean into her so close that my lips graze hers, our noses touch while my hands grip her thighs harder in my attempt to remain controlled.

"Caleb…" She whispers dreamily. "I can't."

I remove my hands from her thighs, hoping that she is as disappointed as I am. I care about her so deeply that I would never want to coerce her into anything. I need her to admit it to me and to herself that she feels it too. So, even though it physically pains me to let her go, I know I have to, at least for now.

"I know," I say, sighing and taking a half-step away from her.

When I grab her by the hips, a needy whimper escapes her lips, which starts making my resolve unravel. *I'm so torn right now.* I lower her slowly, feeling as she slides down my naked torso, knowing that she wants my touch now as much as I need hers. When her feet hit the ground, she sways a little, even as she is pinned between me and the wood pile. I caress her cheek with one hand, knowing it's leaving heat.

"Rose…" I whisper emotionally.

"We can't," she says again sadly, a tear going down her cheek.

Silently, I chastise myself for being so impetuous as I pull my hand back but remain face-to-face with her. I can feel the veins pulsing under my eyes, so I know that she can see them, but I won't turn away from her. I want her to see the real me before it's too late.

"We've been out here for hours. That's enough wood for today," I say, trying to dilute the tension.

My body is shaken with little electric shocks as she surprises me, bringing her hand up and running her fingers across my cheek without fear.

"You're not afraid of me anymore."

"I know you won't hurt me," she whispers with a sweet smile.

She keeps her hand on my face confidently, her wrist next to my mouth. I can smell the blood under the skin, and it calls to me, making the heat take over. I know my eyes are flashing dangerously as my body wants to feed again, but I resist the urge because she hasn't said it.

She's showing the trust she has in me, monster and all, and I won't let her down. She doesn't need to know that I'll always be a risk.

Rose

I know I'm playing a dangerous game, tempting the savage part of Caleb, but I need to see for myself the degree of control I have over him. That's what I'm telling myself. To be honest, I wouldn't hate if he lost control for both of us with the way he's making me feel.

Lining my wrist up beside his mouth, I ignore that there are people going about their business within eyesight. My heart beats harder with the thought of what I'm about to do, in the open no less. *Who am I?*

"Feed," I order him bravely.

He grins at me in a dangerous and excited way, the change happening instantly, turning his head slowly and without hesitation, sinking his razor-sharp teeth into my wrist.

"Ah," I gasp out as the pain pierces me, realizing that in some twisted way I've started to ache for it.

He keeps his eyes on mine and I don't dare look away from his stunning silver eyes, returning his intense gaze with my own determined one.

"Well, well," Sebastian drawls, stepping out from the shadows beside the wood pile, but not pulling Caleb's eyes off me. "I guess now it makes sense why you're not starving," he adds in a deep voice.

I finally turn my head, looking at Sebastian, seeing a dark desire in his eyes and shooting him an angry glare.

"Ow," I hiss, feeling Caleb remove his teeth from my skin.

He keeps his fingers clasped around my wrist to keep it from bleeding, letting the heat leave him before turning his focus on his brother. My chest is moving harder than normal as I try to regain my composure. I'm sure Sebastian has already noticed.

"What do you want, Sebastian?" Caleb asks with renewed patience.

"Nothing. I was bored. Thought Rose might be too," he says watching me. "Obviously she's not," he finishes with a smirk.

"Satisfied?" I ask rudely as Caleb releases my wrist, pulling his jacket on and carrying his shirt.

"Not even close," Sebastian says suggestively, stepping closer to me.

I feel the warmth in my cheeks at his words, feeling a bit embarrassed for what he saw.

"Oh, don't pretend to be modest now, sweetheart. I know you even like the pain. You're a little twisted and dark it seems," he taunts me.

Caleb grabs my hand and starts pulling me towards the manor and away from his brother.

"Leave her alone, Sebastian," he says tensely over his shoulder.

I can hear Sebastian laughing while we walk away. *What a psycho.* Caleb doesn't slow his pace, holding my hand painfully tight and dragging me with him until we are entering our room in the manor.

He finally lets go of my hand, shutting the door and leaning his head against it with relief.

"What was that about? What did he say?" I ask without looking at him.

He spins around, crushing my body up against the wall in an instant, staring at me feverishly.

"It's not about what he said. You were reckless," he begins angrily, "letting me have you that way."

Fury rises to the surface, threatening to engulf me.

"Excuse me? I was feeding you," I say defensively.

"You weren't just feeding me. You were toying with me," he growls out.

After about thirty seconds, my fury is replaced with a feeling of satisfaction as I comprehend why he's upset with me.

"Wait a minute," I say, grinning. "You're mad I was enjoying myself?"

"No. I'm not," he says, his anger melting away. "I'm upset that Sebastian saw you giving in to me that way."

"Ok, first off, him showing up was not my fault. Secondly, I didn't do anything that I didn't want to do. You're not going to make me feel shame because of that."

His eyes travel between mine, making sense of what I just said. I admitted that I wanted him to touch me, to bite me, and he definitely heard me. It's out there. I can't take it back now. I don't think I'd want to if I could.

Out of nowhere, Caleb shoves back from me and bolts back out the door. I stand there in shock.

I admitted some feelings and he ran.

CHAPTER TWENTY-SIX

Rose

"Are you excited for your birthday tomorrow, miss?" Aamily asks kindly, touching up my makeup for Caleb's induction celebration.

"Sure," I lie.

I should be thrilled about my birthday tomorrow. Any normal person would be. I'm finally turning nineteen. I feel like I've been waiting for this forever. But I'm not excited, I'm consumed with thoughts about what happened a week ago. I let Caleb feed from me, unknowingly let Sebastian witness, and then admitted to Caleb that he means something to me, and he ran. He's been avoiding me all week- wouldn't even feed from me.

He's being ridiculous. I thought this is what he wanted.

"Done," Aamily says proudly, pulling me out of my own head.

I look in the mirror, letting out a breath. My makeup is on point with my dark, smoky eyes, thick black lashes, and perfect black cat-eye. Not to mention the sparkly, nude lip gloss on my lips, and the shimmery highlighting powder on my cheek bones.

My hair has loose curls scattered methodically throughout, my lengths cascading over my shoulders. I look totally glamourous. Aamily definitely went all out for this.

Dropping my bathrobe, I admire the strapless black body suit that fits me like a glove. The sheer, black, floor length skirt flowing around my legs, the thigh slit going all the way to my waist. The dress doesn't leave much to the imagination, and the black tie-up heels only add to the appeal.

I turn to open the bathroom door, hoping that Caleb is waiting for me.

"A word of advice, miss," Aamily says abruptly. "Don't let down your guard."

She pushes the door open, both of us stopping in our tracks, at the person in front us.

"Master Sebastian," Aamily says, bowing and rushing out, leaving me in the room with the psycho.

He smiles softly, taking in my appearance, his eyes travelling up and down me appreciatively. I scowl at him, even though I don't really blame him tonight.

"What are you doing here?" I ask with annoyance.

"Caleb was detained with our father. I've come to escort you."

Of course. He holds out his arm patiently, eyeing me devilishly.

I reluctantly link my arm through his and he pulls me closer right away, smirking triumphantly.

"What?" I ask impatiently.

"You look fit to be a queen," he replies, leading us out into the hallway.

He takes me to a room just off the gallery, which turns out to be a ballroom filled with people who turn unabashedly to stare as we enter.

My head starts buzzing as my chest squeezes, making it harder to breath. My heart starts beating at an unsustainable speed as I feel all eyes on me. I have the sudden urge to run and sway indecisively.

"Just breathe," Caleb says, appearing on my other side.

He rests his hand on the small of my back, the warmth seeping through the thin material and calming me.

"Thank you," Caleb says stiffly, nodding at Sebastian.

Sebastian doesn't say anything in response, but he nods back at Caleb in private understanding. He removes his arm from mine and walks away swiftly giving me a hesitant look.

"See you later, sweetheart," he says quietly.

He knows something that I don't.

I slowly catch my breath, snatching a glass of champagne from a waiter as he passes by. I drink it greedily, needing some liquid courage.

"Pace yourself," Caleb says, attempting a joke.

"Now you're going to acknowledge my existence," I say bitterly, chugging the rest of my drink.

I discard my empty glass on a passing tray, retrieving a full one. I waste no time throwing it back, aware of Caleb watching me.

I thought I could handle this, but maybe not. I try to walk away from him, feeling the anger bubbling to the surface. He grabs my arm aggressively, pulling me back to him. I drain my glass again, swapping it out for a full one.

"Don't walk away from me," he says warningly.

His control is obviously a little unreliable tonight.

"So, only you can?" I reply furiously, chugging my third drink while Caleb scowls.

"Rose, you look like absolute perfection," William says, his voice dripping in charm, as he approaches beside us.

"Thank you, William," I say appreciatively, finishing my third drink.

"There's some people that would love to meet you," William says, gesturing across the room, while he hands me a new drink and discards my old one.

Caleb holds his arm out for me to link mine through. Instead, I lace my arm through William's, much to his surprise, and take another long drink.

"Shall we?" I ask sweetly.

Caleb

"Trouble in paradise, son?" William taunts me telepathically as he leads Rose across the room. *"No,"* I respond bluntly.

William stops in front of a few members of the council with Rose on his arm. They eye me warily and their eyes graze over her inappropriately. My blood begins to boil.

"Gentlemen, this is Caleb's young woman, Roselyn Parker," William says politely.

"We've heard so much about you," one of the gentlemen says, licking his lips while reaching out a hand to greet her.

Not happening.

Not caring that I come off as an inconsiderate prick, I grab Rose's wrist and drag her away from the men and onto the dance floor, sloshing what's left of her champagne.

"Jesus, Caleb," she says, handing her glass to a waiter and looking back at me with irritation.

She shakes off the wetness on her hand, sending a few drops flying. Glaring at me, she swipes the rest on my shirt, daring me to stop her in an attempt to piss me off. To her disappointment, it doesn't bug me the way she wants, and I simply roll my eyes at her.

"You ignore me all week and then act like this," she says hushed, trying not to draw attention.

"Like what?" I ask, my temper flaring.

If she knew what those men did in their spare time, she wouldn't have been so eager to meet them. I was doing her a favour.

"Like a colossal dick," she shouts, her anger getting the better of her.

A few individuals turn their heads towards us with prying interest. I sigh with frustration. I knew she wouldn't just let it go and now she's angry and looking for a fight. I should have spoken to her before tonight, but I knew that if I did, I wouldn't keep my hands to myself. After all, she admitted she didn't want me to.

Putting my hand on her lower back, I guide her to a hallway just off the ballroom, knowing we can still be heard, but at least no one is gawking at us.

"I'm sorry," I say exasperated, knowing I say it too much.

"You've been avoiding me. Why?"

She stares into my face, her back against the wall, her eyes begging me to either reciprocate her feelings or put an end to it. It'd be better for me to keep her at arm's length, but I'm selfish and I can't stay away.

Rose

He says nothing, too concerned with his inner monologue.

"Caleb, please talk to me," I plead, my anger turning into insecurity.

He stares at me, his gray eyes ablaze, and I find myself wishing I could hear his private thoughts.

"Things will be worse for you if you let yourself care about me," he says in a low, gravelly voice.

"What things?"

"Things. You have to trust me."

There's something he's not telling me, as usual.

"No. You trust me," I say assertively. "I've tried not to care about you. Believe me!" I continue with frustration.

He smirks at my snarky comment. "So have I," he sighs.

My heart speeds up, beating frantically in my chest. This is the most honest and direct conversation we've had maybe ever, but where does that leave us?

Caleb steps forward, pressing me firmly against the wall, his hand cupping my cheek romantically before his lips crash against mine. His other hand is on my waist, digging into my hip bone painfully, but exciting me anyway.

I'm tired of trying to talk myself out of what I want. I want to be his.

"Caleb!" I moan as he kisses down my chin to my neck.

I feel the heat beginning to take us both, neither of us caring that we're exposed in a hallway.

"It's time to welcome my son, Caleb, back home," William's voice echoes through the room, putting an end to our moment.

Caleb stops what he's doing with a low growl, kissing my cheek gently as he retreats. Without smiling, he makes his way over to his father, leaving me to catch my breath and sneak out behind him. Grabbing a drink on the way, I stand at the front, only feet from him. *It's total torture.*

"Long live the dark prince!" William chants with a sadistic grin.

He raises his glass of champagne and blood, toasting in Caleb's direction as everyone, including me, lifts our glasses in unison. The gleam in William's eye makes it impossible to know if his welcome is sincere, or if it's all a show. Either way, I don't trust him, but I gaze longingly at Caleb, catching his eye and playing along anyway.

Caleb's face twitches at William's casual use of 'dark prince', uncomfortable with the memories that come with the title. He raises his glass of scotch gracefully though, gazing at me and then looking at his father.

"Enjoy the party!" William says, nodding at a few men who follow him out of the room. Caleb follows him, a somber look on his face.

I stay back, watching him get farther away from me. I debate following him, but something tells me I shouldn't.

"Having fun?" Sebastian asks, coming out of nowhere and watching after Caleb too.

"Where are they going?" I ask.

"To finish Caleb's induction," he answers nonchalantly, trying to hide the excitement in his voice.

"What does that mean?"

He shrugs at me.

"You'll have to see for yourself," he replies, draining his drink and walking after them.

I quietly move up against the doorframe and peek in. Caleb is standing a metre in front of his father, with Sebastian to his left. The four other councilmen are scattered around them.

Caleb is glaring at William hatefully, already into a discussion.

"Son, you have to share a feed with me tonight to bind the terms of this contract. It's tradition," William says.

"If I must," Caleb says through gritted teeth.

Share a feed? And he's agreeing? *What the hell?*

"If you want it to be from Rose, Sebastian can go fetch her," William says, smirking.

"No," Caleb says adamantly. "I will not give you permission to feed from Rose."

"I figured as much. However, the rules are quite clear. To make it official, you must participate in the feeding," he says cruelly. "I even procured another girl to solve the problem."

He cannot be serious.

Caleb stares his father down with hatred in his eyes as a beautiful young girl approaches him with a flirtatious smile.

Hell no.

I step into the doorway impulsively, my disapproval clear on my face. Caleb looks at me apologetically, understanding that feeding from another girl will cause problems between us, but also knowing he must feed in order to officially take title and secure my safety.

He's stuck between a rock and a hard place, which is exactly what William wants.

Screw him!

"No need to fetch me, I'm here," I say, moving to Caleb's side. "If Caleb's feeding from anyone, it'll be me," I say firmly.

"That's touching," William says emotionlessly. "But he will not be the only one sinking his teeth into you," he adds sinisterly.

"I understand," I say as bravely as I can.

"You don't have to do this, love," Caleb says affectionately, my heart melting at the use of a pet name. "He'll inflict as much pain as he can."

I consider Caleb's warning, but come back to the same choice.

"I want it to be me."

Caleb pulls me in close until I'm right up against him, my breathing accelerating in fear. With my neck exposed to Caleb, my view is aimed at Sebastian, who is watching me with a new look- he's impressed. Out of the corner of my eye, I can see William approach to arm's length, standing taut but disbelieving that I will follow through.

Caleb takes my arm, presenting it wrist-up to William at my side. He takes hold of me, his touch making me flinch.

"Focus on me," Caleb whispers to me tenderly.

"Witness," William says to the room.

Caleb

Gently, I brush the hair off Rose's neck, exposing her skin; then I place my hands on her waist and hold her to me. The heat transforms me instantly, anticipation taking over. I smirk at William victoriously, happy to see the anger in his eyes. His attempts to drive a wedge between myself and Rose has failed and backfired.

I look back to Rose and see the artery pulsing in her neck. I don't know if she is excited or scared, likely both, knowing her. I bring my lips to her neck and place an affectionate kiss. Her breath catches in her chest. I plunge my teeth into her skin as carefully as I can manage, delighting in the clear moan it causes. I can only imagine how jealous it makes everyone.

I feed slowly, feeling her melt into me, her fingers gripping my shirt and trying to pull me closer. She's allowing herself to enjoy me, pleasure and pain.

"Agh," she screams loudly, tensing all over.

My arms go around her, supporting her weight as her knees buckle from the pain that William is delivering now that he has joined in.

After her initial reaction to him, she sobs quietly, her body tense and shuddering with every breath. I feel bad admitting that I'm still enjoying the taste of her blood, but I don't feed long after, pulling away reluctantly but carefully while William continues.

"That's enough," I say to William, caressing her cheek.

"Enough," I say more firmly.

"William!" I shout, feeling a sliver of fear that he won't stop.

Her blood is addictive; I've known this all along.

"Father!" Sebastian shouts nervously, stepping forward and putting a hand on Williams' shoulder, pulling him out of his trance.

He pulls his teeth out aggressively, not worrying about hurting her more. "Delightful," he says, smirking at me.

Rose's eyes lock onto mine, showering me in warmth, her cheeks tinged with pink. I know my bite still hurts her, but it's obvious she has grown to like the pain. Some would say that's a sign of her darkness. Instead of deterring me, *it just thrills me*. But William was deliberately trying to be a savage just to hurt me.

"Are we done?" I ask, my patience fading as Rose closes her eyes and leans into me.

"It's official," Sebastian confirms as William still reels.

I scoop Rose up into my arms, her head resting against my chest as we go to our room.

CHAPTER TWENTY-SEVEN

Rose

Did that really happen? I ask myself, lying in the bed with my eyes still closed. The twinge in my neck and wrist tells me yes. I let Caleb and his father, William, feed from me at the same time to cement their stupid contract. All because I couldn't handle the thought of Caleb with his lips pressed against another girl.

I don't feel the usual heat radiating off Caleb's body on the bed, so I open my eyes. Looking around the room, I realize he's not here. I sit up, wiping sleep from my eyes, last night's dress digging in under my arms.

Grabbing some jeans and a loose sweater top, I head into the bathroom, trying to the erase the memory of William drinking my blood. I brush my teeth, run my fingers through my hair, fix my makeup, and toss the beautiful dress on the floor.

"Happy birthday," Caleb says, a small smile on his lips as I come back into the room.

He's sitting on the bed, a tray in front of him covered in fruit, a cupcake, and a single white rose. I crawl onto the bed, feeling embarrassed about last night. It was easy to feel brave after drinking so much in such a short time.

"Thank you."

He leans across the bed and plants a gentle kiss on my lips, lingering as he pulls away. I want to reach out and pull him back to me, but I don't, feeling more reserved without the alcohol.

"Do you regret it?" he asks tentatively.

I can see it in his eyes; he's scared of what my answer will be.

I reach over, grabbing the rose and twirling it in my fingers. "I don't," I say confidently. "Any of it."

He watches me take some fruit, a grin on his face, his brilliant gray eyes sparkling with excitement. I'm referring to the kissing and touching that happened earlier in the evening, and he knows it.

I shove some more fruit in my mouth, acknowledging how hungry I am, especially after last night.

"I want to show you something," Caleb says.

"Ok."

Against my better judgement, I decide then and there to go wherever he's taking me, without hesitation. Despite the situation that I found myself in last night. *What can I say?*

I grab a handful of blueberries, leaving the rose and the cupcake behind, then take Caleb's outstretched hand. I like this Caleb. He's not afraid of our touch- he even seems to thrive on it.

"Are you sure this is a good idea?" I ask skeptically.

He looks at me seriously but there is also playful mischief present.

"Trust me."

And that's the funny thing, I do, even if I've seen first-hand the meaner side of Caleb.

He leads me into the hall, down the stairs and to the front door. He takes me outside without a coat in the chilly evening air.

The sun is just beginning to set, but no one is walking around the village. Since it's February, there is still a layer of snow on the ground.

"Caleb, it's freezing out here," I say, still without resisting.

"It won't be for long," he replies with a smirk.

We walk hand-in-hand towards the gardens and the hedge maze.

"Where are you taking me?"

I look up at his face and even in the dark, I can see his amusement as he looks straight ahead. Still, he says nothing as we walk beside the hedge maze.

"Caleb, come on," I whine flirtatiously.

"Yes, love," he answers smugly, turning his heated gaze on me.

He knows that the pet name makes me swoon, partly because he drank my blood and partly because he just knows me. As hard as I've tried to resist it, I'm drawn to him like a magnet.

"I could tell you, but that'd ruin the surprise."

"Maybe I know better than to let you surprise me," I say playfully.

"Does it matter?" he asks, still grinning as he backs me up against the hedge. "Because I know that it doesn't."

My heart starts beating rapidly, my breathing sending little puffs of steam up between us in the cold air. I stare up into his eyes, knowing that everything is different between us now.

"You didn't have to do what you did last night. I never would have asked you to do that," he says seriously, more emotion showing in his eyes than I thought he possessed. "But I'm glad it was you," he admits.

He glances down at his feet and then back at me.

"I know."

"But it was also really dangerous," he says softly, placing a hand on either side of my face. "Not so much the act, but what it means."

"What do you mean?" I ask, distracted by his hands on my face.

His hands fall from me, making me almost whimper in want. "William will know everything now."

"Like what?"

He says nothing, looking away from me.

A faraway fearful look takes over him for some reason. I reach out, grasping the front of his shirt and tugging him to me.

"What is it?" I ask sweetly.

"William will know our strengths and weaknesses. He will know just how important you are to me and how far I'm willing to go to protect you," he says. "Because of that, he'll know now more than ever, that I am more of a danger to him than he ever could have imagined. He'll know that I'd trade my life for yours if I thought it would help. He'll know that I know you'll never be safe without me around. And he'll know that you are my reason for breathing and I will never willingly leave you again, simply because I can't stomach the idea of living a life without you," he finishes, breathing raggedly.

"Oh," is all I can say while I process his confession.

In my defense, he did just drop a bomb on me. I always felt like our connection was epic, but I never considered how all-encompassing it would feel for him. He's over nine hundred years old for god's sake.

He doesn't wait for me to say anything, crashing his mouth against mine hectically, needing some form of reassurance that I reciprocate his feelings. I can't bring myself to say it out loud, but my body betrays me, pulling him as close as I possibly can while his hands roam my body greedily. Still, I find myself wanting more- needing more of him.

"Caleb…" I mutter, using all of my willpower to break our kiss.

He pulls back, his forehead resting against mine, his eyes closed as he tries to contain himself. We're both breathing hard, my heart going a mile a minute. He said I was his reason for breathing- what do I say to that? Or that he'll never willingly leave me again. *I'm so confused.* My feelings seem so overwhelming when he's around and yet so manageable when he's not. I depend on his absence, for my sanity.

Noticing my inner struggle, he composes himself, taking my hand and dragging me towards the trees. He pulls me through the darkness like he has his very own flashlight. In minutes we walk into a break in the trees circling a beautiful waterfall cascading down into a pond and river.

I let go of his hand and walk forward in amazement. I can feel the peace and calm here.

It's a sight beyond words. All I can do is stare.

I feel like myself.

Caleb

She stands with her back to me, staring at the waterfall- deep in thought. Her sweater is hanging off one shoulder, exposing the soft skin of her other one. Her tight jeans are showing off every curve, teasing me. And her dark brown hair is down, the loose waves flowing down her back.

She's gorgeous.

"Thank you for bringing me here," she says, turning her head slightly.

The light reflects off the water, highlighting her profile. She looks angelic.

"I thought you'd like it," I say, stepping closer.

I stop, a foot behind her, as she turns back to the water. After a minute I can hear her heartbeat speeding up. I don't know if it's because of her fear of me or because she wants me to touch her. Maybe it's both.

I close the gap between us in half a step, letting her back graze my chest. Her heart quickens more, her back rigid against me.

I don't know how she feels. I don't know if she wants me as much as I want her and it's killing me, but being close to her is not enough anymore.

I reach out, my fingers brushing the hair off her bare shoulder and across her neck. It feels good to touch her without her jerking away from me.

As if by an invisible force, I lean down and delicately kiss the skin of her shoulder, sliding my lips along her warm skin before I pull away. She lets out a shaky breath but does not move to stop me.

Suddenly, she turns around in my arms until she is facing me, her brilliant green eyes searching my face for the truth behind my confession. My hands go to her waist and my touch does all the things to her that I want it to.

"Why are you doing this to me," she asks, a tear rolling down her cheek.

"Because I need to feel you, to touch you," I answer honestly.

"Why?"

"Because pretending I don't want you is too hard," I confess.

"What about what I need?" she asks sweetly.

She slides her hands up my chest and hooks them around my neck, the electricity dragging along the entire path, making my breathing speed up.

"What do you need?"

"You," she says surely.

My adrenaline spikes, the heat pulsating within me. I press my lips against hers savagely, hungrily. My body wants more and more, knowing that it's unfair of me to ask. The fingers on her one hand intertwine through my hair, the fingers on her other hand caressing the back of my neck. Her pulse getting faster still, her chest moving with her ragged breaths.

My hands move from her waist, one wrapping around her, holding her to me tighter, the other one falling and cupping her ass.

She kisses me deeper, her hunger beginning to match mine. She is letting her impulses win, just like me. Losing herself in us, much to my enjoyment.

I let go of her, tugging my shirt up and over my head, not breaking our kiss for more than a second. Then I undo and push my pants down until I'm standing in front of her in my boxer briefs.

She takes a step back, biting her bottom lip nervously, her eyes locked on mine after she looks at all of me. *I love when she does that.*

I step towards her confidently and play at the bottom of her shirt. She smiles at me reassuringly, so I tug it up over her head, knowing the breeze will be chilly, but the water will be warm. I unbutton her jeans, sliding them down her legs. She steps out of them, standing before me in a black bra and underwear.

To keep myself from taking her right here and now, I have to remind myself that no one has ever touched her the way that I intend to…one day soon. There's no need to rush, we can take this slow.

Wrapping both of my arms around her as far as they will go, I slowly back her into the water. Her eyes fly open in surprise.

"It's so warm."

"It's a hot spring," I reply with a chuckle.

Pressing my lips back to hers, we wade out in the water until it is up to my chest. She puts a hand on either of my shoulders, pulling herself up to eye level with me, and smoothly wraps her legs around me, kissing me without concern. A groan escapes my lips as her body settles against mine. The pleasure of her body pressing into mine is almost too good. I feel her lips pull up in a satisfied smile, on mine.

My hands roam freely, enjoying the exploration of every inch of slippery, wet skin that they can. The sun sets completely, but I could care less that William will be waiting for us because I am excited, *in more than one way.*

It occurs to me that maybe she wants this to go further than I can allow it to go tonight. Her body definitely isn't objecting, but I know that it can't. I need to take a breather before my body acts of its' own desires. I won't take anything from her, not when we're still being watched.

It takes every ounce of my willpower to pull away from her and I hate myself the second I do; immediately feeling the loss. I rest my forehead against her cheek, needing some skin contact in some way, wanting nothing more than to return my lips to hers.

"What's wrong?" she asks, her legs still wrapped around me tightly, sensing my mood.

"I need a few minutes to…calm down," I say with a guilty grin. "It's easy for me to lose myself in you."

She smiles and blushes. She knows exactly what I mean, she can feel me-all of me. She can tell what she's doing to me.

She starts tracing circles on my chest over my heart, her eyes sparkling with a wicked gleam, her touch threatening my chivalry.

"Maybe I'm ok with you losing control," she says seductively.

I groan inwardly, resenting my sweet intentions.

Planting a gentle kiss on her soft lips, I whisper "not here." For the briefest moment she looks hurt. "Believe me, I want nothing more, but we can't," I continue.

"Why not?" she asks with a pout.

"Because we're not alone," I explain as she looks around wildly, seeing only shadows.

"I don't see anyone."

"It's Rip and a couple other guards. They're keeping an eye on us," I admit with embarrassment.

At the mention of his name, his eyes glow from the shadows, alerting her of his presence. She shudders in my grip, realizing that I was right.

"That's unnerving," she admits.

"They won't lay a finger on you, I promise," I say, noting a change in her.

"I believe you. I'm just disappointed," she confesses shyly.

I grin at her, feeling the same disappointment, but I always knew that wasn't happening tonight. Although physically, my body is still annoyed with the mood killing guards.

Rose

Letting my legs fall away from Caleb, I tread water a few feet away from him, trying to cool off. I would have given myself to him. It's like I have no control. *It's so frustrating.*

Caleb climbs out of the water, starting a fire on some rocks with stumps sitting around it. After a few minutes, the stumps look dry. Caleb reaches out a hand to help me out. I take a seat around the fire, aware of my soaking underwear and feeling eyes on me.

"Will you tell me more about the prophecy?" I ask nervously.

Caleb watches the fire stiffly for several minutes before answering.

"Yes. What do you want to know?"

"Everything."

All I know is it involves my future children. I watch Caleb's chest rising and falling in the glow of the fire, his muscles tight with focus.

"Before you were born, it was prophesized that Ana would die, and her spirit would inhabit another halfling. This halfling would possess an unheard of ability. The ability to bear children across creatures. These children will go on to have all the power as the beginning of new breeds of creatures and the side that they are on would become the dominant side," he says as gently as he can.

"So, that's why Dalibor and the vampires want me. To have babies with?" I ask incredulously.

I have never heard of a more archaic, barbaric, and offensive purpose in my life. *Seriously, what the hell?*

"No," Caleb answers flatly. "For Dalibor it isn't about the prophecy, he wants to use you to bring Ana back."

"I thought you couldn't bring people back, at least not as they were."

"You can't. And the ritual he's going to use involves black magick, which will cause a lot of death," Caleb explains grimly.

"So, it's the vampires that want to…have babies with me?" I grimace.

"Rose…" Caleb says regretfully. "It's not just the vampires. The halflings, the enchanters, even the werewolves would love that power. But the vampires are the ones who won't treat you like a person. They will make you carry their kind even if that means forcing themselves on you. And you will be their plaything in between. If they tire of you and you're no longer useful, they'll kill you."

"But I'm yours, so I'm safe, right?" I ask in a small voice.

Caleb's fingers rub my cheek lightly, while his eyes stare right into mine with that well-known intensity of his.

Caleb

Staring into the depths of her green eyes, I wonder to myself, how do I tell her that her current safety has an expiry date? That they won't stop until the prophecy is fulfilled? That her safety is merely an illusion?

"For now," I settle on.

"What's that supposed to mean?"

I pull my hand back as her words come out angry and she sits up straighter. Not that I blame her.

"Are you sure you want to know?"

"Jesus, Caleb. I thought we were past all the secrets. Yes, I want to know," she says.

"They'll find a way to kill me to get rid of me and when they do, you'll have their babies," I say bluntly.

"They can't do that. What if I refuse?"

"They can and it won't matter," I say sadly. "But I'm really hard to kill," I add, trying to bring some levity to our conversation.

"What if…what if I have your babies?" she asks, blushing fiercely.

For a moment, I stare at her, surprised that she'd be willing to do that, that she actually considers me the lesser evil. That's when reality hits me.

"I can't give you children, love," I say reluctantly. "Incubus cannot have children. We are the darkness that dead things come from," I add with self-loathing and shame.

I've never given much thought to having kids. I turned incubus before I felt ready, and I never felt the urge to have a family with anyone. But now, saying it out loud hurts for some reason, and watching her process the truth is absolute agony.

She is quiet for a long time, the minutes dragging on and making me feel like I've extinguished this flame between us that I just managed to ignite.

"You're not all darkness," she says, reaching out and squeezing my hand with a sincere smile.

Maybe I haven't lost her!

CHAPTER TWENTY-EIGHT

Caleb

"Rose. Rose," I whisper into her ear as she begins to wake.

It's still early; the sun is just beginning to set, but what I have planned requires everyone to still be asleep.

"I need you to wake up, love," I whisper, running my hand up and down her arm.

"Ugh, no," she groans sleepily, making me chuckle.

"Come on, we have to go," I say, urging her to sit up.

"Why? Where are we going?" she whines.

She throws her legs over the edge of the bed, her eye lids opening and closing slowly. I watch her tug some leggings on under my t-shirt that she wore to bed, and then pull on my hoodie from the floor.

I'm overcome with the same feeling I had at the pond last night- happiness. I'd watched her dress then, too and I'd been amazed that after everything I've done to her, she still lets me touch her. Maybe her affection for me isn't as fragile as I'd believed.

I surprise myself by grabbing her hand and dragging her, half asleep, into the hall, down the stairs, and across the grounds.

It's strange how much easier it is for me to touch her now and how much I crave it.

Rose

His cabin, I realize standing at the front door. The sun is just beginning to set in the distance. He reaches around me and pushes the door open. I cautiously walk in, feeling Caleb right behind me.

I was expecting a big mess, but it looks like it's been clean for quite some time- a fact William was keeping to himself.

"Bloody liar!" Caleb mutters to himself.

Butterflies flutter nervously in my belly at the thought of being alone after what I was willing to do last night. To calm myself down, I look around, taking in the large cabin. A kitchen is in one corner, parallel to a living area and bedroom, with a fireplace separating the two. There are two closed doors, which must be the bathroom, and perhaps a closet. There also appears to be a sunroom off to the side. Surprisingly, it is a very nice place.

Sitting down on the edge of the king size bed, I watch Caleb's muscles ripple as he gets a fire going. He's got the same look on his face that he had at the pond. It's strange seeing him this way.

I fall back into the soft bed and close my eyes. I'm exhausted. I guess living in a constant state of high anxiety, stress, and fear will do that to you.

Caleb clears his throat, drawing my attention to him crouching in front of me, removing my shoes. His piercing gray eyes gaze right into my soul, making my heart race and my stomach flutter.

He kicks his own shoes off and crawls to the top of the bed, folding his arms behind his head. He gives me a satisfied smirk, closing his eyes, and I start making my way up the bed to join him. Dropping down beside him, I turn to him, propping my head up on one hand.

I look into the sunroom, watching the last few slivers of light fade into night, signaling that it's time for the vampires to wake.

"How long will it take before they find us?"

"They probably already know," he says indifferently.

"Are we allowed to be here?"

"That's not for them to decide, this is my home," he says adamantly, peeking out of one eye to gauge my reaction.

I glance around again with a new appreciation for the cabin. *He brought me to his home.*

Before I can rethink what I'm doing, I lean forward and place my hand over his heart; I press my lips gently to his for just a minute. As I pull away, he tenses while my lips linger millimetres from his.

"Don't kiss me here unless you mean it," he says, his eyes opening and gray clouds swirling.

I think about it for a minute, hard. I know that I shouldn't do this. It's unhealthy and wrong to play out our sick little relationship during our captivity but my heart doesn't care. It wants what it wants.

"I do mean it," I say shyly, pressing my lips firmly against his.

His lips automatically part, allowing our kiss to deepen while he cups the back of my head, holding me to him. He pulls me right on top of him so that I'm straddling him. I break our kiss, pulling my head back from him slightly. I run my finger along his neck, over his shoulder and back across his jaw suggestively.

Sure, I've been getting daily doses of blood in my drinks, but I really want Caleb's blood.

"You can feed from me anytime you want," he replies playfully, knowing what I want and showing how comfortable he is with our intimacy.

He tugs his shirt off with ease and offers me his neck. With his half naked body pressed against mine, the heat takes me instantly. I sink my fangs into the soft, warm skin of his neck, my hands squeezing his shoulders as the blood flows down my throat.

His groans encourage me, and I find my fingers toying at his waist band, needing more of him, and surprising myself. I remove my teeth and pull my own shirt off.

I kiss him passionately like I did in Ireland before we had all these secrets between us. Our skin essentially melts together; his fingers dig sharply into my hips even when he pushes me back.

"Do you remember what I said to you last time you kissed me like this?" he asks curiously, looking into my face.

"Yes," I say quickly. A blush creeps into my cheeks, probably noticeable in the crimson glow from the fireplace. "You said that I had to be sure next time because you didn't want to have to stop yourself," I repeat like he just said it.

A smile lights up his face as a flood of relief washes over him. *Of course, I remember, even though it was months ago.* "And..." he prompts me, needing to hear me say it, needing to know that these feelings aren't one-sided.

"And I want you," I say reassuringly.

"What do you want from me?" he asks huskily, unsatisfied with my answer and needing more.

"I want you to be my first," I confess, blushing harder.

He grins excitedly at me, happy to have gotten the answer he wanted.

I have wanted this longer than I care to admit. Every lingering look, every tingling touch, every secret desire, has been leading to this.

He rolls us over gracefully so that he's on top, sliding his pants off easily. He takes mine off next, goosebumps forming where his fingers contact my skin. He wraps an arm around me, holding me up as he adjusts the blankets over us.

I have no idea what I'm doing.

Pausing, he looks at me seriously. "You're sure?" he asks nervously, giving me a glimpse of his vulnerabilities.

"More than anything," I answer, thinking of nothing but him.

I reach out for him, pulling him on top of me by the shoulders. He smiles at me sweetly, obeying my desires.

My hands start shaking a little with nervousness and excitement.

Following my instincts, I remove his underwear, exposing all of him to me. My eyes travel down and take him in, my breath catching in my throat. My eyes return to his and he seems unabashed. His small smile and gaze calm me, and I remove my underwear. He gracefully reaches around me, expertly unclipping my bra. With our remaining clothes on the floor, he positions himself between my legs slowly, gently. His lips return to mine, kissing me roughly; his body grinding against me lustfully.

His hand slides up my torso to my chest, touching me tenderly, his skin hot to the touch. I let out an involuntary moan, reveling in the feeling of his hand caressing me, while a pulsating need ignites in me. He continues to kiss me, his tongue eagerly meeting mine, as my body welcomes his hand. Running his hand back down slowly, his fingers teasingly circle my belly button before continuing down. He gently rubs at me in a way no one has ever touched me before. I moan uncontrollably, heat spreading in my cheeks and chest. He smiles into my lips, pleased with my current state as he increases the intensity of his touch, driving me crazy, my body arching into him reflexively.

Just before I reach the peak, he takes his hand away, my breaths coming out irregularly. He bends down to my ear, all of his body touching my delicate and sensitive areas and spreading little shocks up my spine. My breaths are forced out in little bursts.

"This might hurt at first," he whispers sensitively.

My heart rate accelerates, and I begin to tremble in anticipation. I can feel the pressure from him pressing himself against me, stretching me as he enters, and then the sharp shock as he pushes further inside, making him groan.

"Are you ok?" he asks, stopping with concern.

"Mhmm," I mumble.

He moves gently inside me, mindful not to hurt me. His hands caress me in ways that I couldn't have imagined. A loud moan escapes my lips, one that I can't suppress, my pleasure mounting, building in my depths.

His groans and my moans mix together, as he shakes from the restraint that he is using to keep control and make my first time gentle. *Even though the pain is the furthest thing from my mind right now.*

My moans get louder and more primal as the pleasure builds for me. My breaths come out erratically as he moves faster and harder, chasing his own release. His hand grips tightly on my outer thigh, almost painfully, as he fights to keep control.

I tremble beneath him, teetering on the edge of my euphoria, lost in the pleasure he's giving me. In an instant, the heat overcomes him, turning him. Deliberately, I turn my head, exposing my neck to him, showing him that I want it too. He plunges his fangs into me, causing me to gasp out loud and tense up around him.

He drinks hungrily, devouring me in more ways than one, thrusting into me almost aggressively. He pulls his fangs back abruptly, letting out a growl as the pleasure from his release tears through him, unable to hold it back anymore. His groans push me over the edge into my own climax, pleasure ripping through my body, making me shudder and gasp.

The heat leaves us both, letting our human sides take control once again. Leaving a gentle kiss on my lips affectionately, he moves beside me, breathing heavily and pulls me to his chest while I struggle to calm myself.

My head is on his chest, listening to his steady heartbeat. My fingers trace his ribs as he tenderly strokes my arm.

"Rose...I..." he begins.

I bolt upright, screaming in agony as a searing hot pain tears through my chest. Clutching at my heart, I'm convinced I am dying. Caleb looks on fearfully; understanding flashing through his eyes, followed by an unbelievable sadness. He watches as I collapse back onto the bed and sits frozen beside me. I gasp and sob beside him, trying to pull myself together.

My heart hurts so much, it feels like it's being ripped out of my chest. I sob in disbelief that Caleb is doing nothing to comfort me and scared because all I can think about is Gavin.

"You were bonded?" Caleb asks angrily, not looking at me.

"I..." I manage to stutter out, although I am not calm enough to speak.

"It broke," he continues coldly.

"Oh my god," I whisper, more to myself than him.

"I didn't know you were bonded," he adds, his voice filled with rage, his gray eyes spearing me.

CHAPTER TWENTY-NINE

Rose

I push myself up, still sobbing lightly, my skin slick with sweat from both having sex and the pain still vibrating in my chest. Caleb watches me glaringly as the painful pieces of the puzzle come together.

"Caleb...I...I," I stutter nervously, but stop because I don't know what to say to him when I can so clearly feel Gavin.

"The pain that you felt...that you're feeling," he tries to explain calmly, his emotions betraying him- his voice coming off cruel, "is not just yours," he finishes.

"I don't understand," I lie, fresh tears trailing down my cheeks.

"Yes, you do. You just wish that you didn't," he says, devoid of emotion.

My sobs become harder, shaking my body as I accept what I've done. "I didn't know..." I start defending myself.

"You were told about the seriousness of a bond. You did know," he reminds me coldly. "You felt his heart shattering because you betrayed him," he says, hesitating, "by being with me."

His face is dark, his eyes clouded with fury and disappointment.

"Oh god," I mutter. "Gavin..."

What have I done?

Caleb climbs to his feet, pulling his boxers back on, his eyes flashing dangerously.

"Caleb, I'm sorry," I say, noting how upset he is, but not fully understanding why. "I didn't mean..."

Caleb focuses his heavy gaze on me, the weight of his anger apparent. I clutch the blankets across my chest protectively, bracing for the storm I've unknowingly unleashed.

"You didn't mean to what?" Caleb shouts at me. "You didn't mean to sleep with me?" he continues, visibly hurt. "Or is it that you didn't mean for Gavin to find out?" he spits out furiously.

"What? No. I…"

But in all honesty, I don't know what I mean anymore. I can't excuse what we did because I wanted him. But I didn't want to hurt Gavin, I love him. I can't think straight when it involves Caleb.

Caleb stomps over to a dresser, pulling out a pair of black pants and tugging them on aggressively. He grabs more clothes out of the drawer and throws them on the bed in front of me.

He gives me one last look, his eyes filled with so many emotions- longing, remorse, anger, before he storms over to the couch and lays down with his back to me. I collapse back on the bed in tears.

My first time. *How fitting.*

Caleb

I lay on the couch, seething, with my back to her; overwhelmed with feelings of outrage and hurt.

I know first-hand the consequences and sting of a broken bond. Even centuries later, I'll never forget.

It broke me then.

How could she make me a part of inflicting that pain on someone else? She's a smart girl. She should have known better.

She'll blame me for ruining what should have been one of her most beautiful memories in her life. It should have been a moment she shared with someone she loves, even if that isn't me. I know that, but I was selfish. I'm as much at fault as she is, but I feel so angry with her that I can't take responsibility for my actions. She'll never forgive me.

I'm angry with her for bonding with anyone in the first place. I know she feels deeply for me, that much is clear. Why would she let it get that far with anyone else, let alone Gavin?

After sharing blood, I can feel her emotions as if they were my own. She's devastated and confused.

I can hear her crying to herself in the bed. I hate myself for being pleased about it but part of me wants to punish her for what she has done. It may not have been my first time, but I gave myself to her too.

Rose

When I wake up in the evening, my body aches, physically and emotionally. My eyes feel swollen from crying for hours. *He always makes me cry.* I'm tired of feeling weak and helpless around him.

I glance over to the couch where Caleb was sulking after we slept together. And of course, he's sitting at one end, leaning forward with his elbows on his knees, hands together, face focused and deep in thought, but he's watching me. Instead of making me blush, I return his unreadable gaze with my own angry stare. He really hurt me and I'm going to make him sorry for it. I clutch the blanket around my still naked chest, realizing that there's a better way to hurt him, but it means I have to be ruthless.

"Get dressed. William is expecting us for lunch since we didn't make breakfast," he says, with no concern about how I'm feeling.

Without breaking eye contact, I climb off the bed, hostility dripping off me, and let the blanket fall to the floor, exposing all of me to him. "Whatever you say," I respond coldly.

His surprise shows only for a second as his eyes flash silver but quickly return to gray. I keep my eyes on his, knowing it's affecting him because his shoulders tense, his jaw twitches as he clenches his teeth, and his knuckles turn white with the pressure of his hands crushing together.

He keeps his face neutral, trying to reveal nothing, but I know better. After a minute, I look away, satisfied that I got under his skin. My clothes are folded neatly at the end of the bed. Obviously, Caleb didn't do much in the way of sleeping.

I hope he's tired, I think to myself.

I pull my clothes on, ignoring the feeling of his eyes scorching my flesh. I want him to lust after me; he wouldn't dare make a move now.

Using my fingers to brush out my hair, I turn to him confidently.

"I'm ready," I say, like I didn't just stand naked in front of him.

I look at him as indifferently as I can, and he raises an eyebrow at me, looking amused while he stretches his fingers.

He gestures at the door, straight lipped, and I take the lead.

As soon as we walk in the door, Aamily is there with a brush and quickly brushes my hair.

"Lunch will be served in the sunroom today, Master Caleb," Aamily says, not making eye contact as she finishes my hair.

She leads the way and we follow a few steps behind her. Caleb reaches out and starts lacing his fingers through mine possessively. I'm so upset with him that I don't care if it's for my own protection- I'm not going to make it easy for him.

Surprising him, I pull my hand from his in one swift movement. "Don't touch me," I say through gritted teeth.

His gaze meets mine and despite the fact that I'm shooting daggers out of my eyes, his look is patronizing and bored.

"My lord," Aamily says, bowing to William and stepping out of the way.

Caleb and I enter the room, probably looking very disheveled. I'm wearing the same clothes from yesterday, my hair dried in loose waves around my shoulders, and sleep still in my eyes. Caleb looks the same- angry and perfect. *Asshole.*

The table is small and round, seating only four. For the tiniest moment William looks excited to see us, but his look quickly goes sour. He is sitting beside Sebastian, who's watching me with a huge grin. I take the seat next to him so that Caleb can sit next to his father.

"I do believe you were wearing that yesterday," Sebastian says, leaning towards me and grinning from ear to ear.

"Leave the girl alone, Sebastian," William says, sounding thoroughly bored, but I can feel him watching me out of the corner of his eye.

I feel Caleb's hand come down on my leg in what I'm sure he means as a comforting gesture, but out of anger I brush it off without looking at him. I can feel the tension emanating from Caleb, but I refuse to give in. It's an exchange that Sebastian doesn't miss.

"Caleb fell short of your expectations, sweetheart?" Sebastian teases me.

I stare at the food in front of me, utterly embarrassed with his inappropriate questions and comments.

"Piss off," Caleb growls in response.

"Boys," William warns, watching with amusement.

"Have I hit a nerve, brother?" Sebastian gloats without compassion.

Caleb says nothing but grits his teeth.

"I'd be happy to show her a better time," Sebastian says, smirking.

Caleb jumps up from his seat furiously, while Sebastian does nothing but watch, leaning back lazily in his chair.

"That's enough," William says firmly.

A shuffle at the side of the room catches my attention and I notice Rip is standing alert at the wall with two other burly guards.

I'm just one girl. Having them follow me really feels like overkill.

Caleb sits back down reluctantly, breathing rapidly, while Sebastian's eyes land on mine and read my curiosity.

"The guards are not for you…" Sebastian says, grinning excitedly.

"They're for me," Caleb interrupts bluntly.

I look at Caleb finally, his gray eyes already peering into my soul.

"The Caleb we knew was…unpredictable," William says.

"Unpredictable?" Sebastian laughs loudly. "He was an insatiable, brutal prick. A downright savage…" he continues while Caleb twitches uncomfortably. "He was the monster that nightmares are made of…"

Caleb stands from the table suddenly, interrupting Sebastian, and grabs my forearm, pulling me up while I stare at him. "We'll be eating at the cabin from now on," he says, dragging me to the hallway.

"You will eat dinner with us Friday nights, breakfast and dinner on Sundays," William commands us as we leave.

"Can't wait," Caleb says sarcastically.

"Let me go," I shout at Caleb when we get back to his cabin.

He complies, releasing his crushing grip on my arm and I stumble a little on the doorstep.

"I'm going to go chop wood," he says, clearly trying to avoid me.

Whatever. I don't want to see him right now anyway.

The next six weeks crawl by slower than it seems possible. I actually come to enjoy meals on Friday and Sunday because it means I actually get to talk to other people- even if it is William and Sebastian. Caleb goes out of his way to keep his distance from me, doing 'chores' and even going as far as to do some 'work' with his father. When he is around, we hardly speak.

Naturally, I haven't fed him since we spent the night together. I don't know when or how he's feeding, but I'm sure Xomira has something to do with it. *It's not my problem.*

"Come eat," Caleb says, setting plates down on the table in his cabin.

I ignore him for the fourth day, flipping through a magazine mindlessly on the bed, because I have no desire to eat anything that he made for me, even if I am really hungry. Just being around him nauseates me lately. It's a shame really; all the wasted food smells good. I bet that he is actually a great cook, even if he barely eats. *I'll never tell him if he is, though.*

"Not hungry," I lie.

"You haven't eaten in days," Caleb says with frustration.

"What do you care?" I ask rudely, refusing to look at him. "You already got what you wanted."

"Rose…"

"Save it, Caleb!"

"I'll be chopping wood," he growls out.

"That's right, Caleb. Run away!" I shout. "It's what you do best!"

He slams the door behind him, leaving me feeling flustered and furious. I throw my magazine at the back of the door after he's already gone, just because.

CHAPTER THIRTY

Caleb

"So, I'm curious, brother, what exactly did you do to her?" Sebastian asks.

He waltzes up behind me as I bring the ax down, relieving some pent-up frustration. It's not enough. Even though I've been out here for over an hour and I'm dripping in sweat, his voice is still grating in my ears.

I glance at him, rolling my eyes with impatience and saying nothing as I turn back to splitting wood.

"Obviously, you did something to make her suddenly hate you and withdraw from your every touch," he provokes me.

I continue my task, blocking him out the best I can, but failing miserably. "Why do you care?"

"I don't really," he says matter-of-factly. "I'm just curious. I take a twisted pleasure in watching you suffer."

"You're depraved," I say bluntly.

He watches me quietly for a few minutes and I know he's estimating how far he has to push me.

"Was she a terrible fuck?" he teases.

"Don't talk about her that way," I say over my shoulder with a warning.

I resume my wood splitting with added vigor. Thinking about the intimate way she let me touch her tugs at my heart painfully.

"Her blood can't be the problem, because our father didn't seem to mind," he says, "or is it a lack of? Because clearly, she isn't giving you that anymore either. She's had an even more prickly hate on for you in the last few weeks."

It takes all of my strength to ignore him.

"Fine. Don't tell me anything. Maybe she'll have more to say."

He starts walking in the direction of my cabin, pulling my attention away from the wood and thoughts of her blood.

"Stay away from her, Sebastian!" I say, my hand clenching around the ax.

He locks eyes with me, hearing the seriousness in my tone and grinning because of it. *Bloody masochist.*

"Maybe," he says, walking away smugly.

I watch him heading back up to the manor and glance towards my cabin knowing that Sebastian isn't done prying, he's just getting warmed up.

Rose

Knock. Knock.

"Aamily," I say with surprise as I open the door.

I wipe at the tears still on my cheeks. Yes, Caleb left almost two hours ago and I'm still crying. *Don't judge me!*

"Miss Rose are you alright?" she asks, knowing that I've been crying.

"Yes. Of course," I answer, determined to hide the devastation that I'm feeling.

"Miss Xomira wishes to speak with you at the manor."

"Oh. Ok."

I fall in step behind Aamily quietly. I'm not feeling particularly chatty, so the silence suits me just fine. Truth be told, I've been holding on to my own secret and I think talking it out with Xomira is the best thing because it's weighing heavily on me.

If Caleb hadn't been so intent on avoiding me lately, it probably would have come to light, no doubt, during an argument. That seems to be the way we work.

We walk in the front door, the quiet in the house deafening. She leads me to a descending staircase, and stops at the bottom, pointing.

"Down that hall, miss," Aamily says shakily.

I start down the dark hall and see a sliver of light coming through a cracked doorway. Something doesn't feel right. I pause, turning back to Aamily with confusion, but she's already several metres away from me with tears pouring down her face.

"What's going on?"

"I'm so sorry. He made me do it," she sobs, turning and running away.

I stand there completely speechless, not sure who put her up to what. After a minute, I resume my way to the cracked doorway and hear muffled voices from inside.

Peeking in, I see Xomira on her back on the bed, as William climbs on top of her, his mouth coming down on hers in what seems to be a very passionate kiss.

My hands clamp down across my mouth, stifling my shock. I start backing away, unable to watch it go any further. Horrified, I hurry down the hallway, staring at the floor and putting some distance between me and the lovers. When she suggested that I be ruthless to survive, was it really advice from her, or was she William's puppet all along?

"Didn't like what you saw?" Sebastian asks crudely.

Looking behind me, I see that he is standing right there. *Where did he even come from?*

"What do you want?" I ask rudely.

"Honestly?" he asks, raising an eyebrow. "I want to know what it is about you that has Caleb so twisted up inside. You torture him and I want to know how."

"There is something wrong with you," I say hatefully.

Sebastian is a dick, and he likes bending the rules and pushing boundaries. I know that, but I don't think that he would do anything he couldn't come back from, at least not right now. Not without suffering the consequences and wrath of his brother; he wouldn't dare touch me intimately. I guess he could still cause me pain though; this realization makes me noticeably shiver.

"What are you thinking about?" he asks, grinning as he steps closer.

"You can't touch me," I spit out nervously.

"Correction. I shouldn't touch you, but I've never been good with following rules," he says threateningly, stepping closer still.

He reaches out, tracing my collarbone where my shirt hangs off one shoulder. His skin feels cold to the touch compared to Caleb's. My heart accelerates as terror sparks in me.

Caleb

I step out of the steamy shower and into the empty room. A sadness overcomes me when I look at the bed where she'd snuggled into me on countless nights. I hate that I came back to the manor to shower, but I'm so bloody hungry, I don't have the patience or control right now to deal with Rose. I've been avoiding her, but it's not only for the reason she thinks. Her blood has been calling to me louder lately, probably because Xomira has only been able to bring me one blood bag a week. *I'm so hungry.*

I tear my eyes from the bed and step out into the hallway in some fresh clothes, bumping right into Aamily.

"Master Caleb!" she says in surprise, turning her face to the floor. "I'm so sorry. Are you looking for Rose?"

"Have you been crying…" I begin asking. "Wait. Rose is here, at the manor?" I ask in horror.

"I'm so sorry. He made me do it," she wails.

I grab her roughly by her arms, squeezing so tight that my nails pierce her skin. "Who made you do what?" I demand, the heat transforming me into an angry, ravaging beast.

"Master Sebastian," she explains, breaking down.

Then my intuition takes over. Tossing Aamily aside into the wall, I race down into the basement.

Rose

"I told you to stay away from her, Sebastian," Caleb threatens, his eyes silver in full vampire form.

I try to move towards him, but Sebastian is faster and encloses one arm around my neck, keeping me in place.

"Technically, she came to me," he smirks. "I'm only trying to help you, dear brother," he says, dragging a nail across my shoulder and ripping my skin so that a few drops of blood pool.

Instantly, he lets me go, and I turn my head to see him lick his finger with my blood on it. He looks at me in surprise, his smile fading, his eyes darkening, and I swear I can see...fear.

I hear a rush of air, and before I know what's happening, Caleb sinks his teeth into my neck, forcing me up against the wall and crushing the air out of my lungs. *He has been taken over by bloodlust.*

The pain feels like a thousand knives. He intends to kill me, I can feel it. A strangled scream escapes my lips just as Caleb pulls back, releasing his death grip on me, and surprising the hell out of me. He stands there with a horrified look on his face as I collapse to the floor breathless, blood running down my neck and down his chin.

"It's not possible," Caleb whispers to himself.

"What is going on here?" William barks, running down the hall, Xomira at his side.

Xomira drops to my side while William takes in the bloody scene.

"Sebastian. Caleb. I asked you a question."

"Caleb attacked Rose," Sebastian answers while Caleb stands paralyzed, but there is no smugness in his words. "She's...she's pregnant," he adds with disbelief.

"What? How?" William demands.

He doesn't get an answer, though. At that moment, I unravel, convulsing in sobs. I had a feeling weeks ago when I didn't get my period, but I was pleading with the universe for it not to be true. *I can't have a baby with Caleb. This can't be happening.*

I've already broken my blood bond with Gavin. I can't have another man's child as well, especially if that man is Caleb.

"Take her to the cabin," William commands Xomira.

She pulls me up and towards the end of the hallway as I shake uncontrollably.

Caleb

Sebastian's smile is completely gone, replaced by a look I've never seen him wear- remorse. William looks absolutely murderous. If Rose really is carrying my child, it's really going to mess up his plans. I can only imagine what he's thinking.

My child.

I don't know what to think. I never thought this would be a possibility. I don't know how to feel. I am entirely aghast.

"You aren't supposed to be capable of fathering children," William accuses me, although I'm well aware. "You're an incubus," he adds with disgust.

"I know what I am," I reply with irritation, snapping out of my haze.

"Her power..." Sebastian mumbles.

"What about it?" William says through clenched teeth.

"It has to be responsible, or maybe it's because Caleb is...different," Sebastian says in an almost brotherly way.

"What are you blathering about?" William asks.

"Not a vampire, but not quite an incubus," I mutter, figuring it out.

"That's nonsense. Her power must simply be that strong," William says excitedly. "There's one way to know for certain."

"It doesn't matter, we're not going to find out. She's mine," I remind William. "Rose's ability to give life by pro-creating with any creature must mean even..."

"Even a lifeless monster like you," William spits hatefully, finishing my thought.

"It would seem so," I guess.

"This wasn't part of the plan," William hisses to himself, deep in thought.

I know he's talking about his plan to eliminate me, but I'm not going to apologize for throwing a wrench in it.

"I need to talk to Rose," I say desperately.

I've been a complete prick since I took her virginity, which has resulted in something even more complicated. Thing is, she didn't seem all that surprised. Sebastian and my revelation only seemed to confirm what she already knew. She was keeping it from me. *She kept a secret from me.*

William's ruined prophetic plans do not take priority right now.

"Wipe the blood off your face, you look like a savage!" Sebastian suggests as I turn to leave.

I look at him hard for a minute, acknowledging how his words contained advice as well as a smug insult at the same time. *Strange!* He is still un-smiling, but this development has changed things somehow.

William

"How could you let this happen?" I ask furiously. "She was supposed to carry your children!"

"Until Caleb was dead either literally or figuratively, there was no way to seduce her into having my children," Sebastian says defensively.

"You could have forced her. It's not like you haven't before," I remind him with a smirk.

"I didn't want that to be her first time," he says sensitively.

His compassion disappoints me.

"We are vampires, Sebastian. We take what we want! Compassion is a weakness," I say bluntly.

"Yes, father."

"If your children are to rule the entire otherworld, they must come from her. Sympathy will not get you what you want in life," I say harshly.

"You're right."

"Of course, I am." I say with an air of superiority.

"What are we going to do now?" I ask, already knowing the answer.

"Caleb will still die and he will never have a child, even if that means letting him destroy himself," I answer more maliciously than a father should be capable of.

CHAPTER THIRTY-ONE

Caleb

I stop outside the door to my cabin, needing to think for a few minutes, trying to process that Rose is carrying my child. I still don't understand *how* though, much less know how I feel about it. The only thing I'm sure of is that William is definitely losing his shit over this, and I can't say that that doesn't please me.

There's also the fact that I full on assaulted her in a haze of bloodlust. My attack was different tonight and I'm ashamed. It wasn't like in the forest. There was no teasing, or desire or lust involved. The bloodlust was just too much for me. If I hadn't been shocked by the fact that she was pregnant, I probably would have killed her.

I turn the handle, deciding that I've stalled long enough. I owe Rose a conversation at the very least. I can't feel her anymore since I'm not feeding from her, but I don't need to just to know she's probably horrified at this whole situation.

I shut the door gently, not wanting to disturb the girls. Rose is laying on the bed sobbing and shuddering softly, facing away from me, while Xomira strokes her hair. She rises from Rose's side, striding towards me. Stopping beside me, she places her hand on my arm in a supportive manner but doesn't say anything. After a few seconds she continues to the door and lets herself out.

I make my way to the bed, standing next to where Xomira had been; my heart racing. What if I say the wrong thing and make this worse? *I always say the wrong thing to her.* I want to touch her, to comfort her in some way, but she hasn't even wanted me near her. I doubt that my attack will make things any better.

"What do you want, Caleb?" she asks through her tears.

My heart aches hearing that much hatred in her voice. She doesn't want this. She doesn't want to have my child and she doesn't want me. She knew she was pregnant, and she never came to me- I saw it in her eyes. *I only have myself to blame for this.*

"We need to talk," I say with a sigh.

"Obviously," she says sarcastically.

I try not to roll my eyes at her attitude, knowing it'll only make things worse. *If that's even possible.* She's using sarcasm to hide how she's truly feeling, it doesn't take a psychologist to figure that out. I wish she would just talk to me, it hurts that she won't.

I sit on the edge of the bed, noting how her shoulders tense at my close proximity, how her heart starts racing, and how she's fighting to keep her breathing even- and not in a good way.

"I promise I won't hurt you. I'm in control," I say as confidently as I can, trying to reassure myself as much as her.

Rose

I want to believe him. I know he thinks he is in control, but I'm beginning to realize that he's never really in control. He pushes his impulses down, ignoring them as long as he can. But when he just can't keep them at bay anymore, they explode. He's more dangerous than Sebastian, who may be a psycho, but at least he's predictable.

Xomira had been trying to give me some peace, but her presence had been anything but. I saw her with William. I know that she can't be trusted. What is her goal in all of this? And now Caleb is here, after finding out that I'm having his baby, all from our one-night stand that was obviously a terrible idea.

"How long have you known?" he asks, disappointed.

"About three weeks," I confess sadly.

"You should have told me."

"When Caleb? You've been determined to stay as far away from me as you can since we had sex," I shout, facing him. "You said that you couldn't have kids. You lied."

"I shouldn't be able to; I didn't lie to you," he says defensively. "Would it have changed what happened between us?" he asks fearfully.

"Maybe," I lie, trying to hurt him.

It wouldn't have changed things. At one point, I even briefly considered having his kids, and it wasn't purely to keep Sebastian and William away.

Caleb frowns at me for a second. "I don't think it would have," he says confidently. "I'm sorry that you've been dealing with this alone."

"It doesn't matter. It was a mistake," I say with finality.

Caleb

My heart breaks at her words, feeling like she's shoved a knife into it. She can't mean that, but after everything I put her through, I shouldn't be surprised.

"Don't say that."

"Why not? It's the truth," she says with fresh tears starting. "We were never a good idea."

She's wrong. She brings out the best intentions in me for the most part but all I do is hurt her in return.

"You can't judge 'us' right now, not with everything we've had to go through," I argue.

"I think that now is the best time to judge us," she claims. "And honestly, we don't work."

"Don't make this decision now. Love, please…we're having a baby," I plead. "I want this with you."

That's when I finally realize that I really do want this. I want to be a father and I want her to be the mother. I want all the normal things that I thought were never in the cards for me.

"We will have a baby and you will be a father, but…you can't have me," she says with a seriousness that seems out of place for her.

Although my heart is breaking, I recognize a tone in her voice. It's cold, detached, making me wonder if I ever had a chance in the first place or if she was always keeping her heart guarded.

I stare into her eyes, hoping I'll see forgiveness hiding there, but I don't.

Rose

"If you want to be a part of this baby's life, then you will not touch me, for any reason. You will not say sweet things to me, and you will not entertain any idea of 'us'," I say, giving him the ultimatum.

Caleb's fingers twitch like he wants to put his hand on mine or touch me in some way, but he decides not to. *I'm relieved.* I need him more than ever right now, but I also need him to respect my choices.

He pulls the blankets up, tucking me in, and leaves without another word. I break down in painful sobs, curling in on myself and wishing that I was carrying anyone else's baby. Not because I don't believe in his ability to be a good father, but because it would be so much simpler if it was with someone who didn't frustrate me to no end. It could have been with anyone else and we wouldn't have such a strained and complicated relationship.

Caleb

"I guess congratulations are in order," he says, leaning casually against the cabin.

I lunge at Sebastian, slamming his back against the wall aggressively, my fists gripping his shirt. "What the hell were you thinking? I could have killed her," I spit out through clenched teeth.

He makes no effort to push me off, keeping his hands relaxed at his sides. He's either stupid or thinks I won't hurt him, and the dark part of me really wants to hurt him bad.

He smirks at me. "Mind your temper. How can she trust you around her baby if you kill me right here?" he says smugly.

I think about what he says and reluctantly push back from him. I hate to admit it, but he's right. I need to prove that I can control the monster in me.

"Good boy," he taunts.

Planting my feet firmly in place, I clench my jaw. "What. Do. You. Want. Sebastian?" I say, my control wavering.

He turns his back to me, no concern at all that I might kill him.

"Was it bad?" he asks with morbid curiosity.

For a moment I'm confused, but as he glances at the cabin, I realize he means my conversation with Rose.

"What do you think?" I say sarcastically. "I could have killed her and our baby, thanks to you."

"I didn't know she was pregnant," he says innocently.

Like that one truth excuses his sadistic behaviour.

"If she wasn't, I probably would have killed her," I admit.

"Please, you would have stopped."

For whatever reason, he's way more confident in my strength than I am.

"I don't think so."

"I wouldn't have let you. I was just having a little fun," he confesses.

I smirk to myself, mostly at the fact that he thinks he'd have been able to stop me. As soon as he drew her blood, I saw red. I only stopped because I felt the second heartbeat pushing her blood and the sugary taste registered in my brain.

I was paralyzed with shock because I knew instantly that it was mine. Despite the fact that it shouldn't be possible for me, I knew in my heart that it was.

"She doesn't want this. She doesn't want me."

"All due respect brother, she wouldn't have fucked you if she didn't want you," he says with a laugh.

I roll my eyes at him, ignoring his choice of words. His offensive and vulgar vocabulary is all thanks to William. Sebastian wouldn't know real emotion if it punched him in the face these days. A token of our upbringing to be cold, cruel, and calculated at all times. Fortunately, I was raised by my mother first and it stuck.

"It was a perfect, passionate moment of weakness that I made sure to destroy immediately after," I confess. "William would have been proud." I let out a self-deprecating laugh. I guess some of his fathering wore off on me after all. "She was bonded, and I didn't know until it was too late."

"She won't be forgetting her first time anytime soon," Sebastian says, enjoying my misfortune too much.

"Thanks for that," I say snidely.

"You actually love her, don't you?" he asks with disbelief.

"Sebastian, I love her so much that I signed up to be the 'dark prince' again, knowing it would be my death sentence," I reveal, knowing my death has already been set in motion.

"Hmm," he says thoughtfully.

He turns to leave, clearly having gotten enough information to satisfy William for the time being.

"If you're as in love with Rose as you act, then you should know that you should keep a close eye on her. Your whole relationship with her, her blood, and now the baby has our father reeling. He's not done with her."

He quickly walks away, disappearing into the dark and leaving me to my thoughts once again. His warning was no surprise. William raised us, we learnt from the devil himself.

When I go back in, I see that Rose has cried herself to sleep, her eyes red and puffy. She's going to feel like shit in the morning. She looks so innocent when she's sleeping, it's easy to forget how much she hates me in this state. I gently brush the hair off her face, remembering that I'm not supposed to touch her, but also not caring.

I see a vein pulsing in her neck violently and realize suddenly that she's going to need to feed more being pregnant. That's going to be an interesting problem to solve. She won't want to feed from me, but she may not have a choice. *Another reason she can hate me, I guess.* Not that she needs more.

I tear myself away from her and sprawl out on the couch, resigning to watch her from the shadows until sleep takes me.

CHAPTER THIRTY-TWO

Rose

Knock. Knock.

Caleb opens the door and I look up from the book I'm reading on the bed, where I'm keeping a comfortable distance from him.

Sebastian stands on the doorstep, appearing bored, until his eyes fall on me.

"Our father would like to speak to you," he informs Caleb without looking away from me. "Now."

Caleb glances back at me, nervous about leaving, but I stare back at Sebastian, ignoring Caleb's gray eyes.

It's been two weeks since Caleb found out that I was having his baby. Two very emotionally draining, furious weeks. We've finally come to an agreement with the boundaries, but that doesn't seem to make a difference when it comes to the way his eyes pierce me. It wasn't an easy conversation to have; I actually had to threaten him with moving back into the manor just to get him to agree.

In the end, I agreed to stay at the cabin with him where he can keep an over-protective eye on us, but under no circumstances is he allowed to touch me or say any sweet things to me.

"Don't worry, I'll keep an eye on your sweetheart," Sebastian says smugly.

His comment pulls Caleb's gaze from me, thankfully, and I smile to myself as I return to my book.

"Where?" Caleb asks with a resentful tone.

"His study."

He's quiet, contemplating his choices. As the 'dark prince', he knows that he has responsibilities to his father, but he also hates letting me out of his sight.

"I'll be back as soon as I can," he says to me, his eyes on Sebastian.

"Whatever," I say indifferently.

He shoulders by Sebastian roughly.

I hear the door close, but no footsteps follow. My eyes are still on my book, but I can feel him watching me.

"What?" I ask sharply.

Looking up from my book, I'm satisfied to see that he is staring at me. *I was right.*

"Shall we take a walk?"

"Where to?" I ask suspiciously.

"Wherever the night takes us," Sebastian says deviously.

I grin at him, knowing it'll really irritate Caleb if I go, but also knowing that Sebastian is reckless. My safety will always be in question around him.

"Come on, live a little," Sebastian says playfully. "Don't worry, we won't tell Caleb you slipped your leash," he adds, teasing me.

"Fine. Let's go," I say.

He smiles wide in a creepy way, clearly happy to have gotten his way. I pull a hoodie on and walk with Sebastian into the night.

We stroll through the grounds in silence as I breathe in the chilly air. It's refreshing. Being in that cabin with Caleb feels suffocating at times.

"Can I ask you something?"

I look at Sebastian curiously, his tone much more restrained than usual.

"Knowing you, it won't matter what I say. So, what is it?" I ask, sending him a suspicious look.

"Why are you so resistant to Caleb?"

I stop walking in shock. He takes another step before turning to face me. "Excuse me?"

"He's in love with you, anyone can see that. It goes against every ounce of nature in his body, but you have this power over him that compels him to fight it every day. Why do you keep him at arm's length?" he asks seriously.

This is not what I expected from Sebastian.

"Not that it's any of your business, but maybe I just don't feel the same way," I say.

He raises an eyebrow at me. "You're pregnant…with his baby…and you want me to believe that that just happened because you wanted a 'no strings attached' fuck for your first time?" he chuckles.

I roll my eyes at him. "You're disgusting," I say, walking around him, hoping to hide the red in my cheeks.

"Ok, I'm sorry," he claims without any conviction, double stepping to catch up and falling into step beside me.

"Let's pretend for a moment that he didn't knock you up…I've seen you two together. The shared looks, the looks you think are secret. The way you have trouble breathing when he touches you. The fact that you can't keep your hands off each other- the ball, the hedge maze, the hot spring, etcetera…" he gloats, making me blush.

"Stalker much?" I quip, cringing at what he's seen.

"Maybe I like to watch," he says, shrugging his shoulders harmlessly.

"You should be ashamed…" I start.

"Why?" he asks, cutting me off.

"Because we were having private moments," I say, raising my voice.

He laughs off my anger. "Caleb knew I was there- watching. Maybe you don't know him as well as you think."

I scowl at him. "Why does it matter? You've never seemed like the brotherly type."

His grin fades, the mischievous joy disappearing from his eyes.

"We were never good at being brothers, especially when our father started grooming us to transition. He brought out the worst in us. I won't blame him for all of it because we made our own choices, but when he saw the darkness in Caleb, he used it. He conditioned him to be the 'dark prince'; he pushed him harder and harder, but Caleb never broke, always exceeding his expectations. We never had the chance to be friends, I realize that now. William never would have allowed it. He used our competition to his advantage…he still does."

I look at Sebastian standing before me, being so honest and giving me a deeper glimpse into why Caleb is the way he is. I say nothing, just listen.

"Before he met Ana, he was the king of savages, as hard as that might be to believe. He was a beast. Even William was afraid of him. Our father had created a monster more terrifying than he expected. When he met Ana, he was still dark, but he started rebelling against our father's control. Over time, it became more obvious that William wasn't in control of him anymore. But our father couldn't have that. I don't know how he did it, but William was responsible for Ana breaking her bond with Caleb and going to Lord Dalibor- I don't think Caleb knows," he says, my eyes widening in disbelief.

"How could he do that to his son?"

"You think that's bad?" he scoffs. "After the life he had being molded into a psycho, the broken bond destroyed what good was left in him. He was on the edge of being an incubus, and William pushed him over."

"Oh my god," I exclaim in horror. "He turned his son into an incubus."

"He did…until now."

"What do you mean?"

"In all of history, an incubus has never fully reformed. Lord Dalibor dances a fine line between incubus and vampire. He has others do his dirty work for him saving little shreds of his soul. Honestly, we don't even know if it's possible to come back when you've stepped so far over the line. An incubus has one goal, to create death, pain, and suffering. They have zero interest in any kind of human connection, and yet, my brother wants it all with you. The strength and power that shows hasn't gone unnoticed…"

"William." I say rather than ask. "Why are you telling me this?"

He looks at me, his eyes travelling to my belly, hope shining in them.

"If I hadn't been so concerned with being the better son, maybe Caleb wouldn't have lost everything. I don't want history to repeat itself. I don't want that life for my niece or nephew. Caleb has a chance to take back everything that William took from him and be the father we always needed," he says truthfully.

"Sebastian…I don't know what to say."

"Well for starters, say you'll never repeat this to Caleb. I have a reputation to protect," he smirks at me. "Secondly, tell me you'll help keep William from pushing him over the edge again, for your baby's sake."

I'm stuck. I don't want William to manipulate Caleb, but I don't think I can do much, not with the state of our relationship. I wouldn't even say we're friends.

"Is William going to try?"

"What do you think he's been doing?"

I look around at where we are and back to Sebastian. He steps closer to me and I shake my head.

"No way in hell is this playing out the way it did before," I say smartly.

Sebastian laughs, "Can't blame me for trying." He shrugs with indifference. He points into the hedge maze, "I'll give you a head start."

"You wouldn't dare."

"Wouldn't I?" he asks, arching an eyebrow.

I know he's only half-serious now. He just wants someone to play with. After living with William, can I really hold that against him?

I take off into the hedge maze, completely lost after a few turns, but with the silence, cold air, and light heart, I feel free and almost happy. I trek noisily through the paths, not sure where I'm going.

"Hello, sweetheart," Sebastian sing-songs, coming around a corner. "You could try not stepping on all the twigs," he adds insult to injury.

"Shut up," I say.

"Try again," Sebastian encourages me, disappearing again.

I play along, but each time he finds me with ease and lectures me about stepping too loud, stepping on leaves, breathing too loud, biting my nails, the list goes on…

"I thought you were supposed to be the fun one," I whine from my ass on the ground, "but you're a drill sergeant just like your brother."

Sebastian had come running at me from down the path, knocking me flat on my ass. Now I am damp, tired, and cold.

"This is fun," he says, smiling and extending a hand to help me up.

"You and I have very different ideas of fun. Can we be done?"

I take his hand as he easily pulls me to my feet.

"One more time," he says as he backs away.

I tip-toe around several corners, trying my hardest to stay in the shadows just like Sebastian drilled into my head.

I hear leaves rustle around a corner that I just passed and freeze, really wanting to beat him at his own game. He comes around the corner slowly. I jump out of the shadows behind him, startling him enough that he falls down, hitting me in the process.

"Ow," I say, realizing he hit my arm with something.

Looking down I see blood soaking my shirt sleeve where there's a noticeable gash. *He cut me.* My eyes shoot back to him, advancing slowly towards me with a large dagger drawn and a hood covering his face.

"You're not Sebastian," I say fearfully.

Sebastian would never hide his face. He would take pride in cornering me. I trip over my own feet, tumbling to the ground again. The man's weapon flies towards my stomach- my baby.

Out of nowhere, Sebastian appears, kicking the man's hand away from me, making him drop the knife. He and Sebastian have a stare down, as if they recognize each other. It occurs to me that maybe this was all an elaborate trap, and he might work for Sebastian and William. Fear rises in my throat at my own stupidity.

The man glances past Sebastian, smiling threateningly. Sebastian looks over his shoulder at me on the ground, his dark brown eyes glowing dangerously. It'd be easy for him to walk away and keep his hands clean, but I can see it in his eyes- he won't abandon me, he'll defend me. *We're family.*

The man seems to have come to the same realization, because he produces another dagger out of thin air and goes after Sebastian.

My eyes go wide in horror thinking that Sebastian is going to take a knife in the back. Sebastian dodges it at the last second and the two end up wrestling for the dagger. After a few minutes he takes it in his hand and rams it up into the man's chin. With a sickening gurgle and ripping sound, he tears the dagger through his cheek, covering himself in blood. The man drops to the ground, blood pouring everywhere. Sebastian gets to his feet, unbothered by what just went down and stands in front of me.

He looks terrifying covered in blood and mud, adrenaline coursing through him and giving off a restless energy. My breath catches in my throat when the sweet smell of blood hits my nose. I didn't realize how hungry I was until I can't tear my eyes away from it.

"Let's get you out of here," Sebastian says with no emotion.

When I get to my feet, he grabs my wrist, the same way Caleb did the night they took me. He holds it all the way back to the cabin and only lets go when we're safe inside.

I catch a glimpse of us in the mirror inside the door. We're both spattered in mud and blood, him more than me, but my arm is still bleeding.

"Why isn't it healing?" I ask.

"You need to turn and you need blood. You can't starve your creature and expect it to heal you," he answers matter-of-factly. "You need to feed," he says, rolling up his sleeve for me.

My mouth immediately starts watering, the heat starting in my belly. "I can't," I say, turning away from his wrist.

"Why? Because you want to ignore that part of yourself just like my brother," he says rudely. "I thought you were all about hurting him?"

"Yes, Sebastian, I want to hurt him because he hurt me too," I admit, "but feeding from anyone will do that. Feeding from his brother would just be disrespectful," I say.

I want to piss him off, but even I know that that's too far. Besides, I still haven't gained enough control over myself and I can't turn unless I'm turned on. *No way in hell am I admitting that to him.*

Sebastian smirks at me, pleased with my refusal for some reason. He's very observant; it's possible he already knows about my issue.

Just then the cabin door bursts open, shaking as it impacts the wall.

"Why can I smell Rose's blood across the grounds?" Caleb shouts, charging in.

He makes a beeline for me, staring daggers at Sebastian on the way. I put my uninjured arm up to stop him from touching me, and his eyes flash furiously, making Sebastian chuckle.

"Are you alright?" he asks seriously.

"I'm fine," I say.

"Next question. Why are both of you covered in mud and blood? What the hell happened?" he asks impatiently.

"Relax, Caleb," Sebastian says coolly. "We were playing an innocent game of hide-and-seek in the maze and..."

Caleb speeds backwards, grabbing Sebastian at the collar and crushing him into the wall. "You did what?" he shouts, his anger flaring uncontrollably.

"Jesus, Caleb, let him go. What the hell is wrong with you? It's just a game," I yell.

He turns on me with a disbelieving look.

"Hide-and-seek in the maze with Sebastian is never just a game. It was what he did to girls before he fucked them or fed from them," he says, using words I'd never heard him use. "He hunted them like animals in there."

I feel my cheeks going red. Am I really that naïve? I look over to Sebastian who simply shrugs unapologetically. Is that what he was doing, hunting me? I thought he just needed a friend.

Walking forward, I break my own rule by putting my hand on Caleb's arm reassuringly and watching his anger melt away.

His eyes meet mine and his breathing calms. "It wasn't like that."

He releases Sebastian, who straightens his shirt but seems otherwise unfazed, like the snake he is.

"As I was saying, before I was interrupted," he says pointedly at Caleb, "we weren't alone. Some idiot attacked Rose," he says slowly. "He won't make that mistake twice."

"How can you be sure?" he asks with worry.

"Because I almost cut his fucking head right off," Sebastian replies confidently.

As soon as he says it, all I can see is the blood and the hunger is back. My knees threaten to collapse as dizziness and nausea roll over me. I stumble to the couch with Caleb hovering near me but keeping his hands to himself.

His eyes go from my face to my arm, where I'm still bleeding and not healing.

"She needs to feed, brother," Sebastian says, not missing a thing.

Caleb's eyes bore into mine, pleading for me to cooperate. He doesn't have to say anything; I know what he is thinking.

"No."

"You need to feed, Rose," he says with a sigh.

"No, I don't," I claim adamantly.

"Yes, you do."

"Not from you," I say with determination.

He hesitates, an inner struggle visible in his eyes.

"From Sebastian, then."

"I already offered. She refused," he says indifferently. "She's very stubborn."

I roll my eyes at the two men. "I don't want to know what either of you are feeling in your head," I explain vehemently.

Sebastian chuckles as he walks away while I scowl at him. I don't know why he's so content- I won't feed from him either.

I finally look at Caleb- I mean *really* look at him and notice that he is also covered in blood... and it's not mine.

"Wait. Why are you covered in blood?" I ask seriously.

"Don't worry, sweetheart, it's not his blood," Sebastian says, lighting up.

"Well, whose is it?"

"It was just business. It doesn't concern you," he says, a detached look in his eyes.

"Don't do that," I demand. "Don't shut me out."

"You don't need to know," he says firmly.

"I want to know what you did."

"Drop it, Rose," he warns.

"No, tell me," I say, pushing. I want to know just how much freedom he gave the monster.

"I ripped a guy limb from limb, slowly, carefully, making sure he was alive for most of it," he answers darkly. "Satisfied?" he asks, rising from his seat.

For several minutes, I say nothing. All I can think about is how awful William is for making Caleb do such a horrible thing.

"William put you up to it, I'm sure. Having to do that doesn't mean that you've done anything wrong, because it wasn't your choice," I say calmly.

"I know," he says grimly.

"Doesn't it, though? I mean you still murdered someone," Sebastian taunts, "and enjoying it is a totally different thing."

Caleb stands as still as stone at Sebastian's proclamation. Horror snakes its way through my body as I stare at his back. There's no way he enjoyed that. *Is there?*

The smell of fresh blood draws our attention back to Sebastian. He's leaning against the cupboards, dragging a knife across his hand, unflinching. He tips his hand to the side, blood dripping out into a cup below it. I watch mesmerized until he's finished.

He tosses the knife down with a clatter and looks from Caleb to me proudly.

"Problem solved. You're not feeding directly from me, so you won't be 'in my head'," Sebastian says using air quotes. "A loophole, if you will."

Caleb nods to assure me of his honesty. I walk over to Sebastian warily. He hands me the cup with a kind of joy. Anyone else would think he was up to something, but I've figured out that that his face looks consistently sketchy.

I take a cautious sip, unsure what to expect. Surprisingly, it's refreshing and I feel energized immediately.

"I know. I'm yummy," he says playfully, making me smile into the cup.

"Ok, get out," Caleb says, his patience wearing thin.

Sebastian heads for the door while I finish my drink and set it down.

"I have to go anyway, but just so you know, I'm even better at the source."

He ducks out the door with a wink at me, followed by a glass crashing and shattering on the closed door. Caleb threw it in anger, but now he's sitting on the couch, his face in his hands. He looks beyond tired.

Caleb

I breathe easier with Sebastian gone, no longer making suggestive comments at Rose, but I rub at my temples still more tired than ever. With my eyes closed, I try to forget about the crime scene I created for William, without much luck.

I feel the couch dip slightly as Rose sits next to me. I glance at her as she watches me nervously, biting her lower lip. Her bright green eyes look into mine.

"How's your arm?" I ask her patiently, looking but not touching.

She holds it out, "healing really slowly."

The skin on her arm is smoothing out, the blood disappearing as well, but at a glacial pace, her torn and bloody sweater starting to look worse after what she went through. Sebastian's blood is doing the job, but it should have been mine.

"If you turn, it will heal faster."

"I'm fine. I'll wait."

"Suit yourself."

"Are you mad at me?" she asks in a small voice.

"About what...you putting yourself in danger with Sebastian...or you preferring to starve, or choosing to drink his blood rather than drink mine?" I ask, my voice coming out sharper than I meant it to.

She gets up quickly after my response and tries to walk away. Before I can stop myself, my hands fly out, grabbing her and pulling her down on my lap sideways. My arms go around her, holding her tight, needing her in my arms because I'm scared of what I'm becoming again.

To hell with it.

She doesn't fight me or push me away, despite our no touching rule.

I lean the side of my head on her chest just under her chin. I need to feel her, to hear her heartbeat, to remind myself why I'm doing this.

"Sebastian wasn't wrong...I did enjoy the kill tonight," I admit, her heart rate increasing, "not because of the blood, pain, or suffering I caused, but because of the power and control I felt from the fear I created. It's addictive to me. It always has been."

She's quiet, and for a minute I second guess sharing my darkness with her. Suddenly, I feel her fingers stroking the nape of my neck, followed by her cheek resting against the back of my head. She's holding me, comforting me. I relax into her, letting out a long breath.

"I can see what working for your father is doing to you," she whispers to me, "I don't want you to go through this for me. I can find another way."

I lift my head, looking deep into her eyes- soaking in their compassion, my arms keeping her on my lap, cocking my head to the side with confusion.

"I will do whatever it takes...to keep you both safe, love," I say passionately, "even though you hate me."

"Caleb...I don't hate you...I," she gets to her feet in frustration, "I can't handle the control you have over me...it kills me. I can't live that way. I just can't tell you what you want to hear," she says flustered.

I get to my feet, towering over her, consumed with my own pain. Sighing, I retreat to the bathroom, turning the shower on as hot as it will go before I strip down and step in. I embrace the pain, needing to ground myself.

I will protect her no matter what we are to each other.
I love her. She's the mother of my child.

CHAPTER THIRTY-THREE

Rose

I wake up, bolting upright, gasping for air, shaking and sweating. Caleb rushes to my side, refraining from touching me even though I know it's hard for him.

"Another nightmare?"

"Yes," I mutter shakily.

The nightmares started about three weeks ago and they come every time I dare to sleep, making it impossible for me to get a decent night's rest, which is pretty important at two and a half months pregnant. It's not morning; it's the middle of the night, which is our afternoon. I was trying to squeeze in a nap, on account of not being able to sleep.

"Xomira said it's a normal part of pregnancy," Caleb offers.

"Whatever it is, it's awful," I reply coldly.

I tug my shirt down over my developing bump vulnerably as I make my way to the table, where Caleb has every food group available for my choosing.

It's his way of being here for me. I stayed at the cabin with him because he looked like he was going to go on a murder spree when I mentioned staying at the manor.

Also, I want to keep an eye on him. Every time he leaves with William, he comes back covered in blood, his eyes darkening and the clouds swirling.

But I can still feel him watching me and staring at my belly when he thinks I'm not paying attention.

"William would like for us to join him for dinner, says he has a surprise," he says annoyed.

"That can't be good."

"Probably not."

I sigh dramatically, shoving some fresh fruit in my mouth before dragging myself towards the bathroom to freshen up for dinner.

After thirty minutes, I step out wearing a flowy black tank top and skinny faux leather leggings. I put my hair in two French braids and I'm wearing very minimal makeup. I don't want to go. I hate William. Every few days Caleb leaves to do 'business' with him and he comes back haunted. Not to mention the creepy way he eye-stalks me, ever since he drank my blood. *It's weird.*

"Do we have to?" I whine.

"There'll be blood in the drinks," he bribes me.

"Yes, but mine won't have booze," I complain.

Caleb

I'd rather be anywhere than having dinner with William, but he requested our presence for dinner, and I know better than to piss him off before I am ready for an all-out war.

"I'm sorry you can't have booze," I say with a grin.

She ends up pouting, which only makes her cuter, but I know I can't tell her that, so I settle for a telepathic message to our baby, "you have the prettiest mom ever."

The only way to stomach my father is with large amounts of alcohol. At least, that's my coping method, so I do feel bad for her.

"Alright, let's get this over with," she says halfheartedly.

I follow Rose out the door, wanting more than anything to interlock my fingers through hers or wrap my arms around her and my baby, but knowing I'd risk pushing her further away.

So, I don't.

I just follow a foot behind her, my hands twitching with the need to touch her again.

"M-master Caleb. Miss Rose," Aamily stutters out, bowing and not making eye contact.

I can see her trembling in fear that I will take my revenge on her for her part in Sebastian's sick trick, and while I know that she was in a tight spot, I have no sympathy because of what she put Rose through.

"Master William is in the formal dining room tonight."

We don't say anything as we follow her to the dining room, and she disappears as quickly as she can. William is sitting at one end of the table, Sebastian at the other, with four other seats set in between them.

"Four?" Rose asks, sitting between me and Sebastian.

She looks to Sebastian when I don't have an answer for her. It bothers me with how comfortable she's getting with him. He comes to the cabin every few days to keep an eye on Rose and bleed into a cup for her to feed. I don't know how much we can trust him though- he is his father's son.

"Yes. We're expecting company," Sebastian answers excitedly.

William is watching us closely; Rose more than me, and it's making me uncomfortable. Not just because I don't want his eyes on her, but because I know he's up to something.

"Who?" I ask suspiciously.

"My lord," Aamily comes into view at the doorway, bowing.

Xander comes walking into the room and smiles with relief at the sight of me and Rose.

"Xander!" Rose exclaims with the biggest smile I've seen on her face in a long time.

She runs forward and throws herself into his arms. She closes her eyes against his chest, with a giggle, and he holds her tight, glancing at me as if trying to relay a message. William uses a dark magick in his house that allows him to hear even private conversations. Xander knows this, so he can't actually say anything.

I stand to greet my friend, but freeze, because in walks Gavin. He stands back a little-ways, taking in the room, his eyes lingering on Rose- exhaling noticeably in relief. He pries his eyes from her, and they land on me, darkening immediately.

"This is going to be interesting," Sebastian says, overjoyed, taking a long swallow of his drink.

Gavin's lip twitches up into a smirk, as though he heard Sebastian's comment, which he probably did.

Shit. There goes my good behaviour.

Rose

"Gavin?!?" I say in shock, pulling away from Xander.

Happiness swells through me at the sight of him, even though he's not returning my smile. For a minute, I forget that I broke his heart with my betrayal. I throw myself against him, wrapping my arms around his neck. His arms quickly engulf me in warmth, holding me protectively, but he's tense- I can feel it.

I've missed him more than I realized.

"So, you can see that young Rose is not being mistreated in any way," William's voice oozes charm. "Shall we have dinner?" he adds, gesturing to the table.

"We're happy to see her unharmed," Xander replies, giving me another once-over.

"But the Order doesn't understand why the council took so long to approve and accommodate our request for a visit, especially given your claim that Rose was a guest," Gavin says brazenly.

Before William can reply, Xander takes a seat next to him and I start sweating nervously. Do I sit with Caleb or Gavin? I mean Gavin is/was my boyfriend and Caleb is…my…the father of my child. *Oh god.* I'm having Caleb's baby. How do I tell him that?

Caleb seems to read exactly what I'm thinking and after a minute of hesitation, taking pity on my dilemma, he takes the seat next to Xander so that I don't have to choose.

Gavin takes the other seat next to William and I sit beside him, well aware of Caleb's heated gaze from across the table, and Sebastian's intrusive stare beside me.

Someone is going to bleed before dessert. I just know it.

"With all due respect, Xander is not a participating member of 'your Order', nor is he a citizen of our world. We had no reason to allow him in, other than he was a friend of Caleb's," William says in a rehearsed way. "As far as you are concerned, I apologize. Getting the returning prince settled in has kept us busy."

"So, the rumours are true?" Gavin says, shifting his attention to Caleb. "The 'dark prince' will be taking his position back."

The two stare each other down, neither of them willing to be the first to look away. The emotion in their eyes is pure hatred. If possible, it's worse than the issues between Caleb and Morgan.

The tension between Gavin and Caleb is so thick, there's no way anyone is missing it. Sebastian seems overly giddy about it.

William chuckles, "not *will*, has. The agreement has already been sealed."

"Just ask Rose," Sebastian chimes in suggestively.

I shoot daggers at Sebastian. He may be watching out for me and he may be feeding me his blood, but he still likes watching me squirm. I glance at Caleb, who is openly smiling in light of this information as he continues to glare at Gavin. I feel my cheeks turning a violent shade of red, but I refocus my attention on Gavin.

He's here. He came for me. *That matters.*

He turns away from his staring match with Caleb like he's aware that I'm watching him. He reaches out and grabs my hand smoothly, bringing it to his lips and placing a gentle kiss on my knuckles- so many feelings travelling between the two of us. My breath catches in my chest with the warmth from his lips. I've missed him so much. He gives me a small smile and keeps hold of my hand. For a minute it feels like it's just us.

"I don't know Caleb, I think her love for this guy goes beyond the fucking you gave her," Sebastian announces, eyes bright with excitement.

My mouth drops open, my heart dropping in my chest. *What. The. Hell?* Mortified, I run from the room without excusing myself.

Caleb

We all watch as Rose flees from the room in tears. I twitch in my seat with the effort it takes to not run after her. My heart aches for her. It might be true, she might love Gavin more. My love might not be enough now. As much as it hurts to accept, he could be right, but he didn't have to say it in the way he did.

Xander, Gavin, and I snap our focus on Sebastian, grinning twistedly and raising his drink to his lips, unperturbed by the scowls he's receiving.

"Considerate as always Sebastian," I say with disgust.

"He has as much tact as his brother when he broke my neck and took my girlfriend," Gavin says to me with clenched teeth. "Guess you're not so different after all."

William chuckles, rising from his seat with an air of amusement. "On that note, I'll see everyone for breakfast."

William leaves the room and we're all quiet for some time while Gavin glares at me in the hopes that it'll kill me.

"Whatever you want to say, just say it," I growl out at Gavin.

"Why did you come back?" he asks.

"Rose needed me," I say.

"No, she didn't. You were gone for months and she was finally moving on- that's why you came back," he says hatefully. "You hated that she could be happy without you. You came back for you."

"You don't know what you're talking about," I retort at Gavin. "I've been protecting her. If I hadn't come…"

"If you hadn't have come, I could have gotten her out of there and away from this idiot without a broken neck," he spits furiously.

Sebastian scoffs, but we ignore him.

"How would you have done that with your pants down? That's what this is really about, isn't it?" I say smugly. "You're upset that she gave herself to me rather than you?"

"You're an asshole," he claims, standing heatedly. "At least I don't have to manipulate her into being with me."

I get abruptly to my feet, annoyed with his accusation.

"Watch yourself," I warn, my temper blazing. "I didn't manipulate her, she wanted to be with me."

"She was scared," he emphasizes. "You took advantage of the situation that she was in because of your damn father. You're pathetic. You weren't satisfied with destroying her the first time, so you had to try and do it again," he continues, ripping into me.

I clench my hands in fists at my sides, wanting to take out all of my pent-up frustration on him. We stand eye to eye across the table, anger billowing off of us.

"You're one to talk," I reply. "How're you keeping the Order off her back? What'd you promise them?"

"Screw you, Caleb."

I stare at him fuming, my chest moving harshly with force.

"Feel better?" Xander asks, raising his eyebrow. "Maybe someone should check on Rose now?"

"What?! No one's even bleeding," Sebastian says disappointed.

"Shut up Sebastian," I say firmly.

"We're not finished," Gavin says. "Don't worry."

I know all about Gavin and his past but if he really wants to pit our monsters against each other, my money is on me every time.

"Promises, promises," Sebastian exaggerates. "I notice that Rose didn't feed tonight," he says, pointing at Rose's untouched drink. "If she's hungry later, just send her to my room… she knows where it is."

"What?" Gavin exclaims.

"She's not feeding from you?" Xander asks me, confused.

"Ha," Sebastian barks. "He wishes," he says and throws back the rest of his drink. "Enjoy your little reunion."

Sebastian practically skips out, happy with the chaos he started. *Fucking Sebastian.*

Gavin turns to the doorway. "You stole her. Managed to get her to sleep with you…and you still managed to fuck it up," he gloats. "I'm not surprised she'd rather drink that demon's blood over yours," he mutters at me as he leaves after Rose.

I move to stop him and find her first, but Xander's hand clamps down on my shoulder. "Let him," he says, giving me such a look that I stay behind.

Gavin gives me one last dirty look before he goes, and I turn an annoyed glare on Xander.

"What was that about? You suddenly siding with Gavin?" I grind out.

"It's not like that," he responds calmly.

"Then what's it like?" I ask childishly, shaking his hand off angrily.

"He was with us when it happened," he says grimly.

I deduce what he's talking about immediately. "I didn't know they were bonded. She never told me," I say defensively.

"Whether you were aware or not, you owe him. You of all people know what he went through…what he's still going through," Xander says firmly. "It took him weeks to recover. For the first few days, we didn't know if he was going to survive. Even now, he doesn't seem like himself."

"I didn't know," I say defensively.

"If you had, would you still have done it?"

I say nothing and Xander scoffs at me. "What do you want me to say?" I ask, annoyed.

"The same thing I've always wanted from you. The truth. It's the only way you hold onto your humanity. You know that!" Xander stresses. "I can see that you're struggling. I know you well enough to know that."

He's right. He always is, but it doesn't make it any easier to say how I'm really feeling, even when I know he'll have no judgement, only support.

"Where are Jason and Paige?" I ask, avoiding his question.

He sighs, "Jason wanted to be here, but William wouldn't let him come because he's not a halfling," Xander explains, rolling his eyes. "I wouldn't let Paige come. I don't want her anywhere near William."

"I don't blame you."

He shuffles nervously, "we're kind of together," he says, grinning.

I smile at him genuinely, "I'm happy for you, I am," I say, distracted.

"I feel like there's something you're not telling me," he says suspiciously.

"What am I going to do?" I ask incredulously. "If I stand back, they might get back together."

"They were never NOT together. You took her," he reminds me. "So, staying out of the way is exactly what you're going to do."

I let out a deep breath, trying to get a handle on my emotions- my fear. I don't want to lose her. Even when we were apart, she was all I thought about. She's like a magnet and she keeps drawing me in.

"If they work things out, you have to accept that. I've watched them grow together. He's good for her. Even if his intentions were questionable in the beginning, things have changed," Xander says gently.

"Does he love her?"

"Yes," he says without hesitating. "Maybe as much as you."

"I sincerely doubt that," I say confidently.

"I know you find that hard to believe but..." he begins.

"No, you don't understand. No one could love her as much as I do, Xander. Not anymore," I say with a nervous grin, "because she's carrying my baby."

It's such a relief to say it out loud.

"What? How?" he asks in shock.

"Apparently the prophecy included even a monster like me."

The more I say it, the more real it feels. *I'm going to be a dad.*

"Shit..." he replies. "How do you feel about that?" he asks, concerned.

"I never thought I'd be a dad, Xander. It's overwhelming," I admit. "But now, I'm afraid of losing it all by screwing things up with Rose."

"I'm so incredibly happy for you," he says with a smile, pulling me into an excited hug, "but I get your fear. You've never had more to lose, but…you have to consider that maybe you won't be a family in the way you expect," he adds gently.

"Believe me, I know," I say tiredly. "She cringes when I look at her, pulls away from my touch, and she would rather drink Sebastian's blood over mine. It's torture," I explain.

I put my face in my hands, exhausted from the stress, feeling Xander watching me closely.

"What happened between you?" Xander asks, confused.

"I fucked up," I state bluntly, using harsher language than usual, revealing my frustration.

I grab Sebastian's whiskey and blood off the table. I need both if I'm going to relive the exact way in which I destroyed Rose in one of her most vulnerable moments.

"Let's talk in your room."

Xander leads the way to his room, and I follow in silence with dread. As we approach his room, Aamily appears in the hallway. As soon as she sees me, she shifts her eyes to the floor, shrinking away from me as we pass. I glare at her and scowl.

Xander looks back at me curiously, knowing there's a story there.

"What do you mean?" he asks me as soon as I shut the door behind us.

I sigh, "When we slept together, it was amazing, but her bond broke right after. It was horrible- she was in so much pain," I remember. "I knew immediately what was happening. And it felt like it was happening to me all over again. I was overcome with the hurt and despair that a broken bond inflicts, so much that I didn't comfort her or reassure her that giving herself to me doesn't make her a bad person," I say, scolding myself.

"Poor Rose," Xander sympathizes. "You can't punish yourself for feeling too much," he adds.

"She's having my baby, but she can hardly stomach when I look at her," I say grimly. "She flinches whenever I try to touch her. She gave me an ultimatum so that I wouldn't."

"Just because you're not together doesn't mean you can't be a father."

"I know, and I intend to be, but…I don't just want her, I need her. I like who I am more when she's mine," I say shamefully, putting my head in my hands. "I don't want her to be with anyone else."

Xander puts his hand on my shoulder in a show of support, but we sit in silence. I let the sadness rush over me, feeling the hopelessness that usually scares me too much. I'm grateful that he's here.

Breaking our silence, "Just because she won't forgive you now doesn't mean she never will," he says wisely. "You have all the time in the world, and you'll always have Jason and me."

"Thank you," I say appreciatively. "I suppose having more time is the beauty of immortality."

"So, what does the baby mean for Rose? What's your father going to do?" he asks nervously.

"I don't know. He wants me dead and gone, I know that much," I say indifferently. "I don't know what his plans are for Rose or our baby, but someone did attack her already. Sebastian was with her; he killed them."

"Why? What's in it for him?"

"As far as I know, nothing. He found out she was pregnant by accident. He set me up to attack her and I did. When he tasted her blood, he realized, and he looked scared for her and apologetic. He's been different ever since. He's still an ass, but he is treating her like a sister, like she's family."

"He has a soft spot for her," Xander says thoughtfully.

"It would seem that way."

The truth is, I know that William doesn't want Rose to have my baby, but I don't know how far he'll go to change that.

He looks at me compassionately. "What does the baby mean for her escape plan?" he asks delicately.

I think about it for a long minute, a somber realization coming over me. "I can't leave. If I do, William will never stop hunting me down, but whether she's having my baby or not, Rose can't stay here."

"But if you stay, William will find a way to kill you anyway," Xander says, scrunching his eyebrows with concern.

"It doesn't matter, as long as Rose is safe, and you and Jason keep her that way."

Xander just nods at me in grim understanding.

CHAPTER THIRTY-FOUR

Rose

In my hurry to get away from the mortifying situation inside, I rushed outside and now I find myself getting lost in the hedge maze.

"Fuck," I say loudly, overcome with frustration.

"My, my," I hear, my heart suddenly racing as I turn around.

"William," I say, immediately scared.

"I've never heard that word come out of your mouth before," he says.

"Sorry," I lie.

I'm not sorry at all. If anyone deserves that language, it's William.

"Don't be sorry. It reminds me how grown you are," he says.

I try not to flinch, but he managed to make the compliment both creepy and threatening at the same time.

"More grown than both of my sons," he claims.

I watch him standing totally still, his eyes glowing in the moonlight as his eyes rake over me inappropriately. This conversation is feeling more and more like a warning.

"Shouldn't you be defending the 'dark prince'? I'm carrying his baby after all- your grandchild," I remind him sharply.

"That's unfortunate!"

"Excuse me?" I say, taken aback.

"Honestly, I'm surprised you let him touch you, let alone take your virginity," he says rudely.

"It's none of your business," I argue, crossing my arms defiantly.

"My dear, in this world, I'm the king…Everything is my business."

"You're not my king," I say.

He clenches his teeth. "No, but I am Caleb's king, so if you don't want me to make the remainder of his life miserable, you better think twice about being disrespectful."

"What makes you think Caleb would hold any control over me?" I ask smartly.

He chuckles crudely. "If you're willing to let him between your legs, he has enough control over you," he says tactlessly.

My cheeks flush. I'm embarrassed with this conversation.

"You're judging me?" I laugh loudly. "I know about you and Xomira."

"We're discreet, my dear; we aren't hiding it. There's a difference, and we both have needs. Are you jealous?" he taunts, eyes wide with excitement.

"Ew. No," I cringe.

My reaction earns me a glare from him, and I shift uncomfortably, noticing that he's managed to get closer, backing me into an actual corner.

"Caleb won't always be around to protect you," he hints. "I was going to give you to Sebastian but the more I think about it, the more I think it would serve me better to keep you for myself," he says, stepping closer, licking his lips.

He stops a foot from me, taking one of my braids in his fingers, smiling twistedly. While I try not to hyperventilate in front of him, my lungs go into overdrive.

"I'd rather die than be yours."

"I admire your stubborn spirit, it'll be fun to break you," he says threateningly.

He crushes my braid in one hand to intimidate me and I pretend it's not working. I return his venomous stare while he stands disturbingly close for several agonizing minutes.

"Hello, Sebastian," he says, his eyes flicking to one side.

"Father," Sebastian says, coming out of the shadows. "Sorry to interrupt," he adds, looking from William to me.

"We're just having a conversation," he says charmingly. "Isn't that right, dear?" he adds, releasing my hair and stepping back.

I can't bring myself to speak, so I nod. Sebastian eyes me curiously as his father turns and leaves without another word.

"Are you ok?" he asks me after a few minutes.

"Not really," I say with a shaky voice.

"Sebastian!" William shouts.

"Did he hurt you?" he asks, ignoring his father.

"No, he didn't have a chance," I say with gratitude, "but he's terrifying."

Sebastian chuckles sadly, thoughtfully- his silence an agreement.

"Caleb has reasons for hating him," he says matter-of-factly.

I take a deep breath. Then I remember that I'm out here because he insisted on pointing out my romantic life. I look at him, furrowing my brows.

"If you were wondering, dinner was uneventful and disappointingly boring. There was no bloodshed, only the exchange of a few words," Sebastian says, sensing the shift in my mood.

"SEBASTIAN," William shouts hectically.

Sebastian rolls his eyes but heads after his father.

"Don't worry, sweetheart, one of your lovers will be here soon," Sebastian says over his shoulder, teasing me.

"You're not as awful as you want everyone to believe," I say to his back.

He doesn't look back or stop, but I know he heard me. I start wandering around, realizing that the gloves are off with William. He's not going to pretend to be nice anymore.

I drop to my knees and cry.

Gavin

I find Rose just inside the hedge maze, on her knees, crying into her hands. I walk up behind her noisily so she will hear me coming, but for a minute she says nothing.

Then, "I'm so sorry," she says through her tears.

I don't ask what she's sorry for. I know what she's talking about. She felt it too- the unbelievable agony of our bond shattering. It's the worst pain I've ever felt, and I hate that she caused it. I want to believe she had her reasons. Maybe he manipulated her into giving herself to him, but it's hard to imagine that even he would do that to someone when he's been through it himself.

"I know."

Standing up, she turns to face me. Tears stain her cheeks, tinged pink with the cold. I should be more upset with her. I was before I saw her. Now I'm relieved and I just want to hold her because I've missed her.

"Why did you do it?" I ask.

"I...I don't know," she stutters. "I didn't want to hurt you...I thought that I had a plan, but one thing led to another and...I messed up."

She means it. She thought she knew what she was doing. Her sincerity is only a bandage on my broken heart, though. As much as I want to move past this, it's hard to forget.

"I need you to be honest with me. Do you love him?" I ask.

"No...I can't. I barely tolerate him," she answers, sounding unsure. "Caleb is controlling, temperamental, and just mean," she says, trying to convince herself.

I didn't need to ask. She may not realize it yet, but even I recognize the love that they share. It's messy and untamed, but it's there. She does love him, but she's fighting it so hard, she may never admit it.

"Do you love me?" I ask.

"I do," she answers without hesitation.

I feel my lips wanting to grin at how easy it is for her to say she loves me. Stepping forward, I put my hand on her hip and pull her towards me, her tears drying up. Her hands push up against my chest, and her fingers flex over my shirt. I lower my lips, leaving a small gap. She stands on her toes and presses her lips into mine eagerly.

Our kiss is more powerful than I expected, even after all the pain. My heart and body recognize her. Wrapped up in our kiss, we stumble back into a hedge. My hands travel over her body greedily, feeling her curves and wanting more. I want to prove to myself that she is mine.

A pain shoots through my chest as a reminder. It's so sharp I push Rose back, breaking the kiss that I've been craving for months.

"Are you ok?" she asks me nervously.

"I will be, but it's going to take time," I say, catching my breath.

"Is there anything I can do?" she asks seductively.

I smile at her. "You're doing it."

She presses her body back into mine, her hand tracing my jaw. I grab her suddenly, roughly, smashing my lips to hers hungrily.

I realize then just how in love with her I really am. Even though I said I was keeping my guard up, she tore it down, and now I'm hopelessly in love.

I'm not losing her again.

"Will you stay with me tonight?" I ask.

"Of course," she replies.

She takes my hand and I lead her back to the manor, desperate to feel her heart beating next to mine.

Rose

Just as we reach the door to Gavin's room, the door across the hall opens and Caleb steps out. It must be Xander's room.

His eyes pass over Gavin and land on mine.

"I'll give you a minute," Gavin says, clenching his teeth but going into his own room.

Caleb doesn't take his eyes off me as I feel the full weight of his gaze.

"You didn't tell him," he says observantly.

"No," I say, fidgeting uncomfortably.

"You're going to have to eventually."

"I know that, Caleb. I just want one night," I say, annoyed.

"You better do it fast. Sebastian will be more than happy to break the news," he says angrily.

I don't correct him, although I don't think he will be the one to rat me out- not after witnessing my torment tonight.

He storms off down the stairs, probably back to his cabin. He looks furious and hurt, but says nothing.

Volatile dick.

I go into Gavin's room, where he's sitting on the edge of the bed.

"I was worried you weren't going to stay," he says sadly.

I shut the door with a smile, heading towards him, hoping I can dismiss the sadness lingering in his eyes.

"I want to be here with you," I say.

Wrapping my arms around his neck, I kiss him softly to remind him that no matter what has happened, I'm still crazy about him.

His hands wrap around my waist securely, pulling me down on top of him as he falls back on the bed. I love how easily we fit together and how effortless our intimacy is. I want him more than ever now, but I know it can't be tonight. We need time to heal.

Breaking our kiss, I lay my head on his chest, listening to the steady beat of his heart. His fingers entwine in my hair the way they used to.

"I know that a lot has happened," he says.

"It has, but it hasn't changed how I feel about you," I remind him.

"Are you sure?" he asks hesitantly.

"Yes," I say. "But can you forgive me?"

"I forgave you the moment I saw you," he confesses. "My love is not as fragile as you might think."

I hope that's true.

We drift off to sleep in each other's arms, but I wake up in the middle of the night feeling restless.

I stare down at my belly guiltily. I shouldn't have kept this secret and I know it.

I sneak out of Gavin's arms and creep towards the door, only relaxing when I'm on the other side, leaning against it. I need some fresh air.

I find myself standing outside the hedge maze of all places before I know it. I walk in, remembering that I've been attacked every time I am here, and I was saved by Sebastian of all people. He's another guy I won't understand.

Why?

"Can't sleep?" a voice asks, catching me off guard.

"Jesus!" I exclaim, doing a weird jump-spin-stumble that knocks me off my feet so that I start falling back on my ass.

Caleb.

He reaches out and grabs me around the waist, stopping my fall and also pulling me insanely close to him. "Sorry," he says, letting go as I scowl.

I try to erase the blush that crept into my cheeks when he grabbed me and sent little tingles into my skin.

"What are you doing out here anyway?" I ask edgily.

He grins to himself, looking up at the sun, savoring the heat.

"I can't sleep either."

"I'm starting to think you never do," I observe.

He looks at me with amusement in his eyes, a smile tugging at the corners of his lips.

"I don't much, but…I had no reason to stay in the cabin tonight and I love the sun. As an incubus, I always feel cold. Nothing good ever seems to give me the illusion of being warm except feeding, and…you," he says hesitantly.

I feel a bubble of sympathy for him as I come to understand that I torture him and now he's going to be tied to me forever by a child.

"What are we going to do, Caleb?"

"About what?" he replies.

"About the baby. I'm scared," I find myself revealing to him. "How're we going to raise a baby when we're, well…us?"

"We'll figure it out," he says adamantly.

"Even if I'm with Gavin?" I ask, raising an eyebrow.

That makes him pause. He steps towards me, backing me into the hedge and I cross my arms. "He can't love you the way I do," he says softly.

His fingertips brush my hip. My skin blazes with tingles, my body betraying me, a blush rising in my cheeks.

"Caleb…"

He runs his hand up my arm slowly. "How can you deny this?" he asks huskily. "Let me love you."

"Caleb, please," I say breathlessly.

He hears the pleading in my voice and reluctantly steps back from me.

"Why Gavin?" he sighs.

"Because he's sweet and he's honest and he loves me openly and he makes me feel safe. He's nothing like you and he's exactly what I need. So please, let me be happy," I beg.

"It sounds lackluster and disappointing," Caleb argues.

"Passion and fire aren't enough. It's not what I need." Maybe I'm trying to convince myself.

"But it's what you crave; you're just fighting it," Caleb says.

"I want a life with Gavin."

"If that's what you want," he says, tensing, biting his tongue.

He stares at me intensely, saying nothing while the air grows thick around us. And although I love Gavin, the thought crosses my mind to give Caleb another chance and let him touch me in all the delicious ways his eyes are saying that he wants to.

"If you have any hope of salvaging what you and Gavin have, it'll be easier if you beat Sebastian to the punch. He needs to hear about the baby from you," he says, actually sounding compassionate.

He walks away in the direction of his cabin before I can thank him for his advice. I head back before Gavin wakes up to find me missing.

"Morning, gorgeous," Gavin says, kissing me on the nose.

I smile at him groggily, his beautiful brown eyes looking into my face, his finger under my chin softly.

"Morning," I say, my hand gliding up the back of his neck.

I pull his head down, pressing his lips into mine and holding him there. He kisses me softly, timidly at first, but after a few minutes he starts kissing me harder, passionately. I feel his hand move from my chin to my hip, squeezing with desire.

My body arches into him. I want his touch, and I become very aware of the night shirt I'm wearing sitting just below my hips.

Gavin shifts his weight, putting his knee between my legs, so that his body is half on me. My heart beats hard and fast as his hand slips down to the bottom of my shirt, his fingers hitting the bare skin of my thigh.

"I missed you," he whispers, trailing kisses over my shoulder.

"God, I missed you too," I say, a breathy moan escaping my lips.

His entire hand sits on my naked thigh, exciting me as I feel him sliding it up under my night shirt.

The bedroom door opens quickly and Sebastian walks in.

"Oh my god, Sebastian," I hiss at him, scrambling to pull my shirt down before he sees too much.

"No time for fucking, you're late for breakfast," he says casually, with a wink at me.

"Like I said before- tactless," Gavin says.

He gets off the bed reluctantly with a lingering glance at me. I turn bright red and scowl at Sebastian.

"Tell you what sweetheart, I'll take your lover and we'll meet you down there," Sebastian says, shoving Gavin out the door. "You know where to go."

He's not going to tell him. Right?

Panic takes me and I jump off the bed to get dressed in a hurry to hear whatever he's saying. I pull on some jeans and a sweater, throwing my hair up in a messy bun on the way down the hall.

I slow my pace as I go into the dining room for breakfast. Everyone is already sitting at the table except Caleb.

"That was fast…you must really be hungry," Sebastian says, knowing exactly why I rushed.

Gavin smiles at me as I take my seat next to him, shooting a dirty look at Sebastian. It only makes him laugh, though. I hate that he can get under my skin so easy, but nothing seems to bother him.

"Any idea where my dear brother is?" Sebastian asks me.

"Rose was with me last night," Gavin replies smugly before I can answer.

"All night?" Sebastian asks suggestively, raising an eyebrow.

Stalker.

He saw us.

Gavin takes another bite of food, seeming unconcerned, but I can see in his eyes that he's considering the possibilities.

"Sebastian, stop trying to cause problems," William says straight-faced.

"Yes, father," Sebastian says with fake apology.

He doesn't sound like someone who was chastised by his father, more like he was encouraged. I glance from Sebastian to William, and he looks at me at the same time. He smirks at me, a malicious glint in his eye.

I knew it.

He's not discouraging Sebastian at all. He's probably putting him up to it. I glare at him, remembering his threats in the maze.

I turn to Sebastian, giving him a look that I'm hoping comes off tougher than I feel. He could cause a lot of drama with everything he knows, and it hasn't gone unrealized.

Caleb

I walk in late and notice that everyone has already started breakfast. I see Rose immediately. Even with her hair in a mess on top of her head, she looks beautiful.

"So nice of you to bless us with your presence," William says sarcastically.

"Sorry," I say in a monotone.

I'm not sorry; not to him. I had met with Xomira and gratefully drank the blood bag she brought me. I tear my eyes from Rose, trying not to stare too long and draw attention. I sit between Xander and Sebastian, feeling her bright green eyes watching me curiously.

"We were just asking Rose where you were," Sebastian says, chuckling.

I look to Xander to see exactly what I missed. His eyes are closed and he's shaking his head in disappointment at my brother. Obviously, he's trying to mess with me, or Rose, or both.

I simply scoff at him, peering across the table at Rose to see how she's holding up. She looks edgy, understandably so.

"We have some business to handle today. I expect your help, Caleb."

Of course, he does. I nod tightly. What father wouldn't enjoy watching his son rip someone apart?

I avoid looking at Rose now, knowing she'll be observing me closely. She said that she could see what it does to me, handling my father's business. Every time takes me one step closer to losing myself completely. I thought I'd have a plan by now, but short of killing everyone, I've got nothing.

"Rose, my dear, what are your plans today?" William pretends to care.

She turns her eyes on him, hatred raining out and I know right away by the look on her face that he said or did something to her.

"*What did you say to her?*" I ask William privately.

"*What are you blubbering about?*" he dodges my question with a question.

"*You heard me. What did you say to her?*" I ask angrily.

"I will be with Gavin," she says, like it should be obvious.

"*Nothing she wasn't already aware of,*" he says smugly.

"*I swear to god if you touched her...*" I say furiously.

"*Only a little...she didn't say stop,*" he says twistedly.

"Of course, you should enjoy your visit with Gavin and Xander while they're still here," William says indifferently.

The public conversation draws me out of our private one because I knew this was coming and they aren't going to be happy about it.

"What are you talking about?" Gavin asks, troubled.

Rose's features change from pissed off to scared in seconds. She doesn't want them to go. She doesn't want Gavin to go.

"Your visit expires tomorrow; it isn't indefinite," Sebastian says rudely.

"Since Rose also doesn't belong here and is also a guest, she's free to leave with us, right?" Gavin asks defensively.

"Of course, but...I assumed that Rose would be staying a little longer, given her condition," William says offhandedly.

I see the horror dance through Rose's eyes as she gives William a pleading look. My heart seizes for her, knowing she wanted to be the one to tell Gavin.

"What condition?" Gavin asks, confused.

"*Don't say anything, please!*" I beg William on Rose's behalf.

"*I wouldn't dare...Sebastian.*"

My eyes fly to Sebastian's face, "*please, Sebastian.*"

He hesitates, his smug smile gone.

"*Sebastian...Now!*" William commands.

Sebastian's eyes show remorse briefly, then his appearance turns stony.

"The baby, of course," he deadpans. "The baby shouldn't be taken away from his father, the dark prince."

Rose's face drains of colour while Gavin looks around the table to gauge if this is real. He looks at me and finally to Rose, watching as it sinks in.

Fuck.

CHAPTER THIRTY-FIVE

Rose

After the truth sinks in, Gavin lunges across the table at Caleb, knocking him to the floor. Dishes, drinks, and food go flying everywhere as William still sits in his chair, drink in hand, watching the commotion with amusement.

Punch after punch, Gavin continues to pummel Caleb without getting a hit back, but neither has turned from their human form. Gavin is usually so calm and laid-back and he's never jealous. *What is happening?*

"We have to stop this," I say to Xander with fear.

Arms come out of nowhere, grabbing my wrist and keeping me away from the brawl. "Sebastian, let me go."

"Sorry, sweetheart."

"No. They need this," Xander says seriously, coming to stand beside me. He nods at Sebastian and he releases my wrist quickly.

It doesn't make sense to me. What possible good can come from kicking someone's ass?

"This is stupid," I say to no one in particular.

Caleb

His hands close around my neck as my chair tips backwards from the force. I saw it coming before he lunged. It was in his eyes.

I push him off me and get to my feet. I could easily win a physical fight if I turn, but it won't make my relationship better with her if I do. I push away my selfish pride, letting him do what he needs- knowing I deserve it.

"*You fucking prick!*" he screams at me.

He clocks me in the face with a right hook. Rage makes my blood start boiling, but I bury it as deep as I can.

"It wasn't enough to take her from me? You had to screw her and get her pregnant?"

He hits me in the face again with his left, making me stumble back a step.

"Why couldn't you just leave her alone?" he asks hatefully, punching me in the gut.

I feel my anger churning with every hit.

"Why don't you tell her the truth? Why you started coming around?"

"Shut up! It doesn't matter," he says.

He pulls me close, face-to-face, our noses almost touching, threateningly.

"If it didn't matter, you would have told her," I say reasonably.

"Go ahead, tell her. It's not why I stayed."

"You love her."

It's not a question, just an observation.

"Why aren't you fighting back?" he asks angrily.

"I deserve everything you're doing. There's nothing I could say to excuse what I've done, and it would be unfair for me to try to defend my behaviour," I admit.

"Taking responsibility or not, you're still a fucking monster," he says, giving me another right hook and making me taste blood.

Wiping blood from my chin, the heat threatening to explode, *"I love her,"* I say calmly.

"Fuck you!" he says, giving me a hard push back.

He stands breathing hard and glaring at me with so much hate.

Rose

Caleb wipes the remaining blood off his lip, the wound having already healed. Gavin is breathing heavily, a desire for violence in his eyes.

"Please stop," I say in a small voice.

Caleb looks at me right away, appearing calmer than me- we lock eyes. I want to ask him if he's alright, but I can't speak. After a minute Gavin turns to me, anger still in his eyes. He looks between me and Caleb and then takes off out of the room.

I run after him without a second thought, catching up to him in the hallway. "Gavin," I say, stopping him in his tracks.

He's got his back to me and he's standing rigidly.

Approaching him slowly, "feel better?" I ask, trying to lighten the mood.

Turning to face me, "if there is any hope for us, he can't be in your life," he says coldly.

"What? How can you expect me to choose?" I stare incredulously.

"I can't share you," he says, his eyes desperate.

"You don't have to; I'm yours."

He shakes his head side-to-side, "you're not only mine."

"What do you want me to do? He's the father of my baby."

"It's me or him," he says, giving me an impossible ultimatum.

I stand there in shock. *He can't be serious* but staring into his eyes I realize that he is very serious.

He begins to walk away, defeated. "I don't know what to say," I blurt out in frustration.

"Your silence says it all," he says unforgivingly.

I watch him walk out the door, not knowing what to do. I feel my anger bubbling to the surface. *This is all Sebastian's fault.*

I stomp back to the dining room. Everyone looks at me, Sebastian indifferently, Xander and Caleb with sympathy, and William with satisfaction.

"So, what's it going to be, sweetheart? You going to keep the dark prince from his child," Sebastian taunts.

Of course, they overheard, "Fuck you, Sebastian."

Sebastian laughs off my outburst, unfazed by my aggressive language- which only pisses me off more. I fume at him in my head, trying to get a grip.

"That language is unbecoming of a young lady," William says.

"It's also unbecoming of a young lady to let another man in between her legs," Sebastian says smugly.

That's it.

I leap at Sebastian and try to punch him, ignoring the heat in my cheeks. He catches my fist in the air and shoves me back hard, the smile completely gone from his face- replaced by contempt. His eyes gleam alarmingly.

I lunge back at him, wanting to rip out all of his hair, but strong arms go around my waist and hold me back.

"Let it go, love," Caleb whispers into my ear, sending shivers down my spine.

William rises from his seat and heads out the door smirking at me, Sebastian right behind him.

I wait until they are out of sight before pushing away from Caleb angrily. "Don't call me that and don't touch me."

Caleb stares at me hard, annoyed with my unwillingness to forgive him. I glare at him to remind him of my unfaltering resolve. Xander watches us with concern but says nothing.

Caleb takes a step towards me. "Why are you so angry with me?"

"You shouldn't need to ask," I say, glaring at him.

I hurry past him, feeling the sting of new tears forming in my eyes. I wipe at them roughly, heading towards the front door. I need to get out of here.

"Rose, stop," Caleb says, following me down the hall.

"Just leave me alone, Caleb," I plead.

I finally get to the front door and pull back on the doorknob. I barely get it open before he comes up behind me and puts his palm out, slamming the door shut. His hand drops from the door, but he stands right behind me, his body uncomfortably close to mine. I stare at the wall, my breath coming out unevenly, trying to collect my thoughts.

After a few minutes, I turn to face him, the tears still running down my cheeks. I'm sure he can see the sadness in my eyes. He's standing close, too close, towering over me.

"I tried to stop them from saying anything," he says.

His eyes are pleading with me to believe him, but how can I? He wanted Gavin gone as well, from this world and from my life.

I scrunch my eyes at him in disbelief. "Yeah, I'm sure you did," I reply sarcastically.

My heart beats harder looking into his gray eyes, dark and cloudy.

"I did!" he says adamantly. "You think I like seeing you this way, when you won't let me comfort you or touch you in anyway? I didn't want him to find out that way either, because I don't want you to have to go through this."

"But you did want him gone?" I ask accusingly.

He stares at me intensely for a minute, seeing the anger sitting below the surface, and thinking through his response.

"Of course, I wanted him gone. You're carrying my baby," he says passionately. "You're supposed to be mine," he adds, more soft-spoken.

"But I'm not yours," I say bluntly. "I'll never be yours."

Caleb punches the wall beside me angrily, his hand going right through in his rage. His head drops to the floor while his chest rises and falls forcibly. He pulls his hand out, revealing a few shallow cuts already healing and leaving blood on his hand.

"Only because you're too stubborn to admit that you love me as much as I love you," he says, bringing his eyes to mine. "You're keeping your heart guarded from me…why?"

I don't know what to say to that. I hadn't expected him to call me on my behaviour. In order to be ruthless, I have to keep my heart protected, especially from him.

"Maybe you're wrong."

"I'm not."

He brings his other hand to my cheek, trailing it over my jaw, down my neck, across my shoulder, and down my side until his hand is gripping my hip possessively. Tingles follow his fingers.

My breath catches in my chest at his touch; my heart accelerates in response. *My body is a traitorous bitch.* He smirks, knowing that I'm just denying my feelings for him. The heat rises in my cheeks, making them flush.

He leans in to whisper in my ear, his body pressed against mine.

"Deny it all you want, love, but you and I both know the truth."

He pulls away, taking all those amazing tingles with him. He glances back, nodding at Xander who is watching us with interest. He gracefully steps beside me, opening the door and disappearing.

Xander walks up to me casually, like he didn't just witness a rare intimate moment between his friend and me.

"He's different now…with you," Xander states.

"What do you mean?" I ask curiously.

"His darkness is growing, but he's embracing it instead of fighting it. It shows in the way he touches you and talks to you. He's making his desires more obvious."

"Is that a bad thing?"

Xander watches me carefully before answering. "Yes," he says honestly. "We should talk. Come with me."

Xander takes me into the trees to the hot spring where Caleb took me. We walk in silence, but I can tell that he has a lot to say. His body is radiating tension as he starts a fire.

"I'm sorry to bring you all the way out here. I wanted to speak in private," he says, fussing with the fire.

"I don't know how private it is, even out here," I say skeptically.

Xander turns and smiles at me, "the guards stopped following us outside the treeline."

"What about the stalker?" I ask with distaste.

Xander looks at me confused for a minute. "Sebastian?" he asks, grinning. "As far as I know, he went with Caleb and William on business."

He leaves the fire alone finally, sitting next to me while the flame dances in his eyes.

"How are you…really?" he asks with sincerity.

I consider my auto response of 'fine' but somehow I feel like he already knows that would be a complete lie.

"I feel like I'm in hell."

He nods and smiles like my response is exactly what he expected.

"Congratulations on the baby," he says sincerely.

"Thank you!" I say, holding my belly reflexively.

"Do you want to talk about it?" he asks sensitively.

I feel my cheeks flush at the memory of Caleb and me naked, "No."

He grins comfortably. "I'm sorry that Paige isn't here for a talk. I didn't want her near William."

"I get it. Wait. Are you two an item?" I ask, smiling hard.

"Yes," he says confidently.

"That's awesome."

"Thank you. So, what do you know about Caleb's feedings lately?"

"Nothing," I say bluntly.

I shudder at how cold my words are and how little I'm pretending to care about Caleb's dietary needs.

"I know that you and him are…complicated right now. I'm not going to argue or try to explain his point of view because I know it's not going to matter, but you need to understand the situation. Caleb is existing in a state of constant hunger. The blood that he's getting is hardly keeping his monster under control. He's very slowly starving himself because he won't feed from anyone but you."

"That's not on me," I say defensively.

"I'm not blaming you," he sighs, "but I'm going to be forced to leave tomorrow and I need you to understand that Caleb isn't himself anymore."

"What are you talking about?"

"You must have noticed that every time he gets back from business with William, his mood is darker. He's withdrawn, his temper is shorter, and his eyes are darkening and cloudy," he says.

Of course, I've noticed. I'm not that self-absorbed.

"I have."

"Then you've also noticed that he's more impulsive when it comes to you. He touches you more, says intimate things, and takes advantage of getting you alone?" he asks.

"Yes," I agree shyly. "But what does it all mean?"

"It means he's…he's turning again. He's embracing his incubus," he says with worry and sadness.

"W-what do I do? How can I help him?"

"There's nothing you can do. He needs to keep himself in control, which would be easier if he fed regularly, but if William keeps using him, he's not going to make it much longer. Even with the baby as incentive. He feels like he has no chance with you now, and you were always the reason he fought so hard."

I let out the breath I didn't know I was holding. I wanted to blame Caleb for Gavin leaving, and for everything I'm going through, but he needs my compassion.

Letting out a huff, I say, "It's my own fault. I thought I had to keep him close without getting involved."

We fall silent, his eyes never leaving mine. The silence makes me feel awkward.

"You were trying to control him," he accuses.

"Just like William," I admit guiltily.

Maybe I'm not as bad as William. I was just trying to survive, but Xander doesn't disagree with me right away.

"You're not William. He's a demented sociopath."

"Was what William said true?" I ask, earning a puzzled look from Xander. "Am I free to leave?"

It takes all my courage to ask the question I know would affect his friend the most. Especially since it would mean running away and leaving everyone else to clean up the mess.

"Technically, he cannot make you stay without forcing the halflings to go to war with the vampires," he answers simply, "but he will find a way to keep you here and make it seem like your choice. I know William."

I know first-hand that he's right. William already threatened me with Caleb's well-being. It shouldn't matter to me anymore. *But it does.*

"I'm so confused," I say sadly, tears falling again. "It's so easy to love Gavin but I think…I think I love Caleb too, only I can't bring myself to admit it to him or myself. I don't know what to do."

Xander pulls me into a bear hug, "no one can tell you what to do. You're going to have to decide for yourself."

"That's not helpful," I say with a self-deprecating laugh. "Why is it so complicated?"

"Love always is."

I stare into the flames of the fire flickering in the moonlight, trying to sort out my own feelings in the quiet.

Xander walked me back to Gavin's room before going to wait for Caleb. I can smell him on the pillow as I lay face down- crying. In my desperate attempt to keep him close to me, I curled up in his bed. Also, I didn't want to be at Caleb's when he got back even more than I didn't want to be alone.

Sitting next to Gavin' s empty chair at breakfast hurts me in ways I can't explain. When he came for me, I thought it was going to be ok. That we could work out whatever happened, that we could move past my mistakes. I realize now that it was naïve of me.

"Good morning, sweetheart," Sebastian says annoyingly.

I glare at him, feeling more and more like this is my permanent face since I make it so often.

He's staring at me with a smug grin. I turn back to my meal, take a sip of blood and orange juice, and try to tune out the world.

"Security said that the halfling left our world yesterday," he taunts me. "I hope he said goodbye."

He gives me a smirk, knowing that Gavin did not say goodbye, and it makes me want to punch him in the face.

"Shut up Sebastian," Caleb says darkly.

I risk looking up at him, only to meet his eyes as they are already locked onto me. His meal is untouched, but his whiskey is empty. He's watching me intensely, his gray eyes dark and cloudy as usual.

I can see it now that Xander has said it- he's changing. A brief spark of fear starts inside me. Am I safe? *I'm scared.*

Sebastian takes in Caleb and seems to rethink an argument with him. He goes back to his meal sulking, which makes me happy.

"After breakfast, I will escort you to the portal," William says to Xander.

He hides his eagerness well, but we all know better. Xander nods politely, looking from Caleb to me. His eyes linger on mine and I can see the concern.

We eat for another twenty minutes in silence before William rises to his feet. Xander scowls but does the same; Caleb does as well. Xander gives Caleb a hug that carries so many feelings. I feel the tears burning behind my eyes. Xander comes around the table and envelops me in his arms tightly. "Watch out for yourself," he whispers into my ear before pulling away.

I watch him follow William reluctantly as a tear escapes down my cheek and I let out a gentle sob.

"Aww, you going to miss your friend, sweetheart?" Sebastian teases.

"Fuck off, Sebastian," I blurt out.

Caleb and Sebastian both look at me like I've grown a second head because of my choice of words. If anyone has ever deserved that language, Sebastian is on that list. *I'm so done with his attitude.*

I wipe the tear from my cheek, Caleb's eyes piercing my soul while I do. I don't care; I'm not embarrassed or ashamed- not anymore. Things have to change, because I don't know how long I'm going to be here.

CHAPTER THIRTY-SIX

Caleb

I push the door open just enough that I can see her still asleep in the bed. She's been staying in Gavin's room since he bolted. I thought she'd come back to my cabin after he left, but she didn't. It'd be easier to keep an eye on her and protect her if she did. I know she won't, though. Something changed between us again. *And not for the better.*

She's laying on her back and my eyes wander to her growing bump- my baby. At five and half months pregnant, it's definitely obvious now, especially on her small frame.

"Caleb, stop lurking. It's creepy," she says sleepily, her eyes still closed.

Pushing the door open, I step inside.

"I thought you were sleeping," I say apologetically.

Opening her eyes, she turns her head towards me standing just inside the doorway.

"And that somehow makes your behaviour less creepy?" she asks sarcastically, smiling at me.

My lips twitch in amusement. When did her sense of humour become so dark? I guess carrying my child and being trapped here with us has changed her more than I thought.

I don't think it's a bad thing.

"How did you know it was me?" I ask curiously.

Her eyes open all the way, taking me in. I watch the colour rise in her cheeks as she flushes with embarrassment.

"I...I just know," she says shyly.

She climbs out of the bed wearing a t-shirt that barely sits below her butt with her pregnant belly.

I can't keep my eyes off the hem of her shirt as she walks around the bed, coming closer to me before she disappears into the bathroom. I shake my head, rub the back of my neck, and chastise myself for behaving like a typical guy. I know better than that, but I can't help it. I haven't touched her in months. *I miss her!*

"So, what do you need?" she asks me, coming out of the bathroom.

She's wearing pants, much to my disappointment.

"You missed breakfast," I say.

"And?" she asks rudely, putting her hands on her hips.

"And…I wanted to see if you'd have lunch with me."

"Oh. Yeah, I could eat," she replies.

We walk side by side back to my cabin for lunch. Neither one of us want to share a table with William or Sebastian any more than necessary.

Once inside the cabin I start making bacon, eggs, hash-browns, and cutting up some fruit for her. She sits tensely on the couch and watches me.

"How have you been feeling?" I ask, making small talk.

"Fine," she says curtly.

I stop my chopping and look back at her in disbelief, my eyes hovering over her belly. She scowls at me and puts a pillow on her lap, hiding the bump from my view.

Turning back to the food, I start frying up the bacon, eggs, and hash browns. "Sure, you are…" I say smartly.

"Ok smartass, obviously I feel like shit. I'm nausous, hungry, tired, achy, and needy all the time," she admits angrily.

I look over to her again, raising an eyebrow. "Needy?" I smirk.

She blushes profusely, refusing to look me in the eye. She clearly didn't mean to tell me that part.

"It's your fault I'm like this," she says.

"What? Pregnant?" I ask with feigned shock. "I didn't do anything you didn't want," I add, making her roll her eyes.

I load up a plate with all the food and take it to her at the couch.

"Thank you," she says gratefully.

"I don't regret it," I say confidently.

She cocks her head to the side like she doesn't believe me. "Any of it?" she asks, putting more food in her mouth.

"Only the way I handled your broken bond," I confess.

She gazes at me with surprise, "really?"

"I don't regret making love to you and I definitely don't hate that you're having my baby," I tell her easily, staring at her hungrily as memories come flooding back.

"Where was all this honesty when it mattered?" she asks indifferently.

I recognize the cold look in her eyes, noting that our playful conversation is over. My eyes fall to her belly again and I feel an overwhelming desire to put my hand on top.

"Can you not stare at me that way, please?" she says harshly.

"Jesus, Rose, you're more combative than usual," I sigh.

"Sorry...It turns out I don't sleep well alone," she says tiredly.

I notice it now, the dark circles around her eyes. I remember the times she'd fallen asleep in my arms before I screwed everything up.

"Come lie down," I offer.

I walk to my bed, pull the covers down, and pat the mattress next to me invitingly.

"Caleb, what are you doing?" she asks suspiciously.

"Can you just trust me?"

There are a lot of reasons why she shouldn't listen to me. Even I'll admit that my actions aren't entirely pure. I want to prove to her that she needs me for something. And to be honest, I need her- to feel her, to hold her. It's been too long. She hesitates for a few minutes before coming to the bed with me. Lying down next to me, I pull her into my arms and begin stroking her hair lovingly.

"Caleb..." she begins.

"Shh," I say quietly. "Just close your eyes."

She stops protesting and gives in, releasing a long sigh as she relaxes into me. She feels so warm and for just a minute, I feel the familiar heat. I'm careful to touch her as little as possible, knowing full-well that she's likely to change her mind.

She must be tired to let me hold her.

I hear her breathing slow down along with her heartbeat and I know exactly when she falls asleep, but I don't move. I stay where I am and enjoy the feel of her body against mine.

I let my fingers drift up and down her bare arm, enjoying the softness of her skin, and I let her sleep.

Rose

When I wake up it's still dark out, but I feel strangely refreshed. I can feel his breath on the back of my neck and then I realize I'm in his cabin, in his bed, and he's still here- sleeping peacefully with his arms wrapped around me. *I don't hate it.*

I take a few minutes to enjoy how safe I feel, but the overwhelming urge to pee happens. So, I shimmy out of bed to relieve myself. When I come out of the bathroom, I approach the bed and try to wiggle back into his arms. It's awkward with a belly.

He chuckles with his eyes still closed, lifts his arm, and pulls me back into him. "I thought you'd never ask," he whispers, nuzzling into my hair.

"I didn't ask," I say smugly.

He smiles, his gray eyes opening and burning into me. "You didn't have to," he says sweetly.

I hold his gaze, feeling more at peace than I have in months, and loving the adoring way he's watching me.

"What time is it?" I ask.

"Almost time for breakfast?" he guesses.

"I slept all day and night?" I gasp, sitting up in shock.

"You were exhausted," he says, eyeing my belly with a look of longing.

I pause, leaning back in the pillows. "Give me your hand."

He does without a second of hesitation and I take it in mine. Lifting my shirt, exposing my belly, I place his hand palm down where the kicking is currently happening. He looks from my belly to me in amazement. Sliding closer, he gently lays his head down beside his hand.

He needed this, to feel close to his baby. To remind him of what he's holding on for. I've kept him away long enough. I know it's not fair.

We stay like that for an hour, long after the baby has gone to sleep. He turns and kisses my belly delicately.

"Let's go get some food," he says, tearing himself away.

He looks almost happy again and it makes my heart swell as he puts his hand on my lower back and leads me out.

Caleb

"Well, don't you two look cozy," Sebastian says, trying to bait us.

I look at him, finding myself completely unfazed. I spent the morning with Rose curled up in my arms and just when I thought it couldn't get any better, she placed my hand on her belly and I felt my baby moving. Nothing can destroy the mood I'm in.

"Morning, Sebastian," I say politely.

"*You're in an awfully good mood,*" he says privately.

"*I am, aren't I?*" I respond, rubbing it in.

"*She let you fuck her again?*" he asks.

I scowl more at the way he uses his choice of words than at the words themselves, but I have more patience for him right now.

I sit beside William, and Rose sits between Sebastian and me.

"*No, Sebastian. She didn't let me fuck her again,*" I say with a smile.

"*Too bad. I hear pregnancy makes them fun,*" he teases.

"*If it's not already fun, you're not doing it right,*" I fire back.

"*Touché,*" he says, grinning.

"Enough…" William says out loud, clearly sick of our banter.

Rose opens her mouth to ask what he's talking about. My eyes find hers and I give her a small shake of my head, hoping she will understand that she shouldn't say anything to draw attention to herself. There had been an edge to William's voice; one I haven't heard in centuries. The last time I heard it, a lot of people died. She frowns at me, but closes her mouth.

We eat our breakfast in silence for several more minutes. By 'we,' I mostly mean Rose. Both William and Sebastian's plates remain untouched, which is unnerving since they usually eat something. Mine, of course, is mostly untouched, save for a bite or two. Rose's whole plate is almost empty, and I fight back a grin.

"I think we've had enough breakfast. Join me in my study for a drink," William says abruptly, pushing back from the table.

It wasn't a question, but a command. I know the difference, unfortunately. William rarely asks questions.

After William disappears into the hallway, I lock eyes with Rose, nodding to signal that we are going to obey. Rose pauses beside me while I drain the rest of my drink. I lace my fingers through hers as we head to the study with Sebastian following silently behind us.

Her face tightens at my touch and she looks reluctant but buries it. I'm only doing it to keep her close. I have a bad feeling about this.

Inside the study, William is pouring drinks. Sebastian follows us in, standing just off to the side of the doorway. William hands me a scotch with blood, Rose gets a coke and blood, Sebastian takes a whiskey and blood, and William takes the same.

He hasn't given me blood at all since I've been here and although I'm suspicious, I drink it. So does Rose.

"You two are full of surprises," William says.

He glances at our interlaced fingers, a look of disgust written on his face. He's not even trying to disguise it.

"What's your problem?" Rose demands.

His eyes flicker to Rose's face at the sound of her voice. She flinches slightly under the weight of his gaze, but he doesn't approach her. He just smiles at her in a sickeningly sweet way, and it's definitely worse.

"I don't have a problem, my dear, but you two…you two have problems, and my guess is you always will," he taunts her.

"That doesn't concern you," she spits back at him.

She pulls her hand out of mine, stepping towards him furiously.

"That's where you're wrong," he says threateningly.

"We had a deal," I say furiously.

His gaze switches to me, his smirk turning into a sneer.

"Don't act like you didn't know this was coming. You knew your time with her had an expiry date," he watches me, waiting for me to deny it.

"Of course, I knew."

"What?" Rose says, horrified.

"You've served your purpose but thank you for dealing with those loose ends for me. Watching you tear those people apart limb from limb, peeling the flesh from their bones, and torturing them on my behalf, almost made me proud to call you son…almost," he laughs.

I notice Rose watching me with concern. She knew I was doing some bad things for him, she even knew I enjoyed the bloodshed, but I think she just realized what exactly that meant.

"Apparently, I live to serve," I say sarcastically.

"Well, your service is no longer required," William replies.

"Caleb…" Rose mutters, but I keep my eyes on William.

Rose

Something feels off.

Out of nowhere, I'm hit by a wave of nausea. "Caleb," I say softly, but he's too busy arguing.

I immediately start sweating and swaying on my feet. My heart is racing so fast it hurts. "Caleb…" I whisper, holding my belly.

I grab onto Caleb as my legs give out. Without missing a beat, he supports my weight. He stops arguing when he realizes something is wrong.

I stare up into his striking gray eyes, the dark taking hold. "Caleb, I don't feel so good," I say slurring my words.

"Rose…Rose," he shouts at me with so much fear.

The world fades to black and the cold creeps in, even with Caleb's warmth wrapped around me.

Caleb

When William and Sebastian don't even flinch at what's happening, I assume that this is their doing.

"Rose…What did you give her?" I ask angrily.

I lay her on the floor gently, push the hair out of her face, and turn my anger on them.

"She'll be fine," Sebastian says, coming near us.

"Maybe," William adds. "Potions are so unpredictable."

My head starts to feel foggy and my heart starts beating faster. I crouch on the floor next to Rose, looking her over nervously and bracing my hands on the ground. Whatever they gave her, they gave it to me too, but it's not working as quickly with me.

"You can't drug her. She's pregnant," I fume.

Sebastian is standing next to Rose. He bends down in a small show of compassion and puts his hand against her belly.

"The baby?" I ask steadily.

He doesn't answer me, just moves his hand to a different spot on her tummy with a look of concentration on his face.

"What about my baby?" I demand.

"They're both fine," Sebastian offers to calm me, removing his hand from her.

"For now…" William insinuates at his plans.

William is glaring at Sebastian, probably disgusted that he would even bother to check the baby and show even a shred of compassion.

A burning pain starts building in my stomach, bringing me to my knees. The pain keeps building and I sweat more, scrunching my eyebrows with the effort to control it.

"Don't fight it. It only gets worse," Sebastian says, gloating as he comes behind me.

"You're going to regret this," I say.

"Unlikely," William replies confidently.

Rip comes through into the room, stopping beside Sebastian. His eyes skim over the scene in the room, remaining casual and unperturbed. I shouldn't be surprised. He helped me with some of William's bidding.

Sebastian is looking right at me. "Break his neck," he tells Rip coolly.

Rip stalks over to me, pulling me to my feet and locking one arm around my neck. He pushes his other hand against the side of my head, trying to snap my neck, but even in my weakened state I'm putting up a fight.

"It didn't have to be this way," William says after being silent for so long.

I grunt against Rip, feeling the stabbing pain of my neck detaching. *I can't win this one.*

The pain sears through me and the world turns to black.

"Ugh," I groan, coming to.

"Welcome back, brother," Sebastian says twistedly.

I look around at the cement walls around us and notice that my hands are shackled high above my head. Rip is standing back against the opposite wall and Sebastian is beside me, chaining Rose to the wall and locking her hands above her head.

"Get away from her," I snarl out, trying to pull my head together.

"Relax. I won't touch her…while she is unconscious," he jeers.

He snickers, glancing over at me before resuming his task with Rose.

"That bloody hurt," I complain through gritted teeth.

Sebastian turns his attention to me, coming to a stop in front of me after finishing with Rose. Rip shifts uncomfortably with Sebastian standing so close to me. If I wasn't chained to the wall, it would make sense, but the reality is that I am, so there's not much I can do. He chuckles coldly at me. "Yes, I know," he says. "I remember all those times you broke my neck, making me unavailable when our father called on us. Anything to make yourself the best son in his eyes."

His voice is laced with resentment from his memories of our youth, even though they are flawed. More accurately, it's his memories of our father.

"You don't know what you're taking about," I say, sighing.

"Sure. For someone who hated our way of life so much, you sure fit the role of 'the dark prince' effortlessly," he accuses me.

"It wasn't without sacrifice," I remind him bitterly.

He throws his head back and laughs. "Don't pretend it wasn't a choice."

"What was I supposed to do? Let him corrupt you more?"

"You think I couldn't handle it after all those years?" he scoffs.

Sebastian's mother had died at birth, so he'd never had anyone to shield him from William's cruelty. I'd grown up with my mother; she had been kind and loving, so when she died and I moved in with William, I knew how terrible his treatment of his son was. Sebastian was still my brother and I wanted to protect him, even if that meant becoming the monster that our father wanted me to be. At least if he was focused on me, he left Sebastian alone. I thought that I could handle it. *I was wrong.*

"I didn't want you to have to," I say compassionately.

"And you thought sabotaging me at every turn was the better option," Sebastian says incredulously.

"I…" I start, pausing when I hear a door open and close.

Footsteps echo towards us as William comes walking into sight.

"Caleb, I didn't think you'd be awake yet," William says observantly.

"Sorry to disappoint," I say smugly.

He approaches me and stops, closer than Sebastian dared to be, but William thrives off intimidation more than actual violence. That's what he is attempting to do- intimidate me.

"Oh, I'm not disappointed," he smirks, turning and continuing towards Rose. "I don't mind if you watch."

He drags his fingers down her neck and across her collarbone while she hangs limply, her head slumped forward.

"Get your fucking hands off her," I say aggressively, straining against the chains uselessly.

He doesn't take his beady eyes off Rose though, just looks her over enthusiastically.

"Watch your tone boy! You're being disrespectful," he says.

"I think we're past the pretense of being a happy family, William," I say, tugging at my shackles.

He grins to himself. "Yes, I suppose we are."

He raises his hand back to her shoulder, stabbing his nail into her flesh and drawing a small amount of blood.

She doesn't even flinch, still being that deeply unconscious. He brings his finger to his lips, sucking the blood off greedily. I feel my blood boiling at the sight but try not to let it show.

"This doesn't bother you, does it?" he taunts, knowing damn well it does. "You and Sebastian used to share your girls all the time," he reminds me.

"Caleb isn't like that anymore, father. Especially where Rose is concerned," Sebastian says, rolling his eyes. "He won't share her for feeding or fucking."

"Shame it's no longer his choice," William says.

They're both right. There was a time when Sebastian and I would share, but that was a long time ago. Things are different with Rose; she's mine.

"So, what is this? Why is Rose here?" I ask furiously, annoyed with the pointless banter.

William peels his eyes from Rose and looks at me with intrigue. "That's your big question- why is Rose here?" he laughs. "You've really accepted that claiming Rose as yours meant signing your own death warrant just to buy more time?"

"More time with a girl that can barely tolerate you at the best of times…" Sebastian adds laughing.

"You really are just a stupid boy consumed with delusions of love," he spits.

"I would make the same choice every time," I say confidently.

William's grin disappears as he walks back towards me and I know what happens next isn't going to be pleasant.

I feel the weapon pierce my torso just below my ribs, while he glares at me with dead eyes. "You're such a disappointment," he hisses at me. He doesn't pull it out so I can heal, but instead twists it in deeper, watching me cringe and sweat in pain. He leaves the weapon protruding from my body painfully, sneering at me.

"Such a waste," he mutters.

He walks past me, pausing next to Rip. "I want it to hurt. Make him bleed, but keep him alive," he instructs before leaving.

Of course, he's not staying to get his own hands dirty.

CHAPTER THIRTY-SEVEN

Caleb

"You're a fool," Sebastian says, leering.

Rip is rolling up his sleeves a few steps behind, an intimidation tactic that I've used many times before.

"Why is that?" I ask monotonously.

I'm asking, but I really don't care what he thinks.

"You knew about the prophecy, so you knew our father would eventually go after her, yet you still fell for her," he says.

"And?" I ask rudely.

"She doesn't have the slightest idea who you really are," he says, trying to hold back his laughter. "You play the part of a boy scout, but how long do you think you can keep your real self from her? Faking it won't change it."

"Maybe you don't know me anymore," I say defensively.

"You're really determined to change who you are. Fine," he shrugs.

"I have changed." I'm not sure who I'm trying to convince.

"Even before you turned incubus, masochism was always your thing. I guess some old habits never die," he says. "I suppose that makes everything make more sense."

"I guess so," I say with resentment.

Rip walks up, pushing Sebastian aside, and sneers at me. We've tortured dozens of people together for William and now he's doing the same to me.

Some would call that karma.

He grabs hold of the object sticking out of me near my ribs. Twisting it, he tilts it up into my ribs forcefully until I hear a sickening crunch, followed by a searing pain through my ribs.

I cringe against the pain, choosing not to satisfy him with outward cries, but it hurt me, and he knows it. The sweat on my brow proves it.

He pulls the object out roughly. I stare him down unflinchingly while blood soaks my shirt and drips on the cement floor.

Rip walks away, one hand covered in blood. I can already feel my rib healing, the wound sealing. He heads towards a table that I'm just now noticing. I watch him throw the weapon down only to pick up another.

"What is the point of this?" I ask, regaining my composure. "I'm not exactly new to pain."

"No, but it's not just about pain…he wants you to bleed."

Rip pulls a sharp knife down my arm, cutting my skin open and letting the blood pour to the floor. I grunt in discomfort before it starts to close. The white-hot pain starts to subside.

"Why not just kill me? That's what he wants, isn't it?" I ask tiredly.

"All in good time, brother," Sebastian says.

Rip wastes no time plunging the knife into my chest, opposite my heart. It tears through my skin and muscle easily, slicing through the bone and puncturing my lung with a sharp stab. I grunt in pain and turn my face towards Rose.

Please let her stay asleep, I don't want her to witness this.

Her hair hangs in front of her drooping head, so I'm unable to read her face. Instead, my eyes fall to her belly. I try to dull the pain by remembering how soft and warm her belly had been when she'd let me feel my baby's kicks.

But I can't ignore it when the knife is ripped back out, leaving me coughing and breathing roughly with a damaged lung. The pain is enough that it pulls me out of my pleasant memories and back into the present.

I feel the heat raging beneath my surface, trying desperately to be released, but I refuse to react. I glare at Rip, feeling my own twisted need to inflict pain and suffering.

"If we really wanted to hurt him, we'd do something to his girl," Rip says, pointing the knife at Rose.

"Don't touch her," I threaten darkly, reacting before thinking.

Sebastian glances at Rose, amusement clouding his face. "Alas, she's off limits for now. We have our orders- make him bleed."

Rip scowls with disappointment and stomps back to his torture table. I release a deep breath with relief as my lung slowly begins to heal.

"You realize your death stops nothing. Our father will do as he pleases with Rose once you're gone," Sebastian tells me.

"I trust that you won't let him," I counter.

"Why on earth would I get in his way?" he asks.

"Because you care," I say bluntly.

"You think that I care about you?" he says, laughing.

"Not me, but I know you care about her, Sebastian, and I know your word is solid," I say kindly. "William has done his worst to bleed all of the good out of you, but he hasn't succeeded yet. You fed her your blood…"

"So? Maybe I'm trying to manipulate her into falsely trusting me."

I scowl at him. "You're not. I've never known you to share your blood ever. William always said it was too emotional and he said that that was a weakness. Or has that changed?"

"No…" he says, annoyed.

Rip comes back over with a hammer. He pulls his arm back, preparing to smash me with it.

"You're wrong," Sebastian says.

Rip brings the hammer down on my right side, crushing my lungs and breaking several ribs. I groan and cough up blood, letting it run down my chin. My breathing becomes laboured. They just stand there watching me suffer.

It takes several agonizing minutes before I start healing this time. The blood loss is finally taking a toll on me.

Rip walks away, leaving Sebastian to watch me sweat.

He smirks at me, "you still think I give a shit?"

"You're trying awfully hard to make me think otherwise," I say smugly.

Rip comes back with a small pipe looking object with jagged nails. He wears an unnerving smile.

"May I?" Sebastian asks Rip, his hand out expectantly.

Rip hands him the weapon hesitantly, clearly disappointed.

"You're trying too hard," I provoke him intentionally.

He slams the object into my stomach with more force than I expected. I gasp and cough, cringing in pain. If I wasn't shackled, I'd be doubled over. The pipe is sticking out of me, letting blood run out and pool at my feet. I close my eyes, tipping my head back, searching for relief while Rip starts packing up.

"Don't say I fucking care," Sebastian says, slowly walking away.

They leave me in the dark hanging next to a still unconscious Rose. I sigh with relief that I get a break now, although pain still overwhelms me.

It isn't easy keeping my creature under control during torture and I'm exhausted. Was I wrong about Sebastian caring? *I hope not.*

Rose

I awake with a gasp, trembling. I'm in a dimly lit cement room. My hands are locked in chains above my head and I'm barely standing on my tip toes against a brick wall.

The last thing I remember is collapsing in the study with Caleb, Sebastian, and William. I felt funny after having that drink- there must have been something in it.

There is a slight pain in my shoulder and looking down, I see the small, curved wound resembling a fingernail.

"H-hello," I say softly.

"Rose…"

I turn my head to the side, my eyes adjusting to the darkness, and I find Caleb shackled up to the wall there, blood smeared on his skin and clothes- his feet in a large puddle of what I can only assume is blood.

"Caleb," I say, terrified. "Are you ok?"

"I've been better," he answers smartly.

His voice is strained and weak, but that's unsurprising- that's a lot of blood he's standing in. My eyes start to focus and zone in on the piece of metal in his stomach.

"Are you ok?" he asks, his eyes flying from my belly to my face.

"I think so," I reply, feeling a tiny kick in my tummy. "Where are we? What's happening?"

Caleb opens his mouth to answer me, but he doesn't have a chance. A door creaks open and slams shut as footsteps grow louder. I watch where the sound is coming from in fear, feeling my heartbeat pick up the pace and the air forcing itself out of my lungs.

William comes around the corner with Sebastian following him obediently, looking slightly unsettled.

"Oh, good. You're both awake," William grins.

A shiver involuntarily travels through my body like cold fingers. I try to put on a tough face, but I'm shaken as shit, so pretending is hard. I knew the gloves were off, but I wasn't expecting this. I know that there are a few ways to play this and I'd prefer the way least likely to trigger his cruel side.

"What are you doing?" I ask, playing the unknowing innocent.

"Oh Rose, willful ignorance is not a good look for you," Sebastian says, amused, not buying into my words.

I give him a look that could kill, making William laugh loudly.

"I never understood the attraction between you and Caleb," William admits, walking closer, "but it is becoming more and more clear. After all, the apple didn't fall far from the tree."

"Caleb couldn't be more different than you!" I say adamantly, ignoring his confession of his attraction to me.

"Are you sure about that, sweetheart?" Sebastian chimes in.

"He hasn't exactly been forthcoming about his past, has he?"

I turn to look at Caleb, feeling my confidence cracking.

"Don't listen to them, love," Caleb says weakly. "They're trying to get under your skin."

William walks over to Caleb, and I tense with worry. He reaches out and grabs the object protruding from his gut. With a sadistic grin, he rips it out.

Caleb winces, but holds back a sound.

"Leave him alone! What's wrong with you?" I ask angrily.

He moves from Caleb to me with a few steps. My anger morphs into fear when I look in his eyes. I try to pull my arms down reflexively, but they don't budge. I feel panicked for a moment as my heartbeat quickens, and he notices- grinning sickly.

"Sebastian, come here," William orders, still smiling.

Sebastian comes to a stand-still beside his father. They are both facing me, and I give them my best tough girl stare, but inside I'm shaking with terror. My chest is also rising and falling too dramatically for me to entirely pull off the whole brave façade.

"What are you doing?" I ask nervously.

Sebastian looks at me, his smile not as enthusiastic as it once was, but William grins harder, which sends an icy chill through me.

"You look hungry, Sebastian," he says suggestively.

"I always am," Sebastian replies quickly.

"Well, please," he gestures to me, "she is delectable."

Sebastian's gaze shoots to his father. I watch suspicion, confusion, and excitement flicker through his face.

"I thought you decided to keep her for yourself," Sebastian says warily.

"Unlike your brother, I know how to share," William replies.

Fear claws at me as his words sink in. *They're going to feed from me.*

I watch his features change as he closes the distance between us, hunger and desire shining in his eyes. I whimper helplessly as Caleb pulls uselessly at his chains. He looks into my eyes and sees my fear, giving him pause.

"I made a very generous offer, Sebastian, but it will expire. Don't be ungrateful," William says, trying to manipulate him.

"Seb, please?" Caleb implores him.

Still, he hesitates, standing intimidatingly close to me, but not actually touching me. Regardless, my heart is racing.

"If you're not going to, I…" William begins.

Sebastian moves quickly, not letting William finish, pushing my head to the side roughly but still gently. I feel his hot breath on my shoulder for only a second as he pushes himself against me. His nose hovers in my neck for a few seconds before his fangs pierce my skin.

My eyes are clenched shut, bracing me for the pain. It is nowhere near as bad as I expected.

William grabs Sebastian by the shoulder, snarling, and rips him from me painfully. He throws him backwards and he stumbles a few feet but catches his balance. He stares at his father furiously at having been interrupted.

"You're pathetic," William says viciously.

He shoves my head the opposite way aggressively, so that I'm looking at Caleb. I see the anger in his eyes, and I know what's about to happen, but I don't have time to prepare.

He drives his fangs into my neck carelessly, a scream erupting from my throat. It's excruciating and feels like he's sucking the life out of me. I'm vaguely aware of the threats and profanities that Caleb is yelling, but it feels far away. After several terrifying minutes he tears his teeth out, making me gasp. Taking a step back, he rakes his gaze over me inappropriately.

"You are more delicious than I remember," William says.

"I'm going to fucking kill you," Caleb threatens.

I turn my attention to him to reassure him that I am alright, but what I see makes my heart skip a beat. His eyes are almost pitch-black.

"Caleb…" I whisper in a small voice.

He looks at me, seething in anger even at my image. His incubus nature is trying to take him away. *I'm losing him.*

"Caleb, please come back to me," I plead.

His breathing slows as he closes his eyes in effort. When he opens them, they're still a charcoal opaque.

"Now that sounded more like the Caleb we used to know," William says merrily. "Why don't you tell her the truth before you're not around?"

At William's statement, he looks away from my gaze, making me feel worried. "What is he talking about?"

"I'm not the person I've led you to believe," he says with an overwhelming anguish.

"What do you mean?" I ask, my heart racing.

"This is all my fault," Caleb says, looking at me sadly.

"What are you talking about?"

"I'm sorry, Rose," he says breathlessly.

"Don't say that," I say firmly. "Don't say it like a goodbye…not again…not now," I add, tears falling.

"Once you hear the truth, you'll want it to be a goodbye. I'll never be the man you deserve, and I should have accepted that sooner," he says, shaking his head. "I was selfish. I thought I could change all of who I was and alter our reality, and that would make you want me, but that wasn't fair to you," he confesses.

"What does that have to do with anything?" I ask, confused.

He goes silent, leaving me with more questions than answers.

Stepping in, "Didn't you wonder why he showed up the same night we did…just minutes before? How I knew how long he had been without blood? Or why I invited him out with us that night at the hotel?" Sebastian asks.

I think back to the night they took me- the way Sebastian had looked at him in my apartment, how they had been unsurprised to see each other, and now it starts to seem odd.

I look from William to Sebastian and finally to Caleb, and it clicks.

"You weren't a prisoner," I say, realizing the awful truth.

"Of course not; he was simply on a short leash," William says like it should have been obvious.

I stare at Caleb, frowning. *He played me again.* He says nothing in his own defense, confirming my nightmare. My stomach is twisted in knots and I feel like I am going to be sick.

"No," I say, looking away from him, and not wanting to believe it.

"Come on sweetheart, you think we would have let him deal with you at your apartment, be at the motel with you, or let him take you through the portal…think about it. All the signs were there, you just didn't want to see it," he says with disappointment.

William smirks at me, "you don't look so good, Rose. I guess ignorance was bliss," he says teasing me.

"How is this possible?" I whisper.

"It's simple, sweetheart. He came home."

"He wanted you away from that halfling, so we struck a deal. The guards were to ensure that he followed through on his end," William says, wiping my remaining blood from his chin.

"What was the deal?" I ask, looking at the floor to keep myself together.

"He would become the 'dark prince' once again in exchange for claiming you exclusively for six months, after which he knew we'd kill him and you'd become ours," William explains indifferently.

"B-but…" I stutter out, looking down at my belly.

"Yes. The baby was not part of the plan," he answers with disgust.

"Still want to spill tears for him?" Sebastian taunts.

I glance at Caleb hanging beside me in a puddle of blood, appearing defeated. I have heard everything I need to.

"You seriously have nothing to say?" I ask angrily.

Caleb finally looks up at me.

"There's nothing to say. It destroyed me seeing you in Gavin's arms the night you ran. I tried to let you go, but I couldn't. Coming home was supposed to be a distraction, but my self-serving nature won out. I made a deal to get him out of the picture and get you alone," he confesses with no emotion. "My only condition was that they treat you fairly after."

"Oh, how considerate of you," I say sarcastically.

"They were coming regardless of my presence. I still tried to protect you," he argues coldly.

"You are unbelievable!" I continue to cry.

I do not even recognize him anymore. I look away from him, ashamed and embarrassed that I couldn't see it when it is so obvious. Indignation consumes me and makes me feel reckless.

"He is not so different after all," William says proudly, "almost makes me want him alive. Almost."

What a dick!

Caleb

In my peripheral vision, I see William signal to Rip, more than likely to bring me right near death so that he can deliver the final blow. That is the way he works- he has everyone else do the hard, dirty bits. Just like he did with me.

I glance at Rose before Rip gets to me. She's staring at the floor, devastated with my betrayal again. *Why do I keep doing this to her?* Her lips twitch, a mix of anger and sadness warring inside her.

A hard fist lands in my still healing gut, pulling my thoughts away from Rose. Pain spikes through me, and the familiar feeling of hopelessness and rage swirls. An intense desire to maim and kill threatens to overwhelm me.

I gasp and cough, choking on my own blood. I watch out of the corner of my eye, but Rose doesn't even flinch or look at me.

Suddenly, an explosion rocks the ceiling above us, sending dust and debris floating down. It wasn't a typical explosion, not in our world. It was done with magick. That can only mean one thing…they've come back for her finally. I was beginning to wonder if Xander was going to be able to pull it off. I look at Rose, but she doesn't seem to understand that it has everything to do with her.

William and Sebastian do though, and they share a knowing look.

"What's the matter, William? Another hitch in your plan?" I say.

William scowls at me and goes to Rose with a look of desperation on his face. He's careless when he is desperate. He produces a key and starts unlocking Rose's shackles.

"What are you doing?" I ask, my voice full of concern.

He had wanted Rose to watch me endure torture, revealing my betrayal so that she felt the same darkness that he had nurtured in me and Sebastian. Then she would almost encourage my elimination. That is, until enough time went by and she started to see the cruelty, forcing her to live with the guilt and driving her into a deeper darkness.

He is a sick man!

Moving her is not part of the plan.

"Taking her somewhere we won't be bothered," William says with a dangerous gleam in his eyes.

"Like hell. I'm not going anywhere with you, asshole," she says with more fire than anyone expected.

She struggles against William's manhandling, refusing to make it easy for him. *That's my girl.* I see it cross his mind, a fraction of a second before it happens. His arm darts out and his fist connects with her cheek bone. There is a disgusting cracking noise and she starts falling limply to the ground before I can yell.

He actually knocked her out.

"What the fuck? That was not part of the deal," I say, grinding my teeth.

"The deal's changing," he snarls, dipping down and letting her fall onto his shoulder.

"You can't do that," I argue.

"Watch me."

"What do you want us to do with him?" Sebastian asks, gesturing at me indifferently. Another smaller explosion rings out above us, followed by a few screams.

"Kill him, of course," he answers, hurrying to the door with Rose slumped over his shoulder.

As soon as William is out of the room, I give Sebastian a hard look.

"Get me down, Sebastian," I order firmly.

He puts his arm out, stopping Rip's approach, earning him a sneer from his loyal guard.

"Why? I thought you'd accepted your fate, brother," he says.

Ignoring another closer explosion, "I have, but this was not what we agreed on," I reason. "He is going to hurt her now- he has no choice."

"And whose fault is that? You know that it was Xander that arranged this after his visit," Sebastian says glaring at me. "You were never going to let any of us have her, were you?" he asks, realization dawning on him.

Now it's my turn to smirk in a victorious way.

"Of course not, you know me better than that," I remind him obnoxiously. He gives me an impressed look. "Can we go after them now please?"

Just then, the door busts off its hinges and the fight from upstairs moves into the small torture room.

Several people are swinging weapons, some are wielding magick; it is absolute chaos. I fight against my shackles, wanting to join into the fight and shed some blood.

Out of thin air, an ax comes flying at my face. It stops just shy of cleaving my head in two. It presses into my cheek and spills more of my blood.

"Fuck! Cutting it kind of close, aren't you," I say, watching a cut on his own cheek heal quickly as my own does at a much slower rate.

"Stop bitching," Sebastian says, dropping the ax. "I stopped it, didn't I? I had to deal with Rip first. He did not approve of the plan."

He pulls out a key and undoes my chains. I rub my wounds and see Rip laying on the floor, his head ripped clean off. "Prick," I mutter, still raw at the pain he inflicted. I look at the violence, grinning enthusiastically.

"He was my favourite guard, just so you know," Sebastian tells me.

"Sorry," I say, trying to sound genuine.

"No, you're not," Sebastian says incredulously.

My lips twitch into a grin. He is right; I couldn't care less about Rip. I start towards the nearest duo, fighting instinctively.

"No time," Sebastian instructs. "Do you want to help Rose or not?"

I hesitate for just a moment at the thought of biting into someone and ripping a few arms off. It would be very satisfying, but there is no time to indulge my savage needs.

Rose needs me. She will likely not want me anywhere near her ever again, but if she survives this, it will be worth it.

Sebastian and I slip out of the room, heading deeper into the tunnels in the basement. William will have gone this way to avoid the brawling and sneak out a hidden door.

"So, what's the plan now?" Sebastian asks we jog down the hall.

"We find them, and I kill William," I say plainly.

"And our deal?" he asks curiously.

"Our deal still stands. Once William is dead, I'll decline the throne and it'll pass to you, making you the next king, as planned…but Rose is to be untouched and free to do as she pleases."

"And what if you are disallowed to refuse the throne?" he asks seriously.

I stop in the hall, forcing Sebastian to a stop as well near the exiting door.

Looking him in the eye, "I'm aware that our deal depends on you becoming king. I'll keep my word," I say with severity. "They won't dispute your claim in the event of my death."

He nods in grim understanding.

CHAPTER THIRTY-EIGHT

Rose

I wake up with my back scraping on the bark of a tree, the left side of my jaw throbbing painfully. My arms are tied at my sides, the rope wrapped tightly around the tree, uncomfortably so.

The trees are tall and cut off most of the sky, but enough shows to tell me it's dark. However, the sky is beginning to lighten, and I can make out William crouching with his back to me, fiddling with something.

"William, why are we here?" I ask nervously.

His back straightens at the sound of my voice.

"Rose, you're awake!" he says, avoiding my question.

"Where are we?"

He stands up and spins to face me. "Somewhere we won't be bothered," he smiles threateningly.

"Why?" I ask, noticing the object in his hands.

A knife.

"If I told you, that would ruin the surprise," he smiles innocently.

He approaches me slowly, menacingly.

"Please, don't do this," I sob fearfully.

"And what is it you think I'm going to do, my dear?" he asks twistedly.

"I don't know."

He walks closer, my heart beating harder with every step he takes. He knows that he is scaring the shit out of me, but that's his goal.

"You are trembling, but you don't know why?" he asks amused.

"You are scaring me," I admit.

"Don't be afraid my dear, I have a plan."

A plan? What the hell does that mean?

In seconds, the heat fully takes him, his brown eyes shining and the veins pulsing under his eyes.

I cry out as he attacks my neck without warning.

He drinks greedily, recklessly, letting it dribble down my neck. The pain is immense, making my knees buckle. If I wasn't tied to the tree, I'd be on the ground. He releases me roughly.

I feel my strength starting to crack the more he touches me. He looks into my eyes before leaning into my ear and whispering.

"You know it doesn't have to hurt. I can make it feel really good if you let me," he says, trying to seduce me.

I can't say anything as I try to catch my breath, not out of excitement, but out of terror. *I don't see a way out of this.*

He strokes my cheek and I turn my face away from him, repulsed. *Big mistake.*

He wastes no time biting into my neck again, using his version of seduction. His hands find my waist and he presses up against me. The feel of his body makes my blood run cold.

Sensing that he's not having the effect on me that he wants, he pulls away with frustration. I gasp in pain, feeling like my neck is barely being held together.

"You're fighting it, Rose," William says, gritting his teeth.

A twig snaps behind me, drawing Williams' attention. He shifts slightly, peering over my shoulder.

"You can't really be surprised that she is," Sebastian says from behind me in the trees.

"Sebastian…what are you doing here?" he asks with suspicion.

"Maybe I've come to finish feeding," he replies.

He sounds different- mischievous and playful. It's a tone he does not usually give his father. Can William hear it too?

"Is that all?" William asks, raising an eyebrow.

I suck in a sharp breath as a form comes into view over William's shoulder, approaching silently from the tree line. *Caleb.*

"Caleb…you're supposed to be dead," William says, sensing Caleb's presence after my sharp inhale of breath.

William turns to face Caleb, seeming to be more annoyed than concerned, which I do not get because the look on Caleb's face is deadly. With his ever-changing eyes, he looks one hundred percent the predator.

I can see him now, the real him, and it's kind of scary.

Caleb

She can see me for who I am now, at least more so than before. I can feel it in her gaze, but all I can see is the mess William has made of her neck as the scent of her blood assaults my senses and threatens to turn me into a monster.

Before you transition fully, the only way to heal is if you let the heat take you and turn into your creature. Rose's problem is that she can't control her ability to turn yet.

I tear my eyes from Rose. "You broke our deal…" I say, watching William intently.

"It seems that you two have made one of your own," he assumes, gesturing at Sebastian, who had been creeping closer.

"Does that make you nervous?" I ask, unable to hide my excitement.

"Hardly," he replies bluntly. "Should I be?"

"I would be if I were you," Sebastian says darkly from beside Rose. *He's good at sneaking around unnoticed.*

The heat is trying to claim me as the anger rushes through my veins.

Quietly, a large, muscle-bound guard comes back into view from the shadows. He tenses as he takes in the scene in front of him.

Of course, he is not unprotected, but it makes no difference. It would take two or three guards to slow me down, and there's still Sebastian.

"One guard will only piss me off," I say confidently.

"You think I haven't considered that?"

Another guard comes into the clearing with Aamily thrown over his shoulder. He drops her on the ground where she stays in a heap, crying. She's not stupid enough to try running, and judging by the smell, she's also wounded. He goes on the defensive quickly, locating his boss and reading his face for instructions.

We are physically outnumbered, but that doesn't mean anything when it comes to our fighting skills. Sebastian and I are hands down the best fighters, and in incubus form I can walk out of a fight that is three to one. But using my incubus form is risky, especially when I've lost most of my blood. If I turn, I might lose control and that puts Rose at risk.

Sebastian shares a look with me but doesn't turn. He knows that I will wait until the last possible second, and he doesn't want to give William any reason to think we feel threatened.

"This isn't going to end the way you want, boys," William brags.

"I like our odds," I say calmly.

"I beg to differ," Sebastian chimes in. "Your entire guard is locked in battle with the halflings and the enchanters. Your reign is coming to an end, father."

"There will be no talking your way out of this one, William," I add.

The gleam in William's eyes terrifies me. It's the spark of a man out of options and he knows it.

He quickly steps behind Rose, holding his hand around her throat, mayhem written on his face.

This is exactly what I was afraid of.

"She is no use to anyone if you kill her," Sebastian says, a little too indifferently for my liking.

"Don't do something you will regret," I say through gritted teeth.

"That's the difference between you and me, Caleb. I regret nothing," William says maliciously.

William's eyes twitch in the smallest way towards Rose, signaling for his guards to jump into action. The biggest guard lunges after me, but in the split second it takes him to make impact, I've already allowed the heat to take me, turning me into a killer.

The guard that tossed Aamily to the ground goes after Sebastian. He doesn't react as fast as I did, and turns once he is in the guard's grip. I know that he is capable, so I turn my attention back to my opponent.

I am vaguely aware of William as he approaches Rose, caressing her cheek and stroking her hair, but his guard stands between us.

"Come on Caleb! Surely you can handle more blood on your hands," William says, provoking me.

I growl at this because I know that he is trying to push me over the edge again, but the part of me that is too far gone wants to be surrounded in death, his specifically.

William withdraws a knife from somewhere.

Big mistake!

What little restraint I was clinging to leaves the moment the blade shines in the moonlight. I surprise the guard when he lunges at me again, tearing his arm off with ease. He drops to his knees screaming in agony, but I don't stop there. Positioning myself behind him, I pull up on his chin, ripping the flesh of his neck as he feebly fights with one arm. I don't show mercy, even as he begs for his life, not until I'm holding his head separate from his body, covered in his blood.

"There he is," William says, smiling wickedly.

I drop the man's head, mesmerized by all of the blood. William is watching me excitedly.

Sebastian finally gets the upper hand in his fight, snapping the guard's neck like a twig and smiling ruthlessly. He takes in the carnage behind me, looking at me with concern.

Stepping behind Rose, he puts the knife to her throat. "Ah, ah, ah. If either of you come any closer, I will slit her throat," he says.

Rose whimpers, trembling with the knife against her neck. My incubus still has me in its claws, and I glare at William, feeling less afraid for Rose than I should. William can see it too.

"Get the knife away from her throat," I tell him.

"Not yet."

"What do you mean, not yet?" Sebastian asks suspiciously.

He points his eyes at Aamily, who is still on the ground sobbing.

"Kill her!"

"Caleb, don't," Rose pleads with me.

"What is the point of this?" I ask, annoyed.

"Humour me," William insists.

I hesitate about showing my desire to spill more blood, because Rose obviously does not want me to. Sebastian sees it and stalks towards Aamily with purpose.

"A broken neck will not suffice," he informs Sebastian.

Sebastian rolls his eyes before moving behind Aamily.

"Please, Master Sebastian, I did everything you asked," Aamily cries.

He doesn't seem to have any reservations at all as he steps into position, pinning her arms down and pulling her chin up. It takes a minute; she's more of a fighter than you'd expect, but soon there's the inevitable wet ripping sound of her head coming off her body.

"Happy?" Sebastian asks dully.

"Ecstatic," William replies.

"What was the point of that?" I ask.

William smirks at us, "to let Rose see that she is surrounded by monsters. You both get off on death and violence as much as me, maybe more. So, thank you for proving that you are both as savage as you claim I am."

Privately, William elaborates. *"You did not disappoint."*

I look at Roses' face. She is horrified and so disappointed in our behaviour. So am I.

I watch as William unexpectedly plunges the knife into her belly, into my baby. She lets out a piercing scream as blood gushes out around the blade. Rage blooms in my chest and all I can see and feel is my need for revenge. William bolts and I stand frozen, torn between setting chase and running to Rose's side.

Rose

The pain is agonizing, more so when Caleb takes off after William, leaving me to bleed.

Sebastian watches Caleb with concern and surprise as he races away.

"Sebastian, the baby," I say with worry as he rushes to my side.

His eyes are showing fear as he looks down at the knife jutting out of me, his hands hovering near it.

"This is going to hurt," he says bluntly.

I cry out as he removes the knife slowly while my wound continues hemorrhaging. He uses the knife to cut the rope tying me to the tree, supporting my weight as my knees buckle.

He lowers me carefully to the ground. "You have to turn, Rose, so that you will heal," he says with urgency, putting steady pressure on my gushing wound.

"I can't," I say weakly.

"You have to. You're dying," he says with exasperation.

"I can't," I say, sobbing harder.

"Why the hell not?" he demands with frustration.

"Because she can't control it," Caleb says, appearing out of nowhere.

"You came back?" I say, tears filling my eyes in fear.

He crouches down beside Sebastian and me, putting a hand on my belly, "I am so sorry, love, I should have stayed with you," he says.

I flinch under his fingers, remembering that he played a part in taking me captive. A big part. An unforgivable part.

"Just go away, Caleb," I say tiredly.

He looks at me with understanding, but I know that he's not going to go away, not until he knows if the baby and I are ok and maybe not even then. He says nothing, but he removes his hand from my belly.

I stare into his dark gray eyes, feeling myself and my baby weaken.

Caleb

I meet Rose's gaze and I can feel something in that look that never used to be there. It's making her so sad.

"Let me help you," I say reassuringly.

"*How are you going to help her?*" Sebastian asks privately.

"*I can help her turn.*"

"*How?*" he asks curiously.

"No. You can't," she says, panicking as the heat rises in her cheeks.

"Rose, please…be reasonable," I plead.

"*I have to make her… needy.*"

"*You think you can do that…now?*" he asks with disbelief.

"No," she says firmly.

"*I have to try.*"

"Leave me alone," she says, swatting my hand away.

"*Then you are going to have to do it against her will, because there is no time for this. She's bleeding out.*"

I look at her, renewed determination in my eyes. She sees it.

"Caleb, I can't. I don't want to want you," she says through tears. "You can't feed me. You have already lost too much. You'll die," she adds, hoping to deter me.

"But you won't, so it doesn't matter," I say honestly.

"It does matter. I'm not a killer…I'm not you!" she says hurtfully.

"I am sorry," I whisper.

Ignoring her attempts to push me away, I raise my hand tenderly. My fingers trace her jaw lovingly as I pepper her neck with kisses. She tries weakly to push me away, but I feel her heartbeat accelerate as I slide my hand down her side, grabbing at her hip. My lips crash into hers, my tongue finding hers immediately, and I kiss her like my life depends on it.

Thing is, her life does.

Rose

The heat builds in my belly as I grab his shirt, pulling him against me harder. His hands roam my body automatically, and maybe a part of me hates it, but I also can't get enough. I grind my body up into him, needing more of him. As much as I want him not to touch me, my body always responds to him. And even though I know why he's doing this, it is still working.

I turn into my halfling form, my fangs dropping automatically. I bite into his neck in a less than gentle way. *He asked for this,* I remind myself. Hearing his hiss of pain, I pull him closer, feeling powerful.

I feel the warmth spread through my body as I take some of his blood. The pain from the knife wound starts to fade as it tingles and heals.

"Ahem," Sebastian clears his throat.

I remove my teeth and push Caleb back to find Sebastian watching with interest. Caleb growls in response to being interrupted. I am breathing heavily, but I try to hide it. I shove him further away using my halfling strength. He rolls back onto his ass looking somewhat annoyed with me but also grinning smugly as a little blood dribbles out of the puncture wounds on his neck.

"I told you no," I say pointedly at Caleb.

"I had to," he says adamantly. "Is my baby ok?"

I had forgotten all about our baby, consumed with the blood. Now I put my hands on my belly protectively, squeezing my eyes shut tight and trying to feel the slightest movement. After a few tense minutes, it starts, my lips turning into a genuine smile. "The baby is fine," I say out loud.

Caleb lets out a breath in relief, but Sebastian looks troubled.

"Are you sure you are alright?" Caleb asks seriously.

"I am fine," I reassure them both.

CHAPTER THIRTY-NINE

Rose

Caleb gets to his feet, extending a hand for me. I refuse to take it. All of my anger and blame floods back. I glare at him with all the pissed off energy I've been holding onto.

I am still in my halfling form, covered in blood as three people come barreling through trees into the clearing with us.

"Oh my god," I exclaim.

I throw myself into the arms of Xander and Paige at the same time, not caring that I am drenched in blood or that they are too. They hold me and I sigh in relief. After a minute, Jason joins our group hug and I start to involuntarily cry.

They let me cry for a few minutes, "Rose, look at you," Paige says after having my bump squished up against her.

I step out of the embrace, letting them see my baby bump, and I smile sadly. Paige smiles back at me.

"Xander told us you were pregnant, but I never considered how much time had gone by," she says happily.

I look down at my belly, rubbing it tenderly. I love my baby already, but I hate Caleb for being the father, because he shouldn't be. He manipulated me. I see that now.

"Rose, what's wrong?" Xander asks, sensing that something is off.

They all stare at me, waiting for me to explain. I can feel Caleb's eyes on me, and I just can't find my words.

"Caleb may or may not have lied to get between her legs," Sebastian says crudely.

"Jesus, Sebastian," I say, blushing.

Jason steps around Paige, giving Sebastian a dirty look.

"Why are you here?" he asks coldly.

Sebastian chuckles, "don't worry, I'm leaving. I have to go clean up William's mess anyway," he says, brushing past me.

"Thank you," I say sincerely.

I know it makes no sense to the others, but he stayed with me when I thought I was dying. And in his own sick and twisted way, he was there for me several other times.

"Anytime, sweetheart," he says suggestively, disappearing into the trees.

"What the hell was he talking about?" Xander asks uncomfortably.

He is staring at me, waiting for me to elaborate, but with every passing second, it is harder to keep the tears at bay.

"It's not what you think…" Caleb begins.

Xander interrupts him. "We don't want to hear your side right now," he says shortly.

I can't stop a tear from escaping and I wipe it hastily from my cheek.

Jason approaches me and lifts his hand a little. "May I?" he asks.

All I can do is nod my approval. Jason takes my hand in his, closing his eyes in concentration. I feel grateful that he can do this and save me from having to say it all.

He opens his eyes after a few minutes and I meet them. "I'm so sorry," he says letting my hand go.

He turns to Caleb, and walks towards him aggressively. He lifts his hand to place it on Caleb's shoulder, but he takes a quick step back out of reach.

"This is not necessary," Caleb says, staring his friend down.

Jason steps towards him. "It really is," he replies.

Caleb lets him connect with his shoulder, but Jason doesn't close his eyes and relax. He keeps his eyes locked on Caleb, growing tenser with every passing second. Finally, he drops his hand, backing away hunched over, gasping for air.

"I tried to stop you," Caleb says smugly.

Jason looks at him with disgust, clearly affected by whatever he felt.

"What happened?" Xander asks.

"You do not want to know. His mind isn't a pretty place right now," Jason says breathlessly.

"I think it's best if you give Rose some space," Xander says warily.

Caleb grins arrogantly. "Of course you do, but does Rose feel the same way?" he asks.

I glare at him, "I do."

My eyes are filled with tears as I stare at Caleb, the man who has kept secrets, broken my trust, shattered my heart, and made me question if he manipulated me into carrying his child, and now I feel numb.

"Fine," he says, leaving reluctantly.

I watch him walk away, feeling my body relax as he goes.

"Are you alright?" Paige asks me, linking her arm through mine.

I look at her sadly. "Not really, but I'm going to have to be," I say, touching my belly.

"Come on, Rose, we will take you home," Paige says, taking my hand.

"Actually," I begin nervously. "I want to stay here."

"Caleb's not safe!" Jason states, glaring in the direction that Caleb went.

Shaking my head, I tell them "I am not going to stay with Caleb. Just at the manor…until the baby is born."

"We can protect you, if that is what you are worried about," Jason assures me.

"We can," Xander says, agreeing with his friend.

I know that they are capable of protecting me, but Caleb is making me nervous with his cruel attitude. I don't want his friends to have to choose between us if he gets worse. They are a family.

"I know you would, but he's your friend, and he is going to need you both," I say thoughtfully. "Sebastian is a prick, but he isn't a danger to me."

"Is there nothing we can say to change your mind?" Paige asks.

"Not about this," I say honestly.

Xander walks past me. "I guess we need to go find Sebastian, work out some ground rules," he says with annoyance.

"This is a bad idea," Jason says.

Paige and I walk arm in arm, following Xander through the trees, with Jason following behind us. The sunrise lights the sky ablaze.

After a few silent minutes, she says "Gavin is the one who arranged this whole rescue with the halflings."

"He is?" I ask, surprised.

"Yes," Xander chimes in. "In fact, we should check in with him."

"He came too?" I ask, my voice full of girlish hope.

"He did, but he wanted to avoid Caleb," Jason replies.

I don't blame him. I would also like to avoid Caleb.

"He was really worried about you," Paige adds.

We walk the rest of the way in silence while my heart starts fluttering at the mention of Gavin coming back for me. He left here so abruptly and so angrily. I assumed he hated me.

When we reach the manor, Sebastian is standing outside with three pompous looking older gentlemen. They all look at me with curiosity as we approach, even as the dead bodies of the fallen are taken away.

Sebastian cocks his head to the side as we stop just a little way away.

"I think it best we don't interrupt them," Xander says.

Sebastian starts heading towards us. "Nonsense. We are finished for the day, right gentlemen?"

I recognize two of the men from the vampire council, with not a drop of blood on them. They sneer at me before walking away. The third gentlemen follows Sebastian over to us as well.

"Rose, this is Christoph Oberman, the high-chair of the enchanters," Sebastian informs me.

"Hello," I manage.

"Rose, it is a pleasure to meet you, my dear," the man says smoothly. "Are you well?" he adds, gesturing at all the blood all over me.

"Oh…yes. I am fine."

Seeming satisfied with my answer, he nods politely at me, turning his attention on Jason.

"Jason, a word please?" he asks.

With a small nod, Jason walks away with Christoph, leaving me with Xander, Paige, and Sebastian.

"What was that about?" I ask nosily.

"Christoph is probably trying to recruit him. His ability is extremely useful," Sebastian says, not trying to hide his enthusiasm. "Anyway, is there something you need?" he adds with boredom.

"I have a favour to ask," I say, suddenly nervous.

"Oh, really? What is that?"

"I want to stay here until I have my baby," I say.

"You're kidding," he says skeptically.

"She's not," Xander jumps in.

"Why?" he asks suspiciously.

"Because, despite your asshole tendencies, I feel safe here. Safe from Dalibor and William and safe from Caleb," I blurt out.

"I see," is all he says. "Some would call you foolish."

"Maybe."

His look is hard and assessing, his brown eyes thoughtful while he considers my request. He gently grabs my arm, pulling me away from the others, much to Xander's dismay.

"Is this really what you want, sweetheart?" Sebastian asks me, confused.

"Yes," I respond with no hesitation.

"I'm a dick. You have said so yourself," he says with amusement. "Why on Earth would you want to stay when they can probably keep you just as safe as I can?"

"Because…when I fed from Caleb tonight, I felt it, his darkness. He's going to turn all the way. And when he does, I may not even be safe. I don't want to put his friends in the position where they have to…" I trail off.

"Kill him?" Sebastian finishes seriously. "And you are so sure I will if it comes to it?"

"I am."

"And that makes you want to stay here? You do know that that is not normal, right?" he says, smirking.

"I never claimed that I was normal," I respond with a grin.

"Lord Dalibor and William, I can guarantee, but Caleb will likely be around. This is his home too until he does something to change that. I'll do my best to limit your contact, and I promise I will protect you from him when it matters, but he's an extremely powerful incubus," Sebastian says honestly.

"Is that a yes?" I ask.

He shakes his head in disbelief. "It's your funeral," he says, shrugging.

I turn around to head back to the others only to see that Gavin is standing near them in discussion with another older gentleman. He's talking to the man, but his eyes are on me, making my breath catch in my chest.

Gavin shakes the man's hand, patting him on the arm and heading directly for me. As he approaches, he glances past me and I remember that Sebastian is standing behind me.

"Give me a minute."

Sebastian listens without any smart remarks and walks around me, rejoining Xander and Paige.

"Hey," he says in greeting.

"Hey," I reply shyly.

"I am relieved you're alright. You are ok, right?" he says, gesturing at the blood all over me.

"What? Oh yeah, I am fine."

"Good," he replies.

He brings his hand up, brushing the hair from my face and tucking it behind my ear, his hand lingering on my cheek.

"I didn't expect to see you here again," I say, my smile fading.

"I know. I am sorry for the way I left. The ultimatum I gave you was unfair. I let my jealousy get the best of me," he says, planting a gentle kiss on my lips. "Can you forgive me?"

"Can you?" I ask, glancing at my belly.

He takes in my bump for a minute. "I want to," he smiles genuinely. "I'm trying. Maybe one day you will carry my baby," he adds intimately.

I smile at the idea of what we have to do in order for that to happen and I feel the blush creeping in.

"You should know that I am staying here for a while, under Sebastian's protection."

His jaw tenses and for a minute it looks like he's going to argue.

He doesn't.

"If you need anything, call me," he responds.

I stand up on my tip toes, tossing my arms around his neck, my stomach fluttering nervously. His hands sit on my hips, flexing possessively. He bends his head down, his lips grazing mine, "I've missed you," he whispers.

His lips press against mine and although it feels like we were never apart, there's also a shadow in what we had. We can't go back to what we once were. "I've missed you too," I say, pulling away sadly.

He laces his hand with mine, filling me with warmth as we head back. The sun is now bright in the sky.

Jason is back with the others when we regroup. I can't help smiling like a schoolgirl even though the night was filled with death and devastation.

"We will see you in a couple weeks," Paige announces.

"Sebastian is graciously allowing us to check in from time to time," Jason says, rolling his eyes.

"We will see you soon," Xander assures me.

"Take care of her," Gavin warns Sebastian.

He kisses me delicately, unashamed of the intimate moment, before letting go of my hand and leaving with the others. I whisper my goodbyes as a tear rolls down my cheek.

"Touching…can I get some sleep now?" Sebastian says, rolling his eyes and gesturing for me to walk ahead of him.

I sigh loudly. *What have I gotten myself into?*

"Evening," Sebastian says.

"Evening," I say, taking my seat beside Sebastian.

We are sitting in the sunroom, giving us a beautiful view of the full moon. I have been here for just over a week and already things have become familiar and reliable. Everyday, the table is set for two at every meal. Sebastian is around most days and when he is not, he has guards on me at all times.

"You look like shit," Sebastian says straightforwardly.

"Thanks. You are so sweet," I snip.

"Are you not feeling well?" he asks.

"Honestly? Not really."

I take a sip of my coke and blood, but almost spit it out when Caleb comes walking in. He takes in the guard standing against the wall before sitting down at the table beside me.

Although I knew he was skulking around, I have not seen him since THAT night. I see Sebastian eyeing him warily, but I remember what he said about this being Caleb's home too. I guess this was inevitable.

"Hello, brother," Sebastian says with suspicion. "What are you doing?"

Caleb smiles twistedly at his brother. "I came to see how you were getting along with the mother of my child."

I glance at him, his eyes dark and dangerous. His eyes rake over me hungrily, teasing me as a blush rises in my cheeks.

"We are getting along famously," Sebastian taunts.

My eyes widen a little. Does he really think it a smart idea to provoke his brother? *Psycho.*

"Like one big happy family!" Caleb says grinning. "Rose, can we talk…alone?"

I stammer, searching for an inoffensive reply.

"Do you really think that that is a wise idea?"

Sebastian looks right at Caleb, who quickly peels his attention from me. My heart thumps in my chest. I don't want to be alone with him. I don't trust the look in his eyes.

Caleb lets out a low growl, proving what I suspected all along. They are having a conversation that I was not privy to.

"I'm not going to fucking hurt her," Caleb shouts furiously.

He gets up from the table so fast that his chair falls backwards. He gazes at me, meeting my eyes before he storms off.

After we hear the front door slam, I ask "do I want to know?"

"It was nothing. We argued about his current state and my concerns," he admits.

"Do you think he would hurt me?" I ask curiously.

"I think he believes he won't, but the dark in him is unpredictable."

"I used to think that you were unpredictable," I say.

"And now?" he asks questioningly.

I laugh to myself, "now I still think you are a psycho, but things have changed," I say, touching my belly.

He chuckles, "why don't you go lie down?"

"I think I will."

I leave dinner without taking a single bite and I head back to my room not feeling any better.

I crawl into my bed, the lightning is beginning to crash outside, but sleep takes me immediately.

My fingers drag along the stone walls in the basement hallway while my feet take me clumsily forward. I can feel the sweat on my forehead, my heart pounding, my breathing shallow. As thunder pounds the manor, I find myself standing in the doorway to Sebastian's room in my tank top and pajama pants.

He is sleeping shirtless on top of the blankets. An empty bottle of whiskey sits on his bedside table.

"Sebastian," I mutter, but it comes out a whisper and he doesn't even twitch. "Sebastian," I say softly again, bracing myself on the door frame.

He shoots up in the bed, "Rose? You're bleeding," he says in surprise.

He rushes to me just as I collapse, my own blood soaking my pants. I know what is happening. I am losing my baby. He scoops me up in his arms, taking me to his bed and laying me down gently.

A guard appears at the door, "Yes, sir."

"Fetch Xomira, it is an emergency," Sebastian barks.

The guard disappears and I feel Sebastian sweep the sweat caked hair from my forehead, "Hang on, Rose. I got you!"

I try to fight, but the world fades to black.

"Thank you, Xomira," I hear Sebastian say in the hall before footsteps lead further away.

My eyes feel swollen when I do open them, and everything hurts. I am still in Sebastian's room and the lights are out. I try to remember what happened, but it is blurry at best. I can smell the lingering smell of blood though- my blood. I gingerly place my hand on my belly, feeling the emptiness and flatness where the baby should be.

Devastated, I choke on my sob before it escapes my throat, making a strange noise erupt from my throat.

"Rose?" Sebastian says, coming into the dark room.

He sits on the edge of the bed while my silent sobs shake my body.

"I lost the baby, didn't I?"

"I'm afraid so," he says softly.

There is no playfulness in his voice, no smugness or cruelty. He is genuinely sad for me.

"How?" I ask between sobs.

He puts his hand on my shoulder in support, "when William stabbed you, the knife had been laced with a poison made with dark magick," he explains.

"But I felt fine after I healed," I remind him.

"Feeding from Caleb immediately slowed it down some, but nothing could be done," he says.

"Am I dying?" I ask indifferently.

"No. Xomira made an antidote, and you have fed," he informs me, "but you are going to feel pretty rough for a while."

"Did I bite someone? Who did I feed from?" I ask, worried about the fact that I can't remember.

He chuckles. "No, you didn't," he says, grabbing the empty whiskey bottle from his bedside table, which is now tinged red with blood, "it was my blood."

"Does he know?" I ask.

"Not yet. No one has seen him since dinner."
I curl up more in the blankets, the exhaustion deep in my bones.
"Do you mind if I go back to sleep?" I ask sweetly.
"No, of course not," he answers, squeezing my shoulder.
He quietly leaves the room and I cry myself to sleep.

CHAPTER FORTY

Caleb

Knock. Knock.

"Come in, Sebastian," I say, sensing who it is.

He enters and quietly shuts the door behind him. I am sitting on my couch, a scotch in one hand, a newspaper in the other. The sun went down a couple hours ago, signaling our start to the day.

"You have been absent for almost twenty-four hours," he says curiously.

"Are you keeping tabs on me?" I ask, amused.

"I would be a fool not to," he says bluntly.

He's not wrong. If the roles were reversed and he was walking the knife's edge of being a threat, I would also know his whereabouts at all times.

Putting down the newspaper, I look at him and I can see it etched in his face- concern and remorse.

My smile fades fast. "What is it?" I say nervously. "Is it Rose?"

Panicking, I drop my drink, my glass shattering on the floor. I rush the door, but Sebastian pushes me back forcefully.

"Stop…STOP," Sebastian yells at me. "Calm down, she is sleeping."

I breathe rapidly, huffing while Sebastian keeps his hands on my chest, his eyes wide, praying with me to relax.

I step back from him, still feeling the fingers of fear scratching at me.

He sighs, stepping around me and grabbing the bottle of scotch on my counter. Opening it, he takes a long gulp, setting me more on edge. He turns back to me, holding out the bottle.

"Something did happen, though," he says.

I fly at him, putting my hands around his throat aggressively, pushing him back into the counter.

"If you touched her, I promise I'll fucking kill you," I snarl, pressing into his throat so hard that my nails draw blood.

"I didn't…fucking…touch her," he chokes out.

I release my hold on his neck, the anger settling as he catches his breath.

"Drink," he says, thrusting the bottle at me. "You are going to need it."

"What happened?" I ask, taking the bottle and chugging it.

"William," he says simply. "The knife that he stabbed Rose with had been laced in a poison created with dark magick," he continues.

"No," I whisper, taking another long swallow.

"She lost the baby," Sebastian says grimly.

"NO," I yell, whipping the bottle across the room.

It impacts the wall and busts into pieces, spraying scotch everywhere.

"I have to talk to her," I say adamantly.

I make for the door, but Sebastian grabs my arm and makes me pause.

"Do you really believe that seeing you like this will make it any easier on her?" he asks firmly.

"I have to," I spit out.

"No. Take a couple days- feed, maim, kill. Do what you got to do to get your shit together; maybe then seeing her won't devastate her more," he says in a less than kind way.

"That was my baby," I say, fighting back tears.

"And I am truly sorry for your loss, brother," he says.

Sebastian starts heading for my door silently with nothing more to say.

"I will watch after her for you," he says over his shoulder.

"Careful, Sebastian, it almost sounds like you care," I say.

My remark should have made me smile, but it didn't. I feel like I can't breathe, and the pain in my chest is unbearable. I slam my fists through the counter, feeling overwhelmed with sadness.

That was my baby- my chance to be a father, my reason to keep Rose close, and just like that, it has been taken from me.

I will hunt him down. He will die by my hands- painfully, gruesomely.

CHAPTER FORTY-ONE

Rose

I am sitting on the window bench, staring out into the rain, my arms wrapped too far around my empty belly. I am lost in thought watching the rain fall. I am wearing a crop top and underwear under a dirty bathrobe. I hear the door open slowly, but I do not look because I just do not care.

"You haven't come out of this room in three days," Sebastian says.

"So?"

"You look like shit," he says arrogantly.

"You sure know how to make a girl blush," I reply sarcastically, not peeling my eyes away from the window.

"You need to feed, you need to eat, you need to shower," he says, the concern is clear in his voice. "Killing yourself won't bring your baby back."

I glance at him, rolling my eyes, "I'm aware, Sebastian."

Sebastian storms across the room, pulling my attention away from the window, a strange look in his eyes.

"Go away. I just want to be alone," I say, annoyed.

He scowls at me, "that is all you ever want."

Sebastian stares at me for several minutes and finally growls as he throws me over his shoulder and stomps back across the room.

"Sebastian, what are you doing?" I whine with zero energy.

"What needs to be done," he says.

He takes me into the bathroom and puts me down on my feet carefully. He quickly undoes my bathrobe and manhandles it off me, leaving me standing in my crop top and underwear.

"What the hell?" I ask. "What? Sad girls turn you on?" I add sarcastically.

"Don't flatter yourself," he says coldly.

Within seconds the heat overtakes him and he uses his own teeth to tear a spot out of his wrist, wincing as he does. "Drink," he says, thrusting his wrist in my face.

I frown at him but bring his wrist to my lips because I am hungry and seeing the blood makes it worse. I drink greedily for several minutes until I notice that Sebastian is looking a little pale. I pull away and his wrist finishes healing.

"I thought you didn't let people feed from you," I say.

"I made an exception. Don't let it go to your head," he says indifferently.

"Thank you," I say softly.

Sebastian smirks playfully, "don't thank me yet," he says.

"What? Why?"

He shoves me hard backwards into the shower. "You need to scrub. I'll see you for dinner."

He spins the dial, turning the shower on cold.

"You are a jerk," I yell as he walks away laughing.

I turn the shower warmer and watch the water run down my legs and going down the drain. I do not care that I am still partially clothed. I start sobbing, my tears blending with the water. I cry for the loss of the baby that I did not know I wanted.

For at least half an hour, I just stand there like a zombie- mourning.

Caleb

"Why am I here?" I ask impatiently.

I stand in the doorway to what was once Williams' study with the two moronic guards that Sebastian sent to collect me. Sebastian is leaning casually on the desk.

"Good evening to you too brother," he says with mock insult.

"Whatever. What do you want Sebastian?"

He sighs, eyeing his guards behind me. They step back only a foot or so like they are ready to attack if the time comes.

"Your less fun than usual," he says with disappointment.

"My baby died, the mother does not want me, and you basically told me to stay away from her. Should I be happy?"

Sebastian chuckles, "honestly, I didn't think you would listen."

He may not have thought I would listen, but I am not an idiot, he did expect me to listen. He is Lord now.

"If you were really unconcerned with my obedience, Rip 2.0 and his clone would not be standing here, breathing down the back of my neck right now," I say, gesturing behind me.

"If I was truly concerned with your cooperation, brother, there would be more than two. They are here as a cautionary reminder," he says with a smirk.

"A cautionary reminder?"

"Surely, you are aware of your own situation?"

"What are you rambling on about?" I sigh.

"You're turning again. You have been trying to fight it, but you are losing. It is only a matter of time."

"Don't try to soften the blow," I growl sarcastically.

Of course, I have noticed. I am colder, short-tempered and starving all the time. It would be impossible not to notice.

"You know that is not my style."

"So why am I here?"

"Rose."

"What about her?" I ask narrowing my eyes.

"She is not coping well."

"She just lost her baby. She needs time," I snarl.

"No. She needed you but you can't be trusted not to rip her apart anymore," he accuses.

I do not correct him because he is not wrong. Even Rose has not been safe from my disturbing thoughts lately.

I give a self-deprecating laugh, "is that why you summoned me? To rub in the reminder of how badly I failed her?"

"No," Sebastian steps closer to me. "I let Rose stay because I had hoped that having her close would help you to stave off this darkness this time, so that you did not lose however many more years. Assuming you can beat this again, but I see now that it is pointless."

"Save it," I say bluntly. "You had other motives as well."

Sebastian smirks at me, confirming what I said.

"Maybe, but it doesn't change the fact that I wanted to help you."

"So, now what?"

"Now…you need to go say goodbye to her before you can't. You owe her that. I practically had to force feed her my blood and force her into the shower. She is probably still there. Try and make things better before it is too late," he adds.

I wish he was wrong, but he is not. I cannot stay here anymore, even if it fills me with an unimaginable pain to leave.

It is a lost cause. I am a lost cause.

"You have twenty minutes. Don't do anything stupid."

With some hesitation, I head for the hallway to go to Rose.

Stopping in the doorway, "will you keep her safe?" I ask over my shoulder.

"She may stay as long as she wants and I will check in on her when she chooses to leave," he reassures me.

Rose

Strong arms slide around my waist, supporting my weight. I let myself step back against their chest, needing the comfort and finding the familiar searing heat from their skin.

Caleb.

"What are you doing?" I ask monotonously.

"Sebastian was worried about you," he replies.

"How did I not pick up on that when he shoved me into a cold shower?"

His chest rumbles with a laugh, "Sebastian likes to handle things in his own way," he says. "I'm worried about you too."

"I'm fine," I lie.

"You are not. You're grieving and so am I," he says darkly.

His arms tighten around me and for a minute I regret sending him away. I wiggle in his grip, turning to face him, looking into his face and then I remember. It's not just the lies. It is because of what we lost and the fact that he's fighting a battle within himself. He has to do it alone, and I can't handle the hopelessness that I feel when I see his face.

He removes his arms from around me and grabs the shampoo, lathering my hair and massaging my scalp with his fingers. After, he puts some conditioner in my hair and starts spreading it with care.

He gathers my wet hair, sweeping it to one side, and whispers "I wanted this more than I knew, for you to be the mother of my child."

Then he grabs the soap and starts washing my back, his slippery fingers sliding under my shirt slowly. He crouches down, washing each of my legs. His fingers travel smoothly across my skin.

I look down at him as he caresses my legs, wet and naked except for a pair of boxer briefs and it suddenly feels overwhelmingly intimate. I start to come undone.

"Stop," I say, my breathing becoming more rapid.

He stands up straight, towering over me, his dark eyes gazing intensely. "Stop what?"

"Stop taking care of me…stop *loving* me," I say awkwardly.

"Well, someone has to…you're not doing it," he argues.

"I need time to feel this loss, and you stepping in and treating me with so much compassion is unbearable."

He stares at me. "You know, I'm dealing with this loss too."

"After what you did, you do not get to touch me like I am yours despite what we both lost," I say venomously, turning off the water.

He sighs, "I was just trying to be there for you."

"Well, I don't want you to."

Caleb places his hand on my belly affectionately, remembering what we almost had. "I lost everything," he says sadly, his eyes filling up with tears.

I have never seen him cry before. I did not even know he could, to be honest.

I cannot comfort him and tell him that he will have another chance because it would be a lie. It has to be me, or it can't happen. *How cruel is that?*

"I'm sorry," I say, a single tear escaping down my cheek.

"This is not your fault," he says adamantly.

I hear it, but I do not entirely believe it. Maybe I could give him enough reason to cling on to his humanity if I could be with him, but I can't give myself to him no matter my feelings.

"I cannot give you what you want...what you need," I say, my voice devoid of all emotion.

"I know," he says with defeat.

He pulls on his shirt and pants that he discarded on the floor, turning back to me. His eyes are darker- even the white part looks gray.

I stand there dripping, half naked and awkward.

The way he is staring at me, I know. He is leaving for good this time. I want him to leave me alone, but don't want him going off the handle.

"Caleb, please, don't leave; not like this," I plead, hands clenching the front of his shirt, tears pouring down my cheeks.

"Give me a reason to stay," Caleb begs me, his eyes turning a hollow black as he slips away from me.

"What do you want me to say?"

"You know what I want you to say."

His voice is dark, gravelly, forced. He is fighting a losing battle to hold onto his humanity. He has suffered too much loss- his child, his chance to be a father, me...himself. It is all too much for him.

"Caleb...I can't." I say, sobs racking my body.

His head droops and he releases a breath like he had been holding it for hours. The entire world goes still and quiet. Several minutes pass and he raises his head back up, his eyes completely black, no white left.

He is gone.

Without looking back, he walks away as I watch him disappear, slumping to the ground, crying from the feeling of despair taking over my body.

Caleb.

Caleb

All I can see...all I can feel...is the darkness inviting me into a hell that I am all too familiar and comfortable with. Its depths pull me back in after

I have clawed my way out.

I will always be fighting this darkness, suspended in a place where I come off as cold and cruel when I know that I should care more. A place where I cannot feel the warmth of life.

I walk away, leaving Rose in a heap on the floor. I never meant to let her down, but that is all I seem to do.

It is better this way.

Goodbye, love.

Sebastian

Rose comes in promptly at dinner time and sits next me. I don't know what Caleb said to her, but she looks better. Her hair and makeup look good. She is wearing some faux leather leggings and a black blouse that shows off enough that I check her out shamelessly.

"I take it you approve," she says indifferently to my gawking.

I chuckle lowly, "clearly," I admit.

She goes for her refreshment before even glancing at her food. She seems different, her presence feels different.

"Caleb?"

She looks directly at me, her eyes betraying her hurt, her pain, her loss. And I see a dark twinkle that was not there before.

"He is gone," she says bluntly.

I realize than that a piece of her has died, she will never be the same and my family is to blame. We all played a part.

RATE THE BOOK

Thank you for reading Dark Magick, book #3 in the Dark Shadows series. Please take a few minutes to review this novel on Amazon or Goodreads. Visit my Facebook page, @Author.Erica.Richer or follow me on Twitter, @EricaRicher and Instagram, @richererica, for updates on upcoming books.

ABOUT THE AUTHOR

Erica Richer is determined to give her readers an intense, emotional journey by writing about strong, passionate characters. She loves adventuring into a good book and wants everyone to experience a book that they just can't put down.